CRA

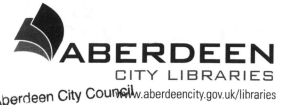

ABERDEEN
CITY LIBRARIES

Aberdeen City Council www.aberdeencity.gov.uk/libraries
Cornhill Library
Tel 696209

Return to . . . .
or any other Aberdeen City Library
Please return/renew this item by the last day shown. Items may also be renewed
by phone or online

CR 1/15

KU-525-529

WITHDRAWN

articles, including several on Mary Wollstonecraft. She has edited
Pride and Prejudice for Penguin Classics, and Frances Burney's
Evelina for Oxford World's Classics, and is the General Editor of
Jane Austen's novels in Oxford World's Classics.

X000 000 040 5825

ABERDEEN CITY LIBRARIES

OXFORD WORLD'S CLASSICS

*For over 100 years Oxford World's Classics have brought
readers closer to the world's great literature. Now with over 700
titles—from the 4,000-year-old myths of Mesopotamia to the
twentieth century's greatest novels—the series makes available
lesser-known as well as celebrated writing.*

*The pocket-sized hardbacks of the early years contained
introductions by Virginia Woolf, T. S. Eliot, Graham Greene,
and other literary figures which enriched the experience of reading.
Today the series is recognized for its fine scholarship and
reliability in texts that span world literature, drama and poetry,
religion, philosophy and politics. Each edition includes perceptive
commentary and essential background information to meet the
changing needs of readers.*

OXFORD WORLD'S CLASSICS

JANE AUSTEN

Persuasion

Edited by
JAMES KINSLEY

With an Introduction and Notes by
DEIDRE SHAUNA LYNCH

OXFORD
UNIVERSITY PRESS

OXFORD
UNIVERSITY PRESS

Great Clarendon Street, Oxford OX2 6DP

Oxford University Press is a department of the University of Oxford.
It furthers the University's objective of excellence in research, scholarship,
and education by publishing worldwide in

Oxford New York

Auckland Bangkok Buenos Aires Cape Town Chennai
Dar es Salaam Delhi Hong Kong Istanbul Karachi Kolkata
Kuala Lumpur Madrid Melbourne Mexico City Mumbai Nairobi
São Paulo Shanghai Taipei Tokyo Toronto

Oxford is a registered trade mark of Oxford University Press
in the UK and in certain other countries

Published in the United States
by Oxford University Press Inc., New York

Introduction and Explanatory Notes © Deidre Shauna Lynch 2004
Bibliography, Chronology, Appendices B, C, and D © Vivien Jones 2003

The moral rights of the authors have been asserted

Database right Oxford University Press (maker)

First published as World's Classics paperback 1980
Reissued as an Oxford World's Classic paperback 1998
New edition 2004

All rights reserved. No part of this publication may be reproduced,
stored in a retrieval system, or transmitted, in any form or by any means,
without the prior permission in writing of Oxford University Press,
or as expressly permitted by law, or under terms agreed with the appropriate
reprographics rights organizations. Enquiries concerning reproduction
outside the scope of the above should be sent to the Rights Department,
Oxford University Press, at the address above

You must not circulate this book in any other binding or cover
and you must impose this same condition on any acquirer

British Library Cataloguing in Publication Data

Data available

Library of Congress Cataloging in Publication Data

Data available

ISBN 978-0-19-953555-2

5

Typeset in Ehrhardt
by RefineCatch Limited, Bungay, Suffolk
Printed in Great Britain by
Clays Ltd., St Ives plc

CONTENTS

ACKNOWLEDGEMENTS

I wish to thank Vivien Jones, Judith Luna, Tom Keirstead, and Adela Pinch for the help they gave me in preparing this edition and for their wise advice and patience. Mary Favret, Richard Nash, and Robert Anderson both asked good questions and helped me find good answers, and Ana Owusu-Tyo's work as a research assistant was invaluable. I completed the latter stages of work on this edition during a research leave granted by the Department of English, Indiana University, and I am grateful for that gift of time.

INTRODUCTION

On 8 August 1815, English newspapers took note of the departure for Saint Helena of HMS *Northumberland* and, with it, a prisoner. He was Napoleon Bonaparte, whose army had been defeated at Waterloo just weeks before, in a bloody battle (almost 50,000 killed) that brought to a close more than two decades of warfare between Britain, France, and their allies. The former Emperor of the French would spend the remainder of his life incarcerated on that tiny South Atlantic island. In 1821 he died there, almost unremarked. Even before the *Northumberland* left British waters, however, Bonaparte had become a has-been: a relic of a past that Europe was resolutely putting behind it. By the summer of 1815, an era of aftermath had arrived.

On the same day that her contemporaries learned of Bonaparte's journey into exile, Jane Austen began to write *Persuasion*, the last of her completed works, and the one in which, according to Virginia Woolf, the novelist embarked on her 'voyage of discovery'.[1] With this characterization Woolf added her authoritative voice to the chorus of commentators who since the nineteenth century have identified *Persuasion* as a work of exceptional innovation and experiment, one in which Austen heads somewhere new. Having encountered four works from her pen, her audience might in 1815 have believed that they knew just what characters, style, and story line an 'Austen novel' would involve. *Persuasion*, however, is different.

For a start, Anne Elliot, its heroine, is, at 27, older than her predecessors, and old enough, in the period's idiom for sex appeal, to have lost 'her bloom' (p. 11). Disconcertingly, *Persuasion* presents us with a heroine who has completed her growing-up. Anne has already internalized—too well, one could argue—the lessons of prudence and self-restraint that most heroines of the period learn only as their stories conclude. This is why, in the conferences about her family's financial troubles which give us our first glimpse of this heroine, we see Anne, in what we soon recognize as a typical gesture, hardening herself to 'affronts' (p. 33). Her concerns over the plans her family hatches in these opening chapters go unvoiced, because it 'would be

---

[1] *The Common Reader*, new edn. (London: Hogarth, 1937), 180.

most right, and most wise, and, therefore, must involve least suffering, to go with the others' (p. 32): that line of reasoning suggests,
sadly, that Anne accepts *some* suffering as an inevitability. However,
as the novel proceeds it becomes clear that Austen will not co-
operate with her heroine's resolution to define herself as a has-been.
This heroine hopes that she has 'outlived the age of blushing'; Anne
seems to aspire to put 'the age of emotion' behind her too (p. 44).
Outwardly, then, Anne may look like a model girl ('almost too good
for me', Austen herself opined).[2] But the unspoken script of her
mental life is, we find, tremulous with passion. In fact, nothing else
Austen published approximates the language of psychological tumult
that *Persuasion* pioneers to convey the feel of the many moments in
the story when Anne is all but overcome by a heady compound of
remembrance, hope, anxiety, and erotic longing.

Many readers have been struck by the energetic, agitated prose—
anticipating Virginia Woolf, it is said, more than it recalls Samuel
Johnson—that Austen uses to convey the wordless dramas of Anne's
inner life.[3] Readers have, furthermore, associated this shift in style
with a transformation in the novelist's understanding of society. For
the upshot of the discussions of the Elliot finances that begin *Persuasion* is that Anne's father, spendthrift Sir Walter, is obliged to vacate
his house. Because he must retrench his expenses, Kellynch Hall,
though Elliot property for generations, must be rented to others.
Austen's glowing depictions of the country houses of Pemberley and
Donwell Abbey, in *Pride and Prejudice* and *Emma*, glorified a social
order made stable by the gentleman's inheritance of landed property.
But *Persuasion*, valuing the activities of the professional classes more
than the traditions of the country house set, recognizes relocation as
a way of life. Its crucial scenes happen in rented rooms. Its most
admirable characters are figures like Admiral and Mrs Croft, Sir
Walter's tenants, who move into Kellynch only to find themselves
regretting the snug quarters they formerly occupied aboard Royal
Navy ships. The Crofts are transients by profession, not permanent
residents. In associating *Persuasion* with voyages of discovery, Woolf
might, in fact, have been noticing how Austen takes the symbolic

---

[2] Letter to Fanny Knight, 23–5 March 1817, *Jane Austen's Letters*, 3rd edn., collected
and ed. Deirdre Le Faye (Oxford and New York: Oxford University Press, 1995), 335.
[3] Norman Page, in J. David Grey *et al.* (eds.), *The Jane Austen Companion* (New York:
Macmillan, 1986), 262–3.

value formerly belonging to her country houses and reattaches it, in this novel, to Navy frigates and carriages speeding down country lanes. *Pride and Prejudice* grants Elizabeth Bennet the chance to tour Darcy's handsome house and discover there, just in time, that 'to be mistress of Pemberley might be something' (vol. III, ch. i). *Persuasion*, inaugurating a new, unsettled mode of domesticity, grants its heroine the chance to study the co-operative spirit in which the Crofts steer their carriage (p. 78). This heroine ends this book 'the mistress', not of a country house, but of the latest thing in transportation: 'a very pretty landaulette' (p. 201).

The modernity of *Persuasion* does not, however, reside exclusively with this emphasis on movement or on looking ahead to new social vistas. For all its innovations, *Persuasion* also takes an interest, in ways that are equally modern, in looking backward: in reviewing and historicizing. The novel's wisdom is to insist that there can be no change of place, no experience of new scenes and faces, without the practices of leave-taking that people use to put the past behind them.

Sir Walter Elliot's nostalgia for the good old days is obvious as soon as the first paragraph depicts his reading habits: when Anne's father picks up the *Baronetage*, it is to use this who's-who list of gentry genealogies in order to take note once again of how few really old families have survived to the present-day and in order to re-indulge his snobbish 'contempt' for the new, ancestor-less baronets ('the almost endless creations of the last century') who have taken their place (p. 9). But even the Navy men and their wives, the figures of social change in *Persuasion*, indulge a taste for reminiscing and 'recurring to former days' (p. 84): Austen portrays them regaling their dinner companions with yarns in which they retrace past voyages and fight past battles over again. Begun on the day when Austen's contemporaries were declaring decades of war 'history', *Persuasion* represents Austen's investigation into these uses of retrospection. Austen asks whether the past might be recalled and memories kept alive without disturbing that peace. She asks about how people keep faith with their memories and whether it is possible to be true to the past without living *in* it—without isolating oneself from the dynamism of historical change.

In posing such questions, Austen was recognizably addressing issues of the moment. Britons inhabiting the 'new world order' of 1815 were, in unprecedented ways, invited to see themselves as time-travellers who had crossed a threshold and passed into a new historical era. During the years of the French Revolution and the two decades of war that followed, the very pace at which history happened appeared to have accelerated. More 'history' had been happening, more quickly, and the past seemed to have receded more rapidly into the distance than it had before. This new experience of time had contradictory consequences. On the one hand, Britons' solicitude about preserving links with a vanishing cultural heritage led to the establishment of museums and of programmes of architectural restoration that aspired to return the nation's old buildings to their past condition. At the same time such preservationism could seem beside the point, for the past had, for many people, become irrevocably distant from, because distinct from, the present. The past had become, as the historian David Lowenthal writes, 'a foreign country'.[4] The second decade of the nineteenth century is, in fact, when the concepts of historical *period* (a word that only then comes to designate a delimited slice of time possessed of its own distinctive character) and of *anachronism* (a term for what is untimely, for what is out of place in the contemporary moment) first enjoy real currency in British culture. These are concepts propagated in the new literary forms developed in the wake of the Battle of Waterloo in 1815: the era's 'tales of the times', its investigations of 'the spirit of the age', as well as the 'historical novels'—with their settings in bygone times— that had been brought into prominence by Sir Walter Scott's best-selling series of Waverley Novels.

Persuasion both assists with, and reacts against, the new tasks of historicizing and of periodizing that literature was being called on to perform after 1815. It too aims to investigate the past so as to specify the historical location of the present. At the same time, *Persuasion*'s interest in reminiscence—in the persistence of the past as memory—supplies Austen with the device that she uses in order to revise, to exquisite effect, the marriage plot. Austen, with glorious assurance, constructs *Persuasion* as a sequel. Readers' sense that Austen in her last book is taking fiction somewhere new is in part a function of how, centred as it is on a grown-up heroine who begins where other heroines end, *Persuasion* reads as a follow-up to the typical 'Austen

---

[4] David Lowenthal, *The Past is a Foreign Country* (Cambridge: Cambridge University Press, 1986). Lowenthal's title quotes the opening of the 1953 novel by L. P. Hartley, *The Go-Between*.

novel'. Some eight years before the story begins, in a sequence of events that the narrator characterizes as a 'little history of sorrowful interest' (p. 28), Anne Elliot met Captain Frederick Wentworth of the Royal Navy. Soon, since 'he had nothing to do, and she had hardly any body to love,' they pledged their love (p. 26). But Anne submitted to duty, and, 'persuaded to believe the engagement a wrong thing,' gave Wentworth up: 'He had left the country in consequence.' The speed with which Austen recounts the story and arranges for it to reach 'its close' (p. 28) is remarkable. It almost suggests that by 1815 that storyline of youthful romance feels to her slightly dull—as if what interests Austen now is how people who have pasts do their loving. But if Austen dispenses briskly with the 'little history' which accounts for Anne's sense of herself as a has-been, the novel that picks up her story eight years on, when a long-awaited peace brings Wentworth back to England and back into Anne's life, is constructed nonetheless so that the feelings of these characters refer repeatedly to memories of this earlier history:

His profession qualified him, his disposition led him, to talk; and '*That* was in the year six;' '*That* happened before I went to sea in the year six,' occurred in the course of the first evening they spent together; and . . . Anne felt the utter impossibility, from her knowledge of his mind, that he could be unvisited by remembrance any more than herself. (p. 55)

Remembrance presents itself as a return visitor, in a novel that has redefined romance as a matter of return: first Wentworth's return from the sea and then at last—in the foregone conclusion, which Austen somehow has arranged so that it feels like a bolt from the blue and a prodigious stroke of luck—his return to Anne. By working in this double time-frame, by arranging for the backward look of retrospection to pull against the forward momentum of plot, Austen gives life to the abstractions of her contemporaries' philosophies of history. Take, for instance, the narrator's comment in Chapter IV that Anne 'had been forced into prudence in her youth, she learned romance as she grew older—the natural sequel of an unnatural beginning' (p. 30). Here Austen signals how her narrative will be inverting the usual schemes through which her novels of courtship or of female development sort out prelude from aftermath. But this sentence also challenges conventional expectations about the work of time in ways that may signal Austen's wish to complicate our ways of delimiting the present from the past, a new era from an old one. By recounting a story of second chances, granting its heroine 'a second spring of youth and beauty' (p. 101) in ways that seem magically to run time backward, *Persuasion* makes readers think hard about what it means to close the book on the past. And the process of plotting Wentworth and Anne's way *back* to happiness, of revising that earlier, foreshortened 'little history' of failed union as a story of *re*union, necessarily raises discomfiting questions about how different people measure time and how, categorized as History, particular experiences of time count, and at the expense of others. *Persuasion* invites readers to wonder, for a start, if a man who 'had nothing to do' and a woman who 'had hardly any body to love' will prove to have been telling and keeping time in sync, according to the same calendar.

Past and Present

In order to survive the heartache caused by Wentworth's return not only to England, but back into her own social circle, Anne reminds herself that time matters. On the first evening on which they are to meet, Anne reasons to herself that it is natural that time should advance and that people should change:

Eight years, almost eight years had passed, since all had been given up. How absurd to be resuming the agitation which such an interval had banished into distance and indistinctness! What might not eight years do? Events of every description, changes, alienations, removals,—all, all must be comprised in it; and oblivion of the past—how natural, how certain too! . . .

   Alas! with all her reasonings, she found, that to retentive feelings eight years may be little more than nothing. (p. 53)

While it records Anne's struggle with her feelings, this passage testifies to her possession of a constant heart. Austen doesn't require Anne to confess outright that she has never ceased to love Wentworth. This is testimony enough that neither her severing of their engagement, nor the years of solitude that followed, have altered anything in Anne's feelings. The case for Anne's constancy to Wentworth is made here almost through the syntax of the passage alone. The jagged rhythms of the prose mime the intensity of Anne's yearning. They register how, far from being able to consign their story to the temporally remote epoch which is conjured up through that reference to 'distance and indistinctness', Anne finds herself stirred all over again by Wentworth's presence. For Anne in 1814, it is natural that 1806 should feel like yesterday.

With this episode in Chapter VII, the book sets in motion with its readers the debate weighing the virtues and pains of romantic constancy which its characters soon take up themselves. Virtues *and* pains—because, as Anne says in her famous defence of women's steadfastness in *Persuasion*'s conclusion, no man should 'covet' the ability to 'love longest' that she ascribes to the female sex. Nothing is 'enviable' about the lot of the woman who, like Anne herself, still loves 'when hope is gone' (p. 189). As early as the opening chapters, Austen's audience gets the wherewithal to test out that proposition: we are soon able to contrast Anne with Henrietta Musgrove, who finds Wentworth, though a newcomer to Uppercross society, 'more agreeable . . . than any individual among [her] male acquaintance, who had been at all a favourite before' (p. 48) and who, in expressing this opinion, blithely consigns her earlier romantic feelings for her cousin Charles to the category of ancient history. Further on in the novel, Wentworth's friend Captain Benwick, introduced when he is mourning his fiancée's sudden death, will disappoint the onlookers who felt that this star-crossed 'little history of his private life', coupled with his enthusiasm for Scott's and Byron's poetry, equipped him to be a paragon of melancholy romantic fidelity (p. 81). With unseemly dispatch, Captain Benwick will forget his dead fiancée and shed his melancholy. He will fall in love, over the same poetry, with Louisa Musgrove.

Nevertheless, this moment in Chapter VII which demonstrates both that Anne's love of Wentworth has been revived and that it never died also makes painfully apparent the grim truth about the context for such constancy. In Anne's world, time unsettles more than it preserves. At this point in the novel, Austen asks us to prize the 'retentive' heart which doesn't let go, but, at the same time, much in the novel, by emphasizing the inevitability of 'changes, alienations, removals', urges the high costs of such constancy and the wisdom of adaptability. Throughout her novel's first volume especially, Austen attends to the losses that come with the passage of years. She catalogues with merciless attention time's ravages on furniture (as with the 'faded sofa' at Uppercross Cottage, which, with the other drawing-room furniture, had 'been gradually growing shabby, under the influence of four summers and two children' (p. 35) and also its ravages on people's bodies.

In *Persuasion* people age. Faces acquire wrinkles and bodies break down. '[S]ailors do grow old betimes,' Mrs Clay says, as she obsequiously points out the disadvantages that men working in a profession face when one compares their looks to those of a leisured man like Sir Walter (p. 22). This doesn't always seem to be the case. That first time he calls at Uppercross, Anne determines that the eight years that have 'destroyed her youth and bloom' have merely made Captain Wentworth *more* like himself, more handsome, more manly (p. 53). A reference to Captain Harville's lameness (p. 82) in fact represents one of the novel's very few acknowledgements that Navy men face graver dangers than the damage (on which Sir Walter especially likes to dwell) that the weather might do to their complexions. If we read that limp as the after-effect of a war wound, the reference may serve as a muted reminder that the lot of the men at war who are even unluckier than Harville is to die as well as to 'grow old betimes'. Such reminders are exceptional, however: *Persuasion* generally keeps a guarded silence about the fact that wounding and killing have for two decades represented the vocation of the Captain Harvilles and Wentworths of this world. But that discretion about wartime carnage is offset, all the same, by the fact that security of life and limb is a precarious thing even under the peace that has brought the surviving sailors home.[5] At the start of Volume I Anne's young nephew Charles has a close call when he falls and breaks his collarbone. At the end of the volume, Louisa Musgrove mistimes her daredevil leap from the Cobb and is injured gravely in consequence. There seem almost to be as many storms to weather on shore as at sea—as much likelihood there, as in the theatre of war, that time will cut young lives short, and as many testimonies to the frailty of the bodies housing those lives.

Still, *Persuasion* also yields an alternative account of what time can perform—Austen concedes that time can also renew, that, even while it alienates, removes, or hurts, it also brings the future. This is, for instance, the account that Anne absorbs when she observes with

---

[5] On *Persuasion*'s stress on physical vulnerability see John Wiltshire, *Jane Austen and the Body: 'The Picture of Health'* (Cambridge: Cambridge University Press, 1992), 155–96.

surprise her old school friend Mrs Smith's 'disposition to be comforted' and 'power of turning readily from evil to good' and when she recognizes how Mrs Smith, though another of the novel's victims of mischance, might be better than she is at actually living *in* time. Mrs Smith manages to combine the 'submissive spirit' that Anne herself cultivates with an 'elasticity of mind' (p. 125).

A similar orientation to time can be discerned when *Persuasion*'s narrator describes the homes at Uppercross and, noting that the Musgrove family, like its two houses, were 'in a state of alteration, perhaps of improvement', (pp. 37–8) conspicuously declines any opportunity to lament the passing of things:

To the Great House accordingly they went, to sit the full half hour in the old-fashioned square parlour, with a small carpet and shining floor, to which the present daughters of the house were gradually giving the proper air of confusion by a grand piano forte and a harp, flower-stands and little tables placed in every direction. Oh! could the originals of the portraits against the wainscot, could the gentlemen in brown velvet and the ladies in blue satin have seen what was going on. (p. 37)

The style Austen chooses for this depiction of the alterations wrought by time is not that of elegy. Instead, passing fashions in clothing and furnishings are annotated and made meaningful as the stuff of what we might call social history. The description evokes a longer timeline than a 'full half hour'. In depicting the parlour almost as a museum or memorial to the changing tastes of multiple eras, Austen enlists the several generations of Musgroves in a long-term process of upward mobility.

This insistence that to be at home in Uppercross is to live through modernization would have seemed to contemporary readers a sign of Austen's interest in her era's new historical novels. As modern scholars observe, this historical fiction operated precisely to domesticate history; in the wake of the extraordinarily eventful quarter-century of the French Revolution and the Napoleonic wars, years that saw politics and warfare become in new ways *mass* experiences, this genre worked to redefine what would count as a 'historical subject', so that history no longer seemed something made exclusively through the actions of Great Men engaged in high politics. This is not to say that *Persuasion* is a historical novel in the manner, for example, of *Waverley, or, 'Tis Sixty Years Since* (1814),

Sir Walter Scott's fictionalization of the Jacobite Rebellion of 1745.
In ways that for ever altered the British novel, *Waverley* grafted the
history book onto the *Bildungsroman*: Scott simultaneously traced his
fictional hero's journey of self-discovery and chronicled the British
nation's journey through an episode of historical transition.[6]
Austen's engagement with historical subjects is of course much more
indirect. When they decide Britain's fate at the Battle of Trafalgar, a
turning point in the war with Napoleonic France, the Navy men of
Persuasion do the deed off-stage, after all: Trafalgar takes place
before the first phase of the romance between Anne and Wentworth
commences. And, even though she is able to bank on her original
audience's knowledge that the historical record had made Navy captains (a group including two of Austen's own brothers) the nation's
epitome of glamour, Austen has too much tact to portray, for
example, her fictional Wentworth being rewarded for his valour at
the Battle of Saint Domingo by a real Horatio Nelson. Scott, by
contrast, had arranged to portray his hero, Edward Waverley, keeping company with the actual leader of the Jacobite forces, Prince
Charles Edward Stuart.

Nonetheless, much in *Persuasion* suggests how responsive Austen
was to the arrangements her fellow novelists were developing to
portray the complex interconnections between individual lives and
larger social structures, as well as to portray the private sphere,
where everyday lives are led by ordinary people, as a site of national historical formation. *Persuasion*'s heightened attention to the historicity
of the domestic details it uses for scene-setting works, in fact, to
similar effect as another of the innovations that makes this Austen
novel stand apart from the others. This is the specificity with which
Austen measures out the time—whether by the half-hour or week—
that the fictional action occupies and the remarkable exactness with
which—beginning at the moment in Chapter I where the narrator
glosses a reference to 'this present time' with the words 'the summer
of 1814' (p. 13)—she identifies the chronological moment at which
that action unfolds. The consequence is that when, for instance, we

---

[6] When Captain Benwick and Anne mention Scott in their discussion of the poetry
'of the present age' (p. 84), Austen invites her audience to make a connection between
her own novels and his. Despite the anonymous publication of *Waverley*, the work in
which Scott first moved from poetry onto Austen's own literary turf, Austen had had no
trouble identifying its author: the authorship of *Waverley* was an open secret (*Letters*,
277).

learn in Chapter III that the tenant for Kellynch is likely to belong to
the Navy because in summer 1814 the 'peace [is] turning . . . [the]
Navy Officers ashore' (p. 20), we see private life being rendered in
terms that pointedly call up a crucial phase of the nation's public
history.

Austen takes pains to lodge the story of Anne's recovery of happiness in the interstices of the historical record, so that it is framed on
both sides by great public events. In fact, the span of time in which
Wentworth and Anne renew their romance coincides almost exactly
with the temporary respite from war which began for Britain with
the Treaty of Paris, signed in June 1814, and which terminated
abruptly with Napoleon's escape from the island of Elba and return
to Paris in February and March 1815. By Michaelmas, 29 September, 1814, Kellynch Hall has been turned over to the Crofts (p. 43).
Captain Wentworth, their first visitor, has returned to England and
into Anne's life by October. The characters' fateful visit to Lyme
occurs in November, an excursion to the seaside that is 'entirely out
of . . . season' (p. 84). On 1 February 1815 Mary begins penning the
letter to Anne, by this time a resident of Bath, which includes the
astonishing news of the engagement between Louisa Musgrove and
Captain Benwick (p. 132); the Crofts carry the letter with them when
they travel to Bath. '[U]nshackled and free' and ready to profit from
rather than regret Louisa's inconstancy (p. 136), Wentworth follows
the Crofts there even before they have the chance to promote the
city's virtues as a place for meeting girls (p. 140). His first appearance in Bath's wet, wintry streets and first encounter with Anne,
who finds then that 'Time had changed him' (p. 142), also occur in
February. Within weeks, Wentworth's journey to Bath is repeated by
the two Uppercross families and Captain Harville: the hunting season has ended in the countryside, so Charles Musgrove is searching
for something to do, and it is time to shop for his sisters' wedding
trousseaus (p. 174). Well before winter ends, the majority of Austen's
characters have been reassembled in time for the climactic scenes at
the city's White Hart Inn.[7]

[7] Through these measures, significantly, Austen makes the resumption of warfare
that followed Napoleon's return to Paris on 20 March 1815 into an event that lies just
beyond the frame of the novel, and in the characters' immediate future. It appears likely
that Anne and Wentworth will be married by the time that the Battle of Waterloo is
fought in June: the Navy in fact was not remobilized that spring, and, as Admiral Croft
says when he tells Anne the history of his own marriage, 'sailors . . . cannot afford to
make long courtships in time of war' (pp. 77–8).

By pointedly situating the action of *Persuasion* within time, insist-ing that it matters where we are in history, Austen proposes that large-scale historical processes help determine how private indi-viduals work out their destinies. This means that, even as *Persuasion* invites readers to get romantic about people with steadfast hearts, it likewise acknowledges, in more hardheaded fashion, that Wentworth in 1815 has become an attractive marriage prospect exactly because, in many respects, the entire nation has moved on since 1806. His rise through the ranks and the wealth he has acquired through that pro-fessional skill exemplify the historical fact that Sir Walter laments: that war and the infusion of wealth that war has brought have served as the 'means of bringing persons of obscure birth into undue distinction' (p. 22).

But history is at issue in the novel's private plots in a second way. By framing *Persuasion* as a sequel, giving it a plot that unfolds under the shadows cast by a prior story, Austen at once obliged Anne and Wentworth to assess the influence of the past and called on her contemporary audience, those new arrivals in a new post-Waterloo world, to grapple along with the characters with the changes wrought by the years that had slipped away since 1806. In order to get past the deadlock of that 'perpetual estrangement' that makes their interchanges at Uppercross so painfully stiff and ceremonious (p. 55), Anne and Wentworth must reach an accommodation about how they will understand the past.

Anne has spent eight years in re-evaluating what her 19-year-old self did in sacrificing her chances for happiness. She has, heartbreak-ingly, had little else to do. Before the novel opens, Anne has con-cluded that Lady Russell's advice about Wentworth was mistaken: 'she should yet have been a happier woman in maintaining the engagement' (p. 29), but she also concludes (and to the end persists in this belief) that she herself was right to be persuaded by her affection for and duty to her friend. For Wentworth, this sort of retrospection occurs belatedly, within the compressed time-frame of the novel, and in a roundabout way. His reintroduction into the book and appearance in Bath in the second volume follow a period in which, off-stage, he has been reviewing the autumn of 1814 and, particularly, the events crowded into the day and a half at Lyme. He has been reflecting on the generosity and presence of mind Anne demonstrated when Louisa was injured and on what that near-tragedy suggests about the headstrong self-confidence that he had commended in Louisa, which he has prized in himself, and which he has hated Anne for lacking. After this review Wentworth appears to have been prompted to return in memory to an earlier time still and to reopen the closed book of the 'little history of sorrowful interest'.

Austen proposes that such reinterpretation of the past can alter the future. Recognizing the past as the place in time that also harbours unfulfilled wishes and unrealized possibilities (things that might have been, as well as those that had to have been) is the first step in revising the narratives we use to set out the origins of the present. It can make these narratives turn out otherwise. When in autumn 1814 Wentworth returns to England, he has already made up his mind about the past's meanings. He knows, he believes, how *that* story turned out. He remembers selectively and uses remembrance merely to nurse his grievances. The sole passage of narrative adopting his point of view suggests as much: 'He had not forgiven Anne Elliot. She had used him ill; deserted and disappointed him; and worse, she had shewn a feebleness of character in doing so, which his own decided, confident temper could not endure' (p. 54). But, in the aftermath of the visit to Lyme (which Austen seems designedly to have scheduled so that it would be *un*timely and 'out of season'), *Persuasion* grants memory a role that involves releasing buried potentiality and not just affirming the inevitability of things as they are. Wentworth, the 'decided' character, learns a lesson about the virtue of keeping open those possibilities that make the future uncertain and undecided, instead of a done deal.

In the penultimate chapter, he recalls how jealous he felt when, after arriving in Bath, he witnessed Mr Elliot's attentions to Anne and confesses that 'the late knowledge I had acquired of your character . . . was [then] overwhelmed, buried, lost in those earlier feelings which I had been smarting under year after year' (p. 197). His language here transposes the positions of the late and the early, and makes the present something dead and buried and memory its undertaker. *Persuasion* in its entirety manifests a comparable willingness to perplex time—to tinker with its logic of linearity and irreversibility. That past which the characters thought was finished not only returns, it returns transformed and renewed by reinterpretation. We learn, for instance, that, retroactively, Wentworth is able to resee the woman whose 'weakness and timidity' he deplored first in 1806, and, all over again, when memory of that earlier hurt was revived in 1814, as having always appeared to him a character 'maintaining the loveliest medium of fortitude and gentleness' (p. 194). In another rewriting of the past that Anne accepts with good grace, Wentworth claims now that this woman who, only months before, appeared to him to be haggard with age and so changed he might not have known her again (p. 53), is someone who, to his admiring eye, 'could never alter' (p. 196).

Persuasion might be said, then, to represent historical fiction in keeping with two understandings of the term. It is the vehicle for Austen's history of the recent past as an epoch of transition and also for her enquiry into what, in a time of transition, the backward glance of the historian might be good for. The reinterpretation of their past that enables Anne and Wentworth to begin again must have invited Austen's original audience to engage in parallel historical reflections of their own. This was a complex task. If military victory, the expansion of the empire, and the influx of wealth from the spoils of war had ushered Britons into a modern era of aftermath, the arrival of this modernity also seemed, strangely, to have restored the political status quo. The year 1815 saw, in fact, the re-establishment across Continental Europe of the old despotic monarchies that had been deposed first by the French Revolutionaries and then by Napoleon's occupying armies; even in celebrating Britain's triumph in the war, many recognized that this victory had signed the death warrant for the possibilities for political transformation that had been opened up by the Revolutions of 1789. In this context, in which history's forward march also felt, uncannily, like a move backward, in which the advent of a new era had resuscitated moribund political formations and made fossilized dynasties like France's Bourbons into historical actors once again, the statements *Persuasion* makes—about the pleasures of memory, about devoted hearts that resist change, and about romance's relationship to lovers' nostalgia for the way they were—were necessarily that much more charged. This may be why Austen had to complicate the terms under which Anne and Wentworth recover their past so that, even in returning to 1806, they might remain open to the future that is on its way. This may be why, through her attention to the new vistas opened up by social change, she had to suggest, ultimately, that her characters have both revived the past and renewed it, 'more exquisitely happy, perhaps, in their reunion, than when it had been first projected; more tender, more tried, more fixed in a knowledge of each other's character, truth, and attachment' (p. 194). We would be wrong to think of the happy ending to this love story as having merely been delayed for eight years: Austen's point is that this is a different love story, in another time.

The Power of Precedents

In insisting, in the historicist spirit of Sir Walter Scott's historical fiction, that it matters what year it is, *Persuasion* sets itself against the *Baronetage*, the book in which this novel's own Sir Walter seeks consolation for the umpteenth time, at the moment when we readers open our own book:

this was the page at which the favourite volume always opened:

'ELLIOT OF KELLYNCH HALL.

'Walter Elliot, born March 1, 1760, married, July 15, 1784, Elizabeth, daughter of James Stevenson . . .; by which lady (who died 1801) he has issue Elizabeth, born June 1, 1785; Anne, born August 9, 1787; a still-born son, Nov. 5, 1789; Mary, born Nov. 20, 1791.' . . .

Then followed the history and rise of the ancient and respectable family, in the usual terms: how it had been first settled in Cheshire . . . exertions of loyalty, and dignity of baronet, in the first year of Charles II., with all the Marys and Elizabeths they had married; forming altogether two handsome duodecimo pages. (p. 9)

Like *Persuasion*'s author, who, as we have seen, carefully pinpoints her story's chronology, the compilers of the *Baronetage* prize exactitude of dating. So does Sir Walter, who customizes the Elliot entry by writing in even more dates. But unlike *Persuasion*, the *Baronetage* aspires to bring time to a standstill. In its scheme of things, only one thing about national history is really worth knowing: that nothing that happened was momentous enough to disrupt the bloodlines whose continuity the *Baronetage* celebrates. Anne's ability, on the second occasion in the book on which she speaks, to retrieve from memory details about Admiral Croft's career ('in the Trafalgar action, and . . . [stationed] in the East Indies since' (p. 24)) bears witness to how, since Wentworth's departure, she has found some consolation in reading the 'navy lists and newspapers' (p. 29) in which he might be mentioned. But this reading has something in common with her memories of her short-lived engagement, which continually occupy her thoughts, but which are never spoken of by the few people privy to the secret of the past: this reading is another thing that isolates her. While her family has cultivated their obliviousness to history, with the result that after two decades of war the names of admirals still mean nothing to them, Anne has had the chronicles of public life—history's raw materials—all to herself.

Reading Sir Walter's favourite entry in the who's-who over his shoulder, we notice how the same names get repeated in it generation after generation: the pattern encompasses even the new blue blood entering the lineage through 'all the Marys and Elizabeths [the Elliots] married'. Those repetitions suggest the resistance to new possibility that distinguishes Elliot life. Because Anne, a good listener, is so useful a sounding-board for the other characters (none of them intuiting that she might have grievances of her own to air), she often finds herself uncomfortably privy to the knowledge that to people like the Musgroves her sisters and father look stiff-necked and silly in their preoccupation with 'precedence' (p. 42). The word contains a pun that hovers over *Persuasion*'s discussion of the hold the past has on the present and to its related discussion of the hold books have on their readers. 'Precedence', as the Musgroves use the term when they complain to Anne, refers to the petty rules that dictate, for instance, who should give way to whom when people in polite society enter a dining room or carriage. (This etiquette works in favour of the daughter of a baronet, and so Mary Musgrove insists on upholding it.) But Austen also invokes 'precedence' as she demonstrates how, in the *Baronetage*'s scheme of things, the present is understood merely as perpetuating precedents set in the past. Valuing individuals' birth rather than their achievements, the *Baronetage* depicts a world in which people lead their lives along lines set out in a story which is already written.

Even as she writes a book about a heroine's self-determination, Austen reminds her audience that books may write us. In a novel in which several characters (from Sir Walter, to Anne, to Captain Benwick, and, following her accident, Louisa Musgrove) seek out opportunities to lose themselves in books, Sir Walter Elliot's 'book of books' (p. 12) stands, in fact, as Austen's Exhibit A in her investigation of the influence that words written down in the past wield over the present. As the critic Adela Pinch argues, *Persuasion* connects readers' indebtedness to books to the pressures exerted by a person of influence like Lady Russell, rumoured to be 'able to persuade a person to any thing!' (p. 87): that indebtedness similarly raises the question of the extent to which individuals' thoughts and desires can be their own.[8] Louisa and Benwick fall 'in love over poetry', after all— and Anne comes close to concluding, flippantly, that poetry—and their second-hand experience of the romantic feelings of the poets—made these two people fall in love (p. 135). One approach *Persuasion* uses to explore how people live in time is to probe the paradoxical way in which books, though esteemed for transcending the immediacy of experience, still persuade readers that they are scripts for living.

The tension built into *Persuasion*'s plotting is the effect of readers' worry that the *Baronetage*—that volume of precedents, commemorating the Elliots' life of 'sameness and . . . elegance . . . prosperity and . . . nothingness' (p. 14)—might give Austen her script. For *Persuasion* is plotted, provocatively, in a manner recalling the narrative patterns of many eighteenth-century novels: books such as Henry Fielding's *Joseph Andrews* or Clara Reeve's *The Old English Baron* in which legitimate heirs go missing, are found, and finally, in scenes of jubilant family reunion, are restored to the estates that are their birthright. (In his novels Sir Walter Scott resurrected this plot, finding in its linking of the generations and of past and future a way of compromising between his commitment to ideas of historical progress and his longing to turn back the clock.)[9] In Austen's near-parodic version of this restoration plot, the lead role goes to Mr William Walter Elliot, heir presumptive to Sir Walter's entailed estate. When *Persuasion* opens, Mr Elliot is a fading memory, banished to the past for his immunity to Anne's older sister's charms and his marriage outside his class. (Elizabeth, the narrator explains, 'could not admit him to be worth thinking of again' (p. 13).) We have known him therefore only as so many words inscribed into Sir

---

[8] 'Lost in a Book: Austen's *Persuasion*', in *Strange Fits of Passion: Epistemologies of Emotion, Hume to Austen* (Stanford, Calif.: Stanford University Press, 1996), 139.

[9] On Scott's use of this plot, and *Persuasion*'s repudiation of that use, see Jane Millgate, '*Persuasion* and the Presence of Scott', *Persuasions: Journal of the Jane Austen Society of North America*, 15 (1993), 184–95.

Walter's 'book of books', but as soon as that writing comes to life in Volume II of Austen's book, as soon as Mr Elliot returns to the family fold in a homecoming that counterbalances Wentworth's return from the sea, Austen teases readers with the possibility that Mr Elliot's story might conscript Anne. She might end up the heroine of a restoration plot: Mr Elliot is guaranteed the estate, but he might also win the competition for the girl and get his 'wishes that [her] name might never change' (p. 152). Anne *is* named Anne, but we worry that, even so, she might not prove the exception to the disheartening rule set out in the *Baronetage*'s list of 'all the Marys and Elizabeths'—the rule that every woman's story is predestined to repeat every other's (p. 9).

That this sort of reincarnation of the past could be Anne's fate adds resonance to the wording the narrator uses in the scene in Volume I that sees Anne, the Musgroves, and Wentworth taking a country walk to Winthrop, the home of the Musgroves' cousin Charles. To numb her pain when she overhears a flirtatious conversation between Wentworth and Louisa Musgrove, Anne tries repeating to herself the lines of poetry with which earlier she had 'occupied her mind', but, in the event, the narrator explains, finds it impossible to '*fall into a quotation again*' (pp. 71–2; emphasis added). This scene suggests some conflicting accounts of what books can do for the bookish. The reader altogether absorbed by 'the sweets of poetical despondence' (p. 72) has erected a buffer between herself and the world. Anne is not that reader, but the fact that she even hopes to find in 'musings and quotations' the wherewithal to 'occup[y] her mind' (p. 71) should not be discounted: *Persuasion* throughout broods on the difference it makes to the relationship between the sexes that men have occupations and women, at least of Anne's class, do not. (Remember how Anne explains her belief that Captain Benwick will recover from his bereavement sooner than she will recover from her loss of Wentworth. Benwick will 'rally' because he is younger than she is 'in feeling, if not in fact; younger as a man' (p. 82), and because, as a man, he has a 'profession, pursuits, business', as Anne comments later to Captain Harville, to 'take [him] back into the world' (p. 187).) On the other hand, however, *Persuasion* does not disguise the costs of Anne's 'fall[s] into quotation'. Anne's tendency to define herself as a looker-on rather than a participant, her preference for 'solitude and reflection' (p. 69), her need to abstract herself

from the agitations of the present moment, make readers feel especially tender toward her. For one thing, we alone are aware of the
inner life going on beneath that quiet exterior; for another, Anne's
pensiveness as she gets lost in her thoughts resembles our own state
as we lose *our* selves in Austen's book. But these traits in Anne's
character also amount to a declaration that she has given up on the
future and resigned herself to living off musings, quotations, and
memories. And when Mr Elliot brings a second, competing marriage
plot into the novel, Anne risks become a quotation herself, another in
a long line of Lady Elliots of Kellynch Hall.

Lady Russell embraces this prospect. She longs, she says to Anne,
'to look forward and see you occupying your dear mother's place'
and see the title of Lady Elliot 'revived' again in Anne, who is, she
declares, her 'mother's self in countenance and disposition' (pp.
129–30). This vision of a future which would restore and replicate
the past, a vision in which, enticingly, Kellynch figures as property
transmitted along matrilineal rather than patrilineal lines, triggers
the only instance in the novel when the sense of right that Anne has
developed in eight years of reviewing the past looks vulnerable to
outside interference. 'For a few moments her imagination and her
heart were bewitched' (p. 130). Anne has reason to be stirred by
Lady Russell's nostalgic longing. She felt deeply the loss of her
mother. So she understands that Lady Russell's match making is
more than another manifestation of the 'prejudices on the side of
ancestry' that did such damage in 1806 (p. 15); it continues in
another form Lady Russell's own mourning for the lost past she
shared with a woman to whom she was, as Chapter I advises,
strongly attached (p. 10).

But Anne has never felt much for Mr Elliot. She has been curious
about his motives for renewing family ties. She has observed with
mingled vexation and amusement his belated conversion to ideas
about the value of rank that she herself contravenes when she main-
tains, despite paternal disapproval, her ties with impoverished Mrs
Smith. Flattering as they are, Mr Elliot's attentions represent therefore nothing but 'unwelcome obtrusiveness' (p. 170). They arouse
Wentworth's envy and cause him to hang back just when he should
advance. They delay the only story whose climax we care about. It is
not a disappointment but a relief when the revelations delivered by
Mrs Smith and her friend Nurse Rooke bring Mr Elliot's story to an

abrupt close. Cynical, self-serving motives, Chapter ix of Volume II reveals, explain his sudden outburst of family feeling. He has reconciled himself with his relations only to prevent Mrs Clay from snaring Sir Walter: if Sir Walter married again and the union produced a son and heir, his own inheritance would be prevented.

The unmasking of Mr Elliot has so little impact that one could reasonably conclude that his main function in the book is, by amorously eyeing Anne as she walks on the causeway at Lyme, to get Wentworth looking in her direction as well (p. 87). Another hypothesis is possible: perhaps Austen needs to arrange for two figures—first, Wentworth, then Mr Elliot—to return, in order to distinguish between two modes of restoring the past. To propose that Wentworth and Anne are more happy eight years on than when their union was 'first projected' (p. 194) is, after all, to suggest that this couple has used the shadows cast by the passing of things to make something new. Austen needs to confirm that the arc of return which her storyline traces should not be equated with immunity to change. One detail suggests the political stakes of making this distinction. In the *Baronetage*'s record of family history, the place that Mr Elliot now occupies was assigned, in the paragraph as it 'originally stood from the printer's hands', to the Elliot heir who was to have been born in the revolutionary year of 1789. Austen has conjured Mr Elliot into life as the substitute for that stillborn son, whose birth announcement ('Nov. 5, 1789') does poignant double duty as his obituary (p. 9).

Or perhaps *Persuasion* must contrast possible restoration plots because Austen has concerns about how easy it is to see restoration of the past as women's work—and so deny women access to the dynamism of historical life. In Volume I, while her father and Elizabeth relinquish their responsibilities as landed gentry and make the move to Bath, Anne is left behind at Kellynch, where she diligently does the work of preservation: 'making a duplicate of the catalogue of my father's books and pictures' (p. 36). To be in thrall to the family heirlooms seems typical of Anne's plight. But Sir Walter's land agent, Mr Shepherd, makes a statement suggesting women in general are susceptible to being saddled with the care of the past. Touting Mrs Croft as Kellynch's tenant, he declares a childless lady like her 'the very best preserver of furniture in the world' (p. 24).

In Volume I Wentworth also subscribes to this coercive account of women's ideal relationship to time and past precedents, as the conversation overheard by Anne as they walk to Winthrop attests. Praising Louisa for her single-minded self-confidence, complaining about timorous, persuadable characters (and so secretly complaining, we infer, about Anne), Wentworth declares: 'It is the worst evil of too yielding and indecisive a character, that no influence over it can be depended on.—You are never sure of a good impression being durable. Every body may sway it' (p. 74). Wentworth is inconsistent when he identifies the problem with persuadableness. In his understanding of over-anxious characters who second-guess themselves and change their minds, the problem is not simply their susceptibility to influence. Wentworth *wants* to influence women. But the possible disappointment with a persuadable woman, he seems to say, is that, once impressed, she remains open to new impressions, rather than being faithful to the earlier one, and (like the 'lady' imagined by Mr Shepherd) preserving it. His view resembles that of William Wordsworth in 'Tintern Abbey', another great Romantic-period exploration of the work of time: a woman—Anne or Wordsworth's sister Dorothy—is to be a mirror in which a man might yet 'behold . . . what [he] was once'.[10] But in their receptivity, the persuadable characters whom Wentworth deplores might be said to live *in* time.[11] Depending on context, 'inconstancy' can be just another name for an openness to change.

Anne in fact is less intent on preserving the traditions of an 'ancient family' like her own (p. 103) than she is curious about the globetrotting that Mrs Croft has done under the Navy's auspices (p. 61), about the elasticity of mind that enables Mrs Smith, though crippled and confined to two small rooms, to find 'employment which carried her out of herself' (p. 125), about Mrs Rooke's working life as 'a nurse by profession' (p. 126). These women's lives might well remind her, by way of contrast, of how restricted and homebound her own life at Kellynch was. For all its romance, *Persuasion* has something unromantic to say about love and narrow horizons. In commenting in her opening that Anne had not been able to recover from her loss of Wentworth in 1806 because 'she had been too

---

[10] William Wordsworth, 'Lines written a few miles above Tintern Abbey', l. 121.

[11] Susan Morgan argues with Wentworth's reasoning at greater length and to wonderful effect in *In the Meantime: Character and Perception in Jane Austen's Fiction* (Chicago: University of Chicago Press, 1980), 166–82.

dependant on time alone; no aid had been given in change of place'
(p. 28), Austen audaciously raises the possibility—explored again
when Captain Harville and Anne hold their debate on constancy in
the penultimate chapter—that a woman's emotional fidelity might
simply be the symptom of her physical immobility.[12] No 'novelty or
enlargement of society' assisted Anne in the effort of putting 1806
behind her (p. 28), and yet, as she observes to Harville, 'continual
occupation and change soon weaken impressions'. *Persuasion*'s promotion of the mobile, active lives of sailors over the landed,
immobile life of gentlemen, of naval chronicles over the *Baronetage*,
evidences Austen's attention to recent history. But the novel makes it
hard to say whether women's lives conform to the same calendar as
men's and whether, in 1815, a new historical era has dawned for
them as well. What if, as Anne suggests, their role is still to 'live at
home, quiet, confined, [where] our feelings prey upon us' (p. 187)?

'No . . . examples in books': An Unscripted Future

This amazing conversation between Anne and Harville, which forms
the climax to the novel, is made that much more tense and dramatic
by our knowledge that Wentworth, in his corner of the drawing-
room at the White Hart Inn, hears it all. During her debate with
Harville, Anne voices some powerful social criticism. She proposes
that if, as Harville asserts, men and women have different natures it
must be because the sexes are granted unequal opportunities,
because social codes put men and women in different relations to
occupation and change. And, as this debate develops, and as it
becomes clear that Anne, in asserting her sex's capacity to love 'longest, when . . . hope is gone', is also speaking out and telling her *own*
story (p. 189), Austen returns to the issue of books' hold on their
readers. Harville states to Anne that in nearly every book he opens he
finds proofs that women are the changeable sex who do not love as
faithfully as men. 'I could bring you fifty quotations in a moment on
my side the argument' (p. 188). (Invoking the teachings of literature,
he momentarily forgets the lessons of events: the counter-example
furnished, in his own household, by Benwick, who proposed to Louisa only months after the death of his first fiancée, Harville's sister.)

---

[12] As Monica F. Cohen notes in *Professional Domesticity and the Victorian Novel*
(Cambridge: Cambridge University Press, 1998), 25.

In response, Anne questions the authority Harville grants to books as archives of received wisdom. Her words send the novel back full circle to its opening image of Sir Walter with pen in hand annotating 'the book of books': 'if you please, no reference to examples in books. Men have had every advantage of us in telling their own story . . . the pen has been in their hands' (p. 188).

This is not the final verdict *Persuasion* delivers on what books do to and for readers. Austen has Anne's and Harville's debate about constancy conclude in a draw, she begins the next chapter hinting that she's uncertain whether the story she's told is 'bad morality' (p. 199), and, in the same relativistic spirit, she keeps her options open in assessing the value of reading. Austen neither requires us to trust in books (or readers), nor requires us to distrust them. If Anne rejects the second-hand experience obtained in reading when Harville wants to authorize his argument with 'examples from books', she herself has earlier recommended a course of reading to Captain Benwick, thinking that he would benefit from acquaintance with 'examples of moral and religious endurance' (p. 85). Certainly, *Persuasion* does not endorse the anxious attitude toward books that Charles Musgrove expresses when he concludes that Benwick's reading 'has done him no harm, for he has fought as well as read' (p. 176). Instead, Austen often shakes up just those gendered oppositions—between manly deeds and womanly words, heroic activity and timorous inaction—which Charles relies on when he reasons that Benwick's war service might compensate for the book-love that has impaired Benwick's masculinity. Remember that the private reading with which Anne has occupied her mind in her years of loneliness is first made visible when Anne uses her knowledge of Navy lists to supply details about Admiral Croft's career. When, with this passage, *Persuasion* begins its discussion of reading, Austen doesn't do as Charles does. She doesn't separate solitary reading from the public service performed by men of action; she puts them into proximity. This entails reconceptualizing the female reader—a figure satirists had long pictured as idle, self-indulgent, and socially irresponsible—in significant ways.

Persuasion illuminates nineteenth-century women's history by suggesting, through its references to the 'navy lists and newspapers' that give Anne her 'authority' (p. 29), how journalism, and the new profession of the war correspondent especially, had made the international conflicts of the era into wars one might read about. Those wars had 'home' fronts in ways that wars never had before. As battles waged in distant lands became a story consumed in British parlours, amid families' daily routines, and as the nation's military struggle came to be understood through the demands it made on private persons, gender roles were revised in ways that made the identity of the patriot compatible with that of the domestic woman. Austen's characterization of Anne registers that domestication of war. It shows that by 1815 it was possible to value feminine reading as a vehicle of feminine patriotism.[13]

Persuasion concludes in this spirit, with two sentences that assert the national relevance of a woman's private virtues. Those sentences are the novelist's parting tribute to her heroine, but, memorializing the end of an era, they also acknowledge the war effort of the nation of readers who on a daily basis had been perusing the papers and paying and repaying a 'tax of quick alarm':

[Wentworth's] profession was all that could ever make [Anne's] friends wish [her] tenderness less; the dread of a future war all that could dim her sunshine. She gloried in being a sailor's wife, but she must pay the tax of quick alarm for belonging to that profession which is, if possible, more distinguished in its domestic virtues than in its national importance. (p. 203)

The carefully chosen metaphor alludes to the new taxation schemes that the British Crown had introduced as war measures, another innovation that linked the fates of private persons more tightly to the fate of the nation. Austen may wonder whether, given their different relations to remembrance and forgetting, men and women can ever occupy the same place on the timeline of national history, but there is no doubt that, in ways that distinguish her from previous Austen heroines, Anne belongs to the nation—to the 'us' she gestures toward when, in her first words in the novel, she speaks up for the sailors' claims to the nation's gratitude: 'The navy . . . who have done so much *for us*, have at least an equal claim with any other set of men, for all the comforts and all the privileges which any home can give' (p. 21; emphasis added). Anne belongs to that 'us' in part

---

[13] See Linda Colley, *Britons: Forging the Nation, 1707–1837* (New Haven: Yale University Press, 1992), 250–62, and Mary A. Favret, 'War Correspondence: Reading Romantic War', *Prose Studies*, 19 (1996), 173–85.

because Austen's syntax has granted her an occupation. '[S]he must pay the tax of quick alarm for belonging to that profession.' The novel's surprising last sentence—which surprises not least by jolting us out of the past tense and into the present—attaches the word 'profession', not to the word sailor, as one might expect, but rather to sailor's wife. It is as though Austen is imagining that those years of vigilant study of newspapers and Navy lists have given Anne an occupation in earnest, remedying the lack of occupations for women that she laments in conversation with Harville. Perhaps in wrapping up *Persuasion* in this manner, Austen means to gesture toward a new value system in which readerly feeling can count, and be rewarded, as work.

The most magnanimous of the rewards received by the readers in, and of, *Persuasion* is dispensed in the chapter just before this one. One proof of the generosity with which Austen treats her readers is that when her book's longed-for happy ending arrives, this climax takes form, thrillingly, as a scene of reading. Austen organizes Chapter xi of Volume II so that it shifts from dialogue—Harville's and Anne's debate about constancy, and, before that, Mrs Musgrove's and Mrs Croft's conversation about long engagements (p. 186)—to the written word. This last-minute swerve almost takes us unawares. The letter of business that, while Anne and Harville were conversing, had seemed to be engrossing Wentworth in his own corner of the room proves to be merely the cover for the love letter he has been writing to Anne:

he drew out a letter from under the scattered paper, placed it before Anne with eyes of glowing entreaty fixed on her for a moment, and hastily collecting his gloves, was again out of the room, almost before Mrs. Musgrove was aware of his being in it—the work of an instant!

The revolution which one instant had made in Anne, was almost beyond expression. (p. 190)

Happiness is salvaged from mischance as soon as Anne's eyes 'devour' Wentworth's declaration of unfailing constancy. His tone is urgent. Happiness must be seized now or never: 'Tell me not that I am too late, that such precious feelings are gone for ever' (p. 191). The intimate effect that the device of the included letter creates for us—for as Anne reads we read too and are plunged into joyful agitation just as she is—is one of the boons of the scene.

It makes this chapter's healing of the lovers' rift feel that much more miraculous, and that much more fragile, to learn that it took Austen two attempts to craft it. In the middle of July 1816, Austen wrote a tenth and an eleventh chapter for the second volume of her novel, and on 16 July, wrote 'FINIS' at the bottom of what she took to be its last page. Two days later she came back to add an additional paragraph and to write 'FINIS' one more time. But she remained dissatisfied and, over the next three weeks, composed two new chapters, adding that scene of debate and letter-writing that goes on in the Musgroves' rooms at the inn, and reincorporating some of the original Chapter XI in what is now the novel's final chapter.

The chapters that Austen threw out (reproduced here in Appendix A) do not include a letter or much conversation. Austen's draft makes the *rapprochement* between Anne and Wentworth the consequence of an exchange of meaningful looks. Admiral Croft has commissioned Wentworth to investigate whether the gossip about the imminent marriage between Anne and Mr Elliot is true and whether, if it is, the couple will wish to live at Kellynch. When the Admiral contrives to leave her tête-à-tête with Wentworth, Anne denies the rumour, Wentworth looks at her keenly, and, then, 'Her Countenance did not discourage'. 'It was a silent, but a very powerful Dialogue,' the narrator says: 'on his side, Supplication, on her's acceptance' (p. 207). This is too easy. Anne's hard-won eloquence in her conversation with Harville is one thing that makes Austen's rewritten Chapter XI so compelling by comparison. Plainly, Austen sought to do more than recount how a heroine finds romantic happiness; she also wished to recount how she breaks her silence. It is Wentworth who, in the revision, repeats Anne's experience during Volume I's walk to Winthrop and who occupies as she did the vulnerable position of the silenced eavesdropper ('I can listen no longer in silence,' he writes (p. 191), anxious to be heard, but this is only the start of his letter, and listen longer he does).

Critical commentary on *Persuasion* traditionally made much of the fact that Austen composed it while in the early stages of the disease that would end her life in July 1817, five months before the novel was published. The assumption that Anne's melancholy about missed chances and lost youth must express Austen's own regrets predisposed many commentators to discover a mood of wistful nostalgia in Austen's final work. Austen, too, is supposed to be savouring while she can 'the sweets of poetical despondence' and 'fall[ing] into a quotation' (p. 72). But at its climax there is nothing autumnal or gently resigned about *Persuasion*.

Woolf was right to associate the novel, instead, with a voyage launched onto uncharted seas. Wentworth's letter, the critic Mary Favret observes, 'shocks like a thunderclap'.[14] Austen choreographs the scene of Wentworth's proposal so that, as Anne reads his letter, she sinks 'into the chair which [Wentworth] had occupied, succeeding to the very spot where he had leaned and written' (pp. 190–1). These arrangements eliminate the time-lag, the safe interval for reflection, that normally separates a writer from a reader. They reconnect reading to the immediacy, urgency, and discomposing energies of speech. To similar effect, *Persuasion* opens out onto the time-frame of the contemporary in its last sentence. Austen, it is worth recalling, begins this sentence by writing 'She *gloried* in being a sailor's wife,' but forgoes the past tense that is conventional for novels when she continues, 'she *must* pay the tax of quick alarm' (p. 203; emphases added). This shift in tense unsettles, just a bit, the storybook settlement—the 'happily ever after'—that we expect from, and which is put in place by, Austen's marriage plot. It leaves us rather in a risky state in which nothing is a done deal and '[a]ny thing [is] possible'—Anne's own situation following 'the revolution' precipitated by the letter (p. 190).

'The revolution which one instant had made in Anne, was almost beyond expression.' In this sentence, the choice of the word 'revolution' works as so much else in *Persuasion* does—to place Anne in the midst of the historical life of an era that had just begun and did not know where it was going.

---

[14] Mary A. Favret, *Romantic Correspondence: Women, Politics and the Fiction of Letters* (Cambridge: Cambridge University Press, 1994), 166.

NOTE ON THE TEXT

Persuasion and *Northanger Abbey* were published together by John Murray in December 1817 (title-page 1818) in a four-volume edition of 2,500 copies. The edition also included the 'Biographical Notice of the Author' by Austen's brother Henry. The first American editions (1,250 copies each) were published by Carey and Lea of Philadelphia in 1832–3. Mme Isabelle de Montolieu translated *Persuasion* as *La Famille Elliot* (1821, 1828). The manuscript of *Persuasion* does not survive and Austen did not live to see the work through the press herself. What does survive in Austen's own hand from the writing of *Persuasion* is her original version of the ending (see Appendix A). The text of this was first printed by her nephew J. E. Austen-Leigh in the second edition of his *A Memoir of Jane Austen* in 1871 and subsequently edited by R. W. Chapman in 1926. A full account of the emendations and erasures in the manuscript, and of the variants, may be found in *The Oxford Illustrated Jane Austen* (1969), v. 274–85.

All six novels were included in Bentley's cheap Standard Novels series (6s. a volume) in 1833 (repr. 1866, 1869, 1878–9, 1882). Since the first Everyman's Library edition introduced by R. Brinley Johnson (London, 1892; rev. edn. Mary Lascelles, London and New York, 1962–4), the six major novels have been reissued in cheap collected editions in (for example) Oxford World's Classics, Everyman, Penguin, Virago. The standard edition of the novels is that of R. W. Chapman (illustrated; 6 vols.; Oxford 1923–54; rev. Mary Lascelles, 1965–7), with commentaries and appendices. The Oxford English Novels series issued the six major novels in 1970–1, based on the standard edition, in which Chapman's textual apparatus was revised and his emendations reconsidered by James Kinsley (see Textual Notes, p. 227).

The present edition reproduces the Oxford English Novels text, which is based on the first edition.

SELECT BIBLIOGRAPHY

Letters and Biography

Jane Austen's Letters, 3rd edn., collected and ed. Deirdre Le Faye (Oxford and New York: Oxford University Press, 1995).

Austen-Leigh, James Edward, *A Memoir of Jane Austen and Other Family Recollections*, ed. Kathryn Sutherland, Oxford World's Classics (Oxford: Oxford University Press, 2002).

Austen-Leigh, William, and Austen-Leigh, Richard Arthur, *Jane Austen: A Family Record* (1913), revised and enlarged Deirdre Le Faye (London: The British Library, 1989).

Fergus, Jan, *Jane Austen: A Literary Life* (Basingstoke: Macmillan, 1991).

Honan, Park, *Jane Austen: Her Life* (London: Weidenfeld and Nicolson, 1987).

Nokes, David, *Jane Austen: A Life* (London: Fourth Estate, 1997).

Tomalin, Claire, *Jane Austen: A Life* (London: Viking, 1997).

Tucker, George Holbert, *A Goodly Heritage: A History of Jane Austen's Family* (Manchester: Carcanet, 1983).

Historical and Literary Contexts

Colley, Linda, *Britons: Forging the Nation, 1707–1837* (New Haven and London: Yale University Press, 1992).

Copeland, Edward, *Women Writing About Money: Women's Fiction in England, 1790–1820* (Cambridge: Cambridge University Press, 1995).

Davidoff, Leonore, and Hall, Catherine, *Family Fortunes: Men and Women of the English Middle Class, 1780–1850* (1987; rpt. London: Routledge, 1994).

Guest, Harriet, *Small Change: Women, Learning, Patriotism, 1750–1810* (Chicago and London: University of Chicago Press, 2000).

Herzog, Don, *Poisoning the Minds of the Lower Orders* (Princeton: Princeton University Press, 1998).

Kelly, Gary, *English Fiction of the Romantic Period 1789–1830* (London: Longman, 1989).

Pearson, Jacqueline, *Women's Reading in Britain 1750 1835. A Dangerous Recreation* (Cambridge: Cambridge University Press, 1999).

Richardson, Alan, *Literature, Education, and Romanticism: Reading as Social Practice, 1780–1832* (Cambridge: Cambridge University Press, 1994).

Shoemaker, Robert B., *Gender in English Society, 1650–1850: The Emergence of Separate Spheres?* (London and New York: Longman, 1998).

Vickery, Amanda, *The Gentleman's Daughter: Women's Lives in Georgian England* (New Haven and London: Yale University Press, 1998).

Critical Works on Jane Austen

Brown, Julia Prewitt, *Jane Austen's Novels: Social Change and Literary Form* (Cambridge, Mass.: Harvard University Press, 1979).

Butler, Marilyn, *Jane Austen and the War of Ideas* (1975; rpt. Oxford: Oxford University Press, 1987).

Byrne, Paula, *Jane Austen and the Theatre* (London: Hambledon and London, 2002).

Collins, Irene, *Jane Austen and the Clergy* (London: Hambledon Press, 1994).

Copeland, Edward, 'What is a Competence? Jane Austen, her Sister Novelists, and the 5%'s', *Modern Language Studies*, 9 (1979), 161–8.

—— and McMaster, Juliet (eds.), *The Cambridge Companion to Jane Austen* (Cambridge: Cambridge University Press, 1997).

Duckworth, Alistair, *The Improvement of the Estate: A Study of Jane Austen's Novels* (Baltimore: Johns Hopkins University Press, 1971).

Favret, Mary A., 'Jane Austen and the Look of Letters', in *Romantic Correspondence: Women, Politics and the Fiction of Letters* (Cambridge: Cambridge University Press, 1993).

Galperin, William H., *The Historical Austen* (Philadelphia: University of Pennsylvania Press, 2003).

Gilbert, Sandra, and Gubar, Susan, 'Inside the House of Fiction: Jane Austen's Tenants of Possibility', in *The Madwoman in the Attic: The Woman Writer and the Nineteenth-Century Literary Imagination* (New Haven and London: Yale University Press, 1979).

Grey, David, Litz, A. Walton, and Southam, Brian (eds.), *The Jane Austen Handbook: With a Dictionary of Jane Austen's Life and Works* (London: Athlone Press, 1986).

Harding, D. W., 'Regulated Hatred: An Aspect of the Work of Jane Austen', *Scrutiny*, 8 (1940), rpt. in Monica Lawlor (ed.), *Regulated Hatred and Other Essays on Jane Austen* (London: Athlone Press, 1998).

Harris, Jocelyn, *Jane Austen's Art of Memory* (Cambridge: Cambridge University Press, 1989).

Johnson, Claudia L., *Jane Austen: Women, Politics and the Novel* (Chicago and London: University of Chicago Press, 1988).

—— *Equivocal Beings: Politics, Gender, and Sentimentality in the 1790s: Wollstonecraft, Radcliffe, Burney, Austen* (Chicago and London: University of Chicago Press, 1995).

Jones, Vivien, *How to Study a Jane Austen Novel*, 2nd edn. (Basingstoke: Macmillan Press, 1997).

Kaplan, Deborah, *Jane Austen Among Women* (Baltimore and London: Johns Hopkins University Press, 1992).

Kirkham, Margaret, *Jane Austen: Feminism and Fiction* (Brighton: Harvester Press, 1983).

Lascelles, Mary, *Jane Austen and Her Art* (Oxford: Oxford University Press, 1939).

Looser, Devoney (ed.), *Jane Austen and Discourses of Feminism* (Basingstoke: Macmillan, 1995).

Lynch, Deidre Shauna, 'Jane Austen and the Social Machine', in *The Economy of Character: Novels, Market Culture, and the Business of Inner Meaning* (Chicago and London: University of Chicago Press, 1998).

—— (ed.), *Janeites: Austen's Disciples and Devotees* (Princeton and Oxford: Princeton University Press, 2000).

Miller, D. A., 'The Danger of Narrative in Jane Austen', in *Narrative and its Discontents: Problems of Closure in the Traditional Novel* (Princeton: Princeton University Press, 1981).

Moler, Kenneth L., *Jane Austen's Art of Allusion* (Lincoln, Neb.: University of Nebraska Press, 1968).

Monaghan, David, *Jane Austen: Structure and Social Vision* (London: Macmillan, 1980).

Morgan, Susan, *In the Meantime: Character and Perception in Jane Austen's Fiction* (Chicago: University of Chicago Press, 1980).

Mudrick, Marvin, *Jane Austen: Irony as Defense and Discovery* (Berkeley and London: University of California Press, 1968).

Phillipps, K. C., *Jane Austen's English* (London: Deutsch, 1970).

Piggott, Patrick, *The Innocent Diversion: A Study of Music in the Life and Writings of Jane Austen* (London, 1979).

Poovey, Mary, *The Proper Lady and the Woman Writer: Ideology as Style in the Works of Mary Wollstonecraft, Mary Shelley, Jane Austen* (Chicago and London: University of Chicago Press, 1984).

Sales, Roger, *Jane Austen and Representations of Regency England* (London: Routledge, 1994).

Southam, B. C., *Jane Austen's Literary Manuscripts: A Study of the Novelist's Development through the Surviving Papers* (Oxford: Oxford University Press, 1964).

—— *Jane Austen: The Critical Heritage*, 2 vols. (London and New York: Routledge and Kegan Paul, 1968, 1987).

—— *Jane Austen and the Navy* (London and New York: Hambledon and London, 2000).

Stafford, Fiona, 'Jane Austen', in Michael O'Neill (ed.), *Literature of the Romantic Period: A Bibliographical Guide* (Oxford: Clarendon Press, 1998).

Stewart, Maaja A., *Domestic Realities and Imperial Fictions: Jane Austen's Novels in Eighteenth-Century Contexts* (Athens, Ga. and London: University of Georgia Press, 1993).

Tanner, Tony, *Jane Austen* (Basingstoke: Macmillan, 1987).

Tave, Stuart, *Some Words of Jane Austen* (Chicago and London: University of Chicago Press, 1973).

Thompson, James, *Between Self and World: The Novels of Jane Austen* (University Park, Pa.: Pennsylvania State University Press, 1988).

Tuite, Clara, *Romantic Austen: Sexual Politics and the Literary Canon* (Cambridge: Cambridge University Press, 2002).

Waldron, Mary, *Jane Austen and the Fiction of her Time* (Cambridge: Cambridge University Press, 1999).

Wallace, Tara Ghoshal, *Jane Austen and Narrative Authority* (Basingstoke: Macmillan, 1995).

Williams, Raymond, *The Country and the City* (Oxford: Oxford University Press, 1973).

Wiltshire, John, *Jane Austen and the Body: 'The Picture of Health'* (Cambridge: Cambridge University Press, 1992).

Websites

http://www.pemberley.com/   *The Republic of Pemberley.*

http://www.jasna.org/   *The Jane Austen Society of North America.*

http://www.ils.unc.edu/~mohas/austenpathfinder.htm   Mohanty, Suchi, *Jane Austen: A Pathfinder.*

Critical Works on Persuasion

Auerbach, Nina, ' "Brave New World": Evolution and Revolution in *Persuasion*', in *Romantic Imprisonment: Women and Other Glorified Outcasts* (New York: Columbia University Press, 1985), 38–54.

Cohen, Monica F., 'Persuading the Navy Home: Austen and Professional Domesticism', in *Professional Domesticity in the Victorian Novel* (Cambridge: Cambridge University Press, 1998), 12–43.

Dames, Nicholas, 'Austen's Nostalgics', *Representations*, 73 (2001), 117–43.

Favret, Mary A., 'Being True to Jane Austen', in John Kucich and Dianne F. Sadoff (eds.), *Victorian Afterlife* (Minneapolis: University of Minnesota Press, 2000), 64–82.

Giordano, Julia, 'The Word as Battleground in Jane Austen's *Persuasion*', in Carol J. Singley and Susan Elizabeth Sweeney (eds.), *Anxious Power: Reading, Writing, and Ambivalence in Narrative by Women* (Albany, NY: State University of New York Press, 1993), 107–24.

Heydt-Stevenson, Jill, ' "Unbecoming Conjunctions": Mourning the Loss of Landscape and Love in *Persuasion*', *Eighteenth-Century Fiction*, 8: 1 (1995), 51–71.

Johnson, Judy Van Sickle, 'The Bodily Frame: Learning Romance in *Persuasion*', *Nineteenth-Century Fiction*, 38 (1983), 43–61.

O' Farrell, Mary Ann, 'Mortifying Persuasions: The Worldliness of Jane Austen', in *Telling Complexions: The Nineteenth-Century English Novel and the Blush* (Durham, NC and London: Duke University Press, 1997), 28–57.

Pinch, Adela, 'Lost in a Book: Jane Austen's *Persuasion*', in *Strange Fits of Passion: Epistemologies of Emotion, Hume to Austen* (Stanford, Calif.: Stanford University Press, 1996), 137–63.

Richardson, Alan, 'Of Heartache and Head Injury: Minds, Brains, and the Subject of *Persuasion*', in *British Romanticism and the Science of the Mind* (Cambridge: Cambridge University Press, 2001), 93–113.

Simons, Judy (ed.), *'Mansfield Park' and 'Persuasion'*, New Casebooks (London: Macmillan, 1997).

Stewart, Garrett, ' "Whomsoever It May Concern": Austen's Open Letters to the Reader', in *Dear Reader: The Conscripted Audience in Nineteenth-Century British Fiction* (Baltimore and London: Johns Hopkins University Press, 1996), 89–112.

Warhol, Robyn, 'The Look, the Body, and the Heroine: A Feminist-Narratological Reading of *Persuasion*', *Novel: A Forum on Fiction*, 26 (1992), 5–21.

Further Reading in Oxford World's Classics

Austen, Jane, *Catharine and Other Writings*, ed. Margaret Anne Doody and Douglas Murray.

—— *Emma*, ed. James Kinsley and Adela Pinch.

—— *Mansfield Park*, ed. James Kinsley and Jane Stabler.

—— *Northanger Abbey, Lady Susan, The Watsons, and Sanditon*, ed. James Kinsley, John Davie, and Claudia L. Johnson.

—— *Pride and Prejudice*, ed. James Kinsley.

—— *Sense and Sensibility*, ed. James Kinsley.

Austen-Leigh, James Edward, *A Memoir of Jane Austen and Other Family Recollections*, ed. Kathryn Sutherland.

A CHRONOLOGY OF JANE AUSTEN

Life	*Historical and Cultural Background*
1775	(16 Dec.) born in Steventon, Hampshire, seventh child of Revd George Austen (1731–1805), Rector of Steventon and Deane, and Cassandra Austen, née Leigh (1739–1827)	American War of Independence begins.
1776		American Declaration of Independence; James Cook's third Pacific voyage.
1778		France enters war on side of American revolutionaries. Frances Burney, *Evelina*
1779	Birth of youngest brother, Charles (1779–1852); eldest brother James (1765–1819) goes to St John's College, Oxford; distant cousin Thomas Knight II and wife Catherine, of Godmersham in Kent, visit Steventon and take close interest in brother Edward (1767–1852)	Britain at war with Spain; siege of Gibraltar (to 1783); Samuel Crompton's spinning mule revolutionizes textile production.
1781	Cousin Eliza Hancock (thought by some to be natural daughter of Warren Hastings) marries Jean-François Capot de Feuillide in France	Warren Hastings deposes Raja of Benares and seizes treasure from Nabob of Oudh.
1782	Austens put on first amateur theatricals	Frances Burney, *Cecilia* William Gilpin, *Observations on the River Wye* William Cowper, *Poems*
1783	JA, sister Cassandra (1773–1845), and cousin Jane Cooper are tutored by Mrs Cawley in Oxford then Southampton until they fall ill with typhoid fever; death of aunt Jane Cooper from typhoid; brother Edward formally adopted by the Knights; JA's mentor, Anne Lefroy, moves into neighbourhood	American independence conceded at Peace of Versailles; Pitt becomes Prime Minister.

	Life	Historical and Cultural Background
1784	Performance of Sheridan's *The Rivals* at Steventon	India Act imposes some parliamentary control on East India Company; Prince Regent begins to build Brighton Pavilion; death of Samuel Johnson.
1785	Attends Abbey House School, Reading, with Cassandra	William Cowper, *The Task*
1786	Brother Francis (1774–1865) enters Royal Naval Academy, Portsmouth; brother Edward on Grand Tour (to 1790); JA and Cassandra leave school for good	William Gilpin, *Observations, Relative Chiefly to Picturesque Beauty . . . particularly the Mountains, and Lakes of Cumberland, and Westmoreland*
1787	Starts writing 'Juvenilia' (to 1793); cousin Eliza de Feuillide visits Steventon; performance of Susannah Centlivre's *The Wonder* at Steventon	American constitution signed.
1788	*The Chances* and *Tom Thumb* performed at Steventon; brother Henry (1771–1850) goes to St John's College, Oxford; brother Francis sails to East Indies on HMS *Perseverance*; cousins Eliza de Feuillide and Philadelphia Walter attend Hastings's trial	Warren Hastings impeached for corruption in India; George III's first spell of madness.
1789	James and Henry in Oxford produce periodical, *The Loiterer* (to Mar. 1790); JA begins lifelong friendship with Martha Lloyd and sister Mary when their mother rents Deane Parsonage	Fall of the Bastille marks beginning of French Revolution.
1790	(June) completes 'Love and Freindship'	Edmund Burke, *Reflections on the Revolution in France* [Mary Wollstonecraft], *Vindication of the Rights of Men*
1791	Brother Charles enters Royal Naval Academy, Portsmouth; Edward marries Elizabeth Bridges and they live at Rowling, Kent	Parliament rejects bill to abolish slave trade. James Boswell, *Life of Johnson* Ann Radcliffe, *The Romance of the Forest*

Life	*Historical and Cultural Background*
1792	Writes 'Lesley Castle' and 'Evelyn', and begins 'Catharine, or the Bower'; Lloyds leave Deane to make way for James and first wife, Anne Matthew; cousin Jane Cooper marries Capt. Thomas Williams, RN; sister Cassandra engaged to Revd Tom Fowle	France declared a republic; Warren Hastings acquitted. Mary Wollstonecraft, *Vindication of the Rights of Woman* Clara Reeve, *Plans of Education*
1793	Writes last of 'Juvenilia'; birth of eldest nieces, Fanny and Anna, daughters of brothers Edward and James; brother Henry joins Oxford Militia	Execution of Louis XVI of France and Marie Antoinette; revolutionary 'Terror' in Paris; Britain declares war on France.
1794	Probably working on *Lady Susan*; Cousin Eliza de Feuillide's husband guillotined in Paris	Suspension of Habeas Corpus; 'Treason Trials' of radicals abandoned by government when juries refuse to convict; failure of harvests keeps food prices high. Uvedale Price, *Essays on the Picturesque* Ann Radcliffe, *The Mysteries of Udolpho*
1795	Writes 'Elinor and Marianne' (first draft of *Sense and Sensibility*); death of James's wife; JA flirts with Tom Lefroy, as recorded in first surviving letter	George III's coach stoned; Pitt's 'Two Acts' enforce repression of radical dissent.
1796	Visits Edward at Rowling; (Oct.) begins 'First Impressions'; subscribes to Frances Burney's *Camilla*	Frances Burney, *Camilla* Regina Maria Roche, *Children of the Abbey* Jane West, *A Gossip's Story*
1797	Marriage of James to Mary Lloyd; (Aug.) completes 'First Impressions'; Cassandra's fiancé dies of fever off Santo Domingo; begins revision of 'Elinor and Marianne' into *Sense and Sensibility*; George Austen offers 'First Impressions' to publisher Cadell without success; Catherine Knight gives Edward possession of Godmersham; marriage of Henry and Eliza de Feuillide	Napoleon becomes commander of French army; failure of French attempt to invade by landing in Wales; mutinies in British Navy, leaders hanged. Ann Radcliffe, *The Italian*

	Life	Historical and Cultural Background
1798	Starts to write 'Susan' (later *Northanger Abbey*); visits Godmersham; death in driving accident of cousin Lady Williams (Jane Cooper)	Irish Rebellion; defeat of French fleet at Battle of the Nile; French army lands in Ireland; further suspension of Habeas Corpus. Elizabeth Inchbald, *Lovers' Vows*, translation of play by Kotzebue
1799	Visit to Bath; probably finishes 'Susan'; aunt, Mrs Leigh-Perrot, charged with theft and imprisoned in Ilchester Gaol	Napoleon becomes consul in France. Hannah More, *Strictures on the Modern System of Female Education* Jane West, *A Tale of the Times*
1800	Stays with Martha Lloyd at Ibthorpe; trial and acquittal of Mrs Leigh-Perrot	French conquer Italy; British capture Malta; food riots; first iron-frame printing press; copyright law extended to Ireland. Elizabeth Hamilton, *Memoirs of Modern Philosophers*
1801	Austens move to Bath on George Austen's retirement; James and family move into Steventon Rectory; first of series of holidays in West Country (to 1804), during one of which thought to have had brief romantic involvement with a man who later died; Henry resigns from Oxford Militia and becomes banker and Army agent in London	Slave rebellion in Santo Domingo led by Toussaint L'Ouverture; Nelson defeats Danes at Battle of Copenhagen; Act of Union joins Britain and Ireland. Maria Edgeworth, *Belinda*
1802	Visits Godmersham; accepts, then the following morning refuses, proposal of marriage from Harris Bigg-Wither; revises 'Susan'	L'Ouverture's slave rebellion crushed by French; Peace of Amiens with France; founding of William Cobbett's *Political Register*.
1803	With brother Henry's help, 'Susan' sold to publishers Crosby & Co. for £10	Resumption of war with France.
1804	Starts writing *The Watsons*; (Dec.) death of Anne Lefroy in riding accident	
1805	(Jan.) death of George Austen; stops working on *The Watsons*	Battle of Trafalgar. Walter Scott, *The Lay of the Last Minstrel*

	Life	*Historical and Cultural Background*
1806	Austens leave Bath; visit relations at Adlestrop and Stoneleigh; Martha Lloyd becomes member of Austen household after death of mother; brother Francis marries Mary Gibson	French blockade of Continental ports against British shipping; first steam-powered textile mill opens in Manchester. Lady Morgan, *The Wild Irish Girl*
1807	JA, Cassandra, and Mrs Austen take lodgings with Frank and wife in Southampton; brother Charles marries Fanny Palmer in Bermuda	France invades Portugal; slave-trading by British ships outlawed. George Crabbe, *Poems*
1808	JA visits Godmersham; death of Edward's wife Elizabeth after giving birth to eleventh child	France invades Spain; beginning of Peninsular War. Debrett, *Baronetage* (*Peerage* first published 1802) Hannah More, *Coelebs in Search of a Wife* Walter Scott, *Marmion*
1809	(Apr.) attempts unsuccessfully to make Crosby publish 'Susan', writing under pseudonym 'Mrs Ashton Dennis' ('M.A.D.'); visits Godmersham; (July) moves, with Cassandra, Martha, and Mrs Austen, to house owned by Edward at Chawton, Hampshire	British capture Martinique and Cayenne from France.
1810	Publisher Egerton accepts *Sense and Sensibility*	British capture Guadeloupe, last French West Indian colony; riots in London in support of parliamentary reform. Walter Scott, *The Lady of the Lake*
1811	Stays with Henry and Eliza in London to correct proofs of *Sense and Sensibility*; (Oct.) *Sense and Sensibility*, 'by a Lady', published on commission; begins *Mansfield Park*; revises 'First Impressions' into *Pride and Prejudice*	Prince of Wales becomes Regent; Luddite anti-machine riots in North and Midlands. Mary Brunton, *Self-Control*
1812	Copyright of *Pride and Prejudice* sold to Egerton for £110; Edward's family take name of Knight at death of Catherine Knight	United States declare war on Britain; French retreat from Moscow; Lord Liverpool becomes Prime Minister after assassination of Spencer Perceval.

Life	Historical and Cultural Background
1813	(Jan.) *Pride and Prejudice* published to great acclaim; JA stays in London to nurse Eliza; death of Eliza; in letter, expresses her hatred for Prince Regent; finishes *Mansfield Park*; second editions of *Sense and Sensibility* and *Pride and Prejudice*	British invasion of France after Wellington's success at Battle of Vittoria. Byron, *The Giaour, The Bride of Abydos* Robert Southey, *Life of Nelson*
1814	(21 Jan.) begins *Emma*; (Mar. and Nov.) visits brother Henry in London, sees Kean play Shylock; (May) Egerton publishes *Mansfield Park* on commission, sold out in six months; death of Fanny Palmer Austen, brother Charles's wife, after childbirth; marriage of niece Anna Austen to Ben Lefroy	Napoleon defeated and exiled to Elba; George Stevenson builds first steam locomotive; Edmund Kean's first appearance at Drury Lane. Mary Brunton, *Discipline* Frances Burney, *The Wanderer* Byron, *The Corsair* Maria Edgeworth, *Patronage* Walter Scott, *Waverley*
1815	(29 Mar.) completes *Emma*; begins *Persuasion*; invited to dedicate *Emma* to the Prince Regent; visits Henry in London; (Dec.) *Emma* published by Murray	Napoleon escapes; finally defeated at Battle of Waterloo and exiled to St Helena; Humphry Davy invents miners' safety lamp.
1816	'Susan' bought back from Crosby and revised as 'Catherine'; failure of Henry's bank; second edition of *Mansfield Park*; (Aug.) JA completes *Persuasion*; health beginning to fail	Post-war slump inaugurates years of popular agitation for political and social reform.
1817	(Jan.–Mar.) works on *Sanditon*; moves, with Cassandra, to Winchester, to be closer to skilled medical care; (15 July) writes last poem 'When Winchester Races'; (18 July, 4.30 a.m.) dies in Winchester, buried in Winchester Cathedral; (Dec.) publication (dated 1818) of *Northanger Abbey* and *Persuasion*, together with brother Henry's 'Biographical Notice'	Attacks on Prince Regent at opening of Parliament; death of his only legitimate child, Princess Charlotte.

PERSUASION

BIOGRAPHICAL NOTICE
OF
THE AUTHOR

[By Henry Austen]

THE following pages are the production of a pen which has already contributed in no small degree to the entertainment of the public. And when the public, which has not been insensible to the merits of 'Sense and Sensibility,' 'Pride and Prejudice,' 'Mansfield Park,' and 'Emma,' shall be informed that the hand which guided that pen is now mouldering in the grave, perhaps a brief account of Jane Austen will be read with a kindlier sentiment than simple curiosity.

Short and easy will be the task of the mere biographer. A life of usefulness, literature, and religion, was not by any means a life of event. To those who lament their irreparable loss, it is consolatory to think that, as she never deserved disapprobation, so, in the circle of her family and friends, she never met reproof; that her wishes were not only reasonable, but gratified; and that to the little disappointments incidental to human life was never added, even for a moment, an abatement of good-will from any who knew her.

Jane Austen was born on the 16th of December, 1775, at Steventon, in the county of Hants. Her father was Rector of that parish upwards of forty years. There he resided, in the conscientious and unassisted discharge of his ministerial duties, until he was turned of seventy years. Then he retired with his wife, our authoress, and her sister, to Bath, for the remainder of his life, a period of about four years. Being not only a profound scholar, but possessing a most exquisite taste in every species of literature, it is not wonderful that his daughter Jane should, at a very early age, have become sensible to the charms of style, and enthusiastic in the cultivation of her own language. On the death of her father she removed, with her mother and sister, for a short time, to Southampton, and finally, in 1809, to the pleasant village of Chawton, in the same county. From this place she sent into the world those novels, which by many have been placed on the same shelf as the works of a D'Arblay and an Edge-worth.* Some of these novels had been the gradual performances of her previous life. For though in composition she was equally rapid and correct, yet an invincible distrust of her own judgement induced her to withhold her works from the public, till time and many per-usals had satisfied her that the charm of recent composition was dissolved. The natural constitution, the regular habits, the quiet and happy occupations of our authoress, seemed to promise a long suc-cession of amusement to the public, and a gradual increase of reputa-tion to herself. But the symptoms of a decay, deep and incurable,* began to shew themselves in the commencement of 1816. Her decline was at first deceitfully slow; and until the spring of this present year, those who knew their happiness to be involved in her existence could not endure to despair. But in the month of May, 1817, it was found advisable that she should be removed to Win-chester for the benefit of constant medical aid, which none even then dared to hope would be permanently beneficial. She supported, dur-ing two months, all the varying pain, irksomeness, and tedium, attendant on decaying nature, with more than resignation, with a truly elastic cheerfulness. She retained her faculties, her memory, her fancy, her temper, and her affections, warm, clear, and unimpaired, to the last. Neither her love of God, nor of her fellow creatures flagged for a moment. She made a point of receiving the sacrament before excessive bodily weakness might have rendered her perception unequal to her wishes. She wrote whilst she could hold a pen, and with a pencil when a pen was become too laborious. The day preceding her death she composed some stanzas* replete with fancy and vigour. Her last voluntary speech conveyed thanks to her medical attendant; and to the final question asked of her, purporting to know her wants, she replied, 'I want nothing but death.'

She expired shortly after, on Friday the 18th of July, 1817, in the arms of her sister, who, as well as the relator of these events, feels too surely that they shall never look upon her like again.

Jane Austen was buried on the 24th of July, 1817, in the cathedral church of Winchester, which, in the whole catalogue of its mighty dead, does not contain the ashes of a brighter genius or a sincerer Christian.

Of personal attractions she possessed a considerable share. Her stature was that of true elegance. It could not have been increased without exceeding the middle height. Her carriage and deportment were quiet, yet graceful. Her features were separately good. Their assemblage produced an unrivalled expression of that cheerfulness, sensibility, and benevolence, which were her real characteristics. Her complexion was of the finest texture. It might with truth be said, that her eloquent blood spoke through her modest chccks.* Her voice was extremely sweet. She delivered herself with fluency and precision. Indeed she was formed for elegant and rational society, excelling in conversation as much as in composition. In the present age it is hazardous to mention accomplishments. Our authoress would, prob- ably, have been inferior to few in such acquirements, had she not been so superior to most in higher things. She had not only an excellent taste for drawing, but, in her earlier days, evinced great power of hand in the management of the pencil. Her own musical attainments she held very cheap. Twenty years ago they would have been thought more of, and twenty years hence many a parent will expect their daughters to be applauded for meaner performances. She was fond of dancing, and excelled in it. It remains now to add a few observations on that which her friends deemed more important, on those endowments which sweetened every hour of their lives.

If there be an opinion current in the world, that perfect placidity of temper is not reconcileable to the most lively imagination, and the keenest relish for wit, such an opinion will be rejected for ever by those who have had the happiness of knowing the authoress of the following works. Though the frailties, foibles, and follies of others could not escape her immediate detection, yet even on their vices did she never trust herself to comment with unkindness. The affectation of candour is not uncommon; but she had no affectation. Faultless herself, as nearly as human nature can be, she always sought, in the faults of others, something to excuse, to forgive or forget. Where extenuation was impossible, she had a sure refuge in silence. She never uttered either a hasty, a silly, or a severe expression. In short, her temper was as polished as her wit. Nor were her manners inferior to her temper. They were of the happiest kind. No one could be often in her company without feeling a strong desire of obtaining her friendship, and cherishing a hope of having obtained it. She was tranquil without reserve or stiffness; and communicative without intrusion or self-sufficiency. She became an authoress entirely from taste and inclination. Neither the hope of fame nor profit mixed with

her early motives.* Most of her works, as before observed, were composed many years previous to their publication. It was with extreme
difficulty that her friends, whose partiality she suspected whilst she
honoured their judgement, could prevail on her to publish her first
work. Nay, so persuaded was she that its sale would not repay the
expense of publication, that she actually made a reserve from her
very moderate income to meet the expected loss. She could scarcely
believe what she termed her great good fortune when 'Sense and
Sensibility' produced a clear profit of about £150. Few so gifted were
so truly unpretending. She regarded the above sum as a prodigious
recompense for that which had cost her nothing. Her readers, perhaps, will wonder that such a work produced so little at a time when
some authors have received more guineas than they have written
lines. The works of our authoress, however, may live as long as those
which have burst on the world with more éclat. But the public has
not been unjust; and our authoress was far from thinking it so. Most
gratifying to her was the applause which from time to time reached
her ears from those who were competent to discriminate. Still, in
spite of such applause, so much did she shrink from notoriety, that
no accumulation of fame would have induced her, had she lived, to
affix her name to any productions of her pen. In the bosom of her
own family she talked of them freely, thankful for praise, open to
remark, and submissive to criticism. But in public she turned away
from any allusion to the character of an authoress. She read aloud
with very great taste and effect. Her own works, probably, were
never heard to so much advantage as from her own mouth; for she
partook largely in all the best gifts of the comic muse. She was a
warm and judicious admirer of landscape, both in nature and on
canvass. At a very early age she was enamoured of Gilpin on the
Picturesque,* and she seldom changed her opinions either on books
or men.

Her reading was very extensive in history and belles lettres; and
her memory extremely tenacious. Her favourite moral writers were
Johnson in prose, and Cowper in verse.* It is difficult to say at what
age she was not intimately acquainted with the merits and defects of
the best essays and novels in the English language. Richardson's
power of creating, and preserving the consistency of his characters,
as particularly exemplified in 'Sir Charles Grandison,'* gratified the
natural discrimination of her mind, whilst her taste secured her from

the errors of his prolix style and tedious narrative. She did not rank any work of Fielding quite so high.* Without the slightest affectation she recoiled from every thing gross. Neither nature, wit, nor humour, could make her amends for so very low a scale of morals.

Her power of inventing characters seems to have been intuitive, and almost unlimited. She drew from nature; but, whatever may have been surmised to the contrary, never from individuals.

The style of her familiar correspondence was in all respects the same as that of her novels. Every thing came finished from her pen; for on all subjects she had ideas as clear as her expressions were well chosen. It is not hazarding too much to say that she never dispatched a note or letter unworthy of publication.

One trait only remains to be touched on. It makes all others unimportant. She was thoroughly religious and devout; fearful of giving offence to God, and incapable of feeling it towards any fellow creature. On serious subjects she was well-instructed, both by reading and meditation, and her opinions accorded strictly with those of our Established Church.

London, Dec. 13, 1817

POSTSCRIPT

SINCE concluding the above remarks, the writer of them has been put in possession of some extracts from the private correspondence of the authoress. They are few and short; but are submitted to the public without apology, as being more truly descriptive of her temper, taste, feelings, and principles than any thing which the pen of a biographer can produce.

The first extract is a playful defence of herself from a mock charge of having pilfered the manuscripts of a young relation.*

'What should I do, my dearest E. with your manly, vigorous sketches, so full of life and spirit? How could I possibly join them on to a little bit of ivory,* two inches wide, on which I work with a brush so fine as to produce little effect after much labour?'

The remaining extracts are from various parts of a letter written a few weeks before her death.

'My attendant is encouraging, and talks of making me quite well. I live chiefly on the sofa, but am allowed to walk from one room to the other. I have been out once in a sedan-chair, and am to repeat it, and be promoted to a wheel-chair as the weather serves. On this subject I will only say further that my dearest sister, my tender, watchful, indefatigable nurse, has not been made ill by her exertions. As to what I owe to her, and to the anxious affection of all my beloved family on this occasion, I can only cry over it, and pray to God to bless them more and more.'

She next touches with just and gentle animadversion on a subject of domestic disappointment. Of this the particulars do not concern the public. Yet in justice to her characteristic sweetness and resignation, the concluding observation of our authoress thereon must not be suppressed.

'But I am getting too near complaint. It has been the appointment of God, however secondary causes may have operated.'

The following and final extract will prove the facility with which she could correct every impatient thought, and turn from complaint to cheerfulness.

'You will find Captain —— a very respectable, well-meaning man, without much manner, his wife and sister all good humour and obligingness, and I hope (since the fashion allows it) with rather longer petticoats than last year.'*

London, Dec. 20, 1817.

VOLUME I

CHAPTER I

SIR WALTER ELLIOT, of Kellynch-hall, in Somersetshire, was a man who, for his own amusement, never took up any book but the Baronetage;* there he found occupation for an idle hour, and consolation in a distressed one; there his faculties were roused into admiration and respect, by contemplating the limited remnant of the earliest patents;* there any unwelcome sensations, arising from domestic affairs, changed naturally into pity and contempt, as he turned over the almost endless creations of the last century*—and there, if every other leaf were powerless, he could read his own history with an interest which never failed—this was the page at which the favourite volume always opened:

'ELLIOT OF KELLYNCH-HALL.

'Walter Elliot, born March 1, 1760, married, July 15, 1784, Elizabeth, daughter of James Stevenson, Esq. of South Park, in the county of Gloucester; by which lady (who died 1801) he has issue Elizabeth, born June 1, 1785; Anne, born August 9, 1787; a still-born son, Nov. 5, 1789; Mary, born Nov. 20, 1791.'

Precisely such had the paragraph originally stood from the printer's hands; but Sir Walter had improved it by adding, for the information of himself and his family, these words, after the date of Mary's birth—'married, Dec. 16, 1810, Charles, son and heir of Charles Musgrove, Esq. of Uppercross, in the county of Somer-set,'—and by inserting most accurately the day of the month on which he had lost his wife.

Then followed the history and rise of the ancient and respectable family, in the usual terms: how it had been first settled in Cheshire; how mentioned in Dugdale*—serving the office of High Sheriff,* representing a borough in three successive parliaments, exertions of loyalty, and dignity of baronet, in the first year of Charles II.,* with all the Marys and Elizabeths they had married; forming altogether two handsome duodecimo* pages, and concluding with the arms and motto: 'Principal seat, Kellynch hall, in the county of Somerset,' and Sir Walter's hand-writing again in this finale:

'Heir presumptive,* William Walter Elliot, Esq., great grandson of the second Sir Walter.'

Vanity was the beginning and the end of Sir Walter Elliot's character; vanity of person and of situation. He had been remarkably handsome in his youth; and, at fifty-four, was still a very fine man. Few women could think more of their personal appearance than he did; nor could the valet of any new made lord be more delighted with the place he held in society. He considered the blessing of beauty as inferior only to the blessing of a baronetcy; and the Sir Walter Elliot, who united these gifts, was the constant object of his warmest respect and devotion.

His good looks and his rank had one fair claim on his attachment; since to them he must have owed a wife of very superior character to any thing deserved by his own. Lady Elliot had been an excellent woman, sensible and amiable; whose judgment and conduct, if they might be pardoned the youthful infatuation which made her Lady Elliot, had never required indulgence afterwards.—She had humoured, or softened, or concealed his failings, and promoted his real respectability for seventeen years; and though not the very happiest being in the world herself, had found enough in her duties, her friends, and her children, to attach her to life, and make it no matter of indifference to her when she was called on to quit them.—Three girls, the two eldest sixteen and fourteen, was an awful legacy* for a mother to bequeath; an awful charge rather, to confide to the authority and guidance of a conceited, silly father. She had, however, one very intimate friend, a sensible, deserving woman, who had been brought, by strong attachment to herself, to settle close by her, in the village of Kellynch; and on her kindness and advice, Lady Elliot mainly relied for the best help and maintenance of the good principles and instruction which she had been anxiously giving her daughters.

This friend, and Sir Walter, did *not* marry, whatever might have been anticipated on that head by their acquaintance.—Thirteen years had passed away since Lady Elliot's death, and they were still near neighbours and intimate friends; and one remained a widower, the other a widow.

That Lady Russell, of steady age and character, and extremely well provided for, should have no thought of a second marriage, needs no apology to the public, which is rather apt to be unreasonably discontented when a woman *does* marry again, than when she does *not*; but Sir Walter's continuing in singleness requires explanation.—Be it known then, that Sir Walter, like a good father, (having met with one or two private disappointments in very unreasonable applications) prided himself on remaining single for his dear daughters' sake.* For one daughter, his eldest, he would really have given up any thing, which he had not been very much tempted to do. Elizabeth had succeeded, at sixteen, to all that was possible, of her mother's rights and consequence; and being very handsome, and very like himself, her influence had always been great, and they had gone on together most happily. His two other children were of very inferior value. Mary had acquired a little artificial importance, by becoming Mrs. Charles Musgrove; but Anne, with an elegance of mind and sweetness of character, which must have placed her high with any people of real understanding, was nobody with either father or sister: her word had no weight; her convenience was always to give way;—she was only Anne.

To Lady Russell, indeed, she was a most dear and highly valued god-daughter, favourite and friend. Lady Russell loved them all; but it was only in Anne that she could fancy the mother to revive again.

A few years before, Anne Elliot had been a very pretty girl, but her bloom had vanished early; and as even in its height, her father had found little to admire in her, (so totally different were her delicate features and mild dark eyes from his own); there could be nothing in them now that she was faded and thin, to excite his esteem. He had never indulged much hope, he had now none, of ever reading her name in any other page of his favourite work. All equality of alliance must rest with Elizabeth; for Mary had merely connected herself with an old country family of respectability and large fortune, and had therefore *given* all the honour, and received none: Elizabeth would, one day or other, marry suitably.

It sometimes happens, that a woman is handsomer at twenty-nine than she was ten years before; and, generally speaking, if there has been neither ill health nor anxiety, it is a time of life at which scarcely any charm is lost. It was so with Elizabeth; still the same handsome Miss Elliot that she had begun to be thirteen years ago; and Sir

Walter might be excused, therefore, in forgetting her age, or, at least, be deemed only half a fool, for thinking himself and Elizabeth as blooming as ever, amidst the wreck of the good looks of every body else; for he could plainly see how old all the rest of his family and acquaintance were growing. Anne haggard, Mary coarse, every face in the neighbourhood worsting; and the rapid increase of the crow's foot about Lady Russell's temples had long been a distress to him.

Elizabeth did not quite equal her father in personal contentment. Thirteen years had seen her mistress of Kellynch Hall, presiding and directing with a self-possession and decision which could never have given the idea of her being younger than she was. For thirteen years had she been doing the honours, and laying down the domestic law at home, and leading the way to the chaise and four,* and walking immediately after Lady Russell out of all the drawing-rooms and dining-rooms in the country. Thirteen winters' revolving frosts had seen her opening every ball* of credit which a scanty neighbourhood afforded; and thirteen springs shewn their blossoms, as she travelled up to London with her father, for a few weeks annual enjoyment of the great world. She had the remembrance of all this; she had the consciousness of being nine-and-twenty, to give her some regrets and some apprehensions. She was fully satisfied of being still quite as handsome as ever; but she felt her approach to the years of danger, and would have rejoiced to be certain of being properly solicited by baronet-blood within the next twelvemonth or two. Then might she again take up the book of books with as much enjoyment as in her early youth; but now she liked it not. Always to be presented with the date of her own birth, and see no marriage follow but that of a youngest sister, made the book an evil; and more than once, when her father had left it open on the table near her, had she closed it, with averted eyes, and pushed it away.

She had had a disappointment, moreover, which that book, and especially the history of her own family, must ever present the remembrance of. The heir presumptive, the very William Walter Elliot, Esq. whose rights had been so generously supported by her father, had disappointed her.

She had, while a very young girl, as soon as she had known him to be, in the event of her having no brother, the future baronet, meant to marry him; and her father had always meant that she should. He had not been known to them as a boy, but soon after Lady Elliot's death Sir Walter had sought the acquaintance, and though his overtures had not been met with any warmth, he had persevered in seeking it, making allowance for the modest drawing back of youth; and in one of their spring excursions to London, when Elizabeth was in her first bloom, Mr. Elliot had been forced into the introduction.

He was at that time a very young man, just engaged in the study of the law; and Elizabeth found him extremely agreeable, and every plan in his favour was confirmed. He was invited to Kellynch Hall; he was talked of and expected all the rest of the year; but he never came. The following spring he was seen again in town, found equally agreeable, again encouraged, invited and expected, and again he did not come; and the next tidings were that he was married. Instead of pushing his fortune in the line marked out for the heir of the house of Elliot, he had purchased independence by uniting himself to a rich woman of inferior birth.

Sir Walter had resented it. As the head of the house, he felt that he ought to have been consulted, especially after taking the young man so publicly by the hand. 'For they must have been seen together,' he observed, 'once at Tattersal's,* and twice in the lobby of the House of Commons.' His disapprobation was expressed, but apparently very little regarded. Mr. Elliot had attempted no apology, and shewn himself as unsolicitous of being longer noticed by the family, as Sir Walter considered him unworthy of it: all acquaintance between them had ceased.

This very awkward history of Mr. Elliot, was still, after an interval of several years, felt with anger by Elizabeth, who had liked the man for himself, and still more for being her father's heir, and whose strong family pride could see only in *him*, a proper match for Sir Walter Elliot's eldest daughter. There was not a baronet from A to Z, whom her feelings could have so willingly acknowledged as an equal. Yet so miserably had he conducted himself, that though she was at this present time, (the summer of 1814,) wearing black ribbons for his wife,* she could not admit him to be worth thinking of again. The disgrace of his first marriage might, perhaps, as there was no reason to suppose it perpetuated by offspring, have been got over, had he not done worse; but he had, as by the accustomary intervention of kind friends they had been informed, spoken most disrespectfully of them all, most slightingly and contemptuously of the very blood he belonged to, and the honours which were hereafter to be his own. This could not be pardoned.

Such were Elizabeth Elliot's sentiments and sensations; such the cares to alloy, the agitations to vary, the sameness and the elegance, the prosperity and the nothingness, of her scene of life—such the feelings to give interest to a long, uneventful residence in one country circle, to fill the vacancies which there were no habits of utility abroad, no talents or accomplishments for home, to occupy.

But now, another occupation and solicitude of mind was beginning to be added to these. Her father was growing distressed for money. She knew, that when he now took up the Baronetage, it was to drive the heavy bills of his tradespeople, and the unwelcome hints of Mr. Shepherd, his agent,* from his thoughts. The Kellynch property was good, but not equal to Sir Walter's apprehension of the state required in its possessor. While Lady Elliot lived, there had been method, moderation, and economy, which had just kept him within his income; but with her had died all such right-mindedness, and from that period he had been constantly exceeding it. It had not been possible for him to spend less; he had done nothing but what Sir Walter Elliot was imperiously called on to do; but blameless as he was, he was not only growing dreadfully in debt, but was hearing of it so often, that it became vain to attempt concealing it longer, even partially, from his daughter. He had given her some hints of it the last spring in town; he had gone so far even as to say, 'Can we retrench? does it occur to you that there is any one article in which we can retrench?'—and Elizabeth, to do her justice, had, in the first ardour of female alarm, set seriously to think what could be done, and had finally proposed these two branches of economy: to cut off some unnecessary charities, and to refrain from new-furnishing the drawing-room; to which expedients she afterwards added the happy thought of their taking no present down to Anne, as had been the usual yearly custom. But these measures, however good in themselves, were insufficient for the real extent of the evil, the whole of which Sir Walter found himself obliged to confess to her soon afterwards. Elizabeth had nothing to propose of deeper efficacy. She felt herself ill-used and unfortunate, as did her father; and they were neither of them able to devise any means of lessening their expenses without compromising their dignity, or relinquishing their comforts in a way not to be borne.

There was only a small part of his estate that Sir Walter could dispose of; but had every acre been alienable,* it would have made no difference. He had condescended to mortgage as far as he had the power, but he would never condescend to sell. No; he would never disgrace his name so far. The Kellynch estate should be transmitted whole and entire, as he had received it.

Their two confidential friends, Mr. Shepherd, who lived in the neighbouring market town, and Lady Russell, were called on to advise them; and both father and daughter seemed to expect that something should be struck out by one or the other to remove their embarrassments and reduce their expenditure, without involving the loss of any indulgence of taste or pride.

CHAPTER II

MR. SHEPHERD, a civil, cautious lawyer, who, whatever might be his hold or his views on Sir Walter, would rather have the *disagreeable* prompted by any body else, excused himself from offering the slightest hint, and only begged leave to recommend an implicit deference to the excellent judgment of Lady Russell,—from whose known good sense he fully expected to have just such resolute measures advised, as he meant to see finally adopted.

Lady Russell was most anxiously zealous on the subject, and gave it much serious consideration. She was a woman rather of sound than of quick abilities, whose difficulties in coming to any decision in this instance were great, from the opposition of two leading principles. She was of strict integrity herself, with a delicate sense of honour; but she was as desirous of saving Sir Walter's feelings, as solicitous for the credit of the family, as aristocratic in her ideas of what was due to them, as any body of sense and honesty could well be. She was a benevolent, charitable, good woman, and capable of strong attachments; most correct in her conduct, strict in her notions of decorum, and with manners that were held a standard of good-breeding. She had a cultivated mind, and was, generally speaking, rational and consistent—but she had prejudices on the side of ancestry; she had a value for rank and consequence, which blinded her a little to the faults of those who possessed them. Herself, the widow of only a knight,* she gave the dignity of a baronet all its due;

and Sir Walter, independent of his claims as an old acquaintance, an attentive neighbour, an obliging landlord, the husband of her very dear friend, the father of Anne and her sisters, was, as being Sir Walter, in her apprehension entitled to a great deal of compassion and consideration under his present difficulties.

They must retrench; that did not admit of a doubt. But she was very anxious to have it done with the least possible pain to him and Elizabeth. She drew up plans of economy, she made exact calculations, and she did, what nobody else thought of doing, she consulted Anne, who never seemed considered by the others as having any interest in the question. She consulted, and in a degree was influenced by her, in marking out the scheme of retrenchment, which was at last submitted to Sir Walter. Every emendation of Anne's had been on the side of honesty against importance. She wanted more vigorous measures, a more complete reformation, a quicker release from debt, a much higher tone of indifference for every thing but justice and equity.

'If we can persuade your father to all this,' said Lady Russell, looking over her paper, 'much may be done. If he will adopt these regulations, in seven years he will be clear; and I hope we may be able to convince him and Elizabeth, that Kellynch-hall has a respectability in itself, which cannot be affected by these reductions; and that the true dignity of Sir Walter Elliot will be very far from lessened, in the eyes of sensible people, by his acting like a man of principle. What will he be doing, in fact, but what very many of our first families have done,—or ought to do?—There will be nothing singular in his case; and it is singularity which often makes the worst part of our suffering, as it always does of our conduct. I have great hope of our prevailing. We must be serious and decided—for, after all, the person who has contracted debts must pay them; and though a great deal is due to the feelings of the gentleman, and the head of a house, like your father, there is still more due to the character of an honest man.'

This was the principle on which Anne wanted her father to be proceeding, his friends to be urging him. She considered it as an act of indispensable duty to clear away the claims of creditors, with all the expedition which the most comprehensive retrenchments could secure, and saw no dignity in any thing short of it. She wanted it to be prescribed, and felt as a duty. She rated Lady Russell's influence highly, and as to the severe degree of self-denial, which her own conscience prompted, she believed there might be little more difficulty in persuading them to a complete, than to half a reformation. Her knowledge of her father and Elizabeth, inclined her to think that the sacrifice of one pair of horses would be hardly less painful than of both, and so on, through the whole list of Lady Russell's too gentle reductions.

How Anne's more rigid requisitions might have been taken, is of little consequence. Lady Russell's had no success at all—could not be put up with—were not to be borne. 'What! Every comfort of life knocked off! Journeys, London, servants, horses, table,—contractions and restrictions every where. To live no longer with the decencies even of a private gentleman! No, he would sooner quit Kellynch-hall at once, than remain in it on such disgraceful terms.'

'Quit Kellynch-hall.' The hint was immediately taken up by Mr. Shepherd, whose interest was involved in the reality of Sir Walter's retrenching, and who was perfectly persuaded that nothing would be done without a change of abode.—'Since the idea had been started in the very quarter which ought to dictate, he had no scruple,' he said, 'in confessing his judgment to be entirely on that side. It did not appear to him that Sir Walter could materially alter his style of living in a house which had such a character of hospitality and ancient dignity to support.—In any other place, Sir Walter might judge for himself; and would be looked up to, as regulating the modes of life, in whatever way he might choose to model his household.'

Sir Walter would quit Kellynch-hall;—and after a very few days more of doubt and indecision, the great question of whither he should go, was settled, and the first outline of this important change made out.

There had been three alternatives, London, Bath,* or another house in the country. All Anne's wishes had been for the latter. A small house in their own neighbourhood, where they might still have Lady Russell's society, still be near Mary, and still have the pleasure of sometimes seeing the lawns and groves of Kellynch, was the object of her ambition. But the usual fate of Anne attended her, in having something very opposite from her inclination fixed on. She disliked Bath, and did not think it agreed with her—and Bath was to be her home.

Sir Walter had at first thought more of London, but Mr. Shepherd felt that he could not be trusted in London, and had been skilful enough to dissuade him from it, and make Bath preferred. It was a much safer place for a gentleman in his predicament:—he might there be important at comparatively little expense.—Two material advantages of Bath over London had of course been given all their weight, its more convenient distance from Kellynch, only fifty miles, and Lady Russell's spending some part of every winter there; and to the very great satisfaction of Lady Russell, whose first views on the projected change had been for Bath, Sir Walter and Elizabeth were induced to believe that they should lose neither consequence nor enjoyment by settling there.

Lady Russell felt obliged to oppose her dear Anne's known wishes. It would be too much to expect Sir Walter to descend into a small house in his own neighbourhood. Anne herself would have found the mortifications of it more than she foresaw, and to Sir Walter's feelings they must have been dreadful. And with regard to Anne's dislike of Bath, she considered it as a prejudice and mistake, arising first from the circumstance of her having been three years at school there, after her mother's death, and, secondly, from her happening to be not in perfectly good spirits the only winter which she had afterwards spent there with herself.

Lady Russell was fond of Bath in short, and disposed to think it must suit them all; and as to her young friend's health, by passing all the warm months with her at Kellynch-lodge, every danger would be avoided; and it was, in fact, a change which must do both health and spirits good. Anne had been too little from home, too little seen. Her spirits were not high. A larger society would improve them. She wanted her to be more known.

The undesirableness of any other house in the same neighbourhood for Sir Walter, was certainly much strengthened by one part, and a very material part of the scheme, which had been happily engrafted on the beginning. He was not only to quit his home, but to see it in the hands of others; a trial of fortitude, which stronger heads than Sir Walter's have found too much.—Kellynch-hall was to be let. This, however, was a profound secret; not to be breathed beyond their own circle.

Sir Walter could not have borne the degradation of being known to design letting his house.—Mr. Shepherd had once mentioned the word, 'advertise;'—but never dared approach it again; Sir Walter spurned the idea of its being offered in any manner; forbad the slightest hint being dropped of his having such an intention; and it was only on the supposition of his being spontaneously solicited by some most unexceptionable applicant, on his own terms, and as a great favour, that he would let it at all.

How quick come the reasons for approving what we like!—Lady Russell had another excellent one at hand, for being extremely glad that Sir Walter and his family were to remove from the country. Elizabeth had been lately forming an intimacy, which she wished to see interrupted. It was with a daughter of Mr. Shepherd, who had returned, after an unprosperous marriage, to her father's house,* with the additional burthen of two children. She was a clever young woman, who understood the art of pleasing; the art of pleasing, at least, at Kellynch-hall; and who had made herself so acceptable to Miss Elliot, as to have been already staying there more than once, in spite of all that Lady Russell, who thought it a friendship quite out of place, could hint of caution and reserve.

Lady Russell, indeed, had scarcely any influence with Elizabeth, and seemed to love her, rather because she would love her, than because Elizabeth deserved it. She had never received from her more than outward attention, nothing beyond the observances of complaisance,* had never succeeded in any point which she wanted to carry, against previous inclination. She had been repeatedly very earnest in trying to get Anne included in the visit to London, sensibly open to all the injustice and all the discredit of the selfish arrangements which shut her out, and on many lesser occasions had endeavoured to give Elizabeth the advantage of her own better judgment and experience—but always in vain; Elizabeth would go her own way—and never had she pursued it in more decided opposition to Lady Russell, than in this selection of Mrs. Clay; turning from the society of so deserving a sister to bestow her affection and confidence on one who ought to have been nothing to her but the object of distant civility.

From situation, Mrs. Clay was, in Lady Russell's estimate, a very unequal, and in her character she believed a very dangerous companion—and a removal that would leave Mrs. Clay behind, and bring a choice of more suitable intimates within Miss Elliot's reach, was therefore an object of first-rate importance.

CHAPTER III

'I MUST take leave to observe, Sir Walter,' said Mr. Shepherd one morning at Kellynch Hall, as he laid down the newspaper 'that the present juncture is much in our favour. This peace* will be turning all our rich Navy Officers ashore. They will be all wanting a home. Could not be a better time, Sir Walter, for having a choice of tenants, very responsible tenants. Many a noble fortune has been made during the war. If a rich Admiral were to come in our way, Sir Walter—'

'He would be a very lucky man, Shepherd,' replied Sir Walter, 'that's all I have to remark. A prize indeed* would Kellynch Hall be to him; rather the greatest prize of all, let him have taken ever so many before—hey, Shepherd?'

Mr. Shepherd laughed, as he knew he must, at this wit, and then added,

'I presume to observe, Sir Walter, that, in the way of business, gentlemen of the navy are well to deal with. I have had a little knowledge of their methods of doing business, and I am free to confess that they have very liberal notions,* and are as likely to make desirable tenants as any set of people one should meet with. Therefore, Sir Walter, what I would take leave to suggest is, that if in consequence of any rumours getting abroad of your intention— which must be contemplated as a possible thing, because we know how difficult it is to keep the actions and designs of one part of the world from the notice and curiosity of the other,—consequence has its tax—I, John Shepherd, might conceal any family-matters that I chose, for nobody would think it worth their while to observe me, but Sir Walter Elliot has eyes upon him which it may be very difficult to elude—and therefore, thus much I venture upon, that it will not greatly surprise me if, with all our caution, some rumour of the truth should get abroad—in the supposition of which, as I was going to observe, since applications will unquestionably follow, I should think any from our wealthy naval commanders particularly worth attending to—and beg leave to add, that two hours will bring me over at any time, to save you the trouble of replying.'

Sir Walter only nodded. But soon afterwards, rising and pacing the room, he observed sarcastically,

'There are few among the gentlemen of the navy, I imagine, who would not be surprised to find themselves in a house of this description.'

'They would look around them, no doubt, and bless their good fortune,' said Mrs. Clay, for Mrs. Clay was present; her father had driven her over, nothing being of so much use to Mrs. Clay's health as a drive to Kellynch: 'but I quite agree with my father in thinking a sailor might be a very desirable tenant. I have known a good deal of the profession; and besides their liberality, they are so neat and careful in all their ways! These valuable pictures of yours, Sir Walter, if you chose to leave them, would be perfectly safe. Every thing in and about the house would be taken such excellent care of! the gardens and shrubberies would be kept in almost as high order as they are now. You need not be afraid, Miss Elliot, of your own sweet flower-garden's being neglected.'

'As to all that,' rejoined Sir Walter coolly, 'supposing I were induced to let my house, I have by no means made up my mind as to the privileges to be annexed to it. I am not particularly disposed to favour a tenant. The park would be open to him of course, and few navy officers, or men of any other description, can have had such a range; but what restrictions I might impose on the use of the pleasure-grounds, is another thing. I am not fond of the idea of my shrubberies being always approachable; and I should recommend Miss Elliot to be on her guard with respect to her flower-garden. I am very little disposed to grant a tenant of Kellynch Hall any extraordinary favour, I assure you, be he sailor or soldier.'

After a short pause, Mr. Shepherd presumed to say,

'In all these cases, there are established usages which make every thing plain and easy between landlord and tenant. Your interest, Sir Walter, is in pretty safe hands. Depend upon me for taking care that no tenant has more than his just rights. I venture to hint, that Sir Walter Elliot cannot be half so jealous for his own, as John Shepherd will be for him.'

Here Anne spoke,—

'The navy, I think, who have done so much for us, have at least an equal claim with any other set of men, for all the comforts and all the privileges which any home can give. Sailors work hard enough for their comforts, we must all allow.'

'Very true, very true. What Miss Anne says, is very true,' was Mr.

Shepherd's rejoinder, and 'Oh! certainly,' was his daughter's; but Sir Walter's remark was, soon afterwards—

'The profession has its utility, but I should be sorry to see any friend of mine belonging to it.'

'Indeed!' was the reply, and with a look of surprise.

'Yes; it is in two points offensive to me; I have two strong grounds of objection to it. First, as being the means of bringing persons of obscure birth into undue distinction, and raising men to honours which their fathers and grandfathers never dreamt of; and secondly, as it cuts up a man's youth and vigour most horribly; a sailor grows old sooner than any other man; I have observed it all my life. A man is in greater danger in the navy of being insulted by the rise of one whose father, his father might have disdained to speak to, and of becoming prematurely an object of disgust himself, than in any other line. One day last spring, in town, I was in company with two men, striking instances of what I am talking of, Lord St. Ives, whose father we all know to have been a country curate, without bread to eat; I was to give place to Lord St. Ives, and a certain Admiral Baldwin, the most deplorable looking personage you can imagine, his face the colour of mahogany, rough and rugged to the last degree, all lines and wrinkles, nine grey hairs of a side, and nothing but a dab of powder at top.—"In the name of heaven, who is that old fellow?" said I, to a friend of mine who was standing near, (Sir Basil Morley.) "Old fellow!" cried Sir Basil, "it is Admiral Baldwin. What do you take his age to be?" "Sixty," said I, "or perhaps sixty-two." "Forty," replied Sir Basil, "forty, and no more." Picture to yourselves my amazement; I shall not easily forget Admiral Baldwin. I never saw quite so wretched an example of what a sea-faring life can do; but to a degree, I know it is the same with them all: they are all knocked about, and exposed to every climate, and every weather, till they are not fit to be seen. It is a pity they are not knocked on the head at once, before they reach Admiral Baldwin's age.'

'Nay, Sir Walter,' cried Mrs. Clay, 'this is being severe indeed. Have a little mercy on the poor men. We are not all born to be handsome. The sea is no beautifier, certainly; sailors do grow old betimes; I have often observed it; they soon lose the look of youth. But then, is not it the same with many other professions, perhaps most other? Soldiers, in active service, are not at all better off: and even in the quieter professions, there is a toil and a labour of the mind, if not of the body, which seldom leaves a man's looks to the natural effect of time. The lawyer plods, quite care-worn; the physician is up at all hours, and travelling in all weather; and even the clergyman—' she stopt a moment to consider what might do for the clergyman;—'and even the clergyman, you know, is obliged to go into infected rooms, and expose his health and looks to all the injury of a poisonous atmosphere. In fact, as I have long been convinced, though every profession is necessary and honourable in its turn, it is only the lot of those who are not obliged to follow any, who can live in a regular way, in the country, choosing their own hours, following their own pursuits, and living on their own property, without the torment of trying for more; it is only *their* lot, I say, to hold the blessings of health and a good appearance to the utmost: I know no other set of men but what lose something of their personableness when they cease to be quite young.'

It seemed as if Mr. Shepherd, in this anxiety to bespeak Sir Walter's good-will towards a naval officer as tenant, had been gifted with foresight; for the very first application for the house was from an Admiral Croft, with whom he shortly afterwards fell into company in attending the quarter sessions at Taunton,* and indeed, he had received a hint of the admiral from a London correspondent. By the report which he hastened over to Kellynch to make, Admiral Croft was a native of Somersetshire, who having acquired a very handsome fortune, was wishing to settle in his own country, and had come down to Taunton in order to look at some advertised places in that immediate neighbourhood, which, however, had not suited him; that accidentally hearing—(it was just as he had foretold, Mr. Shepherd observed, Sir Walter's concerns could not be kept a secret,)—accidentally hearing of the possibility of Kellynch Hall being to let, and understanding his (Mr. Shepherd's) connection with the owner, he had introduced himself to him in order to make particular inquiries, and had, in the course of a pretty long conference, expressed as strong an inclination for the place as a man who knew it only by description, could feel; and given Mr. Shepherd, in his explicit account of himself, every proof of his being a most responsible, eligible tenant.

'And who is Admiral Croft?' was Sir Walter's cold suspicious inquiry.

Mr. Shepherd answered for his being of a gentleman's family, and mentioned a place; and Anne, after the little pause which followed, added—

'He is rear admiral of the white.* He was in the Trafalgar action* and has been in the East Indies since; he has been stationed there, I believe, several years.'

'Then, I take it for granted,' observed Sir Walter, 'that his face is about as orange as the cuffs and capes of my livery.'

Mr. Shepherd hastened to assure him, that Admiral Croft was a very hale, hearty, well-looking man, a little weather-beaten, to be sure, but not much; and quite the gentleman in all his notions and behaviour;—not likely to make the smallest difficulty about terms;—only wanted a comfortable home, and to get into it as soon as possible;—knew he must pay for his convenience;—knew what rent a ready-furnished house of that consequence might fetch;—should not have been surprised if Sir Walter had asked more;—had inquired about the manor;—would be glad of the deputation,* certainly, but made no great point of it;—said he sometimes took out a gun, but never killed;—quite the gentleman.

Mr. Shepherd was eloquent on the subject; pointing out all the circumstances of the admiral's family, which made him peculiarly desirable as a tenant. He was a married man, and without children; the very state to be wished for. A house was never taken good care of, Mr. Shepherd observed, without a lady: he did not know, whether furniture might not be in danger of suffering as much where there was no lady, as where there were many children. A lady, without a family, was the very best preserver of furniture in the world. He had seen Mrs. Croft, too; she was at Taunton with the admiral, and had been present almost all the time they were talking the matter over.

'And a very well-spoken, genteel, shrewd lady, she seemed to be,' continued he; 'asked more questions about the house, and terms, and taxes, than the admiral himself, and seemed more conversant with business. And moreover, Sir Walter, I found she was not quite unconnected in this country, any more than her husband; that is to say, she is sister to a gentleman who did live amongst us once; she told me so herself: sister to the gentleman who lived a few years back, at Monkford. Bless me! what was his name? At this moment I cannot recollect his name, though I have heard it so lately. Penelope, my dear, can you help me to the name of the gentleman who lived at Monkford—Mrs. Croft's brother?'

But Mrs. Clay was talking so eagerly with Miss Elliot, that she did not hear the appeal.

'I have no conception whom you can mean, Shepherd; I remember no gentleman resident at Monkford since the time of old Governor Trent.'

'Bless me! how very odd! I shall forget my own name soon, I suppose. A name that I am so very well acquainted with; knew the gentleman so well by sight; seen him a hundred times; came to consult me once, I remember, about a trespass of one of his neighbours; farmer's man breaking into his orchard—wall torn down—apples stolen—caught in the fact; and afterwards, contrary to my judgment, submitted to an amicable compromise. Very odd indeed!'

After waiting another moment—

'You mean Mr. Wentworth, I suppose,' said Anne.

Mr. Shepherd was all gratitude.

'Wentworth was the very name! Mr. Wentworth was the very man. He had the curacy of Monkford, you know, Sir Walter, some time back, for two or three years. Came there about the year—5, I take it. You remember him, I am sure.'

'Wentworth? Oh! ay,—Mr. Wentworth, the curate of Monkford. You misled me by the term *gentleman*. I thought you were speaking of some man of property: Mr. Wentworth was nobody, I remember; quite unconnected; nothing to do with the Strafford family.* One wonders how the names of many of our nobility become so common.'

As Mr. Shepherd perceived that this connexion of the Crofts did them no service with Sir Walter, he mentioned it no more; returning, with all his zeal, to dwell on the circumstances more indisputably in their favour; their age, and number, and fortune; the high idea they had formed of Kellynch Hall, and extreme solicitude for the advantage of renting it; making it appear as if they ranked nothing beyond the happiness of being the tenants of Sir Walter Elliot: an extraordinary taste, certainly, could they have been supposed in the secret of Sir Walter's estimate of the dues of a tenant.

It succeeded, however; and though Sir Walter must ever look with an evil eye on any one intending to inhabit that house, and think them infinitely too well off in being permitted to rent it on the highest terms, he was talked into allowing Mr. Shepherd to proceed in the treaty, and authorising him to wait on Admiral

Croft, who still remained at Taunton, and fix a day for the house being seen.

Sir Walter was not very wise; but still he had experience enough of the world to feel, that a more unobjectionable tenant, in all essentials, than Admiral Croft bid fair to be, could hardly offer. So far went his understanding; and his vanity supplied a little additional soothing, in the admiral's situation in life, which was just high enough, and not too high. 'I have let my house to Admiral Croft,' would sound extremely well; very much better than to any mere *Mr.*——; a *Mr.* (save, perhaps, some half dozen in the nation,) always needs a note of explanation. An admiral speaks his own consequence, and, at the same time, can never make a baronet look small. In all their dealings and intercourse, Sir Walter Elliot must ever have the precedence.

Nothing could be done without a reference to Elizabeth; but her inclination was growing so strong for a removal, that she was happy to have it fixed and expedited by a tenant at hand; and not a word to suspend decision was uttered by her.

Mr. Shepherd was completely empowered to act; and no sooner had such an end been reached, than Anne, who had been a most attentive listener to the whole, left the room, to seek the comfort of cool air for her flushed cheeks; and as she walked along a favourite grove, said, with a gentle sigh, 'a few months more, and *he*, perhaps, may be walking here.'

CHAPTER IV

He was not Mr. Wentworth, the former curate of Monkford, however suspicious appearances may be, but a captain Frederick Wentworth, his brother, who being made commander in consequence of the action off St. Domingo,* and not immediately employed, had come into Somersetshire, in the summer of 1806; and having no parent living, found a home for half a year, at Monkford. He was, at that time, a remarkably fine young man, with a great deal of intelligence, spirit and brilliancy; and Anne an extremely pretty girl, with gentleness, modesty, taste, and feeling.—Half the sum of attraction, on either side, might have been enough, for he had nothing to do, and she had hardly any body to love; but the encounter of such lavish recommendations could not fail. They were gradually acquainted,

and when acquainted, rapidly and deeply in love. It would be difficult to say which had seen highest perfection in the other, or
which had been the happiest; she, in receiving his declarations and
proposals, or he in having them accepted.

A short period of exquisite felicity followed, and but a short
one.—Troubles soon arose. Sir Walter, on being applied to, without
actually withholding his consent, or saying it should never be, gave it
all the negative of great astonishment, great coldness, great silence,
and a professed resolution of doing nothing for his daughter. He
thought it a very degrading alliance; and Lady Russell, though with
more tempered and pardonable pride, received it as a most
unfortunate one.

Anne Elliot, with all her claims of birth, beauty, and mind, to
throw herself away at nineteen; involve herself at nineteen in an
engagement with a young man, who had nothing but himself to
recommend him, and no hopes of attaining affluence, but in the
chances of a most uncertain profession, and no connexions to secure
even his farther rise in that profession; would be, indeed, a throwing
away, which she grieved to think of! Anne Elliot, so young; known to
so few, to be snatched off by a stranger without alliance or fortune; or
rather sunk by him into a state of most wearing, anxious, youth-
killing dependance! It must not be, if by any fair interference of
friendship, any representations from one who had almost a mother's
love, and mother's rights, it would be prevented.

Captain Wentworth had no fortune. He had been lucky in his
profession, but spending freely, what had come freely, had realized
nothing. But, he was confident that he should soon be rich;—full of
life and ardour, he knew that he should soon have a ship, and soon be
on a station that would lead to every thing he wanted. He had always
been lucky; he knew he should be so still.—Such confidence, powerful in its own warmth, and bewitching in the wit which often
expressed it, must have been enough for Anne; but Lady Russell saw
it very differently.—His sanguine temper, and fearlessness of mind,
operated very differently on her. She saw in it but an aggravation of
the evil. It only added a dangerous character to himself. He was
brilliant, he was headstrong.—Lady Russell had little taste for
wit; and of any thing approaching to imprudence a horror. She
deprecated the connexion in every light.

Such opposition, as these feelings produced, was more than Anne could combat. Young and gentle as she was, it might yet have been possible to withstand her father's ill-will, though unsoftened by one kind word or look on the part of her sister;—but Lady Russell, whom she had always loved and relied on, could not, with such steadiness of opinion, and such tenderness of manner, be continually advising her in vain. She was persuaded to believe the engagement a wrong thing—indiscreet, improper, hardly capable of success, and not deserving it. But it was not a merely selfish caution, under which she acted, in putting an end to it. Had she not imagined herself consulting his good, even more than her own, she could hardly have given him up.—The belief of being prudent, and self-denying principally for *his* advantage, was her chief consolation, under the misery of a parting—a final parting; and every consolation was required, for she had to encounter all the additional pain of opinions, on his side, totally unconvinced and unbending, and of his feeling himself ill-used by so forced a relinquishment.—He had left the country in consequence.

A few months had seen the beginning and the end of their acquaintance; but, not with a few months ended Anne's share of suffering from it. Her attachment and regrets had, for a long time, clouded every enjoyment of youth; and an early loss of bloom and spirits had been their lasting effect.

More than seven years were gone since this little history of sorrowful interest had reached its close; and time had softened down much, perhaps nearly all of peculiar attachment to him,—but she had been too dependant on time alone; no aid had been given in change of place, (except in one visit to Bath soon after the rupture,) or in any novelty or enlargement of society.—No one had ever come within the Kellynch circle, who could bear a comparison with Frederick Wentworth, as he stood in her memory. No second attachment, the only thoroughly natural, happy, and sufficient cure, at her time of life, had been possible to the nice tone of her mind,* the fastidiousness of her taste, in the small limits of the society around them. She had been solicited, when about two-and-twenty, to change her name, by the young man, who not long afterwards found a more willing mind in her younger sister; and Lady Russell had lamented her refusal; for Charles Musgrove was the eldest son of a man, whose landed property and general importance, were second, in that country, only to Sir Walter's, and of good character and appearance; and however Lady Russell might have asked yet for something more, while Anne was nineteen, she would have rejoiced to see her at twenty-two, so respectably removed from the partialities and injustice of her father's house, and settled so permanently near herself. But in this case, Anne had left nothing for advice to do; and though Lady Russell, as satisfied as ever with her own discretion, never wished the past undone, she began now to have the anxiety which borders on hopelessness for Anne's being tempted, by some man of talents and independence, to enter a state for which she held her to be peculiarly fitted by her warm affections and domestic habits.

They knew not each other's opinion, either its constancy or its change, on the one leading point of Anne's conduct, for the subject was never alluded to,—but Anne, at seven and twenty, thought very differently from what she had been made to think at nineteen.—She did not blame Lady Russell, she did not blame herself for having been guided by her; but she felt that were any young person, in similar circumstances, to apply to her for counsel, they would never receive any of such certain immediate wretchedness, such uncertain future good.—She was persuaded that under every disadvantage of disapprobation at home, and every anxiety attending his profession, all their probable fears, delays and disappointments, she should yet have been a happier woman in maintaining the engagement, than she had been in the sacrifice of it; and this, she fully believed, had the usual share, had even more than a usual share of all such solicitudes and suspense been theirs, without reference to the actual results of their case, which, as it happened, would have bestowed earlier prosperity than could be reasonably calculated on. All his sanguine expectations, all his confidence had been justified. His genius and ardour had seemed to foresee and to command his prosperous path. He had, very soon after their engagement ceased, got employ; and all that he had told her would follow, had taken place. He had distinguished himself, and early gained the other step in rank* and must now, by successive captures, have made a handsome fortune. She had only navy lists* and newspapers for her authority, but she could not doubt his being rich;—and, in favour of his constancy, she had no reason to believe him married.

How eloquent could Anne Elliot have been,—how eloquent, at least, were her wishes on the side of early warm attachment, and a cheerful confidence in futurity, against that over-anxious caution which seems to insult exertion and distrust Providence!—She had been forced into prudence in her youth, she learned romance as she grew older—the natural sequel of an unnatural beginning.

With all these circumstances, recollections and feelings, she could not hear that Captain Wentworth's sister was likely to live at Kellynch, without a revival of former pain; and many a stroll and many a sigh were necessary to dispel the agitation of the idea. She often told herself it was folly, before she could harden her nerves sufficiently to feel the continual discussion of the Crofts and their business no evil. She was assisted, however, by that perfect indifference and apparent unconsciousness, among the only three of her own friends in the secret of the past, which seemed almost to deny any recollection of it. She could do justice to the superiority of Lady Russell's motives in this, over those of her father and Elizabeth; she could honour all the better feelings of her calmness—but the general air of oblivion among them was highly important, from whatever it sprung; and in the event of Admiral Croft's really taking Kellynch-hall, she rejoiced anew over the conviction which had always been most grateful to her, of the past being known to those three only among her connexions, by whom no syllable, she believed, would ever be whispered, and in the trust that among his, the brother only with whom he had been residing, had received any information of their short-lived engagement.—That brother had been long removed from the country—and being a sensible man, and, moreover, a single man at the time, she had a fond dependance on no human creature's having heard of it from him.

The sister, Mrs. Croft, had then been out of England, accompanying her husband on a foreign station, and her own sister, Mary, had been at school while it all occurred—and never admitted by the pride of some, and the delicacy of others, to the smallest knowledge of it afterwards.

With these supports, she hoped that the acquaintance between herself and the Crofts, which, with Lady Russell, still resident in Kellynch, and Mary fixed only three miles off, must be anticipated, need not involve any particular awkwardness.

CHAPTER V

ON the morning appointed for Admiral and Mrs. Croft's seeing Kellynch-hall, Anne found it most natural to take her almost daily walk to Lady Russell's, and keep out of the way till all was over; when she found it most natural to be sorry that she had missed the opportunity of seeing them.

This meeting of the two parties proved highly satisfactory, and decided the whole business at once. Each lady was previously well disposed for an agreement, and saw nothing, therefore, but good manners in the other; and, with regard to the gentlemen, there was such an hearty good humour, such an open, trusting liberality on the Admiral's side, as could not but influence Sir Walter, who had besides been flattered into his very best and most polished behaviour by Mr. Shepherd's assurances of his being known, by report, to the Admiral, as a model of good breeding.

The house and grounds, and furniture, were approved, the Crofts were approved, terms, time, every thing, and every body, was right; and Mr. Shepherd's clerks were set to work, without there having been a single preliminary difference to modify of all that 'This indenture sheweth.'*

Sir Walter, without hesitation, declared the Admiral to be the best-looking sailor he had ever met with, and went so far as to say, that, if his own man might have had the arranging of his hair, he should not be ashamed of being seen with him any where; and the Admiral, with sympathetic cordiality, observed to his wife as they drove back through the Park, 'I thought we should soon come to a deal, my dear, in spite of what they told us at Taunton. The baronet will never set the Thames on fire,* but there seems no harm in him:'—reciprocal compliments, which would have been esteemed about equal.

The Crofts were to have possession at Michaelmas,* and as Sir Walter proposed removing to Bath in the course of the preceding month, there was no time to be lost in making every dependant arrangement.

Lady Russell, convinced that Anne would not be allowed to be of any use, or any importance, in the choice of the house which they were going to secure, was very unwilling to have her hurried away so soon, and wanted to make it possible for her to stay behind, till she might convey her to Bath herself after Christmas; but having engagements of her own, which must take her from Kellynch for several weeks, she was unable to give the full invitation she wished; and Anne, though dreading the possible heats of September in all the white glare of Bath, and grieving to forego all the influence so sweet and so sad of the autumnal months in the country, did not think that, every thing considered, she wished to remain. It would be most right, and most wise, and, therefore, must involve least suffering, to go with the others.

Something occurred, however, to give her a different duty. Mary, often a little unwell, and always thinking a great deal of her own complaints, and always in the habit of claiming Anne when any thing was the matter, was indisposed, and foreseeing that she should not have a day's health all the autumn, entreated, or rather required her, for it was hardly entreaty, to come to Uppercross Cottage, and bear her company as long as she should want her, instead of going to Bath.

'I cannot possibly do without Anne,' was Mary's reasoning; and Elizabeth's reply was, 'Then I am sure Anne had better stay, for nobody will want her in Bath.'

To be claimed as a good, though in an improper style, is at least better than being rejected as no good at all; and Anne, glad to be thought of some use, glad to have any thing marked out as a duty, and certainly not sorry to have the scene of it in the country, and her own dear country, readily agreed to stay.

This invitation of Mary's removed all Lady Russell's difficulties, and it was consequently soon settled that Anne should not go to Bath till Lady Russell took her, and that all the intervening time should be divided between Uppercross Cottage and Kellynch-lodge.

So far all was perfectly right; but Lady Russell was almost startled by the wrong of one part of the Kellynch-hall plan, when it burst on her, which was, Mrs. Clay's being engaged to go to Bath with Sir Walter and Elizabeth, as a most important and valuable assistant to the latter in all the business before her. Lady Russell was extremely sorry that such a measure should have been resorted to at all— wondered, grieved, and feared—and the affront it contained to Anne, in Mrs. Clay's being of so much use, while Anne could be of none, was a very sore aggravation.

Anne herself was become hardened to such affronts; but she felt the imprudence of the arrangement quite as keenly as Lady Russell. With a great deal of quiet observation, and a knowledge, which she often wished less, of her father's character, she was sensible that results the most serious to his family from the intimacy, were more than possible. She did not imagine that her father had at present an idea of the kind. Mrs. Clay had freckles, and a projecting tooth, and a clumsy wrist, which he was continually making severe remarks upon, in her absence; but she was young, and certainly altogether well-looking, and possessed, in an acute mind and assiduous pleasing manners, infinitely more dangerous attractions than any merely personal* might have been. Anne was so impressed by the degree of their danger, that she could not excuse herself from trying to make it perceptible to her sister. She had little hope of success; but Elizabeth, who in the event of such a reverse would be so much more to be pitied than herself, should never, she thought, have reason to reproach her for giving no warning.

She spoke, and seemed only to offend. Elizabeth could not conceive how such an absurd suspicion should occur to her; and indignantly answered for each party's perfectly knowing their situation.

'Mrs. Clay,' said she warmly, 'never forgets who she is; and as I am rather better acquainted with her sentiments than you can be, I can assure you, that upon the subject of marriage they are particularly nice; and that she reprobates all inequality of condition and rank more strongly than most people. And as to my father, I really should not have thought that he, who has kept himself single so long for our sakes, need be suspected now. If Mrs. Clay were a very beautiful woman, I grant you, it might be wrong to have her so much with me; not that any thing in the world, I am sure, would induce my father to make a degrading match; but he might be rendered unhappy. But poor Mrs. Clay, who, with all her merits, can never have been reckoned tolerably pretty! I really think poor Mrs. Clay may be staying here in perfect safety. One would imagine you had never heard my father speak of her personal misfortunes, though I know you must fifty times. That tooth of her's! and those freckles! Freckles do not disgust me so very much as they do him: I have known a face not materially disfigured by a few, but he abominates them. You must have heard him notice Mrs. Clay's freckles.'

'There is hardly any personal defect,' replied Anne, 'which an agreeable manner might not gradually reconcile one to.'

'I think very differently,' answered Elizabeth, shortly; 'an agreeable manner may set off handsome features, but can never alter plain ones. However, at any rate, as I have a great deal more at stake on this point than any body else can have, I think it rather unnecessary in you to be advising me.'

Anne had done—glad that it was over, and not absolutely hopeless of doing good. Elizabeth, though resenting the suspicion, might yet be made observant by it.

The last office of the four carriage-horses was to draw Sir Walter, Miss Elliot, and Mrs. Clay to Bath. The party drove off in very good spirits; Sir Walter prepared with condescending bows for all the afflicted tenantry and cottagers who might have had a hint to shew themselves: and Anne walked up at the same time, in a sort of desolate tranquillity, to the Lodge, where she was to spend the first week.

Her friend was not in better spirits than herself. Lady Russell felt this break-up of the family exceedingly. Their respectability was as dear to her as her own; and a daily intercourse had become precious by habit. It was painful to look upon their deserted grounds, and still worse to anticipate the new hands they were to fall into; and to escape the solitariness and the melancholy of so altered a village, and be out of the way when Admiral and Mrs. Croft first arrived, she had determined to make her own absence from home begin when she must give up Anne. Accordingly their removal was made together, and Anne was set down at Uppercross Cottage, in the first stage of Lady Russell's journey.

Uppercross was a moderate-sized village, which a few years back had been completely in the old English style; containing only two houses superior in appearance to those of the yeomen and labourers, —the mansion of the 'squire, with its high walls, great gates, and old trees, substantial and unmodernized—and the compact, tight parsonage, enclosed in its own neat garden, with a vine and a pear-tree trained round its casements; but upon the marriage of the young 'squire, it had received the improvement of a farm-house elevated into a cottage for his residence; and Uppercross Cottage, with its viranda, French windows, and other prettinesses, was quite as likely to catch the traveller's eye, as the more consistent and considerable aspect and premises of the Great House, about a quarter of a mile farther on.

Here Anne had often been staying. She knew the ways of
Uppercross as well as those of Kellynch. The two families were so
continually meeting, so much in the habit of running in and out of
each other's house at all hours, that it was rather a surprise to her to
find Mary alone; but being alone, her being unwell and out of spirits,
was almost a matter of course. Though better endowed than the
elder sister, Mary had not Anne's understanding or temper. While
well, and happy, and properly attended to, she had great good
humour and excellent spirits; but any indisposition sunk her completely; she had no resources for solitude; and inheriting a considerable share of the Elliot self-importance, was very prone to add to
every other distress that of fancying herself neglected and ill-used.
In person, she was inferior to both sisters, and had, even in her
bloom, only reached the dignity of being 'a fine girl.' She was now
lying on the faded sofa of the pretty little drawing-room, the once
elegant furniture of which had been gradually growing shabby,
under the influence of four summers and two children; and, on
Anne's appearing, greeted her with,

'So, you are come at last! I began to think I should never see you. I
am so ill I can hardly speak. I have not seen a creature the whole
morning!'

'I am sorry to find you unwell,' replied Anne. 'You sent me such a
good account of yourself on Thursday!'

'Yes, I made the best of it; I always do; but I was very far from well
at the time; and I do not think I ever was so ill in my life as I have
been all this morning—very unfit to be left alone, I am sure. Suppose
I were to be seized of a sudden in some dreadful way, and not able to
ring the bell! So, Lady Russell would not get out. I do not think she
has been in this house three times this summer.'

Anne said what was proper, and enquired after her husband. 'Oh!
Charles is out shooting. I have not seen him since seven o'clock. He
would go, though I told him how ill I was. He said he should not stay
out long; but he has never come back, and now it is almost one. I
assure you, I have not seen a soul this whole long morning.'

'You have had your little boys with you?'

'Yes, as long as I could bear their noise; but they are so unmanageable that they do me more harm than good. Little Charles does not
mind a word I say, and Walter is growing quite as bad.'

'Well, you will soon be better now,' replied Anne, cheerfully. 'You know I always cure you when I come. How are your neighbours at the Great House?'

'I can give you no account of them. I have not seen one of them to-day, except Mr. Musgrove, who just stopped and spoke through the window, but without getting off his horse; and though I told him how ill I was, not one of them have been near me. It did not happen to suit the Miss Musgroves, I suppose, and they never put themselves out of their way.'

'You will see them yet, perhaps, before the morning is gone. It is early.'

'I never want them, I assure you. They talk and laugh a great deal too much for me. Oh! Anne, I am so very unwell! It was quite unkind of you not to come on Thursday.'

'My dear Mary, recollect what a comfortable account you sent me of yourself! You wrote in the cheerfullest manner, and said you were perfectly well, and in no hurry for me; and that being the case, you must be aware that my wish would be to remain with Lady Russell to the last: and besides what I felt on her account, I have really been so busy, have had so much to do, that I could not very conveniently have left Kellynch sooner.'

'Dear me! what can *you* possibly have to do?'

'A great many things, I assure you. More than I can recollect in a moment: but I can tell you some. I have been making a duplicate of the catalogue of my father's books and pictures. I have been several times in the garden with Mackenzie, trying to understand, and make him understand, which of Elizabeth's plants are for Lady Russell. I have had all my own little concerns to arrange—books and music to divide, and all my trunks to repack, from not having understood in time what was intended as to the waggons. And one thing I have had to do, Mary, of a more trying nature; going to almost every house in the parish, as a sort of take-leave. I was told that they wished it. But all these things took up a great deal of time.'

'Oh! well;'—and after a moment's pause, 'But you have never asked me one word about our dinner at the Pooles yesterday.'

'Did you go then? I have made no enquiries, because I concluded you must have been obliged to give up the party.'

'Oh! yes, I went. I was very well yesterday; nothing at all the matter with me till this morning. It would have been strange if I had not gone.'

'I am very glad you were well enough, and I hope you had a pleasant party.'

'Nothing remarkable. One always knows beforehand what the dinner will be, and who will be there. And it is so very uncomfortable, not having a carriage of one's own. Mr. and Mrs. Musgrove took me, and we were so crowded! They are both so very large, and take up so much room! And Mr. Musgrove always sits forward. So, there was I, crowded into the back seat with Henrietta and Louisa. And I think it very likely that my illness to-day may be owing to it.'

A little farther perseverance in patience, and forced cheerfulness on Anne's side, produced nearly a cure on Mary's. She could soon sit upright on the sofa, and began to hope she might be able to leave it by dinner-time. Then, forgetting to think of it, she was at the other end of the room, beautifying a nosegay; then, she ate her cold meat; and then she was well enough to propose a little walk.

'Where shall we go?' said she, when they were ready. 'I suppose you will not like to call at the Great House before they have been to see you?'

'I have not the smallest objection on that account,' replied Anne. 'I should never think of standing on such ceremony with people I know so well as Mrs. and the Miss Musgroves.'

'Oh! but they ought to call upon you as soon as possible. They ought to feel what is due to you as *my* sister. However, we may as well go and sit with them a little while, and when we have got that over, we can enjoy our walk.'

Anne had always thought such a style of intercourse highly imprudent; but she had ceased to endeavour to check it, from believing that, though there were on each side continual subjects of offence, neither family could now do without it. To the Great House accordingly they went, to sit the full half hour in the old-fashioned square parlour, with a small carpet and shining floor, to which the present daughters of the house were gradually giving the proper air of confusion by a grand piano forte and a harp, flower stands and little tables placed in every direction. Oh! could the originals of the portraits against the wainscot, could the gentlemen in brown velvet and the ladies in blue satin have seen what was going on, have been conscious of such an overthrow of all order and neatness! The portraits themselves seemed to be staring in astonishment.

The Musgroves, like their houses, were in a state of alteration,

perhaps of improvement. The father and mother were in the old
English style, and the young people in the new. Mr. and Mrs. Musgrove were a very good sort of people; friendly and hospitable, not
much educated, and not at all elegant. Their children had more
modern minds and manners. There was a numerous family; but the
only two grown up, excepting Charles, were Henrietta and Louisa,
young ladies of nineteen and twenty, who had brought from a school
at Exeter all the usual stock of accomplishments,* and were now, like
thousands of other young ladies, living to be fashionable, happy, and
merry. Their dress had every advantage, their faces were rather
pretty, their spirits extremely good, their manners unembarrassed
and pleasant; they were of consequence at home, and favourites
abroad. Anne always contemplated them as some of the happiest
creatures of her acquaintance; but still, saved as we all are by some
comfortable feeling of superiority from wishing for the possibility of
exchange, she would not have given up her own more elegant and
cultivated mind for all their enjoyments; and envied them nothing
but that seemingly perfect good understanding and agreement
together, that good-humoured mutual affection, of which she had
known so little herself with either of her sisters.

They were received with great cordiality. Nothing seemed amiss
on the side of the Great House family, which was generally, as Anne
very well knew, the least to blame. The half hour was chatted away
pleasantly enough; and she was not at all surprised, at the end of it,
to have their walking party joined by both the Miss Musgroves, at
Mary's particular invitation.

CHAPTER VI

ANNE had not wanted this visit to Uppercross, to learn that a
removal from one set of people to another, though at a distance of
only three miles, will often include a total change of conversation,
opinion, and idea. She had never been staying there before, without
being struck by it, or without wishing that other Elliots could have
her advantage in seeing how unknown, or unconsidered there, were
the affairs which at Kellynch-hall were treated as of such general
publicity and pervading interest; yet, with all this experience, she
believed she must now submit to feel that another lesson, in the art

of knowing our own nothingness beyond our own circle, was become necessary for her;—for certainly, coming as she did, with a heart full of the subject which had been completely occupying both houses in Kellynch for many weeks, she had expected rather more curiosity and sympathy than she found in the separate, but very similar remark of Mr. and Mrs. Musgrove—'So, Miss Anne, Sir Walter and your sister are gone; and what part of Bath do you think they will settle in?' and this, without much waiting for an answer;—or in the young ladies' addition of, 'I hope *we* shall be in Bath in the winter; but remember, papa, if we do go, we must be in a good situation— none of your Queen-squares for us!'* or in the anxious supplement from Mary, of 'Upon my word, I shall be pretty well off, when you are all gone away to be happy at Bath!'

She could only resolve to avoid such self-delusion in future, and think with heightened gratitude of the extraordinary blessing of having one such truly sympathising friend as Lady Russell.

The Mr. Musgroves had their own game to guard, and to destroy; their own horses, dogs, and newspapers to engage them; and the females were fully occupied in all the other common subjects of house-keeping, neighbours, dress, dancing, and music. She acknowledged it to be very fitting, that every little social commonwealth should dictate its own matters of discourse; and hoped, ere long, to become a not unworthy member of the one she was now transplanted into.—With the prospect of spending at least two months at Uppercross, it was highly incumbent on her to clothe her imagination, her memory, and all her ideas in as much of Uppercross as possible.

She had no dread of these two months. Mary was not so repulsive* and unsisterly as Elizabeth, nor so inaccessible to all influence of hers; neither was there any thing among the other component parts of the cottage inimical to comfort.—She was always on friendly terms with her brother-in-law; and in the children, who loved her nearly as well, and respected her a great deal more than their mother, she had an object of interest, amusement, and wholesome exertion.

Charles Musgrove was civil and agreeable; in sense and temper he was undoubtedly superior to his wife; but not of powers, or conversation, or grace, to make the past, as they were connected together, at all a dangerous contemplation; though, at the same time, Anne could believe, with Lady Russell, that a more equal match might have greatly improved him; and that a woman of real understanding might have given more consequence to his character, and more usefulness, rationality, and elegance to his habits and pursuits. As it was, he did nothing with much zeal, but sport; and his time was otherwise trifled away, without benefit from books, or any thing else. He had very good spirits, which never seemed much affected by his wife's occasional lowness; bore with her unreasonableness sometimes to Anne's admiration; and, upon the whole, though there was very often a little disagreement, (in which she had sometimes more share than she wished, being appealed to by both parties) they might pass for a happy couple. They were always perfectly agreed in the want of more money, and a strong inclination for a handsome present from his father; but here, as on most topics, he had the superiority, for while Mary thought it a great shame that such a present was not made, he always contended for his father's having many other uses for his money, and a right to spend it as he liked.

As to the management of their children, his theory was much better than his wife's, and his practice not so bad—'I could manage them very well, if it were not for Mary's interference,'—was what Anne often heard him say, and had a good deal of faith in; but when listening in turn to Mary's reproach of 'Charles spoils the children so that I cannot get them into any order,'—she never had the smallest temptation to say, 'Very true.'

One of the least agreeable circumstances of her residence there, was her being treated with too much confidence by all parties, and being too much in the secret of the complaints of each house. Known to have some influence with her sister, she was continually requested, or at least receiving hints to exert it, beyond what was practicable. 'I wish you could persuade Mary not to be always fancying herself ill,' was Charles's language; and, in an unhappy mood, thus spoke Mary;—'I do believe if Charles were to see me dying, he would not think there was any thing the matter with me. I am sure, Anne, if you would, you might persuade him that I really am very ill—a great deal worse than I ever own.'

Mary's declaration was, 'I hate sending the children to the Great House, though their grandmamma is always wanting to see them, for she humours and indulges them to such a degree, and gives them so much trash and sweet things, that they are sure to come back sick and cross for the rest of the day.'—And Mrs. Musgrove took the first opportunity of being alone with Anne, to say, 'Oh! Miss Anne, I cannot help wishing Mrs. Charles had a little of your method with those children. They are quite different creatures with you! But to be sure, in general they are so spoilt! It is a pity you cannot put your sister in the way of managing them. They are as fine healthy children as ever were seen, poor little dears, without partiality; but Mrs. Charles knows no more how they should be treated!—Bless me, how troublesome they are sometimes!—I assure you, Miss Anne, it prevents my wishing to see them at our house so often as I otherwise should. I believe Mrs. Charles is not quite pleased with my not inviting them oftener; but you know it is very bad to have children with one, that one is obliged to be checking every moment; "don't do this, and don't do that;"—or that one can only keep in tolerable order by more cake than is good for them.'

She had this communication, moreover, from Mary. 'Mrs. Musgrove thinks all her servants so steady, that it would be high treason to call it in question; but I am sure, without exaggeration, that her upper house-maid and laundry-maid, instead of being in their business, are gadding about the village, all day long. I meet them wherever I go; and I declare, I never go twice into my nursery without seeing something of them. If Jemima were not the trustiest, steadiest creature in the world, it would be enough to spoil her; for she tells me, they are always tempting her to take a walk with them.' And on Mrs. Musgrove's side, it was,—'I make a rule of never interfering in any of my daughter-in-law's concerns, for I know it would not do; but I shall tell *you*, Miss Anne, because you may be able to set things to rights, that I have no very good opinion of Mrs. Charles's nursery-maid: I hear strange stories of her; she is always upon the gad: and from my own knowledge, I can declare, she is such a fine-dressing lady, that she is enough to ruin any servants she comes near. Mrs. Charles quite swears by her, I know; but I just give you this hint, that you may be upon the watch; because, if you see any thing amiss, you need not be afraid of mentioning it.'

Again; it was Mary's complaint, that Mrs. Musgrove was very apt not to give her the precedence that was her due,* when they dined at the Great House with other families; and she did not see any reason why she was to be considered so much at home as to lose her place. And one day, when Anne was walking with only the Miss Musgroves, one of them, after talking of rank, people of rank, and jealousy of rank, said, 'I have no scruple of observing to *you*, how non-sensical some persons are about their place, because, all the world knows how easy and indifferent you are about it: but I wish any body could give Mary a hint that it would be a great deal better if she were not so very tenacious; especially, if she would not be always putting herself forward to take place of mamma. Nobody doubts her right to have precedence of mamma, but it would be more becoming in her not to be always insisting on it. It is not that mamma cares about it the least in the world, but I know it is taken notice of by many persons.'

How was Anne to set all these matters to rights? She could do little more than listen patiently, soften every grievance, and excuse each to the other; give them all hints of the forbearance necessary between such near neighbours, and make those hints broadest which were meant for her sister's benefit.

In all other respects, her visit began and proceeded very well. Her own spirits improved by change of place and subject, by being removed three miles from Kellynch: Mary's ailments lessened by having a constant companion; and their daily intercourse with the other family, since there was neither superior affection, confidence, nor employment in the cottage, to be interrupted by it, was rather an advantage. It was certainly carried nearly as far as possible, for they met every morning, and hardly ever spent an evening asunder; but she believed they should not have done so well without the sight of Mr. and Mrs. Musgrove's respectable forms in the usual places, or without the talking, laughing, and singing of their daughters.

She played a great deal better than either of the Miss Musgroves; but having no voice, no knowledge of the harp, and no fond parents to sit by and fancy themselves delighted, her performance was little thought of, only out of civility, or to refresh the others, as she was well aware. She knew that when she played she was giving pleasure only to herself; but this was no new sensation: excepting one short period of her life, she had never, since the age of fourteen, never since the loss of her dear mother, known the happiness of being listened to, or encouraged by any just appreciation or real taste. In music she had been always used to feel alone in the world; and Mr. and Mrs. Musgrove's fond partiality for their own daughters' per-formance, and total indifference to any other person's, gave her much more pleasure for their sakes, than mortification for her own.

The party at the Great House was sometimes increased by other company. The neighbourhood was not large, but the Musgroves were visited by every body, and had more dinner parties, and more callers, more visitors by invitation and by chance, than any other family. They were more completely popular.

The girls were wild for dancing; and the evenings ended, occasionally, in an unpremeditated little ball. There was a family of cousins within a walk of Uppercross, in less affluent circumstances, who depended on the Musgroves for all their pleasures: they would come at any time, and help play at any thing, or dance any where; and Anne, very much preferring the office of musician to a more active post, played country dances* to them by the hour together; a kindness which always recommended her musical powers to the notice of Mr. and Mrs. Musgrove more than any thing else, and often drew this compliment;—'Well done, Miss Anne! very well done indeed! Lord bless me! how those little fingers of yours fly about!'

So passed the first three weeks. Michaelmas came; and now Anne's heart must be in Kellynch again. A beloved home made over to others; all the precious rooms and furniture, groves, and pro-spects, beginning to own other eyes and other limbs! She could not think of much else on the 29th of September; and she had this sympathetic touch in the evening, from Mary, who, on having occa-sion to note down the day of the month, exclaimed, 'Dear me! is not this the day the Crofts were to come to Kellynch? I am glad I did not think of it before. How low it makes me!'

The Crofts took possession with true naval alertness, and were to be visited. Mary deplored the necessity for herself. 'Nobody knew how much she should suffer. She should put it off as long as she could.' But was not easy till she had talked Charles into driving her over on an early day; and was in a very animated, comfortable state of imaginary agitation, when she came back. Anne had very sincerely rejoiced in there being no means of her going.* She wished, however, to see the Crofts, and was glad to be within when the visit was returned. They came; the master of the house was not at home, but the two sisters were together; and as it chanced that Mrs. Croft fell to the share of Anne, while the admiral sat by Mary, and made himself very agreeable by his good-humoured notice of her little boys, she was well able to watch for a likeness, and if it failed her in the features, to catch it in the voice, or the turn of sentiment and expression.

Mrs. Croft, though neither tall nor fat, had a squareness, upright-ness, and vigour of form, which gave importance to her person. She had bright dark eyes, good teeth, and altogether an agreeable face; though her reddened and weather-beaten complexion, the con-sequence of her having been almost as much at sea as her husband, made her seem to have lived some years longer in the world than her real eight and thirty. Her manners were open, easy, and decided, like one who had no distrust of herself, and no doubts of what to do; without any approach to coarseness, however, or any want of good humour. Anne gave her credit, indeed, for feelings of great consider-ation towards herself, in all that related to Kellynch; and it pleased her: especially, as she had satisfied herself in the very first half minute, in the instant even of introduction, that there was not the smallest symptom of any knowledge or suspicion on Mrs. Croft's side, to give a bias of any sort. She was quite easy on that head, and consequently full of strength and courage, till for a moment electrified by Mrs. Croft's suddenly saying,—

'It was you, and not your sister, I find, that my brother had the pleasure of being acquainted with, when he was in this country.'

Anne hoped she had outlived the age of blushing; but the age of emotion she certainly had not.

'Perhaps you may not have heard that he is married,' added Mrs. Croft.

She could now answer as she ought; and was happy to feel, when Mrs. Croft's next words explained it to be Mr. Wentworth of whom she spoke, that she had said nothing which might not do for either brother. She immediately felt how reasonable it was, that Mrs. Croft should be thinking and speaking of Edward, and not of Frederick; and with shame at her own forgetfulness, applied herself to the knowledge of their former neighbour's present state, with proper interest.

The rest was all tranquillity; till just as they were moving, she heard the admiral say to Mary,

'We are expecting a brother of Mrs. Croft's here soon; I dare say you know him by name.'

He was cut short by the eager attacks of the little boys, clinging to him like an old friend, and declaring he should not go; and being too much engrossed by proposals of carrying them away in his coat pocket, &c. to have another moment for finishing or recollecting what he had begun, Anne was left to persuade herself, as well as she could, that the same brother must still be in question. She could not, however, reach such a degree of certainty, as not to be anxious to hear whether any thing had been said on the subject at the other house, where the Crofts had previously been calling.

The folks of Great House were to spend the evening of this day at the Cottage; and it being now too late in the year for such visits to be made on foot, the coach was beginning to be listened for, when the youngest Miss Musgrove walked in. That she was coming to apologize, and that they should have to spend the evening by themselves, was the first black idea; and Mary was quite ready to be affronted, when Louisa made all right by saying, that she only came on foot, to leave more room for the harp, which was bringing in the carriage.

'And I will tell you our reason,' she added, 'and all about it. I am come on to give you notice, that papa and mamma are out of spirits this evening, especially mamma; she is thinking so much of poor Richard! And we agreed it would be best to have the harp, for it seems to amuse her more than the pianoforte. I will tell you why she is out of spirits. When the Crofts called this morning, (they called here afterwards, did not they?) they happened to say, that her brother, Captain Wentworth, is just returned to England, or paid off, or something, and is coming to see them almost directly; and most unluckily it came into mamma's head, when they were gone, that Wentworth, or something very like it, was the name of poor Richard's captain, at one time, I do not know when or where, but a great while before he died, poor fellow! And upon looking over his letters and things, she found it was so; and is perfectly sure that this must be the very man, and her head is quite full of it, and of poor Richard! So we must all be as merry as we can, that she may not be dwelling upon such gloomy things.'

The real circumstances of this pathetic piece of family history were, that the Musgroves had had the ill fortune of a very troublesome, hopeless son; and the good fortune to lose him before he reached his twentieth year; that he had been sent to sea, because he was stupid and unmanageable on shore; that he had been very little cared for at any time by his family, though quite as much as he deserved; seldom heard of, and scarcely at all regretted, when the intelligence of his death abroad had worked its way to Uppercross, two years before.

He had, in fact, though his sisters were now doing all they could for him, by calling him 'poor Richard,' been nothing better than a thick-headed, unfeeling, unprofitable Dick Musgrove, who had never done any thing to entitle himself to more than the abbreviation of his name, living or dead.

He had been several years at sea, and had, in the course of those removals to which all midshipmen are liable, and especially such midshipmen as every captain wishes to get rid of, been six months on board Captain Frederick Wentworth's frigate,* the Laconia; and from the Laconia he had, under the influence of his captain, written the only two letters which his father and mother had ever received from him during the whole of his absence; that is to say, the only two disinterested letters; all the rest had been mere applications for money.

In each letter he had spoken well of his captain; but yet, so little were they in the habit of attending to such matters, so unobservant and incurious were they as to the names of men or ships, that it had made scarcely any impression at the time; and that Mrs. Musgrove should have been suddenly struck, this very day, with a recollection of the name of Wentworth, as connected with her son, seemed one of those extraordinary bursts of mind which do sometimes occur.

She had gone to her letters, and found it all as she supposed; and the reperusal of these letters, after so long an interval, her poor son gone for ever, and all the strength of his faults forgotten, had affected her spirits exceedingly, and thrown her into greater grief for him than she had known on first hearing of his death. Mr. Musgrove was, in a lesser degree, affected likewise; and when they reached the cottage, they were evidently in want, first, of being listened to anew on this subject, and afterwards, of all the relief which cheerful companions could give.

To hear them talking so much of Captain Wentworth, repeating his name so often, puzzling over past years, and at last ascertaining that it *might*, that it probably *would*, turn out to be the very same Captain Wentworth whom they recollected meeting, once or twice, after their coming back from Clifton;*—a very fine young man; but they could not say whether it was seven or eight years ago,—was a new sort of trial to Anne's nerves. She found, however, that it was

one to which she must enure herself. Since he actually was expected
in the country, she must teach herself to be insensible on such points.
And not only did it appear that he was expected, and speedily, but
the Musgroves, in their warm gratitude for the kindness he had
shewn poor Dick, and very high respect for his character, stamped as
it was by poor Dick's having been six months under his care, and
mentioning him in strong, though not perfectly well spelt praise, as
'a fine dashing felow, only two perticular about the school-master,'*
were bent on introducing themselves, and seeking his acquaintance,
as soon as they could hear of his arrival.

The resolution of doing so helped to form the comfort of their
evening.

CHAPTER VII

A VERY few days more, and Captain Wentworth was known to be at
Kellynch, and Mr. Musgrove had called on him, and come back
warm in his praise, and he was engaged with the Crofts to dine at
Uppercross, by the end of another week. It had been a great disappointment to Mr. Musgrove, to find that no earlier day could be
fixed, so impatient was he to shew his gratitude, by seeing Captain
Wentworth under his own roof, and welcoming him to all that was
strongest and best in his cellars. But a week must pass; only a week,
in Anne's reckoning, and then, she supposed, they must meet; and
soon she began to wish that she could feel secure even for a week.

Captain Wentworth made a very early return to Mr. Musgrove's
civility, and she was all but calling there in the same half hour!—She
and Mary were actually setting forward for the great house, where, as
she afterwards learnt, they must inevitably have found him, when
they were stopped by the eldest boy's being at that moment brought
home in consequence of a bad fall. The child's situation put the visit
entirely aside, but she could not hear of her escape with indifference,
even in the midst of the serious anxiety which they afterwards felt on
his account.

His collar-bone was found to be dislocated, and such injury
received in the back, as roused the most alarming ideas. It was an
afternoon of distress, and Anne had every thing to do at once—the
apothecary to send for—the father to have pursued and informed—

the mother to support and keep from hysterics—the servants to control—the youngest child to banish, and the poor suffering one to attend and soothe;—besides sending, as soon as she recollected it, proper notice to the other house, which brought her an accession rather of frightened, enquiring companions, than of very useful assistants.

Her brother's return* was the first comfort; he could take best care of his wife, and the second blessing was the arrival of the apothecary. Till he came and had examined the child, their apprehensions were the worse for being vague;—they suspected great injury, but knew not where; but now the collar-bone was soon replaced, and though Mr. Robinson felt and felt, and rubbed, and looked grave, and spoke low words both to the father and the aunt, still they were all to hope the best, and to be able to part and eat their dinner in tolerable ease of mind; and then it was, just before they parted, that the two young aunts were able so far to digress from their nephew's state, as to give the information of Captain Wentworth's visit;—staying five minutes behind their father and mother, to endeavour to express how perfectly delighted they were with him, how much handsomer, how infinitely more agreeable they thought him than any individual among their male acquaintance, who had been at all a favourite before—how glad they had been to hear papa invite him to stay dinner—how sorry when he said it was quite out of his power—and how glad again, when he had promised in reply to papa and mamma's farther pressing invitations, to come and dine with them on the morrow, actually on the morrow!—And he had promised it in so pleasant a manner, as if he felt all the motive of their attention just as he ought!—And, in short, he had looked and said every thing with such exquisite grace, that they could assure them all, their heads were both turned by him!—And off they ran, quite as full of glee as of love, and apparently more full of Captain Wentworth than of little Charles.

The same story and the same raptures were repeated, when the two girls came with their father, through the gloom of the evening, to make enquiries; and Mr. Musgrove, no longer under the first uneasiness about his heir, could add his confirmation and praise, and hope there would be now no occasion for putting Captain Wentworth off, and only be sorry to think that the cottage party, probably, would not like to leave the little boy, to give him the meeting.—'Oh, no! as to leaving the little boy!'—both father and mother were in much too strong and recent alarm to bear the thought; and Anne, in the joy of the escape, could not help adding her warm protestations to theirs.

Charles Musgrove, indeed, afterwards shewed more of inclination; 'the child was going on so well—and he wished so much to be introduced to Captain Wentworth, that, perhaps, he might join them in the evening; he would not dine from home, but he might walk in for half an hour.' But in this he was eagerly opposed by his wife, with 'Oh, no! indeed, Charles, I cannot bear to have you go away. Only think, if any thing should happen!'

The child had a good night, and was going on well the next day. It must be a work of time to ascertain that no injury had been done to the spine, but Mr. Robinson found nothing to increase alarm, and Charles Musgrove began consequently to feel no necessity for longer confinement. The child was to be kept in bed, and amused as quietly as possible; but what was there for a father to do? This was quite a female case, and it would be highly absurd in him, who could be of no use at home, to shut himself up. His father very much wished him to meet Captain Wentworth, and there being no sufficient reason against it, he ought to go; and it ended in his making a bold public declaration, when he came in from shooting, of his meaning to dress directly, and dine at the other house.

'Nothing can be going on better than the child,' said he, 'so I told my father just now that I would come, and he thought me quite right. Your sister being with you, my love, I have no scruple at all. You would not like to leave him yourself, but you see I can be of no use. Anne will send for me if any thing is the matter.'

Husbands and wives generally understand when opposition will be vain. Mary knew, from Charles's manner of speaking, that he was quite determined on going, and that it would be of no use to teaze him. She said nothing, therefore, till he was out of the room, but as soon as there was only Anne to hear,

'So! You and I are to be left to shift by ourselves, with this poor sick child—and not a creature coming near us all the evening! I knew how it would be. This is always my luck! If there is any thing disagreeable going on, men are always sure to get out of it, and Charles is as bad as any of them. Very unfeeling! I must say it is very unfeeling of him, to be running away from his poor little boy; talks of his being going on so well! How does he know that he is going on well, or that there may not be a sudden change half an hour hence? I did not think Charles would have been so unfeeling. So, here he is to go away and enjoy himself, and because I am the poor mother, I am not to be allowed to stir;—and yet, I am sure, I am more unfit than any body else to be about the child. My being the mother is the very reason why my feelings should not be tried. I am not at all equal to it. You saw how hysterical I was yesterday.'

'But that was only the effect of the suddenness of your alarm—of the shock. You will not be hysterical again. I dare say we shall have nothing to distress us. I perfectly understand Mr. Robinson's directions, and have no fears; and indeed, Mary, I cannot wonder at your husband. Nursing does not belong to a man, it is not his province. A sick child is always the mother's property, her own feelings generally make it so.'

'I hope I am as fond of my child as any mother—but I do not know that I am of any more use in the sick-room than Charles, for I cannot be always scolding and teazing a poor child when it is ill; and you saw, this morning, that if I told him to keep quiet, he was sure to begin kicking about. I have not nerves for the sort of thing.'

'But, could you be comfortable yourself, to be spending the whole evening away from the poor boy?'

'Yes; you see his papa can, and why should not I?—Jemima is so careful! And she could send us word every hour how he was. I really think Charles might as well have told his father we would all come. I am not more alarmed about little Charles now than he is. I was dreadfully alarmed yesterday, but the case is very different to-day.'

'Well—if you do not think it too late to give notice for yourself, suppose you were to go, as well as your husband. Leave little Charles to my care. Mr. and Mrs. Musgrove cannot think it wrong, while I remain with him.'

'Are you serious?' cried Mary, her eyes brightening. 'Dear me! that's a very good thought, very good indeed. To be sure I may just as well go as not, for I am of no use at home—am I? and it only harasses me. You, who have not a mother's feelings, are a great deal the properest person. You can make little Charles do any thing; he always minds you at a word. It will be a great deal better than leaving him with only Jemima. Oh! I will certainly go; I am sure I ought if I can, quite as much as Charles, for they want me excessively to be acquainted with Captain Wentworth, and I know you do not mind being left alone. An excellent thought of yours, indeed, Anne! I will go and tell Charles, and get ready directly. You can send for us, you know, at a moment's notice, if any thing is the matter; but I dare say there will be nothing to alarm you. I should not go, you may be sure, if I did not feel quite at ease about my dear child.'

The next moment she was tapping at her husband's dressing-room door, and as Anne followed her up stairs, she was in time for the whole conversation, which began with Mary's saying, in a tone of great exultation,

'I mean to go with you, Charles, for I am of no more use at home than you are. If I were to shut myself up for ever with the child, I should not be able to persuade him to do any thing he did not like. Anne will stay; Anne undertakes to stay at home and take care of him. It is Anne's own proposal, and so I shall go with you, which will be a great deal better, for I have not dined at the other house since Tuesday.'

'This is very kind of Anne,' was her husband's answer, 'and I should be very glad to have you go; but it seems rather hard that she should be left at home by herself, to nurse our sick child.'

Anne was now at hand to take up her own cause, and the sincerity of her manner being soon sufficient to convince him, where conviction was at least very agreeable, he had no farther scruples as to her being left to dine alone, though he still wanted her to join them in the evening, when the child might be at rest for the night, and kindly urged her to let him come and fetch her; but she was quite unpersuadable; and this being the case, she had ere long the pleasure of seeing them set off together in high spirits. They were gone, she hoped, to be happy, however oddly constructed such happiness might seem; as for herself, she was left with as many sensations of comfort, as were, perhaps, ever likely to be hers. She knew herself to be of the first utility to the child; and what was it to her, if Frederick Wentworth were only half a mile distant, making himself agreeable to others!

She would have liked to know how he felt as to a meeting. Perhaps indifferent, if indifference could exist under such circumstances. He must be either indifferent or unwilling. Had he wished ever to see her again, he need not have waited till this time; he would have done what she could not but believe that in his place she should have done long ago, when events had been early giving him the independence which alone had been wanting.

Her brother and sister came back delighted with their new acquaintance, and their visit in general. There had been music, singing, talking, laughing, all that was most agreeable; charming manners in Captain Wentworth, no shyness or reserve; they seemed all to know each other perfectly, and he was coming the very next morning to shoot with Charles. He was to come to breakfast, but not at the Cottage, though that had been proposed at first; but then he had been pressed to come to the Great House instead, and he seemed afraid of being in Mrs. Charles Musgrove's way, on account of the child; and therefore, somehow, they hardly knew how, it ended in Charles's being to meet him to breakfast at his father's.

Anne understood it. He wished to avoid seeing her. He had enquired after her, she found, slightly, as might suit a former slight acquaintance, seeming to acknowledge such as she had acknowledged, actuated, perhaps, by the same view of escaping introduction when they were to meet.

The morning hours of the Cottage were always later than those of the other house; and on the morrow the difference was so great, that Mary and Anne were not more than beginning breakfast when Charles came in to say that they were just setting off, that he was come for his dogs, that his sisters were following with Captain Wentworth, his sisters meaning to visit Mary and the child, and Captain Wentworth proposing also to wait on her for a few minutes, if not inconvenient; and though Charles had answered for the child's being in no such state as could make it inconvenient, Captain Wentworth would not be satisfied without his running on to give notice.

Mary, very much gratified by this attention, was delighted to receive him; while a thousand feelings rushed on Anne, of which this was the most consoling, that it would soon be over. And it was soon over. In two minutes after Charles's preparation, the others appeared; they were in the drawing-room. Her eye half met Captain Wentworth's; a bow, a curtsey passed; she heard his voice—he talked to Mary, said all that was right; said something to the Miss Musgroves, enough to mark an easy footing: the room seemed full—full of persons and voices—but a few minutes ended it. Charles shewed himself at the window, all was ready, their visitor had bowed and was gone; the Miss Musgroves were gone too, suddenly resolving to walk to the end of the village with the sportsmen: the room was cleared, and Anne might finish her breakfast as she could.

'It is over! it is over!' she repeated to herself again, and again, in nervous gratitude. 'The worst is over!'

Mary talked, but she could not attend. She had seen him. They had met. They had been once more in the same room!

Soon, however, she began to reason with herself, and try to be feeling less. Eight years, almost eight years had passed, since all had been given up. How absurd to be resuming the agitation which such an interval had banished into distance and indistinctness! What might not eight years do? Events of every description, changes, alienations, removals,—all, all must be comprised in it; and oblivion of the past—how natural, how certain too! It included nearly a third part of her own life.

Alas! with all her reasonings, she found, that to retentive feelings eight years may be little more than nothing.

Now, how were his sentiments to be read? Was this like wishing to avoid her? And the next moment she was hating herself for the folly which asked the question.

On one other question, which perhaps her utmost wisdom might not have prevented, she was soon spared all suspense; for after the Miss Musgroves had returned and finished their visit at the Cottage, she had this spontaneous information from Mary:

'Captain Wentworth is not very gallant by you, Anne, though he was so attentive to me. Henrietta asked him what he thought of you, when they went away; and he said, "You were so altered he should not have known you again."'

Mary had no feelings to make her respect her sister's in a common way; but she was perfectly unsuspicious of being inflicting any peculiar wound.

'Altered beyond his knowledge!' Anne fully submitted, in silent, deep mortification. Doubtless it was so; and she could take no revenge, for he was not altered, or not for the worse. She had already acknowledged it to herself, and she could not think differently, let him think of her as he would. No; the years which had destroyed her youth and bloom had only given him a more glowing, manly, open look, in no respect lessening his personal advantages. She had seen the same Frederick Wentworth.

'So altered that he should not have known her again!' These were words which could not but dwell with her. Yet she soon began to rejoice that she had heard them. They were of sobering tendency; they allayed agitation; they composed, and consequently must make her happier.

Frederick Wentworth had used such words, or something like them, but without an idea that they would be carried round to her. He had thought her wretchedly altered, and, in the first moment of appeal, had spoken as he felt. He had not forgiven Anne Elliot. She had used him ill; deserted and disappointed him; and worse, she had shewn a feebleness of character in doing so, which his own decided, confident temper could not endure. She had given him up to oblige others. It had been the effect of over-persuasion. It had been weakness and timidity.

He had been most warmly attached to her, and had never seen a woman since whom he thought her equal; but, except from some natural sensation of curiosity, he had no desire of meeting her again. Her power with him was gone for ever.

It was now his object to marry. He was rich, and being turned on shore, fully intended to settle as soon as he could be properly tempted; actually looking round, ready to fall in love with all the speed which a clear head and quick taste could allow. He had a heart for either of the Miss Musgroves, if they could catch it; a heart, in short, for any pleasing young woman who came in his way, excepting Anne Elliot. This was his only secret exception, when he said to his sister, in answer to her suppositions,

'Yes, here I am, Sophia, quite ready to make a foolish match. Any body between fifteen and thirty may have me for asking. A little beauty, and a few smiles, and a few compliments to the navy, and I am a lost man. Should not this be enough for a sailor, who has had no society among women to make him nice?'

He said it, she knew, to be contradicted. His bright, proud eye spoke the happy conviction that he was nice; and Anne Elliot was not out of his thoughts, when he more seriously described the woman he should wish to meet with. 'A strong mind, with sweetness of manner,' made the first and the last of the description.

'This is the woman I want,' said he. 'Something a little inferior I shall of course put up with, but it must not be much. If I am a fool, I shall be a fool indeed, for I have thought on the subject more than most men.'

CHAPTER VIII

FROM this time Captain Wentworth and Anne Elliot were repeatedly in the same circle. They were soon dining in company together at Mr. Musgrove's, for the little boy's state could no longer supply his aunt with a pretence for absenting herself; and this was but the beginning of other dinings and other meetings.

Whether former feelings were to be renewed, must be brought to the proof; former times must undoubtedly be brought to the recollection of each; *they* could not but be reverted to; the year of their engagement could not but be named by him, in the little narratives or descriptions which conversation called forth. His profession qualified him, his disposition led him, to talk; and '*That* was in the year six;' '*That* happened before I went to sea in the year six,' occurred in the course of the first evening they spent together: and though his voice did not falter, and though she had no reason to suppose his eye wandering towards her while he spoke, Anne felt the utter impossibility, from her knowledge of his mind, that he could be unvisited by remembrance any more than herself. There must be the same immediate association of thought, though she was very far from conceiving it to be of equal pain.

They had no conversation together, no intercourse but what the commonest civility required. Once so much to each other! Now nothing! There *had* been a time, when of all the large party now filling the drawing-room at Uppercross, they would have found it most difficult to cease to speak to one another. With the exception, perhaps, of Admiral and Mrs. Croft, who seemed particularly attached and happy, (Anne could allow no other exception even among the married couples) there could have been no two hearts so open, no tastes so similar, no feelings so in unison, no countenances so beloved. Now they were as strangers; nay, worse than strangers, for they could never become acquainted. It was a perpetual estrangement.

When he talked, she heard the same voice, and discerned the same mind. There was a very general ignorance of all naval matters throughout the party; and he was very much questioned, and especially by the two Miss Musgroves, who seemed hardly to have any eyes but for him, as to the manner of living on board, daily regulations, food, hours, &c.; and their surprise at his accounts, at learning the degree of accommodation and arrangement which was practicable, drew from him some pleasant ridicule, which reminded Anne of the early days when she too had been ignorant, and she too had been accused of supposing sailors to be living on board without any thing to eat, or any cook to dress it if there were, or any servant to wait, or any knife and fork to use.

From thus listening and thinking, she was roused by a whisper of Mrs. Musgrove's, who, overcome by fond regrets, could not help saying,

'Ah! Miss Anne, if it had pleased Heaven to spare my poor son, I dare say he would have been just such another by this time.'

Anne suppressed a smile, and listened kindly, while Mrs. Musgrove relieved her heart a little more; and for a few minutes, therefore, could not keep pace with the conversation of the others.— When she could let her attention take its natural course again, she found the Miss Musgroves just fetching the navy-list,—(their own navy list, the first that had ever been at Uppercross); and sitting down together to pore over it, with the professed view of finding out the ships which Captain Wentworth had commanded.

'Your first was the Asp, I remember; we will look for the Asp.'

'You will not find her there.—Quite worn out and broken up. I was the last man who commanded her.—Hardly fit for service then.—Reported fit for home service for a year or two,—and so I was sent off to the West Indies.'

The girls looked all amazement.

'The admiralty,' he continued, 'entertain themselves now and then, with sending a few hundred men to sea, in a ship not fit to be employed. But they have a great many to provide for; and among the thousands that may just as well go to the bottom as not, it is impossible for them to distinguish the very set who may be least missed.'

'Phoo! phoo!' cried the admiral, 'what stuff these young fellows talk! Never was a better sloop than the Asp in her day.—For an old built sloop,* you would not see her equal. Lucky fellow to get her!— He knows there must have been twenty better men than himself applying for her at the same time. Lucky fellow to get any thing so soon, with no more interest than his.'*

'I felt my luck, admiral, I assure you;' replied Captain Wentworth, seriously.—'I was as well satisfied with my appointment as you can desire. It was a great object with me, at that time, to be at sea,—a very great object. I wanted to be doing something.'

'To be sure you did.—What should a young fellow, like you, do ashore, for half a year together?—If a man has not a wife, he soon wants to be afloat again.'

'But, Captain Wentworth,' cried Louisa, 'how vexed you must have been when you came to the Asp, to see what an old thing they had given you.'

'I knew pretty well what she was, before that day;' said he, smiling. 'I had no more discoveries to make, than you would have as to the fashion and strength of any old pelisse,* which you had seen lent about among half your acquaintance, ever since you could remember, and which at last, on some very wet day, is lent to yourself.—Ah! she was a dear old Asp to me. She did all that I wanted. I knew she would.—I knew that we should either go to the bottom together, or that she would be the making of me; and I never had two days of foul weather all the time I was at sea in her; and after taking privateers enough to be very entertaining, I had the good luck, in my passage home the next autumn, to fall in with the very French frigate I wanted.—I brought her into Plymouth; and here was another instance of luck. We had not been six hours in the Sound,* when a gale came on, which lasted four days and nights, and which would have done for poor old Asp, in half the time; our touch with the Great Nation* not having much improved our condition. Four-and-twenty hours later, and I should only have been a gallant Captain Wentworth, in a small paragraph at one corner of the newspapers; and being lost in only a sloop, nobody would have thought about me.'

Anne's shudderings were to herself, alone: but the Miss Musgroves could be as open as they were sincere, in their exclamations of pity and horror.

'And so then, I suppose,' said Mrs. Musgrove, in a low voice, as if thinking aloud, 'so then he went away to the Laconia, and there he met with our poor boy.—Charles, my dear,' (beckoning him to her), 'do ask Captain Wentworth where it was he first met with your poor brother. I always forget.'

'It was at Gibraltar,* mother, I know. Dick had been left ill at Gibraltar, with a recommendation from his former captain to Captain Wentworth.'

'Oh!—but, Charles, tell Captain Wentworth, he need not be afraid of mentioning poor Dick before me, for it would be rather a pleasure to hear him talked of, by such a good friend.'

Charles, being somewhat more mindful of the probabilities of the case, only nodded in reply, and walked away.

The girls were now hunting for the Laconia; and Captain Wentworth could not deny himself the pleasure of taking the precious volume into his own hands to save them the trouble, and once more read aloud the little statement of her name and rate, and present non-commissioned class,* observing over it, that she too had been one of the best friends man ever had.

'Ah! those were pleasant days when I had the Laconia! How fast I made money in her.—A friend of mine, and I, had such a lovely cruise together off the Western Islands.*—Poor Harville, sister! You know how much he wanted money—worse than myself. He had a wife.—Excellent fellow! I shall never forget his happiness. He felt it all, so much for her sake.—I wished for him again the next summer, when I had still the same luck in the Mediterranean.'

'And I am sure, Sir,' said Mrs. Musgrove, 'it was a lucky day for *us*, when you were put captain into that ship. *We* shall never forget what you did.'

Her feelings made her speak low; and Captain Wentworth, hearing only in part, and probably not having Dick Musgrove at all near his thoughts, looked rather in suspense, and as if waiting for more.

'My brother,' whispered one of the girls; 'mamma is thinking of poor Richard.'

'Poor dear fellow!' continued Mrs. Musgrove; 'he was grown so steady, and such an excellent correspondent, while he was under your care! Ah! it would have been a happy thing, if he had never left you. I assure you, Captain Wentworth, we are very sorry he ever left you.'

There was a momentary expression in Captain Wentworth's face at this speech, a certain glance of his bright eye, and curl of his handsome mouth, which convinced Anne, that instead of sharing in Mrs. Musgrove's kind wishes, as to her son, he had probably been at some pains to get rid of him; but it was too transient an indulgence of self-amusement to be detected by any who understood him less than herself; in another moment he was perfectly collected and serious; and almost instantly afterwards coming up to the sofa, on which she and Mrs. Musgrove were sitting, took a place by the latter, and entered into conversation with her, in a low voice, about her son, doing it with so much sympathy and natural grace, as shewed the kindest consideration for all that was real and unabsurd in the parent's feelings.

They were actually on the same sofa, for Mrs. Musgrove had most readily made room for him;—they were divided only by Mrs. Musgrove. It was no insignificant barrier indeed. Mrs. Musgrove was of a comfortable substantial size, infinitely more fitted by nature to express good cheer and good humour, than tenderness and sentiment; and while the agitations of Anne's slender form, and pensive face, may be considered as very completely screened, Captain Wentworth should be allowed some credit for the self-command with which he attended to her large fat sighings over the destiny of a son, whom alive nobody had cared for.

Personal size and mental sorrow have certainly no necessary proportions. A large bulky figure has as good a right to be in deep affliction, as the most graceful set of limbs in the world. But, fair or not fair, there are unbecoming conjunctions, which reason will patronize in vain,—which taste cannot tolerate,—which ridicule will seize.

The admiral, after taking two or three refreshing turns about the room with his hands behind him, being called to order by his wife, now came up to Captain Wentworth, and without any observation of what he might be interrupting, thinking only of his own thoughts, began with,

'If you had been a week later at Lisbon, last spring, Frederick, you would have been asked to give a passage to Lady Mary Grierson and her daughters.'

'Should I? I am glad I was not a week later then.'

The admiral abused him for his want of gallantry. He defended himself; though professing that he would never willingly admit any ladies* on board a ship of his, excepting for a ball, or a visit, which a few hours might comprehend.

'But, if I know myself,' said he, 'this is from no want of gallantry towards them. It is rather from feeling how impossible it is, with all one's efforts, and all one's sacrifices, to make the accommodations on board, such as women ought to have. There can be no want of gallantry, admiral, in rating the claims of women to every personal comfort *high*—and this is what I do. I hate to hear of women on board, or to see them on board; and no ship, under my command, shall ever convey a family of ladies any where, if I can help it.'

This brought his sister upon him.

'Oh Frederick!—But I cannot believe it of you.—All idle refinement!—Women may be as comfortable on board, as in the best house in England. I believe I have lived as much on board as most women, and I know nothing superior to the accommodations of a man of war.* I declare I have not a comfort or an indulgence about me, even at Kellynch-hall,' (with a kind bow to Anne) 'beyond what I always had in most of the ships I have lived in; and they have been five altogether.'

'Nothing to the purpose,' replied her brother. 'You were living with your husband; and were the only woman on board.'

'But you, yourself, brought Mrs. Harville, her sister, her cousin, and the three children, round from Portsmouth to Plymouth. Where was this superfine, extraordinary sort of gallantry of yours, then?'

'All merged in my friendship, Sophia. I would assist any brother officer's wife that I could, and I would bring any thing of Harville's from the world's end, if he wanted it. But do not imagine that I did not feel it an evil in itself.'

'Depend upon it they were all perfectly comfortable.'

'I might not like them the better for that, perhaps. Such a number of women and children have no *right* to be comfortable on board.'

'My dear Frederick, you are talking quite idly. Pray, what would become of us poor sailors' wives, who often want to be conveyed to one port or another, after our husbands, if every body had your feelings?'

'My feelings, you see, did not prevent my taking Mrs. Harville, and all her family, to Plymouth.'

'But I hate to hear you talking so, like a fine gentleman, and as if women were all fine ladies, instead of rational creatures. We none of us expect to be in smooth water all our days.'

'Ah! my dear,' said the admiral, 'when he has got a wife, he will sing a different tune. When he is married, if we have the good luck to live to another war, we shall see him do as you and I, and a great many others, have done. We shall have him very thankful to any body that will bring him his wife.'

'Ay, that we shall.'

'Now I have done,' cried Captain Wentworth—'When once married people begin to attack me with, "Oh! you will think very differently, when you are married." I can only say, "No, I shall not;" and then they say again, "Yes, you will," and there is an end of it.'

He got up and moved away.

'What a great traveller you must have been, ma'am!' said Mrs. Musgrove to Mrs. Croft.

'Pretty well, ma'am, in the fifteen years of my marriage; though many women have done more. I have crossed the Atlantic four times, and have been once to the East Indies, and back again; and only once, besides being in different places about home—Cork, and Lisbon,* and Gibraltar. But I never went beyond the Streights*—and never was in the West Indies. We do not call Bermuda or Bahama, you know, the West Indies.'

Mrs. Musgrove had not a word to say in dissent; she could not accuse herself of having ever called them any thing in the whole course of her life.

'And I do assure you, ma'am,' pursued Mrs. Croft, 'that nothing can exceed the accommodations of a man of war; I speak, you know, of the higher rates. When you come to a frigate, of course, you are more confined—though any reasonable woman may be perfectly happy in one of them; and I can safely say, that the happiest part of my life has been spent on board a ship. While we were together, you know, there was nothing to be feared. Thank God! I have always been blessed with excellent health, and no climate disagrees with me. A little disordered always the first twenty-four hours of going to sea, but never knew what sickness was afterwards. The only time that I ever really suffered in body or mind, the only time that I ever fancied myself unwell, or had any ideas of danger, was the winter that I passed by myself at Deal,* when the Admiral (*Captain* Croft then) was in the North Seas. I lived in perpetual fright at that time, and had all manner of imaginary complaints from not knowing what to do with myself, or when I should hear from him next; but as long as we could be together, nothing ever ailed me, and I never met with the smallest inconvenience.'

'Ay, to be sure.—Yes, indeed, oh yes, I am quite of your opinion, Mrs. Croft,' was Mrs. Musgrove's hearty answer. 'There is nothing so bad as a separation. I am quite of your opinion. *I* know what it is, for Mr. Musgrove always attends the assizes,* and I am so glad when they are over, and he is safe back again.'

The evening ended with dancing. On its being proposed, Anne offered her services, as usual, and though her eyes would sometimes fill with tears as she sat at the instrument, she was extremely glad to be employed, and desired nothing in return but to be unobserved.

It was a merry, joyous party, and no one seemed in higher spirits than Captain Wentworth. She felt that he had every thing to elevate him, which general attention and deference, and especially the attention of all the young women could do. The Miss Hayters, the females of the family of cousins already mentioned, were apparently admitted to the honour of being in love with him; and as for Henrietta and Louisa, they both seemed so entirely occupied by him, that nothing but the continued appearance of the most perfect good-will between themselves, could have made it credible that they were not decided rivals. If he were a little spoilt by such universal, such eager admiration, who could wonder?

These were some of the thoughts which occupied Anne, while her fingers were mechanically at work, proceeding for half an hour together, equally without error, and without consciousness. *Once* she felt that he was looking at herself—observing her altered features, perhaps, trying to trace in them the ruins of the face which had once charmed him; and *once* she knew that he must have spoken of her;— she was hardly aware of it, till she heard the answer; but then she was sure of his having asked his partner whether Miss Elliot never danced? The answer was, 'Oh! no, never; she has quite given up dancing. She had rather play. She is never tired of playing.' Once, too, he spoke to her. She had left the instrument on the dancing being over, and he had sat down to try to make out an air which he wished to give the Miss Musgroves an idea of. Unintentionally she returned to that part of the room; he saw her, and, instantly rising, said, with studied politeness,

'I beg your pardon, madam, this is your seat;' and though she immediately drew back with a decided negative, he was not to be induced to sit down again.

Anne did not wish for more of such looks and speeches. His cold politeness, his ceremonious grace, were worse than any thing.

CHAPTER IX

CAPTAIN WENTWORTH was come to Kellynch as to a home, to stay as long as he liked, being as thoroughly the object of the Admiral's fraternal kindness as of his wife's. He had intended, on first arriving, to proceed very soon into Shropshire, and visit the brother settled in that county, but the attractions of Uppercross induced him to put this off. There was so much of friendliness, and of flattery, and of every thing most bewitching in his reception there; the old were so hospitable, the young so agreeable, that he could not but resolve to remain where he was, and take all the charms and perfections of Edward's wife upon credit a little longer.

It was soon Uppercross with him almost every day. The Musgroves could hardly be more ready to invite than he to come, particularly in the morning, when he had no companion at home, for the Admiral and Mrs. Croft were generally out of doors together, interesting themselves in their new possessions, their grass, and their sheep, and dawdling about in a way not endurable to a third person, or driving out in a gig,* lately added to their establishment.

Hitherto there had been but one opinion of Captain Wentworth, among the Musgroves and their dependencies. It was unvarying, warm admiration every where. But this intimate footing was not more than established, when a certain Charles Hayter returned among them, to be a good deal disturbed by it, and to think Captain Wentworth very much in the way.

Charles Hayter was the eldest of all the cousins, and a very amiable, pleasing young man, between whom and Henrietta there had been a considerable appearance of attachment previous to Captain Wentworth's introduction. He was in orders, and having a curacy in the neighbourhood where residence was not required, lived at his father's house, only two miles from Uppercross. A short absence from home had left his fair one unguarded by his attentions at this critical period, and when he came back he had the pain of finding very altered manners, and of seeing Captain Wentworth.

Mrs. Musgrove and Mrs. Hayter were sisters. They had each had money, but their marriages had made a material difference in their degree of consequence. Mr. Hayter had some property of his own, but it was insignificant compared with Mr. Musgrove's; and while the Musgroves were in the first class of society in the country, the young Hayters would, from their parents' inferior, retired, and unpolished way of living, and their own defective education, have been hardly in any class at all, but for their connexion with Uppercross; this eldest son of course excepted, who had chosen to be a scholar and a gentleman, and who was very superior in cultivation and manners to all the rest.

The two families had always been on excellent terms, there being no pride on one side, and no envy on the other, and only such a consciousness of superiority in the Miss Musgroves, as made them pleased to improve their cousins.—Charles's attentions to Henrietta had been observed by her father and mother without any disapprobation. 'It would not be a great match for her; but if Henrietta liked him,—and Henrietta *did* seem to like him.'

Henrietta fully thought so herself, before Captain Wentworth came; but from that time Cousin Charles had been very much forgotten.

Which of the two sisters was preferred by Captain Wentworth was as yet quite doubtful, as far as Anne's observation reached. Henrietta was perhaps the prettiest, Louisa had the higher spirits; and she knew not *now*, whether the more gentle or the more lively character were most likely to attract him.

Mr. and Mrs. Musgrove, either from seeing little, or from an entire confidence in the discretion of both their daughters, and of all the young men who came near them, seemed to leave every thing to take its chance. There was not the smallest appearance of solicitude or remark about them, in the Mansion-house; but it was different at the Cottage: the young couple there were more disposed to speculate and wonder; and Captain Wentworth had not been above four or five times in the Miss Musgroves' company, and Charles Hayter had but just reappeared, when Anne had to listen to the opinions of her brother and sister, as to *which* was the one liked best. Charles gave it for Louisa, Mary for Henrietta, but quite agreeing that to have him marry either would be extremely delightful.

Charles 'had never seen a pleasanter man in his life; and from what he had once heard Captain Wentworth himself say, was very sure that he had not made less than twenty thousand pounds by the war. Here was a fortune at once; besides which, there would be the chance of what might be done in any future war; and he was sure

Captain Wentworth was as likely a man to distinguish himself as any officer in the navy. Oh! it would be a capital match for either of his sisters.'

'Upon my word it would,' replied Mary. 'Dear me! If he should rise to any very great honours! If he should ever be made a Baronet! "Lady Wentworth" sounds very well. That would be a noble thing, indeed, for Henrietta! She would take place of me then, and Henrietta would not dislike that. Sir Frederick and Lady Wentworth! It would be but a new creation, however, and I never think much of your new creations.'

It suited Mary best to think Henrietta the one preferred, on the very account of Charles Hayter, whose pretensions she wished to see put an end to. She looked down very decidedly upon the Hayters, and thought it would be quite a misfortune to have the existing connection between the families renewed—very sad for herself and her children.

'You know,' said she, 'I cannot think him at all a fit match for Henrietta; and considering the alliances which the Musgroves have made, she has no right to throw herself away. I do not think any young woman has a right to make a choice that may be disagreeable and inconvenient to the *principal* part of her family, and be giving bad connections to those who have not been used to them. And, pray, who is Charles Hayter? Nothing but a country curate. A most improper match for Miss Musgrove, of Uppercross.'

Her husband, however, would not agree with her here; for besides having a regard for his cousin, Charles Hayter was an eldest son, and he saw things as an eldest son himself.

'Now you are talking nonsense, Mary,' was therefore his answer. 'It would not be a *great* match for Henrietta, but Charles has a very fair chance, through the Spicers, of getting something from the Bishop in the course of a year or two; and you will please to remember, that he is the eldest son; whenever my uncle dies, he steps into very pretty property. The estate at Winthrop is not less than two hundred and fifty acres, besides the farm near Taunton, which is some of the best land in the country. I grant you, that any of them but Charles would be a very shocking match for Henrietta, and indeed it could not be; he is the only one that could be possible; but he is a very good-natured, good sort of a fellow; and whenever Winthrop comes into his hands, he will make a different sort of place of it, and live in a very different sort of way; and with that property, he will never be a contemptible man. Good, freehold property.* No, no; Henrietta might do worse than marry Charles Hayter; and if she has him, and Louisa can get Captain Wentworth, I shall be very well satisfied.'

'Charles may say what he pleases,' cried Mary to Anne, as soon as he was out of the room, 'but it would be shocking to have Henrietta marry Charles Hayter; a very bad thing for *her*, and still worse for *me*; and therefore it is very much to be wished that Captain Wentworth may soon put him quite out of her head, and I have very little doubt that he has. She took hardly any notice of Charles Hayter yesterday. I wish you had been there to see her behaviour. And as to Captain Wentworth's liking Louisa as well as Henrietta, it is nonsense to say so; for he certainly *does* like Henrietta a great deal the best. But Charles is so positive! I wish you had been with us yesterday, for then you might have decided between us; and I am sure you would have thought as I did, unless you had been determined to give it against me.'

A dinner at Mr. Musgrove's had been the occasion, when all these things should have been seen by Anne; but she had staid at home, under the mixed plea of a head-ache of her own, and some return of indisposition in little Charles. She had thought only of avoiding Captain Wentworth; but an escape from being appealed to as umpire, was now added to the advantages of a quiet evening.

As to Captain Wentworth's views, she deemed it of more consequence that he should know his own mind, early enough not to be endangering the happiness of either sister, or impeaching his own honour, than that he should prefer Henrietta to Louisa, or Louisa to Henrietta. Either of them would, in all probability, make him an affectionate, good-humoured wife. With regard to Charles Hayter, she had delicacy which must be pained by any lightness of conduct in a well-meaning young woman, and a heart to sympathize in any of the sufferings it occasioned; but if Henrietta found herself mistaken in the nature of her feelings, the alteration could not be understood too soon.

Charles Hayter had met with much to disquiet and mortify him in his cousin's behaviour. She had too old a regard for him to be so wholly estranged, as might in two meetings extinguish every past hope, and leave him nothing to do but to keep away from

Uppercross; but there was such a change as became very alarming, when such a man as Captain Wentworth was to be regarded as the probable cause. He had been absent only two Sundays; and when they parted, had left her interested even to the height of his wishes, in his prospect of soon quitting his present curacy, and obtaining that of Uppercross instead. It had then seemed the object nearest her heart, that Dr. Shirley, the rector, who for more than forty years had been zealously discharging all the duties of his office, but was now growing too infirm for many of them, should be quite fixed on engaging a curate; should make his curacy quite as good as he could afford, and should give Charles Hayter the promise of it. The advantage of his having to come only to Uppercross, instead of going six miles another way; of his having, in every respect, a better curacy; of his belonging to their dear Dr. Shirley, and of dear, good Dr. Shirley's being relieved from the duty which he could no longer get through without most injurious fatigue, had been a great deal, even to Louisa, but had been almost every thing to Henrietta. When he came back, alas! the zeal of the business was gone by. Louisa could not listen at all to his account of a conversation which he had just held with Dr. Shirley: she was at window, looking out for Captain Wentworth; and even Henrietta had at best only a divided attention to give, and seemed to have forgotten all the former doubt and solicitude of the negociation.

'Well, I am very glad indeed, but I always thought you would have it; I always thought you sure. It did not appear to me that—In short, you know, Dr. Shirley *must* have a curate, and you had secured his promise. Is he coming, Louisa?'

One morning, very soon after the dinner at the Musgroves, at which Anne had not been present, Captain Wentworth walked into the drawing-room at the Cottage, where were only herself and the little invalid Charles, who was lying on the sofa.

The surprise of finding himself almost alone with Anne Elliot, deprived his manners of their usual composure: he started, and could only say, 'I thought the Miss Musgroves had been here—Mrs. Musgrove told me I should find them here,' before he walked to the window to recollect himself, and feel how he ought to behave.

'They are up stairs with my sister—they will be down in a few moments, I dare say,'—had been Anne's reply, in all the confusion that was natural; and if the child had not called her to come and do something for him, she would have been out of the room the next moment, and released Captain Wentworth as well as herself.

He continued at the window; and after calmly and politely saying, 'I hope the little boy is better,' was silent.

She was obliged to kneel down by the sofa, and remain there to satisfy her patient; and thus they continued a few minutes, when, to her very great satisfaction, she heard some other person crossing the little vestibule. She hoped, on turning her head, to see the master of the house; but it proved to be one much less calculated for making matters easy—Charles Hayter, probably not at all better pleased by the sight of Captain Wentworth, than Captain Wentworth had been by the sight of Anne.

She only attempted to say, 'How do you do? Will not you sit down? The others will be here presently.'

Captain Wentworth, however, came from his window, apparently not ill-disposed for conversation; but Charles Hayter soon put an end to his attempts, by seating himself near the table, and taking up the newspaper; and Captain Wentworth returned to his window.

Another minute brought another addition. The younger boy, a remarkable stout, forward child, of two years old, having got the door opened for him by some one without, made his determined appearance among them, and went straight to the sofa to see what was going on, and put in his claim to any thing good that might be giving away.

There being nothing to be eat, he could only have some play; and as his aunt would not let him teaze his sick brother, he began to fasten himself upon her, as she knelt, in such a way that, busy as she was about Charles, she could not shake him off. She spoke to him— ordered, intreated, and insisted in vain. Once she did contrive to push him away, but the boy had the greater pleasure in getting upon her back again directly.

'Walter,' said she, 'get down this moment. You are extremely troublesome. I am very angry with you.'

'Walter,' cried Charles Hayter, 'why do you not do as you are bid? Do not you hear your aunt speak? Come to me, Walter, come to cousin Charles.'

But not a bit did Walter stir.

In another moment, however, she found herself in the state of being released from him; some one was taking him from her, though he had bent down her head so much, that his little sturdy hands were unfastened from around her neck, and he was resolutely borne away, before she knew that Captain Wentworth had done it.

Her sensations on the discovery made her perfectly speechless. She could not even thank him. She could only hang over little Charles, with most disordered feelings. His kindness in stepping forward to her relief—the manner—the silence in which it had passed—the little particulars of the circumstance—with the conviction soon forced on her by the noise he was studiously making with the child, that he meant to avoid hearing her thanks, and rather sought to testify that her conversation was the last of his wants, produced such a confusion of varying, but very painful agitation, as she could not recover from, till enabled by the entrance of Mary and the Miss Musgroves to make over her little patient to their cares, and leave the room. She could not stay. It might have been an opportunity of watching the loves and jealousies of the four; they were now all together, but she could stay for none of it. It was evident that Charles Hayter was not well inclined towards Captain Wentworth. She had a strong impression of his having said, in a vext tone of voice, after Captain Wentworth's interference, 'You ought to have minded *me*, Walter; I told you not to teaze your aunt;' and could comprehend his regretting that Captain Wentworth should do what he ought to have done himself. But neither Charles Hayter's feelings, nor any body's feelings, could interest her, till she had a little better arranged her own. She was ashamed of herself, quite ashamed of being so nervous, so overcome by such a trifle; but so it was; and it required a long application of solitude and reflection to recover her.

CHAPTER X

OTHER opportunities of making her observations could not fail to occur. Anne had soon been in company with all the four together often enough to have an opinion, though too wise to acknowledge as much at home, where she knew it would have satisfied neither husband nor wife; for while she considered Louisa to be rather the favourite, she could not but think, as far as she might dare to judge from memory and experience, that Captain Wentworth was not in love with either. They were more in love with him; yet there it was not love. It was a little fever of admiration; but it might, probably must, end in love with some. Charles Hayter seemed aware of being slighted, and yet Henrietta had sometimes the air of being divided between them. Anne longed for the power of representing to them all what they were about, and of pointing out some of the evils they were exposing themselves to. She did not attribute guile to any. It was the highest satisfaction to her, to believe Captain Wentworth not in the least aware of the pain he was occasioning. There was no triumph, no pitiful triumph in his manner. He had, probably, never heard, and never thought of any claims of Charles Hayter. He was only wrong in accepting the attentions—(for accepting must be the word) of two young women at once.

After a short struggle, however, Charles Hayter seemed to quit the field. Three days had passed without his coming once to Uppercross; a most decided change. He had even refused one regular invitation to dinner; and having been found on the occasion by Mr. Musgrove with some large books before him, Mr. and Mrs. Musgrove were sure all could not be right, and talked, with grave faces, of his studying himself to death. It was Mary's hope and belief, that he had received a positive dismissal from Henrietta, and her husband lived under the constant dependance of seeing him to-morrow. Anne could only feel that Charles Hayter was wise.

One morning, about this time, Charles Musgrove and Captain Wentworth being gone a shooting together, as the sisters in the cottage were sitting quietly at work, they were visited at the window by the sisters from the mansion-house.

It was a very fine November day, and the Miss Musgroves came through the little grounds, and stopped for no other purpose than to say, that they were going to take a *long* walk, and, therefore, concluded Mary could not like to go with them; and when Mary immediately replied, with some jealousy, at not being supposed a good walker, 'Oh, yes, I should like to join you very much, I am very fond of a long walk,' Anne felt persuaded, by the looks of the two girls, that it was precisely what they did not wish, and admired again the sort of necessity which the family-habits seemed to produce, of every thing being to be communicated, and every thing being to be done together, however undesired and inconvenient. She tried to dissuade Mary from going, but in vain; and that being the case, thought it best to accept the Miss Musgroves' much more cordial invitation to herself to go likewise, as she might be useful in turning back with her sister, and lessening the interference in any plan of their own.

'I cannot imagine why they should suppose I should not like a long walk!' said Mary, as she went up stairs. 'Every body is always supposing that I am not a good walker! And yet they would not have been pleased, if we had refused to join them. When people come in this manner on purpose to ask us, how can one say no?'

Just as they were setting off, the gentlemen returned. They had taken out a young dog, who had spoilt their sport, and sent them back early. Their time and strength, and spirits, were, therefore, exactly ready for this walk, and they entered into it with pleasure. Could Anne have foreseen such a junction, she would have staid at home; but, from some feelings of interest and curiosity, she fancied now that it was too late to retract, and the whole six set forward together in the direction chosen by the Miss Musgroves, who evidently considered the walk as under their guidance.

Anne's object was, not to be in the way of any body, and where the narrow paths across the fields made many separations necessary, to keep with her brother and sister. Her *pleasure* in the walk must arise from the exercise and the day, from the view of the last smiles of the year upon the tawny leaves and withered hedges, and from repeating to herself some few of the thousand poetical descriptions extant of autumn, that season of peculiar and inexhaustible influence on the mind of taste and tenderness, that season which has drawn from every poet, worthy of being read, some attempt at description, or some lines of feeling. She occupied her mind as much as possible in such like musings and quotations; but it was not possible, that when within reach of Captain Wentworth's conversation with either of the Miss Musgroves, she should not try to hear it; yet she caught little very remarkable. It was mere lively chat,—such as any young persons, on an intimate footing, might fall into. He was more engaged with Louisa than with Henrietta. Louisa certainly put more forward for his notice than her sister. This distinction appeared to increase, and there was one speech of Louisa's which struck her. After one of the many praises of the day, which were continually bursting forth, Captain Wentworth added,

'What glorious weather for the Admiral and my sister! They meant to take a long drive this morning; perhaps we may hail them from some of these hills. They talked of coming into this side of the country. I wonder whereabouts they will upset to-day. Oh! it does happen very often, I assure you—but my sister makes nothing of it—she would as lieve be tossed out as not.'

'Ah! You make the most of it, I know,' cried Louisa, 'but if it were really so, I should do just the same in her place. If I loved a man, as she loves the Admiral, I would be always with him, nothing should ever separate us, and I would rather be overturned by him, than driven safely by anybody else.'

It was spoken with enthusiasm.

'Had you?' cried he, catching the same tone; 'I honour you!' And there was silence between them for a little while.

Anne could not immediately fall into a quotation again. The sweet scenes of autumn were for a while put by—unless some tender sonnet, fraught with the apt analogy of the declining year, with declining happiness, and the images of youth and hope, and spring, all gone together, blessed her memory. She roused herself to say, as they struck by order into another path, 'Is not this one of the ways to Winthrop?' But nobody heard, or, at least, nobody answered her.

Winthrop, however, or its environs—for young men are, sometimes, to be met with, strolling about near home, was their destination; and after another half mile of gradual ascent through large enclosures, where the ploughs at work, and the fresh-made path spoke the farmer, counteracting the sweets of poetical despondence, and meaning to have spring again, they gained the summit of the most considerable hill, which parted Uppercross and Winthrop, and soon commanded a full view of the latter, at the foot of the hill on the other side.

Winthrop, without beauty and without dignity, was stretched before them; an indifferent house, standing low, and hemmed in by the barns and buildings of a farm-yard.

Mary exclaimed, 'Bless me! here is Winthrop—I declare I had no idea!——well, now I think we had better turn back; I am excessively tired.'

Henrietta, conscious* and ashamed, and seeing no cousin Charles walking along any path, or leaning against any gate, was ready to do as Mary wished; but 'No,' said Charles Musgrove, and 'No, no,' cried Louisa more eagerly, and taking her sister aside, seemed to be arguing the matter warmly.

Charles, in the meanwhile, was very decidedly declaring his resolution of calling on his aunt, now that he was so near; and very evidently, though more fearfully, trying to induce his wife to go too. But this was one of the points on which the lady shewed her strength, and when he recommended the advantage of resting herself a quarter of an hour at Winthrop, as she felt so tired, she resolutely answered, 'Oh! no, indeed!—walking up that hill again would do her more harm than any sitting down could do her good;' —and, in short, her look and manner declared, that go she would not.

After a little succession of these sort of debates and consultations, it was settled between Charles and his two sisters, that he, and Henrietta, should just run down for a few minutes, to see their aunt and cousins, while the rest of the party waited for them at the top of the hill. Louisa seemed the principal arranger of the plan; and, as she went a little way with them, down the hill, still talking to Henrietta, Mary took the opportunity of looking scornfully around her, and saying to Captain Wentworth,

'It is very unpleasant, having such connexions! But I assure you, I have never been in the house above twice in my life.'

She received no other answer, than an artificial, assenting smile, followed by a contemptuous glance, as he turned away, which Anne perfectly knew the meaning of.

The brow of the hill, where they remained, was a cheerful spot; Louisa returned, and Mary finding a comfortable seat for herself, on the step of a stile,* was very well satisfied so long as the others all stood about her; but when Louisa drew Captain Wentworth away, to try for a gleaning of nuts in an adjoining hedge-row, and they were gone by degrees quite out of sight and sound, Mary was happy no longer; she quarrelled with her own seat,—was sure Louisa had got a much better somewhere,—and nothing could prevent her from going to look for a better also. She turned through the same gate,— but could not see them.—Anne found a nice seat for her, on a dry sunny bank, under the hedge-row, in which she had no doubt of their still being—in some spot or other. Mary sat down for a moment, but it would not do; she was sure Louisa had found a better seat somewhere else, and she would go on, till she overtook her.

Anne, really tired herself, was glad to sit down; and she very soon heard Captain Wentworth and Louisa in the hedge-row, behind her, as if making their way back, along the rough, wild sort of channel, down the centre.* They were speaking as they drew near. Louisa's voice was the first distinguished. She seemed to be in the middle of some eager speech. What Anne first heard was,

'And so, I made her go. I could not bear that she should be frightened from the visit by such nonsense. What!—would I be turned back from doing a thing that I had determined to do, and that I knew to be right, by the airs and interference of such a person?— or, of any person I may say. No,—I have no idea of being so easily persuaded. When I have made up my mind, I have made it. And Henrietta seemed entirely to have made up hers to call at Winthrop to-day—and yet, she was as near giving it up, out of nonsensical complaisance!'

'She would have turned back then, but for you?'

'She would indeed. I am almost ashamed to say it.'

'Happy for her, to have such a mind as yours at hand—After the hints you gave just now, which did but confirm my own observations, the last time I was in company with him, I need not affect to have no comprehension of what is going on. I see that more than a mere dutiful morning-visit to your aunt was in question;—and woe betide him, and her too, when it comes to things of consequence, when they are placed in circumstances, requiring fortitude and strength of mind, if she have not resolution enough to resist idle interference in such a trifle as this. Your sister is an amiable creature; but *yours* is the character of decision and firmness, I see. If you value her conduct or happiness, infuse as much of your own spirit into her, as you can. But this, no doubt, you have been always doing. It is the worst evil of too yielding and indecisive a character, that no influence over it can be depended on.—You are never sure of a good impression being durable. Every body may sway it; let those who would be happy be firm.—Here is a nut,' said he, catching one down from an upper bough. 'To exemplify,—a beautiful glossy nut, which, blessed with original strength, has outlived all the storms of autumn. Not a puncture, not a weak spot any where.—This nut,' he continued, with playful solemnity,—'while so many of its brethren have fallen and been trodden under foot, is still in possession of all the happiness that a hazel-nut can be supposed capable of.' Then, returning to his former earnest tone: 'My first wish for all, whom I am interested in, is that they should be firm. If Louisa Musgrove would be beautiful and happy in her November of life, she will cherish all her present powers of mind.'

He had done,—and was unanswered. It would have surprised Anne, if Louisa could have readily answered such a speech—words of such interest, spoken with such serious warmth!—she could imagine what Louisa was feeling. For herself—she feared to move, lest she should be seen. While she remained, a bush of low rambling holly protected her, and they were moving on. Before they were beyond her hearing, however, Louisa spoke again.

'Mary is good-natured enough in many respects,' said she; 'but she does sometimes provoke me excessively, by her nonsense and her pride; the Elliot pride. She has a great deal too much of the Elliot pride.—We do so wish that Charles had married Anne instead.—I suppose you know he wanted to marry Anne?'

After a moment's pause, Captain Wentworth said,

'Do you mean that she refused him?'

'Oh! yes, certainly.'

'When did that happen?'

'I do not exactly know, for Henrietta and I were at school at the time; but I believe about a year before he married Mary. I wish she had accepted him. We should all have liked her a great deal better; and papa and mamma always think it was her great friend Lady Russell's doing, that she did not.—They think Charles might not be learned and bookish enough to please Lady Russell, and that therefore, she persuaded Anne to refuse him.'

The sounds were retreating, and Anne distinguished no more. Her own emotions still kept her fixed. She had much to recover from, before she could move. The listener's proverbial fate* was not absolutely hers; she had heard no evil of herself,—but she had heard a great deal of very painful import. She saw how her own character was considered by Captain Wentworth; and there had been just that degree of feeling and curiosity about her in his manner, which must give her extreme agitation.

As soon as she could, she went after Mary, and having found, and walked back with her to their former station, by the stile, felt some comfort in their whole party being immediately afterwards collected, and once more in motion together. Her spirits wanted the solitude and silence which only numbers could give.

Charles and Henrietta returned, bringing, as may be conjectured,

Charles Hayter with them. The minutiæ of the business Anne could not attempt to understand; even Captain Wentworth did not seem admitted to perfect confidence here; but that there had been a withdrawing on the gentleman's side, and a relenting on the lady's, and that they were now very glad to be together again, did not admit a doubt. Henrietta looked a little ashamed, but very well pleased;— Charles Hayter exceedingly happy, and they were devoted to each other almost from the first instant of their all setting forward for Uppercross.

Every thing now marked out Louisa for Captain Wentworth; nothing could be plainer; and where many divisions were necessary, or even where they were not, they walked side by side, nearly as much as the other two. In a long strip of meadow-land, where there was ample space for all, they were thus divided—forming three distinct parties; and to that party of the three which boasted least animation, and least complaisance, Anne necessarily belonged. She joined Charles and Mary, and was tired enough to be very glad of Charles's other arm;—but Charles, though in very good humour with her, was out of temper with his wife. Mary had shewn herself disobliging to him, and was now to reap the consequence, which consequence was his dropping her arm almost every moment, to cut off the heads of some nettles in the hedge with his switch; and when Mary began to complain of it, and lament her being ill-used, according to custom, in being on the hedge side, while Anne was never incommoded on the other, he dropped the arms of both to hunt after a weasel which he had a momentary glance of; and they could hardly get him along at all.

This long meadow bordered a lane, which their footpath, at the end of it, was to cross; and when the party had all reached the gate of exit, the carriage advancing in the same direction, which had been some time heard, was just coming up, and proved to be Admiral Croft's gig.—He and his wife had taken their intended drive, and were returning home. Upon hearing how long a walk the young people had engaged in, they kindly offered a seat to any lady who might be particularly tired; it would save her full a mile, and they were going through Uppercross. The invitation was general, and generally declined. The Miss Musgroves were not at all tired, and Mary was either offended, by not being asked before any of the others, or what Louisa called the Elliot pride could not endure to make a third in a one horse chaise.

The walking-party had crossed the lane, and were surmounting an opposite stile; and the admiral was putting his horse into motion again, when Captain Wentworth cleared the hedge in a moment to say something to his sister.—The something might be guessed by its effects.

'Miss Elliot, I am sure *you* are tired,' cried Mrs. Croft. 'Do let us have the pleasure of taking you home. Here is excellent room for three, I assure you. If we were all like you, I believe we might sit four.—You must, indeed, you must.'

Anne was still in the lane; and though instinctively beginning to decline, she was not allowed to proceed. The admiral's kind urgency came in support of his wife's; they would not be refused; they compressed themselves into the smallest possible space to leave her a corner, and Captain Wentworth, without saying a word, turned to her, and quietly obliged her to be assisted into the carriage.

Yes,—he had done it. She was in the carriage, and felt that he had placed her there, that his will and his hands had done it, that she owed it to his perception of her fatigue, and his resolution to give her rest. She was very much affected by the view of his disposition towards her which all these things made apparent. This little circumstance seemed the completion of all that had gone before. She understood him. He could not forgive her,—but he could not be unfeeling. Though condemning her for the past, and considering it with high and unjust resentment, though perfectly careless of her, and though becoming attached to another, still he could not see her suffer, without the desire of giving her relief. It was a remainder of former sentiment; it was an impulse of pure, though unacknowledged friendship; it was a proof of his own warm and amiable heart, which she could not contemplate without emotions so compounded of pleasure and pain, that she knew not which prevailed.

Her answers to the kindness and the remarks of her companions were at first unconsciously given. They had travelled half their way along the rough lane, before she was quite awake to what they said. She then found them talking of 'Frederick.'

'He certainly means to have one or other of those two girls, Sophy,' said the admiral;—'but there is no saying which. He has been running after them, too, long enough, one would think, to make up his mind. Ay, this comes of the peace. If it were war, now, he would have settled it long ago.—We sailors, Miss Elliot, cannot afford to make long courtships in time of war. How many days was it, my dear, between the first time of my seeing you, and our sitting down together in our lodgings at North Yarmouth?'

'We had better not talk about it, my dear,' replied Mrs. Croft, pleasantly; 'for if Miss Elliot were to hear how soon we came to an understanding, she would never be persuaded that we could be happy together. I had known you by character, however, long before.'

'Well, and I had heard of you as a very pretty girl; and what were we to wait for besides?—I do not like having such things so long in hand. I wish Frederick would spread a little more canvas,* and bring us home one of these young ladies to Kellynch. Then, there would always be company for us.—And very nice young ladies they both are; I hardly know one from the other.'

'Very good humoured, unaffected girls, indeed,' said Mrs. Croft, in a tone of calmer praise, such as made Anne suspect that her keener powers might not consider either of them as quite worthy of her brother; 'and a very respectable family. One could not be connected with better people.—My dear admiral, that post!—we shall certainly take that post.'

But by coolly giving the reins a better direction herself, they happily passed the danger; and by once afterwards judiciously putting out her hand, they neither fell into a rut, nor ran foul of a dung-cart; and Anne, with some amusement at their style of driving, which she imagined no bad representation of the general guidance of their affairs, found herself safely deposited by them at the cottage.

CHAPTER XI

THE time now approached for Lady Russell's return; the day was even fixed, and Anne, being engaged to join her as soon as she was resettled, was looking forward to an early removal to Kellynch, and beginning to think how her own comfort was likely to be affected by it.

It would place her in the same village with Captain Wentworth, within half a mile of him; they would have to frequent the same church, and there must be intercourse between the two families. This was against her; but, on the other hand, he spent so much of his time at Uppercross, that in removing thence she might be considered rather as leaving him behind, than as going towards him;

and, upon the whole, she believed she must, on this interesting question, be the gainer, almost as certainly as in her change of domestic society, in leaving poor Mary for Lady Russell.

She wished it might be possible for her to avoid ever seeing Captain Wentworth at the hall;—those rooms had witnessed former meetings which would be brought too painfully before her; but she was yet more anxious for the possibility of Lady Russell and Captain Wentworth never meeting any where. They did not like each other, and no renewal of acquaintance now could do any good; and were Lady Russell to see them together, she might think that he had too much self-possession, and she too little.

These points formed her chief solicitude in anticipating her removal from Uppercross, where she felt she had been stationed quite long enough. Her usefulness to little Charles would always give some sweetness to the memory of her two months visit there, but he was gaining strength apace, and she had nothing else to stay for.

The conclusion of her visit, however, was diversified in a way which she had not at all imagined. Captain Wentworth, after being unseen and unheard of at Uppercross for two whole days, appeared again among them to justify himself by a relation of what had kept him away.

A letter from his friend, Captain Harville, having found him out at last, had brought intelligence of Captain Harville's being settled with his family at Lyme* for the winter; of their being, therefore, quite unknowingly, within twenty miles of each other. Captain Harville had never been in good health since a severe wound which he received two years before, and Captain Wentworth's anxiety to see him had determined him to go immediately to Lyme. He had been there for four-and-twenty hours. His acquittal was complete, his friendship warmly honoured, a lively interest excited for his friend, and his description of the fine country about Lyme so feelingly attended to by the party, that an earnest desire to see Lyme themselves, and a project for going thither was the consequence.

The young people were all wild to see Lyme. Captain Wentworth talked of going there again himself; it was only seventeen miles from Uppercross; though November, the weather was by no means bad; and, in short, Louisa, who was the most eager of the eager, having formed the resolution to go, and besides the pleasure of doing as she liked, being now armed with the idea of merit in maintaining her own way, bore down all the wishes of her father and mother for putting it off till summer; and to Lyme they were to go—Charles, Mary, Anne, Henrietta, Louisa, and Captain Wentworth.

The first heedless scheme had been to go in the morning and return at night, but to this Mr. Musgrove, for the sake of his horses, would not consent; and when it came to be rationally considered, a day in the middle of November would not leave much time for seeing a new place, after deducting seven hours, as the nature of the country required, for going and returning. They were consequently to stay the night there, and not to be expected back till the next day's dinner. This was felt to be a considerable amendment; and though they all met at the Great House at rather an early breakfast hour, and set off very punctually, it was so much past noon before the two carriages, Mr. Musgrove's coach containing the four ladies, and Charles's curricle,* in which he drove Captain Wentworth, were descending the long hill into Lyme, and entering upon the still steeper street of the town itself, that it was very evident they would not have more than time for looking about them, before the light and warmth of the day were gone.

After securing accommodations, and ordering a dinner at one of the inns, the next thing to be done was unquestionably to walk directly down to the sea. They were come too late in the year for any amusement or variety which Lyme, as a public place, might offer; the rooms were shut up, the lodgers almost all gone, scarcely any family but of the residents left—and, as there is nothing to admire in the buildings themselves, the remarkable situation of the town, the principal street almost hurrying into the water, the walk to the Cobb, skirting round the pleasant little bay, which in the season is animated with bathing machines* and company, the Cobb itself, its old wonders and new improvements,* with the very beautiful line of cliffs stretching out to the east of the town, are what the stranger's eye will seek; and a very strange stranger it must be, who does not see charms in the immediate environs of Lyme, to make him wish to know it better. The scenes in its neighbourhood, Charmouth, with its high grounds and extensive sweeps of country, and still more its sweet retired bay, backed by dark cliffs, where fragments of low rock among the sands make it the happiest spot for watching the flow of the tide, for sitting in unwearied contemplation;—the woody varieties of the cheerful village of Up Lyme,* and, above all, Pinny, with its green chasms between romantic rocks,* where the scattered forest trees and orchards of luxuriant growth declare that many a generation must have passed away since the first partial falling of the cliff prepared the ground for such a state, where a scene so wonderful and so lovely is exhibited, as may more than equal any of the resembling scenes of the far-famed Isle of Wight:* these places must be visited, and visited again, to make the worth of Lyme understood.

The party from Uppercross passing down by the now deserted and melancholy looking rooms, and still descending, soon found themselves on the sea shore, and lingering only, as all must linger and gaze on a first return to the sea, who ever deserve to look on it at all, proceeded towards the Cobb, equally their object in itself and on Captain Wentworth's account; for in a small house, near the foot of an old pier of unknown date, were the Harvilles settled. Captain Wentworth turned in to call on his friend; the others walked on, and he was to join them on the Cobb.

They were by no means tired of wondering and admiring; and not even Louisa seemed to feel that they had parted with Captain Wentworth long, when they saw him coming after them, with three companions, all well known already by description to be Captain and Mrs. Harville, and a Captain Benwick, who was staying with them.

Captain Benwick had some time ago been first lieutenant of the Laconia; and the account which Captain Wentworth had given of him, on his return from Lyme before; his warm praise of him as an excellent young man and an officer, whom he had always valued highly, which must have stamped him well in the esteem of every listener, had been followed by a little history of his private life, which rendered him perfectly interesting in the eyes of all the ladies. He had been engaged to Captain Harville's sister, and was now mourning her loss. They had been a year or two waiting for fortune and promotion. Fortune came, his prize-money as lieutenant being great,—promotion, too, came at *last*; but Fanny Harville did not live to know it. She had died the preceding summer, while he was at sea. Captain Wentworth believed it impossible for man to be more attached to woman than poor Benwick had been to Fanny Harville, or to be more deeply afflicted under the dreadful change. He considered his disposition as of the sort which must suffer heavily, uniting very strong feelings with quiet, serious, and retiring manners, and a decided taste for reading, and sedentary pursuits. To finish the interest of the story, the friendship between him and the Harvilles seemed, if possible, augmented by the event which closed all their views of alliance, and Captain Benwick was now living with them entirely. Captain Harville had taken his present house for half a year, his taste, and his health, and his fortune all directing him to a residence unexpensive, and by the sea; and the grandeur of the country, and the retirement of Lyme in the winter, appeared exactly adapted to Captain Benwick's state of mind. The sympathy and good-will excited towards Captain Benwick was very great.

'And yet,' said Anne to herself, as they now moved forward to meet the party, 'he has not, perhaps, a more sorrowing heart than I have. I cannot believe his prospects so blighted for ever. He is younger than I am; younger in feeling, if not in fact; younger as a man. He will rally again, and be happy with another.'

They all met, and were introduced. Captain Harville was a tall, dark man, with a sensible, benevolent countenance; a little lame; and from strong features, and want of health, looking much older than Captain Wentworth. Captain Benwick looked and was the youngest of the three, and, compared with either of them, a little man. He had a pleasing face and a melancholy air, just as he ought to have, and drew back from conversation.

Captain Harville, though not equalling Captain Wentworth in manners, was a perfect gentleman, unaffected, warm, and obliging. Mrs. Harville, a degree less polished than her husband, seemed however to have the same good feelings; and nothing could be more pleasant than their desire of considering the whole party as friends of their own, because the friends of Captain Wentworth, or more kindly hospitable than their entreaties for their all promising to dine with them. The dinner, already ordered at the inn, was at last, though unwillingly, accepted as an excuse; but they seemed almost hurt that Captain Wentworth should have brought any such party to Lyme, without considering it as a thing of course that they should dine with them.

There was so much attachment to Captain Wentworth in all this, and such a bewitching charm in a degree of hospitality so uncommon, so unlike the usual style of give-and-take invitations, and dinners of formality and display, that Anne felt her spirits not likely to be benefited by an increasing acquaintance among his brother-officers. 'These would have been all my friends,' was her thought; and she had to struggle against a great tendency to lowness.

On quitting the Cobb, they all went indoors with their new friends, and found rooms so small as none but those who invite from the heart could think capable of accommodating so many. Anne had a moment's astonishment on the subject herself; but it was soon lost in the pleasanter feelings which sprang from the sight of all the ingenious contrivances and nice arrangements of Captain Harville, to turn the actual space to the best possible account, to supply the deficiencies of lodging-house furniture, and defend the windows and doors against the winter storms to be expected. The varieties in the fitting-up of the rooms, where the common necessaries provided by the owner, in the common indifferent plight, were contrasted with some few articles of a rare species of wood, excellently worked up, and with something curious and valuable from all the distant countries Captain Harville had visited, were more than amusing to Anne: connected as it all was with his profession, the fruit of its labours, the effect of its influence on his habits, the picture of repose and domestic happiness it presented, made it to her a something more, or less, than gratification.

Captain Harville was no reader; but he had contrived excellent accommodations, and fashioned very pretty shelves, for a tolerable collection of well-bound volumes, the property of Captain Benwick. His lameness prevented him from taking much exercise; but a mind of usefulness and ingenuity seemed to furnish him with constant employment within.* He drew, he varnished, he carpentered, he glued; he made toys for the children, he fashioned new netting-needles and pins with improvements,* and if every thing else was done, sat down to his large fishing-net at one corner of the room.

Anne thought she left great happiness behind her when they quitted the house; and Louisa, by whom she found herself walking, burst forth into raptures of admiration and delight on the character of the navy—their friendliness, their brotherliness, their openness, their uprightness; protesting that she was convinced of sailors having more worth and warmth than any other set of men in England; that they only knew how to live, and they only deserved to be respected and loved.

They went back to dress and dine; and so well had the scheme answered already, that nothing was found amiss; though its being 'so entirely out of the season,' and the 'no-thorough-fare of Lyme,'* and the 'no expectation of company,' had brought many apologies from the heads of the inn.

Anne found herself by this time growing so much more hardened to being in Captain Wentworth's company than she had at first imagined could ever be, that the sitting down to the same table with him now, and the interchange of the common civilities attending on it—(they never got beyond) was become a mere nothing.

The nights were too dark for the ladies to meet again till the morrow, but Captain Harville had promised them a visit in the evening; and he came, bringing his friend also, which was more than had been expected, it having been agreed that Captain Benwick had all the appearance of being oppressed by the presence of so many strangers. He ventured among them again, however, though his spirits certainly did not seem fit for the mirth of the party in general.

While Captains Wentworth and Harville led the talk on one side of the room, and, by recurring to former days, supplied anecdotes in abundance to occupy and entertain the others, it fell to Anne's lot to be placed rather apart with Captain Benwick; and a very good impulse of her nature obliged her to begin an acquaintance with him. He was shy, and disposed to abstraction; but the engaging mildness of her countenance, and gentleness of her manners, soon had their effect; and Anne was well repaid the first trouble of exertion. He was evidently a young man of considerable taste in reading, though principally in poetry; and besides the persuasion of having given him at least an evening's indulgence in the discussion of subjects, which his usual companions had probably no concern in, she had the hope of being of real use to him in some suggestions as to the duty and benefit of struggling against affliction, which had naturally grown out of their conversation. For, though shy, he did not seem reserved; it had rather the appearance of feelings glad to burst their usual restraints; and having talked of poetry, the richness of the present age, and gone through a brief comparison of opinion as to the first-rate poets, trying to ascertain whether *Marmion* or *The Lady of the Lake* were to be preferred, and how ranked the *Giaour* and *The Bride of Abydos*,* and moreover, how the *Giaour* was to be pronounced, he shewed himself so intimately acquainted with all the tenderest songs of the one poet, and all the impassioned descriptions of hopeless agony of the other; he repeated, with such tremulous feeling, the various lines which imaged a broken heart, or a mind destroyed by wretchedness, and looked so entirely as if he meant to be understood, that she ventured to hope he did not always read only poetry; and to say, that she thought it was the misfortune of poetry, to be seldom safely enjoyed by those who enjoyed it completely; and that the strong feelings which alone could estimate it truly, were the very feelings which ought to taste it but sparingly.

His looks shewing him not pained, but pleased with this allusion to his situation, she was emboldened to go on; and feeling in herself the right of seniority of mind, she ventured to recommend a larger allowance of prose in his daily study; and on being requested to particularize, mentioned such works of our best moralists,* such collections of the finest letters, such memoirs of characters of worth and suffering, as occurred to her at the moment as calculated to rouse and fortify the mind by the highest precepts, and the strongest examples of moral and religious endurance.

Captain Benwick listened attentively, and seemed grateful for the interest implied; and though with a shake of the head, and sighs which declared his little faith in the efficacy of any books on grief like his, noted down the names of those she recommended, and promised to procure and read them.

When the evening was over, Anne could not but be amused at the idea of her coming to Lyme, to preach patience and resignation to a young man whom she had never seen before; nor could she help fearing, on more serious reflection, that, like many other great moralists and preachers, she had been eloquent on a point in which her own conduct would ill bear examination.

CHAPTER XII

ANNE and Henrietta, finding themselves the earliest of the party the next morning, agreed to stroll down to the sea before breakfast.— They went to the sands, to watch the flowing of the tide, which a fine south-easterly breeze was bringing in with all the grandeur which so flat a shore admitted. They praised the morning; gloried in the sea; sympathized in the delight of the fresh-feeling breeze—and were silent; till Henrietta suddenly began again, with,

'Oh! yes,—I am quite convinced that, with very few exceptions, the sea-air always does good. There can be no doubt of its having been of the greatest service to Dr. Shirley, after his illness, last spring twelvemonth. He declares himself, that coming to Lyme for a month, did him more good than all the medicine he took; and, that being by the sea, always makes him feel young again. Now, I cannot help thinking it a pity that he does not live entirely by the sea. I do think he had better leave Uppercross entirely, and fix at Lyme.—Do not you, Anne?—Do not you agree with me, that it is the best thing he could do, both for himself and Mrs. Shirley?—She has cousins here, you know, and many acquaintance, which would make it cheerful for her,—and I am sure she would be glad to get to a place where she could have medical attendance at hand, in case of his having another seizure. Indeed I think it quite melancholy to have such excellent people as Dr. and Mrs. Shirley, who have been doing good all their lives, wearing out their last days in a place like Uppercross, where, excepting our family, they seem shut out from all the world. I wish his friends would propose it to him. I really think they ought. And, as to procuring a dispensation,* there could be no difficulty at his time of life, and with his character. My only doubt is, whether any thing could persuade him to leave his parish. He is so very strict and scrupulous in his notions; over-scrupulous, I must say. Do not you think, Anne, it is being over-scrupulous? Do not you think it is quite a mistaken point of conscience, when a clergyman sacrifices his health for the sake of duties, which may be just as well performed by another person?—And at Lyme too,—only seventeen miles off,—he would be near enough to hear, if people thought there was any thing to complain of.'

Anne smiled more than once to herself during this speech, and entered into the subject, as ready to do good by entering into the feelings of a young lady as of a young man,—though here it was good of a lower standard, for what could be offered but general acquiescence?—She said all that was reasonable and proper on the business; felt the claims of Dr. Shirley to repose, as she ought; saw how very desirable it was that he should have some active, respectable young man, as a resident curate, and was even courteous enough to hint at the advantage of such resident curate's being married.

'I wish,' said Henrietta, very well pleased with her companion, 'I wish Lady Russell lived at Uppercross, and were intimate with Dr. Shirley. I have always heard of Lady Russell, as a woman of the greatest influence with every body! I always look upon her as able to persuade a person to any thing! I am afraid of her, as I have told you before, quite afraid of her, because she is so very clever; but I respect her amazingly, and wish we had such a neighbour at Uppercross.'

Anne was amused by Henrietta's manner of being grateful, and amused also, that the course of events and the new interests of Henrietta's views should have placed her friend at all in favour with any of the Musgrove family; she had only time, however, for a general answer, and a wish that such another woman were at Uppercross, before all subjects suddenly ceased, on seeing Louisa and Captain Wentworth coming towards them. They came also for a stroll till breakfast was likely to be ready; but Louisa recollecting, immediately afterwards, that she had something to procure at a shop, invited them all to go back with her into the town. They were all at her disposal.

When they came to the steps, leading upwards from the beach, a gentleman at the same moment preparing to come down, politely drew back, and stopped to give them way. They ascended and passed him; and as they passed, Anne's face caught his eye, and he looked at her with a degree of earnest admiration, which she could not be insensible of. She was looking remarkably well; her very regular, very pretty features, having the bloom and freshness of youth restored by the fine wind which had been blowing on her complexion, and by the animation of eye which it had also produced. It was evident that the gentleman, (completely a gentleman in manner) admired her exceedingly. Captain Wentworth looked round at her instantly in a way which shewed his noticing of it. He gave her a momentary glance,—a glance of brightness, which seemed to say, 'That man is struck with you,—and even I, at this moment, see something like Anne Elliot again.'

After attending Louisa through her business, and loitering about a little longer, they returned to the inn; and Anne in passing afterwards quickly from her own chamber to their dining-room, had nearly run against the very same gentleman, as he came out of an adjoining apartment. She had before conjectured him to be a stranger like themselves, and determined that a well-looking groom, who was strolling about near the two inns as they came back, should be his servant. Both master and man being in mourning, assisted the idea. It was now proved that he belonged to the same inn as themselves; and this second meeting, short as it was, also proved again by the gentleman's looks, that he thought hers very lovely, and by the readiness and propriety of his apologies, that he was a man of exceedingly good manners. He seemed about thirty, and, though not handsome, had an agreeable person. Anne felt that she should like to know who he was.

They had nearly done breakfast, when the sound of a carriage, (almost the first they had heard since entering Lyme) drew half the party to the window. 'It was a gentleman's carriage—a curricle—but only coming round from the stable-yard to the front door— Somebody must be going away.—It was driven by a servant in mourning.'

The word curricle made Charles Musgrove jump up, that he might compare it with his own, the servant in mourning roused Anne's curiosity, and the whole six were collected to look, by the time the owner of the curricle was to be seen issuing from the door amidst the bows and civilities of the household, and taking his seat, to drive off.

'Ah!' cried Captain Wentworth, instantly, and with half a glance at Anne; 'it is the very man we passed.'

The Miss Musgroves agreed to it; and having all kindly watched him as far up the hill as they could, they returned to the breakfast-table. The waiter came into the room soon afterwards.

'Pray,' said Captain Wentworth, immediately, 'can you tell us the name of the gentleman who is just gone away?'

'Yes, Sir, a Mr. Elliot; a gentleman of large fortune,—came in last night from Sidmouth,—dare say you heard the carriage, Sir, while you were at dinner; and going on now for Crewkherne,* in his way to Bath and London.'

'Elliot!'—Many had looked on each other, and many had repeated the name, before all this had been got through, even by the smart rapidity of a waiter.

'Bless me!' cried Mary; 'it must be our cousin;—it must be our Mr. Elliot, it must, indeed!—Charles, Anne, must not it? In mourning, you see, just as our Mr. Elliot must be. How very extraordinary! In the very same inn with us! Anne, must not it be our Mr. Elliot; my father's next heir? Pray Sir,' (turning to the waiter), 'did not you hear,—did not his servant say whether he belonged to the Kellynch family?'

'No, ma'am,—he did not mention no particular family; but he

said his master was a very rich gentleman, and would be a baronight
some day.'

'There! you see!' cried Mary, in an ecstacy, 'Just as I said! Heir to
Sir Walter Elliot!—I was sure that would come out, if it was so.
Depend upon it, that is a circumstance which his servants take care
to publish wherever he goes. But, Anne, only conceive how extraordinary! I wish I had looked at him more. I wish we had been aware
in time, who it was, that he might have been introduced to us. What a
pity that we should not have been introduced to each other!—Do
you think he had the Elliot countenance? I hardly looked at him, I
was looking at the horses; but I think he had something of the Elliot
countenance. I wonder the arms did not strike me!* Oh!—the great-
coat was hanging over the pannel, and hid the arms; so it did, otherwise, I am sure, I should have observed them, and the livery too; if
the servant had not been in mourning, one should have known him
by the livery.'

'Putting all these very extraordinary circumstances together,' said
Captain Wentworth, 'we must consider it to be the arrangement of
Providence, that you should not be introduced to your cousin.'

When she could command Mary's attention, Anne quietly tried
to convince her that their father and Mr. Elliot had not, for many
years, been on such terms as to make the power of attempting an
introduction at all desirable.

At the same time, however, it was a secret gratification to herself
to have seen her cousin, and to know that the future owner of Kel
lynch was undoubtedly a gentleman, and had an air of good sense.
She would not, upon any account, mention her having met with him
the second time; luckily Mary did not much attend to their having
passed close by him in their early walk, but she would have felt quite
ill-used by Anne's having actually run against him in the passage,
and received his very polite excuses, while she had never been near
him at all; no, that cousinly little interview must remain a perfect
secret.

'Of course,' said Mary, 'you will mention our seeing Mr. Elliot,
the next time you write to Bath. I think my father certainly ought to
hear of it; do mention all about him.'

Anne avoided a direct reply, but it was just the circumstance
which she considered as not merely unnecessary to be communicated, but as what ought to be suppressed. The offence which had

been given her father, many years back, she knew; Elizabeth's particular share in it she suspected; and that Mr. Elliot's idea always produced irritation in both, was beyond a doubt. Mary never wrote to Bath herself; all the toil of keeping up a slow and unsatisfactory correspondence with Elizabeth fell on Anne.

Breakfast had not been long over, when they were joined by Captain and Mrs. Harville, and Captain Benwick, with whom they had appointed to take their last walk about Lyme. They ought to be setting off for Uppercross by one, and in the meanwhile were to be all together, and out of doors as long as they could.

Anne found Captain Benwick getting near her, as soon as they were all fairly in the street. Their conversation, the preceding evening, did not disincline him to seek her again; and they walked together some time, talking as before of Mr. Scott and Lord Byron, and still as unable, as before, and as unable as any other two readers, to think exactly alike of the merits of either, till something occasioned an almost general change amongst their party, and instead of Captain Benwick, she had Captain Harville by her side.

'Miss Elliot,' said he, speaking rather low, 'you have done a good deed in making that poor fellow talk so much. I wish he could have such company oftener. It is bad for him, I know, to be shut up as he is; but what can we do? we cannot part.'

'No,' said Anne, 'that I can easily believe to be impossible; but in time, perhaps—we know what time does in every case of affliction, and you must remember, Captain Harville, that your friend may yet be called a young mourner—only last summer, I understand.'

'Ay, true enough,' (with a deep sigh) 'only June.'

'And not known to him, perhaps, so soon.'

'Not till the first week in August, when he came home from the Cape,—just made into the Grappler.* I was at Plymouth, dreading to hear of him; he sent in letters, but the Grappler was under orders for Portsmouth. There the news must follow him, but who was to tell it? not I. I would as soon have been run up to the yard-arm.* Nobody could do it, but that good fellow, (pointing to Captain Wentworth.) The Laconia had come into Plymouth the week before; no danger of her being sent to sea again. He stood his chance for the rest—wrote up for leave of absence, but without waiting the return, travelled night and day till he got to Portsmouth, rowed off to the Grappler that instant, and never left the poor fellow for a week; that's what he did, and nobody else could have saved poor James. You may think, Miss Elliot, whether he is dear to us!'

Anne did think on the question with perfect decision, and said as much in reply as her own feelings could accomplish, or as his seemed able to bear, for he was too much affected to renew the subject—and when he spoke again, it was of something totally different.

Mrs. Harville's giving it as her opinion that her husband would have quite walking enough by the time he reached home, determined the direction of all the party in what was to be their last walk; they would accompany them to their door, and then return and set off themselves. By all their calculations there was just time for this; but as they drew near the Cobb, there was such a general wish to walk along it once more, all were so inclined, and Louisa soon grew so determined, that the difference of a quarter of an hour, it was found, would be no difference at all, so with all the kind leave-taking, and all the kind interchange of invitations and promises which may be imagined, they parted from Captain and Mrs. Harville at their own door, and still accompanied by Captain Benwick, who seemed to cling to them to the last, proceeded to make the proper adieus to the Cobb.

Anne found Captain Benwick again drawing near her. Lord Byron's 'dark blue seas'* could not fail of being brought forward by their present view, and she gladly gave him all her attention as long as attention was possible. It was soon drawn per force another way.

There was too much wind to make the high part of the new Cobb pleasant for the ladies, and they agreed to get down the steps to the lower, and all were contented to pass quietly and carefully down the steep flight, excepting Louisa; she must be jumped down them by Captain Wentworth. In all their walks, he had had to jump her from the stiles; the sensation was delightful to her. The hardness of the pavement for her feet, made him less willing upon the present occasion; he did it, however; she was safely down, and instantly, to shew her enjoyment, ran up the steps to be jumped down again. He advised her against it, thought the jar too great; but no, he reasoned and talked in vain; she smiled and said, 'I am determined I will:' he put out his hands; she was too precipitate by half a second, she fell on the pavement on the Lower Cobb, and was taken up lifeless!

There was no wound, no blood, no visible bruise; but her eyes were closed, she breathed not, her face was like death.—The horror of that moment to all who stood around!

Captain Wentworth, who had caught her up, knelt with her in his arms, looking on her with a face as pallid as her own, in an agony of silence. 'She is dead! she is dead!' screamed Mary, catching hold of her husband, and contributing with his own horror to make him immoveable; and in another moment, Henrietta, sinking under the conviction, lost her senses too, and would have fallen on the steps, but for Captain Benwick and Anne, who caught and supported her between them.

'Is there no one to help me?' were the first words which burst from Captain Wentworth, in a tone of despair, and as if all his own strength were gone.

'Go to him, go to him,' cried Anne, 'for heaven's sake go to him. I can support her myself. Leave me, and go to him. Rub her hands, rub her temples; here are salts,—take them, take them.'

Captain Benwick obeyed, and Charles at the same moment, disengaging himself from his wife, they were both with him; and Louisa was raised up and supported more firmly between them, and every thing was done that Anne had prompted, but in vain; while Captain Wentworth, staggering against the wall for his support, exclaimed in the bitterest agony,

'Oh God! her father and mother!'

'A surgeon!' said Anne.

He caught the word; it seemed to rouse him at once, and saying only 'True, true, a surgeon this instant,' was darting away, when Anne eagerly suggested,

'Captain Benwick, would not it be better for Captain Benwick? He knows where a surgeon is to be found.'

Every one capable of thinking felt the advantage of the idea, and in a moment (it was all done in rapid moments) Captain Benwick had resigned the poor corpse-like figure entirely to the brother's care, and was off for the town with the utmost rapidity.

As to the wretched party left behind, it could scarcely be said which of the three, who were completely rational, was suffering most, Captain Wentworth, Anne, or Charles, who, really a very affectionate brother, hung over Louisa with sobs of grief, and could only turn his eyes from one sister, to see the other in a state as insensible, or to witness the hysterical agitations of his wife, calling on him for help which he could not give.

Anne, attending with all the strength and zeal, and thought, which instinct supplied, to Henrietta, still tried, at intervals, to suggest comfort to the others, tried to quiet Mary, to animate Charles, to assuage the feelings of Captain Wentworth. Both seemed to look to her for directions.

'Anne, Anne,' cried Charles, 'what is to be done next? What, in heaven's name, is to be done next?'

Captain Wentworth's eyes were also turned towards her.

'Had not she better be carried to the inn? Yes, I am sure, carry her gently to the inn.'

'Yes, yes, to the inn,' repeated Captain Wentworth, comparatively collected, and eager to be doing something. 'I will carry her myself. Musgrove, take care of the others.'

By this time the report of the accident had spread among the workmen and boatmen about the Cobb, and many were collected near them, to be useful if wanted, at any rate, to enjoy the sight of a dead young lady, nay, two dead young ladies, for it proved twice as fine as the first report. To some of the best-looking of these good people Henrietta was consigned, for, though partially revived, she was quite helpless; and in this manner, Anne walking by her side, and Charles attending to his wife, they set forward, treading back with feelings unutterable, the ground which so lately, so very lately, and so light of heart, they had passed along.

They were not off the Cobb, before the Harvilles met them. Captain Benwick had been seen flying by their house, with a countenance which shewed something to be wrong; and they had set off immediately, informed and directed, as they passed, towards the spot. Shocked as Captain Harville was, he brought senses and nerves that could be instantly useful; and a look between him and his wife decided what was to be done. She must be taken to their house—all must go to their house—and wait the surgeon's arrival there. They would not listen to scruples: he was obeyed; they were all beneath his roof; and while Louisa, under Mrs. Harville's direction, was conveyed up stairs, and given possession of her own bed, assistance, cordials, restoratives were supplied by her husband to all who needed them.

Louisa had once opened her eyes, but soon closed them again, without apparent consciousness. This had been a proof of life, however, of service to her sister; and Henrietta, though perfectly incapable of being in the same room with Louisa, was kept, by the agitation of hope and fear, from a return of her own insensibility. Mary, too, was growing calmer.

The surgeon was with them almost before it had seemed possible. They were sick with horror while he examined; but he was not hopeless. The head had received a severe contusion, but he had seen greater injuries recovered from: he was by no means hopeless; he spoke cheerfully.

That he did not regard it as a desperate case—that he did not say a few hours must end it—was at first felt, beyond the hope of most; and the ecstasy of such a reprieve, the rejoicing, deep and silent, after a few fervent ejaculations of gratitude to Heaven had been offered, may be conceived.

The tone, the look, with which 'Thank God!' was uttered by Captain Wentworth, Anne was sure could never be forgotten by her; nor the sight of him afterwards, as he sat near a table, leaning over it with folded arms, and face concealed, as if overpowered by the various feelings of his soul, and trying by prayer and reflection to calm them.

Louisa's limbs had escaped. There was no injury but to the head.

It now became necessary for the party to consider what was best to be done, as to their general situation. They were now able to speak to each other, and consult. That Louisa must remain where she was, however distressing to her friends to be involving the Harvilles in such trouble, did not admit a doubt. Her removal was impossible. The Harvilles silenced all scruples; and, as much as they could, all gratitude. They had looked forward and arranged every thing, before the others began to reflect. Captain Benwick must give up his room to them, and get a bed elsewhere—and the whole was settled. They were only concerned that the house could accommodate no more; and yet perhaps by 'putting the children away in the maids' room, or swinging a cot somewhere,' they could hardly bear to think of not finding room for two or three besides, supposing they might wish to stay; though, with regard to any attendance on Miss Musgrove, there need not be the least uneasiness in leaving her to Mrs. Harville's care entirely. Mrs. Harville was a very experienced nurse; and her nursery-maid, who had lived with her long and gone about with her every where, was just such another. Between those two, she could want no possible attendance by day or night. And all this was said with a truth and sincerity of feeling irresistible.

Charles, Henrietta, and Captain Wentworth were the three in consultation, and for a little while it was only an interchange of perplexity and terror. 'Uppercross,—the necessity of some one's going to Uppercross,—the news to be conveyed—how it could be broken to Mr. and Mrs. Musgrove—the lateness of the morning,—an hour already gone since they ought to have been off,—the impossibility of being in tolerable time.' At first, they were capable of nothing more to the purpose than such exclamations; but, after a while, Captain Wentworth, exerting himself, said,

'We must be decided, and without the loss of another minute. Every minute is valuable. Some must resolve on being off for Uppercross instantly. Musgrove, either you or I must go.'

Charles agreed; but declared his resolution of not going away. He would be as little incumbrance as possible to Captain and Mrs. Harville; but as to leaving his sister in such a state, he neither ought, nor would. So far it was decided; and Henrietta at first declared the same. She, however, was soon persuaded to think differently. The usefulness of her staying!—She, who had not been able to remain in Louisa's room, or to look at her, without sufferings which made her worse than helpless! She was forced to acknowledge that she could do no good; yet was still unwilling to be away, till touched by the thought of her father and mother, she gave it up; she consented, she was anxious to be at home.

The plan had reached this point, when Anne, coming quietly down from Louisa's room, could not but hear what followed, for the parlour door was open.

'Then it is settled, Musgrove,' cried Captain Wentworth, 'that you stay, and that I take care of your sister home. But as to the rest;—as to the others;—If one stays to assist Mrs. Harville, I think it need be only one.—Mrs. Charles Musgrove will, of course, wish to get back to her children; but, if Anne will stay, no one so proper, so capable as Anne!'

She paused a moment to recover from the emotion of hearing herself so spoken of. The other two warmly agreed to what he said, and she then appeared.

'You will stay, I am sure; you will stay and nurse her;' cried he, turning to her and speaking with a glow, and yet a gentleness, which seemed almost restoring the past.—She coloured deeply; and he recollected himself, and moved away.—She expressed herself most willing, ready, happy to remain. 'It was what she had been thinking of, and wishing to be allowed to do.—A bed on the floor in Louisa's room would be sufficient for her, if Mrs. Harville would but think so.'

One thing more, and all seemed arranged. Though it was rather desirable that Mr. and Mrs. Musgrove should be previously alarmed by some share of delay; yet the time required by the Uppercross horses to take them back, would be a dreadful extension of suspense; and Captain Wentworth proposed, and Charles Musgrove agreed, that it would be much better for him to take a chaise from the inn, and leave Mr. Musgrove's carriage and horses to be sent home the next morning early, when there would be the farther advantage of sending an account of Louisa's night.

Captain Wentworth now hurried off to get every thing ready on his part, and to be soon followed by the two ladies. When the plan was made known to Mary, however, there was an end of all peace in it. She was so wretched, and so vehement, complained so much of injustice in being expected to go away, instead of Anne;—Anne, who was nothing to Louisa, while she was her sister,* and had the best right to stay in Henrietta's stead! Why was not she to be as useful as Anne? And to go home without Charles, too—without her husband! No, it was too unkind! And, in short, she said more than her husband could long withstand; and as none of the others could oppose when he gave way, there was no help for it: the change of Mary for Anne was inevitable.

Anne had never submitted more reluctantly to the jealous and ill-judging claims of Mary; but so it must be, and they set off for the town, Charles taking care of his sister, and Captain Benwick attending to her. She gave a moment's recollection, as they hurried along, to the little circumstances which the same spots had witnessed earlier in the morning. There she had listened to Henrietta's schemes for Dr. Shirley's leaving Uppercross; farther on, she had first seen Mr. Elliot; a moment seemed all that could now be given to any one but Louisa, or those who were wrapt up in her welfare.

Captain Benwick was most considerately attentive to her; and, united as they all seemed by the distress of the day, she felt an increasing degree of good-will towards him, and a pleasure even in thinking that it might, perhaps, be the occasion of continuing their acquaintance.

Captain Wentworth was on the watch for them, and a chaise and four in waiting, stationed for their convenience in the lowest part of the street; but his evident surprise and vexation, at the substitution of one sister for the other—the change of his countenance—the astonishment—the expressions begun and suppressed, with which Charles was listened to, made but a mortifying reception of Anne; or must at least convince her that she was valued only as she could be useful to Louisa.

She endeavoured to be composed, and to be just. Without emulating the feelings of an Emma towards her Henry,* she would have attended on Louisa with a zeal above the common claims of regard, for his sake; and she hoped he would not long be so unjust as to suppose she would shrink unnecessarily from the office of a friend.

In the meanwhile she was in the carriage. He had handed them both in, and placed himself between them; and in this manner, under these circumstances full of astonishment and emotion to Anne, she quitted Lyme. How the long stage would pass; how it was to affect their manners; what was to be their sort of intercourse, she could not foresee. It was all quite natural, however. He was devoted to Henrietta; always turning towards her; and when he spoke at all, always with the view of supporting her hopes and raising her spirits. In general, his voice and manner were studiously calm. To spare Henrietta from agitation seemed the governing principle. Once only, when she had been grieving over the last ill-judged, ill-fated walk to the Cobb, bitterly lamenting that it ever had been thought of, he burst forth, as if wholly overcome—

'Don't talk of it, don't talk of it,' he cried. 'Oh God! that I had not given way to her at the fatal moment! Had I done as I ought! But so eager and so resolute! Dear, sweet Louisa!'

Anne wondered whether it ever occurred to him now, to question the justness of his own previous opinion as to the universal felicity and advantage of firmness of character; and whether it might not strike him, that, like all other qualities of the mind, it should have its proportions and limits. She thought it could scarcely escape him to feel, that a persuadable temper might sometimes be as much in favour of happiness, as a very resolute character.

They got on fast. Anne was astonished to recognise the same hills and the same objects so soon. Their actual speed, heightened by some dread of the conclusion, made the road appear but half as long as on the day before. It was growing quite dusk, however, before they were in the neighbourhood of Uppercross, and there had been total silence among them for some time, Henrietta leaning back in the corner, with a shawl over her face, giving the hope of her having cried herself to sleep; when, as they were going up their last hill, Anne found herself all at once addressed by Captain Wentworth. In a low, cautious voice, he said,

'I have been considering what we had best do. She must not appear at first. She could not stand it. I have been thinking whether you had not better remain in the carriage with her, while I go in and break it to Mr. and Mrs. Musgrove. Do you think this a good plan?'

She did: he was satisfied, and said no more. But the remembrance of the appeal remained a pleasure to her—as a proof of friendship, and of deference for her judgment, a great pleasure; and when it became a sort of parting proof, its value did not lessen.

When the distressing communication at Uppercross was over, and he had seen the father and mother quite as composed as could be hoped, and the daughter all the better for being with them, he announced his intention of returning in the same carriage to Lyme; and when the horses were baited,* he was off.

END OF VOLUME I

VOLUME II

CHAPTER I

THE remainder of Anne's time at Uppercross, comprehending only two days, was spent entirely at the mansion-house,* and she had the satisfaction of knowing herself extremely useful there, both as an immediate companion, and as assisting in all those arrangements for the future, which, in Mr. and Mrs. Musgrove's distressed state of spirits, would have been difficulties.

They had an early account from Lyme the next morning. Louisa was much the same. No symptoms worse than before had appeared. Charles came a few hours afterwards, to bring a later and more particular account. He was tolerably cheerful. A speedy cure must not be hoped, but every thing was going on as well as the nature of the case admitted. In speaking of the Harvilles, he seemed unable to satisfy his own sense of their kindness, especially of Mrs. Harville's exertions as a nurse. 'She really left nothing for Mary to do. He and Mary had been persuaded to go early to their inn last night. Mary had been hysterical again this morning. When he came away, she was going to walk out with Captain Benwick, which, he hoped, would do her good. He almost wished she had been prevailed on to come home the day before; but the truth was, that Mrs. Harville left nothing for any body to do.'

Charles was to return to Lyme the same afternoon, and his father had at first half a mind to go with him, but the ladies could not consent. It would be going only to multiply trouble to the others, and increase his own distress; and a much better scheme followed and was acted upon. A chaise was sent for from Crewkherne, and Charles conveyed back a far more useful person in the old nursery-maid of the family, one who having brought up all the children, and seen the very last, the lingering and long-petted master Harry, sent to school after his brothers, was now living in her deserted nursery to mend stockings, and dress all the blains* and bruises she could get near her, and who, consequently, was only too happy in being allowed to go and help nurse dear Miss Louisa. Vague wishes of getting Sarah thither, had occurred before to Mrs. Musgrove and Henrietta; but without Anne, it would hardly have been resolved on, and found practicable so soon.

They were indebted, the next day, to Charles Hayter for all the minute knowledge of Louisa, which it was so essential to obtain every twenty-four hours. He made it his business to go to Lyme, and his account was still encouraging. The intervals of sense and consciousness were believed to be stronger. Every report agreed in Captain Wentworth's appearing fixed in Lyme.

Anne was to leave them on the morrow, an event which they all dreaded. 'What should they do without her? They were wretched comforters for one another!' And so much was said in this way, that Anne thought she could not do better than impart among them the general inclination to which she was privy, and persuade them all to go to Lyme at once. She had little difficulty; it was soon determined that they would go, go to-morrow, fix themselves at the inn, or get into lodgings, as it suited, and there remain till dear Louisa could be moved. They must be taking off some trouble from the good people she was with; they might at least relieve Mrs. Harville from the care of her own children; and in short they were so happy in the decision, that Anne was delighted with what she had done, and felt that she could not spend her last morning at Uppercross better than in assisting their preparations, and sending them off at an early hour, though her being left to the solitary range of the house was the consequence.

She was the last, excepting the little boys at the cottage, she was the very last, the only remaining one of all that had filled and animated both houses, of all that had given Uppercross its cheerful character. A few days had made a change indeed!

If Louisa recovered, it would all be well again. More than former happiness would be restored. There could not be a doubt, to her mind there was none, of what would follow her recovery. A few months hence, and the room now so deserted, occupied but by her silent, pensive self, might be filled again with all that was happy and gay, all that was glowing and bright in prosperous love, all that was most unlike Anne Elliot!

An hour's complete leisure for such reflections as these, on a dark November day, a small thick rain almost blotting out the very few objects ever to be discerned from the windows, was enough to make the sound of Lady Russell's carriage exceedingly welcome; and yet, though desirous to be gone, she could not quit the mansion-house, or look an adieu to the cottage, with its black, dripping, and comfortless veranda, or even notice through the misty glasses the last humble tenements of the village, without a saddened heart.—Scenes had passed in Uppercross, which made it precious. It stood the record of many sensations of pain, once severe, but now softened; and of some instances of relenting feeling, some breathings of friendship and reconciliation, which could never be looked for again, and which could never cease to be dear. She left it all behind her; all but the recollection that such things had been.

Anne had never entered Kellynch since her quitting Lady Russell's house, in September. It had not been necessary, and the few occasions of its being possible for her to go to the hall she had contrived to evade and escape from. Her first return, was to resume her place in the modern and elegant apartments of the lodge, and to gladden the eyes of its mistress.

There was some anxiety mixed with Lady Russell's joy in meeting her. She knew who had been frequenting Uppercross. But happily, either Anne was improved in plumpness and looks, or Lady Russell fancied her so; and Anne, in receiving her compliments on the occasion, had the amusement of connecting them with the silent admiration of her cousin, and of hoping that she was to be blessed with a second spring of youth and beauty.

When they came to converse, she was soon sensible of some mental change. The subjects of which her heart had been full on leaving Kellynch, and which she had felt slighted, and been compelled to smother among the Musgroves, were now become but of secondary interest. She had lately lost sight even of her father and sister and Bath. Their concerns had been sunk under those of Uppercross, and when Lady Russell reverted to their former hopes and fears, and spoke her satisfaction in the house in Camden-place,* which had been taken, and her regret that Mrs. Clay should still be with them, Anne would have been ashamed to have it known, how much more she was thinking of Lyme, and Louisa Musgrove, and all her acquaintance there; how much more interesting to her was the home and the friendship of the Harvilles and Captain Benwick, than her own father's house in Camden-place, or her own sister's intimacy with Mrs. Clay. She was actually forced to exert herself, to meet Lady

Russell with any thing like the appearance of equal solicitude, on topics which had by nature the first claim on her.

There was a little awkwardness at first in their discourse on another subject. They must speak of the accident at Lyme. Lady Russell had not been arrived five minutes the day before, when a full account of the whole had burst on her; but still it must be talked of, she must make enquiries, she must regret the imprudence, lament the result, and Captain Wentworth's name must be mentioned by both. Anne was conscious of not doing it so well as Lady Russell. She could not speak the name, and look straight forward to Lady Russell's eye, till she had adopted the expedient of telling her briefly what she thought of the attachment between him and Louisa. When this was told, his name distressed her no longer.

Lady Russell had only to listen composedly, and wish them happy; but internally her heart revelled in angry pleasure, in pleased contempt, that the man who at twenty-three had seemed to understand somewhat of the value of an Anne Elliot, should, eight years afterwards, be charmed by a Louisa Musgrove.

The first three or four days passed most quietly, with no circumstance to mark them excepting the receipt of a note or two from Lyme, which found their way to Anne, she could not tell how, and brought a rather improving account of Louisa. At the end of that period, Lady Russell's politeness could repose no longer, and the fainter self-threatenings of the past, became in a decided tone, 'I must call on Mrs. Croft; I really must call upon her soon. Anne, have you courage to go with me, and pay a visit in that house? It will be some trial to us both.'

Anne did not shrink from it; on the contrary, she truly felt as she said, in observing,

'I think you are very likely to suffer the most of the two; your feelings are less reconciled to the change than mine. By remaining in the neighbourhood, I am become inured to it.'

She could have said more on the subject; for she had in fact so high an opinion of the Crofts, and considered her father so very fortunate in his tenants, felt the parish to be so sure of a good example, and the poor of the best attention and relief, that however sorry and ashamed for the necessity of the removal, she could not but in conscience feel that they were gone who deserved not to stay, and that Kellynch-hall had passed into better hands than its owners'.

These convictions must unquestionably have their own pain, and severe was its kind; but they precluded that pain which Lady Russell would suffer in entering the house again, and returning through the well-known apartments.

In such moments Anne had no power of saying to herself, 'These rooms ought to belong only to us. Oh, how fallen in their destination! How unworthily occupied! An ancient family to be so driven away! Strangers filling their place!' No, except when she thought of her mother, and remembered where she had been used to sit and preside, she had no sigh of that description to heave.

Mrs. Croft always met her with a kindness which gave her the pleasure of fancying herself a favourite; and on the present occasion, receiving her in that house, there was particular attention.

The sad accident at Lyme was soon the prevailing topic; and on comparing their latest accounts of the invalid, it appeared that each lady dated her intelligence from the same hour of yester morn, that Captain Wentworth had been in Kellynch yesterday—(the first time since the accident) had brought Anne the last note, which she had not been able to trace the exact steps of, had staid a few hours and then returned again to Lyme—and without any present intention of quitting it any more.—He had enquired after her, she found, particularly;—had expressed his hope of Miss Elliot's not being the worse for her exertions, and had spoken of those exertions as great. —This was handsome,—and gave her more pleasure than almost any thing else could have done.

As to the sad catastrophe itself, it could be canvassed only in one style by a couple of steady, sensible women, whose judgments had to work on ascertained events; and it was perfectly decided that it had been the consequence of much thoughtlessness and much imprudence; that its effects were most alarming, and that it was frightful to think, how long Miss Musgrove's recovery might yet be doubtful, and how liable she would still remain to suffer from the concussion hereafter!—The Admiral wound it all up summarily by exclaiming,

'Ay, a very bad business indeed.—A new sort of way this, for a young fellow to be making love, by breaking his mistress's head!—is not it, Miss Elliot?—This is breaking a head and giving a plaister* truly!'

Admiral Croft's manners were not quite of the tone to suit Lady

Russell, but they delighted Anne. His goodness of heart and simplicity of character were irresistible.

'Now, this must be very bad for you,' said he, suddenly rousing from a little reverie, 'to be coming and finding us here.—I had not recollected it before, I declare,—but it must be very bad.—But now, do not stand upon ceremony.—Get up and go over all the rooms in the house if you like it.'

'Another time, Sir, I thank you, not now.'

'Well, whenever it suits you.—You can slip in from the shrubbery at any time. And there you will find we keep our umbrellas, hanging up by that door. A good place, is not it? But' (checking himself) 'you will not think it a good place, for yours were always kept in the butler's room. Ay, so it always is, I believe. One man's ways may be as good as another's, but we all like our own best. And so you must judge for yourself, whether it would be better for you to go about the house or not.'

Anne, finding she might decline it, did so, very gratefully.

'We have made very few changes either!' continued the Admiral, after thinking a moment. 'Very few.—We told you about the laundry-door, at Uppercross. That has been a very great improvement. The wonder was, how any family upon earth could bear with the inconvenience of its opening as it did, so long!—You will tell Sir Walter what we have done, and that Mr. Shepherd thinks it the greatest improvement the house ever had. Indeed, I must do ourselves the justice to say, that the few alterations we have made have been all very much for the better. My wife should have the credit of them, however. I have done very little besides sending away some of the large looking-glasses from my dressing-room, which was your father's. A very good man, and very much the gentleman I am sure— but I should think, Miss Elliot' (looking with serious reflection) 'I should think he must be rather a dressy man for his time of life.— Such a number of looking-glasses! oh Lord! there was no getting away from oneself. So I got Sophy to lend me a hand, and we soon shifted their quarters; and now I am quite snug, with my little shaving glass in one corner, and another great thing that I never go near.'

Anne, amused in spite of herself, was rather distressed for an answer, and the Admiral, fearing he might not have been civil enough, took up the subject again, to say,

'The next time you write to your good father, Miss Elliot, pray give my compliments and Mrs. Croft's, and say that we are settled here quite to our liking, and have no fault at all to find with the place. The breakfast-room chimney smokes a little, I grant you, but it is only when the wind is due north and blows hard, which may not happen three times a winter. And take it altogether, now that we have been into most of the houses hereabouts and can judge, there is not one that we like better than this. Pray say so, with my compliments. He will be glad to hear it.'

Lady Russell and Mrs. Croft were very well pleased with each other; but the acquaintance which this visit began, was fated not to proceed far at present; for when it was returned, the Crofts announced themselves to be going away for a few weeks, to visit their connexions in the north of the county, and probably might not be at home again before Lady Russell would be removing to Bath.

So ended all danger to Anne of meeting Captain Wentworth at Kellynch-hall, or of seeing him in company with her friend. Every thing was safe enough, and she smiled over the many anxious feelings she had wasted on the subject.

CHAPTER II

THOUGH Charles and Mary had remained at Lyme much longer after Mr. and Mrs. Musgrove's going, than Anne conceived they could have been at all wanted, they were yet the first of the family to be at home again, and as soon as possible after their return to Uppercross, they drove over to the lodge.—They had left Louisa beginning to sit up; but her head, though clear, was exceedingly weak, and her nerves susceptible to the highest extreme of tenderness; and though she might be pronounced to be altogether doing very well, it was still impossible to say when she might be able to bear the removal home; and her father and mother, who must return in time to receive their younger children for the Christmas holidays, had hardly a hope of being allowed to bring her with them.

They had been all in lodgings together. Mrs. Musgrove had got Mrs. Harville's children away as much as she could, every possible supply from Uppercross had been furnished, to lighten the inconvenience to the Harvilles, while the Harvilles had been wanting them to come to dinner every day; and in short, it seemed to have been only a struggle on each side as to which should be most disinterested and hospitable.

Mary had had her evils; but upon the whole, as was evident by her staying so long, she had found more to enjoy than to suffer.— Charles Hayter had been at Lyme oftener than suited her, and when they dined with the Harvilles there had been only a maid-servant to wait, and at first, Mrs. Harville had always given Mrs. Musgrove precedence; but then, she had received so very handsome an apology from her on finding out whose daughter she was, and there had been so much going on every day, there had been so many walks between their lodgings and the Harvilles, and she had got books from the library and changed them so often, that the balance had certainly been much in favour of Lyme. She had been taken to Charmouth too, and she had bathed, and she had gone to church, and there were a great many more people to look at in the church at Lyme than at Uppercross,—and all this, joined to the sense of being so very useful, had made really an agreeable fortnight.

Anne enquired after Captain Benwick. Mary's face was clouded directly. Charles laughed.

'Oh! Captain Benwick is very well, I believe, but he is a very odd young man. I do not know what he would be at. We asked him to come home with us for a day or two; Charles undertook to give him some shooting, and he seemed quite delighted, and for my part, I thought it was all settled; when behold! on Tuesday night, he made a very awkward sort of excuse; 'he never shot' and he had 'been quite misunderstood,'—and he had promised this and he had promised that, and the end of it was, I found, that he did not mean to come. I suppose he was afraid of finding it dull; but upon my word I should have thought we were lively enough at the Cottage for such a heart-broken man as Captain Benwick.'

Charles laughed again and said, 'Now Mary, you know very well how it really was.—It was all your doing,' (turning to Anne.) 'He fancied that if he went with us, he should find you close by; he fancied every body to be living in Uppercross; and when he discovered that Lady Russell lived three miles off, his heart failed him, and he had not courage to come. That is the fact, upon my honour. Mary knows it is.'

But Mary did not give into it very graciously; whether from not considering Captain Benwick entitled by birth and situation to be in love with an Elliot, or from not wanting to believe Anne a greater attraction to Uppercross than herself, must be left to be guessed. Anne's good-will, however, was not to be lessened by what she heard. She boldly acknowledged herself flattered, and continued her enquiries.

'Oh! he talks of you,' cried Charles, 'in such terms,'—Mary interrupted him. 'I declare, Charles, I never heard him mention Anne twice all the time I was there. I declare, Anne, he never talks of you at all.'

'No,' admitted Charles, 'I do not know that he ever does, in a general way—but however, it is a very clear thing that he admires you exceedingly.—His head is full of some books that he is reading upon your recommendation, and he wants to talk to you about them; he has found out something or other in one of them which he thinks—Oh! I cannot pretend to remember it, but it was something very fine—I overheard him telling Henrietta all about it—and then "Miss Elliot" was spoken of in the highest terms!—Now Mary, I declare it was so, I heard it myself, and you were in the other room.—"Elegance, sweetness, beauty," Oh! there was no end of Miss Elliot's charms.'

'And I am sure,' cried Mary warmly, 'it was very little to his credit, if he did. Miss Harville only died last June. Such a heart is very little worth having; is it, Lady Russell? I am sure you will agree with me.'

'I must see Captain Benwick before I decide,' said Lady Russell, smiling.

'And that you are very likely to do very soon, I can tell you, ma'am,' said Charles. 'Though he had not nerves for coming away with us and setting off again afterwards to pay a formal visit here, he will make his way over to Kellynch one day by himself, you may depend on it. I told him the distance and the road, and I told him of the church's being so very well worth seeing, for as he has a taste for those sort of things, I thought that would be a good excuse, and he listened with all his understanding and soul; and I am sure from his manner that you will have him calling here soon. So, I give you notice, Lady Russell.'

'Any acquaintance of Anne's will always be welcome to me,' was Lady Russell's kind answer.

'Oh! as to being Anne's acquaintance,' said Mary, 'I think he is rather my acquaintance, for I have been seeing him every day this last fortnight.'

'Well, as your joint acquaintance, then, I shall be very happy to see Captain Benwick.'

'You will not find any thing very agreeable in him, I assure you, ma'am. He is one of the dullest young men that ever lived. He has walked with me, sometimes, from one end of the sands to the other, without saying a word. He is not at all a well-bred young man. I am sure you will not like him.'

'There we differ, Mary,' said Anne. 'I think Lady Russell would like him. I think she would be so much pleased with his mind, that she would very soon see no deficiency in his manner.'

'So do I, Anne,' said Charles. 'I am sure Lady Russell would like him. He is just Lady Russell's sort. Give him a book, and he will read all day long.'

'Yes, that he will!' exclaimed Mary, tauntingly. 'He will sit poring over his book, and not know when a person speaks to him, or when one drops one's scissors, or any thing that happens. Do you think Lady Russell would like that?'

Lady Russell could not help laughing. 'Upon my word,' said she, 'I should not have supposed that my opinion of any one could have admitted of such difference of conjecture, steady and matter of fact as I may call myself. I have really a curiosity to see the person who can give occasion to such directly opposite notions. I wish he may be induced to call here. And when he does, Mary, you may depend upon hearing my opinion; but I am determined not to judge him beforehand.'

'You will not like him, I will answer for it.'

Lady Russell began talking of something else. Mary spoke with animation of their meeting with, or rather missing, Mr. Elliot so extraordinarily.

'He is a man,' said Lady Russell, 'whom I have no wish to see. His declining to be on cordial terms with the head of his family, has left a very strong impression in his disfavour with me.'

This decision checked Mary's eagerness, and stopped her short in the midst of the Elliot countenance.

With regard to Captain Wentworth, though Anne hazarded no enquiries, there was voluntary communication sufficient. His spirits had been greatly recovering lately, as might be expected. As Louisa

improved, he had improved; and he was now quite a different creature from what he had been the first week. He had not seen Louisa;
and was so extremely fearful of any ill consequence to her from an
interview, that he did not press for it at all; and, on the contrary,
seemed to have a plan of going away for a week or ten days, till her
head were stronger. He had talked of going down to Plymouth for a
week, and wanted to persuade Captain Benwick to go with him; but,
as Charles maintained to the last, Captain Benwick seemed much
more disposed to ride over to Kellynch.

There can be no doubt that Lady Russell and Anne were both
occasionally thinking of Captain Benwick, from this time. Lady Russell could not hear the door-bell without feeling that it might be his
herald; nor could Anne return from any stroll of solitary indulgence
in her father's grounds, or any visit of charity in the village, without
wondering whether she might see him or hear of him. Captain Benwick came not, however. He was either less disposed for it than
Charles had imagined, or he was too shy; and after giving him a
week's indulgence, Lady Russell determined him to be unworthy of
the interest which he had been beginning to excite.

The Musgroves came back to receive their happy boys and girls
from school, bringing with them Mrs. Harville's little children, to
improve the noise of Uppercross, and lessen that of Lyme. Henrietta
remained with Louisa; but all the rest of the family were again in
their usual quarters.

Lady Russell and Anne paid their compliments to them once,
when Anne could not but feel that Uppercross was already quite
alive again. Though neither Henrietta, nor Louisa, nor Charles
Hayter, nor Captain Wentworth were there, the room presented as
strong a contrast as could be wished, to the last state she had seen it in.

Immediately surrounding Mrs. Musgrove were the little Harvilles, whom she was sedulously guarding from the tyranny of the
two children from the Cottage, expressly arrived to amuse them. On
one side was a table, occupied by some chattering girls, cutting up
silk and gold paper; and on the other were tressels and trays, bending
under the weight of brawn and cold pies, where riotous boys were
holding high revel; the whole completed by a roaring Christmas fire,
which seemed determined to be heard, in spite of all the noise of the
others. Charles and Mary also came in, of course, during their visit;
and Mr. Musgrove made a point of paying his respects to Lady

Russell, and sat down close to her for ten minutes, talking with a very raised voice, but, from the clamour of the children on his knees, generally in vain. It was a fine family-piece.

Anne, judging from her own temperament, would have deemed such a domestic hurricane a bad restorative of the nerves, which Louisa's illness must have so greatly shaken; but Mrs. Musgrove, who got Anne near her on purpose to thank her most cordially, again and again, for all her attentions to them, concluded a short recapitulation of what she had suffered herself, by observing, with a happy glance round the room, that after all she had gone through, nothing was so likely to do her good as a little quiet cheerfulness at home.

Louisa was now recovering apace. Her mother could even think of her being able to join their party at home, before her brothers and sisters went to school again. The Harvilles had promised to come with her and stay at Uppercross, whenever she returned. Captain Wentworth was gone, for the present, to see his brother in Shropshire.

'I hope I shall remember, in future,' said Lady Russell, as soon as they were reseated in the carriage, 'not to call at Uppercross in the Christmas holidays.'

Every body has their taste in noises as well as in other matters; and sounds are quite innoxious, or most distressing, by their sort rather than their quantity. When Lady Russell, not long afterwards, was entering Bath on a wet afternoon, and driving through the long course of streets from the Old Bridge to Camden-place, amidst the dash of other carriages, the heavy rumble of carts and drays, the bawling of newsmen, muffin-men and milk-men, and the ceaseless clink of pattens,* she made no complaint. No, these were noises which belonged to the winter pleasures; her spirits rose under their influence; and, like Mrs. Musgrove, she was feeling, though not saying, that, after being long in the country, nothing could be so good for her as a little quiet cheerfulness.

Anne did not share these feelings. She persisted in a very determined, though very silent, disinclination for Bath; caught the first dim view of the extensive buildings, smoking in rain, without any wish of seeing them better; felt their progress through the streets to be, however disagreeable, yet too rapid; for who would be glad to see her when she arrived? And looked back, with fond regret, to the bustles of Uppercross and the seclusion of Kellynch.

Elizabeth's last letter had communicated a piece of news of some interest. Mr. Elliot was in Bath. He had called in Camden-place; had called a second time, a third; had been pointedly attentive: if Elizabeth and her father did not deceive themselves, had been taking as much pains to seek the acquaintance, and proclaim the value of the connection, as he had formerly taken pains to shew neglect. This was very wonderful, if it were true; and Lady Russell was in a state of very agreeable curiosity and perplexity about Mr. Elliot, already recanting the sentiment she had so lately expressed, to Mary, of his being 'a man whom she had no wish to see.' She had a great wish to see him. If he really sought to reconcile himself like a dutiful branch, he must be forgiven for having dismembered himself from the paternal tree.

Anne was not animated to an equal pitch by the circumstance; but she felt that she would rather see Mr. Elliot again than not, which was more than she could say for many other persons in Bath.

She was put down in Camden-place; and Lady Russell then drove to her own lodgings, in Rivers-street.

CHAPTER III

SIR WALTER had taken a very good house in Camden-place, a lofty, dignified situation, such as becomes a man of consequence; and both he and Elizabeth were settled there, much to their satisfaction.

Anne entered it with a sinking heart, anticipating an imprisonment of many months, and anxiously saying to herself, 'Oh! when shall I leave you again?' A degree of unexpected cordiality, however, in the welcome she received, did her good. Her father and sister were glad to see her, for the sake of shewing her the house and furniture, and met her with kindness. Her making a fourth, when they sat down to dinner, was noticed as an advantage.

Mrs. Clay was very pleasant, and very smiling, but her courtesies and smiles were more a matter of course. Anne had always felt that she would pretend what was proper on her arrival; but the complaisance of the others was unlooked for. They were evidently in excellent spirits, and she was soon to listen to the causes. They had no inclination to listen to her. After laying out for some compliments of being deeply regretted in their old neighbourhood, which Anne

could not pay, they had only a few faint enquiries to make, before the
talk must be all their own. Uppercross excited no interest, Kellynch
very little, it was all Bath.

They had the pleasure of assuring her that Bath more than
answered their expectations in every respect. Their house was
undoubtedly the best in Camden-place; their drawing-rooms had
many decided advantages over all the others which they had either
seen or heard of; and the superiority was not less in the style of
the fitting-up, or the taste of the furniture. Their acquaintance
was exceedingly sought after. Every body was wanting to visit
them. They had drawn back from many introductions, and still
were perpetually having cards left by people of whom they knew
nothing.*

Here were funds of enjoyment! Could Anne wonder that her
father and sister were happy? She might not wonder, but she must
sigh that her father should feel no degradation in his change; should
see nothing to regret in the duties and dignity of the resident
land-holder; should find so much to be vain of in the littlenesses of a
town; and she must sigh, and smile, and wonder too, as Elizabeth
threw open the folding-doors, and walked with exultation from
one drawing-room to the other, boasting of their space, at the possibility of that woman, who had been mistress of Kellynch Hall, finding extent to be proud of between two walls, perhaps thirty feet
asunder.

But this was not all which they had to make them happy. They had
Mr. Elliot, too. Anne had a great deal to hear of Mr. Elliot. He was
not only pardoned, they were delighted with him. He had been in
Bath about a fortnight; (he had passed through Bath in November, in
his way to London, when the intelligence of Sir Walter's being settled there had of course reached him, though only twenty-four hours
in the place, but he had not been able to avail himself of it): but he
had now been a fortnight in Bath, and his first object, on arriving,
had been to leave his card in Camden-place, following it up by such
assiduous endeavours to meet, and, when they did meet, by such
great openness of conduct, such readiness to apologize for the past,
such solicitude to be received as a relation again, that their former
good understanding was completely re-established.

They had not a fault to find in him. He had explained away all the
appearance of neglect on his own side. It had originated in misap-

prehension entirely. He had never had an idea of throwing himself off; he had feared that he was thrown off, but knew not why; and delicacy had kept him silent. Upon the hint of having spoken disrespectfully or carelessly of the family, and the family honours, he was quite indignant. He, who had ever boasted of being an Elliot, and whose feelings, as to connection, were only too strict to suit the unfeudal tone of the present day! He was astonished, indeed! But his character and general conduct must refute it. He could refer Sir Walter to all who knew him; and, certainly, the pains he had been taking on this, the first opportunity of reconciliation, to be restored to the footing of a relation and heir-presumptive, was a strong proof of his opinions on the subject.

The circumstances of his marriage too were found to admit of much extenuation. This was an article not to be entered on by himself; but a very intimate friend of his, a Colonel Wallis, a highly respectable man, perfectly the gentleman, (and not an ill-looking man, Sir Walter added) who was living in very good style in Marlborough Buildings, and had, at his own particular request, been admitted to their acquaintance through Mr. Elliot, had mentioned one or two things relative to the marriage, which made a material difference in the discredit of it.

Colonel Wallis had known Mr. Elliot long, had been well acquainted also with his wife, had perfectly understood the whole story. She was certainly not a woman of family, but well educated, accomplished, rich, and excessively in love with his friend. There had been the charm. She had sought him. Without that attraction, not all her money would have tempted Elliot, and Sir Walter was, moreover, assured of her having been a very fine woman. Here was a great deal to soften the business. A very fine woman, with a large fortune, in love with him! Sir Walter seemed to admit it as complete apology, and though Elizabeth could not see the circumstance in quite so favourable a light, she allowed it be a great extenuation.

Mr. Elliot had called repeatedly, had dined with them once, evidently delighted by the distinction of being asked, for they gave no dinners in general; delighted, in short, by every proof of cousinly notice; and placing his whole happiness in being on intimate terms in Camden-place.

Anne listened, but without quite understanding it. Allowances, large allowances, she knew, must be made for the ideas of those who spoke. She heard it all under embellishment. All that sounded extravagant or irrational in the progress of the reconciliation might have no origin but in the language of the relators. Still, however, she had the sensation of there being something more than immediately appeared, in Mr. Elliot's wishing, after an interval of so many years, to be well received by them. In a worldly view, he had nothing to gain by being on terms with Sir Walter, nothing to risk by a state of variance. In all probability he was already the richer of the two, and the Kellynch estate would as surely be his hereafter as the title. A sensible man! and he had looked like a *very* sensible man, why should it be an object to him? She could only offer one solution; it was, perhaps, for Elizabeth's sake. There might really have been a liking formerly, though convenience and accident had drawn him a different way, and now that he could afford to please himself, he might mean to pay his addresses to her. Elizabeth was certainly very handsome, with well-bred, elegant manners, and her character might never have been penetrated by Mr. Elliot, knowing her but in public, and when very young himself. How her temper and understanding might bear the investigation of his present keener time of life was another concern, and rather a fearful one. Most earnestly did she wish that he might not be too nice, or too observant, if Elizabeth were his object; and that Elizabeth was disposed to believe herself so, and that her friend Mrs. Clay was encouraging the idea, seemed apparent by a glance or two between them, while Mr. Elliot's frequent visits were talked of.

Anne mentioned the glimpses she had had of him at Lyme, but without being much attended to. 'Oh! yes, perhaps, it had been Mr. Elliot. They did not know. It might be him, perhaps.' They could not listen to her description of him. They were describing him themselves; Sir Walter especially. He did justice to his very gentlemanlike appearance, his air of elegance and fashion, his good shaped face, his sensible eye, but, at the same time, 'must lament his being very much under-hung,* a defect which time seemed to have increased; nor could he pretend to say that ten years had not altered almost every feature for the worse. Mr. Elliot appeared to think that he (Sir Walter) was looking exactly as he had done when they last parted;' but Sir Walter had 'not been able to return the compliment entirely, which had embarrassed him. He did not mean to complain, however,

Mr. Elliot was better to look at than most men, and he had no objection to being seen with him any where.'

Mr. Elliot, and his friends in Marlborough Buildings, were talked of the whole evening. 'Colonel Wallis had been so impatient to be introduced to them! and Mr. Elliot so anxious that he should!' And there was a Mrs. Wallis, at present only known to them by description, as she was in daily expectation of her confinement; but Mr. Elliot spoke of her as 'a most charming woman, quite worthy of being known in Camden-place,' and as soon as she recovered, they were to be acquainted. Sir Walter thought much of Mrs. Wallis; she was said to be an excessively pretty woman, beautiful. 'He longed to see her. He hoped she might make some amends for the many very plain faces he was continually passing in the streets. The worst of Bath was, the number of its plain women. He did not mean to say that there were no pretty women, but the number of the plain was out of all proportion. He had frequently observed, as he walked, that one handsome face would be followed by thirty, or five and thirty frights; and once, as he had stood in a shop in Bond-street, he had counted eighty-seven women go by, one after another, without there being a tolerable face among them. It had been a frosty morning, to be sure, a sharp frost, which hardly one woman in a thousand could stand the test of. But still, there certainly were a dreadful multitude of ugly women in Bath; and as for the men! they were infinitely worse. Such scarecrows as the streets were full of! It was evident how little the women were used to the sight of any thing tolerable, by the effect which a man of decent appearance produced. He had never walked any where arm in arm with Colonel Wallis, (who was a fine military figure, though sandy-haired) without observing that every woman's eye was upon him; every woman's eye was sure to be upon Colonel Wallis.' Modest Sir Walter! He was not allowed to escape, however. His daughter and Mrs. Clay united in hinting that Colonel Wallis's companion might have as good a figure as Colonel Wallis, and certainly was not sandy-haired.

'How is Mary looking?' said Sir Walter, in the height of his good humour. 'The last time I saw her, she had a red nose, but I hope that may not happen every day.'

'Oh! no, that must have been quite accidental. In general she has been in very good health, and very good looks since Michaelmas.'

'If I thought it would not tempt her to go out in sharp winds, and grow coarse, I would send her a new hat and pelisse.'

Anne was considering whether she should venture to suggest that a gown, or a cap, would not be liable to any such misuse, when a knock at the door suspended every thing. 'A knock at the door! and so late! It was ten o'clock. Could it be Mr. Elliot? They knew he was to dine in Lansdown Crescent. It was possible that he might stop in his way home, to ask them how they did. They could think of no one else. Mrs. Clay decidedly thought it Mr. Elliot's knock.' Mrs. Clay was right. With all the state which a butler and foot-boy could give, Mr. Elliot was ushered into the room.

It was the same, the very same man, with no difference but of dress. Anne drew a little back, while the others received his compliments, and her sister his apologies for calling at so unusual an hour, but 'he could not be so near without wishing to know that neither she nor her friend had taken cold the day before, &c. &c.' which was all as politely done, and as politely taken as possible, but her part must follow then. Sir Walter talked of his youngest daughter; 'Mr. Elliot must give him leave to present him to his youngest daughter'— (there was no occasion for remembering Mary) and Anne, smiling and blushing, very becomingly shewed to Mr. Elliot the pretty features which he had by no means forgotten, and instantly saw, with amusement at his little start of surprise, that he had not been at all aware of who she was. He looked completely astonished, but not more astonished than pleased; his eyes brightened, and with the most perfect alacrity he welcomed the relationship, alluded to the past, and entreated to be received as an acquaintance already. He was quite as good-looking as he had appeared at Lyme, his countenance improved by speaking, and his manners were so exactly what they ought to be, so polished, so easy, so particularly agreeable, that she could compare them in excellence to only one person's manners. They were not the same, but they were, perhaps, equally good.

He sat down with them, and improved their conversation very much. There could be no doubt of his being a sensible man. Ten minutes were enough to certify that. His tone, his expressions, his choice of subject, his knowing where to stop,—it was all the operation of a sensible, discerning mind. As soon as he could, he began to talk to her of Lyme, wanting to compare opinions respecting the place, but especially wanting to speak of the circumstance of their happening to be guests in the same inn at the same time, to give his own route, understand something of hers, and regret that he should have lost such an opportunity of paying his respects to her. She gave him a short account of her party, and business at Lyme. His regret increased as he listened. He had spent his whole solitary evening in the room adjoining theirs; had heard voices—mirth continually; thought they must be a most delightful set of people—longed to be with them; but certainly without the smallest suspicion of his possessing the shadow of a right to introduce himself. If he had but asked who the party were! The name of Musgrove would have told him enough. 'Well, it would serve to cure him of an absurd practice of never asking a question at an inn, which he had adopted, when quite a young man, on the principle of its being very ungenteel to be curious.

'The notions of a young man of one or two and twenty,' said he, 'as to what is necessary in manners to make him quite the thing, are more absurd, I believe, than those of any other set of beings in the world. The folly of the means they often employ is only to be equalled by the folly of what they have in view.'

But he must not be addressing his reflections to Anne alone; he knew it; he was soon diffused again among the others, and it was only at intervals that he could return to Lyme.

His enquiries, however, produced at length an account of the scene she had been engaged in there, soon after his leaving the place. Having alluded to 'an accident,' he must hear the whole. When he questioned, Sir Walter and Elizabeth began to question also; but the difference in their manner of doing it could not be unfelt. She could only compare Mr. Elliot to Lady Russell, in the wish of really comprehending what had passed, and in the degree of concern for what she must have suffered in witnessing it.

He staid an hour with them. The elegant little clock on the mantle-piece had struck 'eleven with its silver sounds,'* and the watchman was beginning to be heard at a distance telling the same tale, before Mr. Elliot or any of them seemed to feel that he had been there long.

Anne could not have supposed it possible that her first evening in Camden-place could have passed so well!

CHAPTER IV

THERE was one point which Anne, on returning to her family, would
have been more thankful to ascertain, even than Mr. Elliot's being in
love with Elizabeth, which was, her father's not being in love with
Mrs. Clay; and she was very far from easy about it, when she had
been at home a few hours. On going down to breakfast the next
morning, she found there had just been a decent pretence on the
lady's side of meaning to leave them. She could imagine Mrs. Clay to
have said, that 'now Miss Anne was come, she could not suppose
herself at all wanted;' for Elizabeth was replying, in a sort of whisper,
'That must not be any reason, indeed. I assure you I feel it none. She
is nothing to me, compared with you;' and she was in full time to
hear her father say, 'My dear Madam, this must not be. As yet, you
have seen nothing of Bath. You have been here only to be useful. You
must not run away from us now. You must stay to be acquainted with
Mrs. Wallis, the beautiful Mrs. Wallis. To your fine mind, I well
know the sight of beauty is a real gratification.'

He spoke and looked so much in earnest, that Anne was not surprised to see Mrs. Clay stealing a glance at Elizabeth and herself. Her
countenance, perhaps, might express some watchfulness; but the
praise of the fine mind did not appear to excite a thought in her
sister. The lady could not but yield to such joint entreaties, and
promise to stay.

In the course of the same morning, Anne and her father chancing
to be alone together, he began to compliment her on her improved
looks; he thought her 'less thin in her person, in her cheeks; her skin,
her complexion, greatly improved—clearer, fresher. Had she been
using any thing in particular?' 'No, nothing.' 'Merely Gowland,'* he
supposed. 'No, nothing at all.' 'Ha! he was surprised at that;' and
added, 'Certainly you cannot do better than continue as you are; you
cannot be better than well; or I should recommend Gowland, the
constant use of Gowland, during the spring months. Mrs. Clay has
been using it at my recommendation, and you see what it has done
for her. You see how it has carried away her freckles.'

If Elizabeth could but have heard this! Such personal praise might
have struck her, especially as it did not appear to Anne that the
freckles were at all lessened. But every thing must take its chance.

The evil of the marriage would be much diminished, if Elizabeth were also to marry. As for herself, she might always command a home with Lady Russell.

Lady Russell's composed mind and polite manners were put to some trial on this point, in her intercourse in Camden-place. The sight of Mrs. Clay in such favour, and of Anne so overlooked, was a perpetual provocation to her there; and vexed her as much when she was away, as a person in Bath who drinks the water,* gets all the new publications, and has a very large acquaintance, has time to be vexed.

As Mr. Elliot became known to her, she grew more charitable, or more indifferent, towards the others. His manners were an immediate recommendation; and on conversing with him she found the solid so fully supporting the superficial, that she was at first, as she told Anne, almost ready to exclaim, 'Can this be Mr. Elliot?' and could not seriously picture to herself a more agreeable or estimable man. Every thing united in him; good understanding, correct opinions, knowledge of the world, and a warm heart. He had strong feelings of family-attachment and family-honour, without pride or weakness; he lived with the liberality of a man of fortune, without display; he judged for himself in every thing essential, without defying public opinion in any point of worldly decorum. He was steady, observant, moderate, candid;* never run away with by spirits or by selfishness, which fancied itself strong feeling; and yet, with a sensibility to what was amiable and lovely, and a value for all the felicities of domestic life, which characters of fancied enthusiasm and violent agitation seldom really possess. She was sure that he had not been happy in marriage. Colonel Wallis said it, and Lady Russell saw it; but it had been no unhappiness to sour his mind, nor (she began pretty soon to suspect) to prevent his thinking of a second choice. Her satisfaction in Mr. Elliot outweighed all the plague of Mrs. Clay.

It was now some years since Anne had begun to learn that she and her excellent friend could sometimes think differently; and it did not surprise her, therefore, that Lady Russell should see nothing suspicious or inconsistent, nothing to require more motives than appeared, in Mr. Elliot's great desire of a reconciliation. In Lady Russell's view, it was perfectly natural that Mr. Elliot, at a mature time of life, should feel it a most desirable object, and what would very generally recommend him, among all sensible people, to be on good terms with the head of his family; the simplest process in the world of time upon a head naturally clear, and only erring in the heyday of youth. Anne presumed, however, still to smile about it; and at last to mention 'Elizabeth.' Lady Russell listened, and looked, and made only this cautious reply: 'Elizabeth! Very well. Time will explain.'

It was a reference to the future, which Anne, after a little observation, felt she must submit to. She could determine nothing at present. In that house Elizabeth must be first; and she was in the habit of such general observance as 'Miss Elliot,' that any particularity of attention seemed almost impossible. Mr. Elliot, too, it must be remembered, had not been a widower seven months. A little delay on his side might be very excusable. In fact, Anne could never see the crape round his hat,* without fearing that she was the inexcusable one, in attributing to him such imaginations; for though his marriage had not been very happy, still it had existed so many years that she could not comprehend a very rapid recovery from the awful impression of its being dissolved.

However it might end, he was without any question their pleasantest acquaintance in Bath; she saw nobody equal to him; and it was a great indulgence now and then to talk to him about Lyme, which he seemed to have as lively a wish to see again, and to see more of, as herself. They went through the particulars of their first meeting a great many times. He gave her to understand that he had looked at her with some earnestness. She knew it well; and she remembered another person's look also.

They did not always think alike. His value for rank and connexion she perceived to be greater than hers. It was not merely complaisance, it must be a liking to the cause, which made him enter warmly into her father and sister's solicitudes on a subject which she thought unworthy to excite them. The Bath paper one morning announced the arrival of the Dowager Viscountess Dalrymple, and her daughter, the Honourable Miss Carteret;* and all the comfort of No.—, Camden-place, was swept away for many days; for the Dalrymples (in Anne's opinion, most unfortunately) were cousins of the Elliots; and the agony was, how to introduce themselves properly.

Anne had never seen her father and sister before in contact with nobility, and she must acknowledge herself disappointed. She had hoped better things from their high ideas of their own situation in life, and was reduced to form a wish which she had never foreseen—

a wish that they had more pride; for 'our cousins Lady Dalrymple and Miss Carteret;' 'our cousins, the Dalrymples,' sounded in her ears all day long.

Sir Walter had once been in company with the late Viscount, but had never seen any of the rest of the family, and the difficulties of the case arose from there having been a suspension of all intercourse by letters of ceremony,* ever since the death of that said late Viscount, when, in consequence of a dangerous illness of Sir Walter's at the same time, there had been an unlucky omission at Kellynch. No letter of condolence had been sent to Ireland. The neglect had been visited on the head of the sinner, for when poor Lady Elliot died herself, no letter of condolence was received at Kellynch, and, consequently, there was but too much reason to apprehend that the Dalrymples considered the relationship as closed. How to have this anxious business set to rights, and be admitted as cousins again, was the question; and it was a question which, in a more rational manner, neither Lady Russell nor Mr. Elliot thought unimportant. 'Family connexions were always worth preserving, good company always worth seeking; Lady Dalrymple had taken a house, for three months, in Laura-place, and would be living in style. She had been at Bath the year before, and Lady Russell had heard her spoken of as a charming woman. It was very desirable that the connexion should be renewed, if it could be done, without any compromise of propriety on the side of the Elliots.'

Sir Walter, however, would choose his own means, and at last wrote a very fine letter of ample explanation, regret and entreaty, to his right honourable cousin. Neither Lady Russell nor Mr. Elliot could admire the letter; but it did all that was wanted, in bringing three lines of scrawl from the Dowager Viscountess. 'She was very much honoured, and should be happy in their acquaintance.' The toils of the business were over, the sweets began. They visited in Laura-place, they had the cards of Dowager Viscountess Dalrymple, and the Hon. Miss Carteret, to be arranged wherever they might be most visible; and 'Our cousins in Laura-place,'—'Our cousins, Lady Dalrymple and Miss Carteret,' were talked of to every body.

Anne was ashamed. Had Lady Dalrymple and her daughter even been very agreeable, she would still have been ashamed of the agitation they created, but they were nothing. There was no superiority of manner, accomplishment, or understanding. Lady Dalrymple had acquired the name of 'a charming woman,' because she had a smile and a civil answer for every body. Miss Carteret, with still less to say, was so plain and so awkward, that she would never have been tolerated in Camden-place but for her birth.

Lady Russell confessed that she had expected something better; but yet 'it was an acquaintance worth having,' and when Anne ventured to speak her opinion of them to Mr. Elliot, he agreed to their being nothing in themselves, but still maintained that as a family connexion, as good company, as those who would collect good company around them, they had their value. Anne smiled and said,

'My idea of good company, Mr. Elliot, is the company of clever, well-informed people, who have a great deal of conversation; that is what I call good company.'

'You are mistaken,' said he gently, 'that is not good company, that is the best. Good company requires only birth, education and manners, and with regard to education is not very nice. Birth and good manners are essential; but a little learning* is by no means a dangerous thing in good company, on the contrary, it will do very well. My cousin, Anne, shakes her head. She is not satisfied. She is fastidious. My dear cousin, (sitting down by her) you have a better right to be fastidious than almost any other woman I know; but will it answer? Will it make you happy? Will it not be wiser to accept the society of these good ladies in Laura-place, and enjoy all the advantages of the connexion as far as possible? You may depend upon it, that they will move in the first set in Bath this winter, and as rank is rank, your being known to be related to them will have its use in fixing your family (our family let me say) in that degree of consideration which we must all wish for.'

'Yes,' sighed Anne, 'we shall, indeed, be known to be related to them!'—then recollecting herself, and not wishing to be answered, she added, 'I certainly do think there has been by far too much trouble taken to procure the acquaintance. I suppose (smiling) I have more pride than any of you; but I confess it does vex me, that we should be so solicitous to have the relationship acknowledged, which we may be very sure is a matter of perfect indifference to them.'

'Pardon me, my dear cousin, you are unjust to your own claims. In London, perhaps, in your present quiet style of living, it might be as you say; but in Bath, Sir Walter Elliot and his family will always be worth knowing, always acceptable as acquaintance.'

'Well,' said Anne, 'I certainly am proud, too proud to enjoy a welcome which depends so entirely upon place.'*

'I love your indignation,' said he; 'it is very natural. But here you are in Bath, and the object is to be established here with all the credit and dignity which ought to belong to Sir Walter Elliot. You talk of being proud, I am called proud I know, and I shall not wish to believe myself otherwise, for our pride, if investigated, would have the same object, I have no doubt, though the kind may seem a little different. In one point, I am sure, my dear cousin, (he continued, speaking lower, though there was no one else in the room) in one point, I am sure, we must feel alike. We must feel that every addition to your father's society, among his equals or superiors, may be of use in diverting his thoughts from those who are beneath him.'

He looked, as he spoke, to the seat which Mrs. Clay had been lately occupying, a sufficient explanation of what he particularly meant; and though Anne could not believe in their having the same sort of pride, she was pleased with him for not liking Mrs. Clay; and her conscience admitted that his wishing to promote her father's getting great acquaintance, was more than excusable in the view of defeating her.

CHAPTER V

WHILE Sir Walter and Elizabeth were assiduously pushing their good fortune in Laura-place, Anne was renewing an acquaintance of a very different description.

She had called on her former governess, and had heard from her of there being an old school-fellow in Bath, who had the two strong claims on her attention, of past kindness and present suffering. Miss Hamilton, now Mrs. Smith, had shewn her kindness in one of those periods of her life when it had been most valuable. Anne had gone unhappy to school, grieving for the loss of a mother whom she had dearly loved, feeling her separation from home, and suffering as a girl of fourteen, of strong sensibility and not high spirits, must suffer at such a time; and Miss Hamilton, three years older than herself, but still from the want of near relations and a settled home, remaining another year at school, had been useful and good to her in a way which had considerably lessened her misery, and could never be remembered with indifference.

Miss Hamilton had left school, had married not long afterwards, was said to have married a man of fortune, and this was all that Anne had known of her, till now that their governess's account brought her situation forward in a more decided but very different form.

She was a widow, and poor. Her husband had been extravagant; and at his death, about two years before, had left his affairs dreadfully involved. She had had difficulties of every sort to contend with, and in addition to these distresses, had been afflicted with a severe rheumatic fever, which finally settling in her legs, had made her for the present a cripple. She had come to Bath on that account, and was now in lodgings near the hot-baths, living in a very humble way, unable even to afford herself the comfort of a servant, and of course almost excluded from society.

Their mutual friend answered for the satisfaction which a visit from Miss Elliot would give Mrs. Smith, and Anne therefore lost no time in going. She mentioned nothing of what she had heard, or what she intended, at home. It would excite no proper interest there. She only consulted Lady Russell, who entered thoroughly into her sentiments, and was most happy to convey her as near to Mrs. Smith's lodgings in Westgate-buildings, as Anne chose to be taken.

The visit was paid, their acquaintance re-established, their interest in each other more than re-kindled. The first ten minutes had its awkwardness and its emotion. Twelve years were gone since they had parted, and each presented a somewhat different person from what the other had imagined. Twelve years had changed Anne from the blooming, silent, unformed girl of fifteen, to the elegant little woman of seven and twenty, with every beauty excepting bloom, and with manners as consciously right as they were invariably gentle; and twelve years had transformed the fine-looking, well-grown Miss Hamilton, in all the glow of health and confidence of superiority, into a poor, infirm, helpless widow, receiving the visit of her former protegeé as a favour; but all that was uncomfortable in the meeting had soon passed away, and left only the interesting charm of remembering former partialities and talking over old times.

Anne found in Mrs. Smith the good sense and agreeable manners which she had almost ventured to depend on, and a disposition to converse and be cheerful beyond her expectation. Neither the dissipations of the past—and she had lived very much in the world, nor the restrictions of the present; neither sickness nor sorrow seemed to have closed her heart or ruined her spirits.

In the course of a second visit she talked with great openness, and Anne's astonishment increased. She could scarcely imagine a more cheerless situation in itself than Mrs. Smith's. She had been very fond of her husband,—she had buried him. She had been used to affluence,—it was gone. She had no child to connect her with life and happiness again, no relations to assist in the arrangement of perplexed affairs, no health to make all the rest supportable. Her accommodations were limited to a noisy parlour, and a dark bed-room behind, with no possibility of moving from one to the other without assistance, which there was only one servant in the house to afford, and she never quitted the house but to be conveyed into the warm bath.—Yet, in spite of all this, Anne had reason to believe that she had moments only of languor and depression, to hours of occupation and enjoyment. How could it be?—She watched—observed—reflected—and finally determined that this was not a case of fortitude or of resignation only.—A submissive spirit might be patient, a strong understanding would supply resolution, but here was something more; here was that elasticity of mind, that disposition to be comforted, that power of turning readily from evil to good, and of finding employment which carried her out of herself, which was from Nature alone. It was the choicest gift of Heaven; and Anne viewed her friend as one of those instances in which, by a merciful appointment, it seems designed to counter-balance almost every other want.

There had been a time, Mrs. Smith told her, when her spirits had nearly failed. She could not call herself an invalid now, compared with her state on first reaching Bath. Then, she had indeed been a pitiable object—for she had caught cold on the journey, and had hardly taken possession of her lodgings, before she was again confined to her bed, and suffering under severe and constant pain; and all this among strangers—with the absolute necessity of having a regular nurse, and finances at that moment particularly unfit to meet any extraordinary expense. She had weathered it however, and could truly say that it had done her good. It had increased her comforts by making her feel herself to be in good hands. She had seen too much of the world, to expect sudden or disinterested attachment any where, but her illness had proved to her that her landlady had a character to preserve, and would not use her ill; and she had been particularly fortunate in her nurse, as a sister of her landlady, a nurse by profession, and who had always a home in that house when unemployed, chanced to be at liberty just in time to attend her.—'And she,' said Mrs. Smith, 'besides nursing me most admirably, has really proved an invaluable acquaintance.—As soon as I could use my hands, she taught me to knit, which has been a great amusement; and she put me in the way of making these little thread-cases, pin-cushions and card-racks, which you always find me so busy about, and which supply me with the means of doing a little good to one or two very poor families in this neighbourhood. She has a large acquaintance, of course professionally, among those who can afford to buy, and she disposes of my merchandize.* She always takes the right time for applying. Every body's heart is open, you know, when they have recently escaped from severe pain, or are recovering the blessing of health, and nurse Rooke thoroughly understands when to speak. She is a shrewd, intelligent, sensible woman. Hers is a line for seeing human nature; and she has a fund of good sense and observation which, as a companion, make her infinitely superior to thousands of those who having only received "the best education in the world," know nothing worth attending to. Call it gossip if you will; but when nurse Rooke has half an hour's leisure to bestow on me, she is sure to have something to relate that is entertaining and profitable, something that makes one know one's species better. One likes to hear what is going on, to be *au fait** as to the newest modes of being trifling and silly. To me, who live so much alone, her conversation I assure you is a treat.'

Anne, far from wishing to cavil at the pleasure, replied, 'I can easily believe it. Women of that class have great opportunities, and if they are intelligent may be well worth listening to. Such varieties of human nature as they are in the habit of witnessing! And it is not merely in its follies, that they are well read; for they see it occasionally under every circumstance that can be most interesting or affecting. What instances must pass before them of ardent, disinterested, self-denying attachment, of heroism, fortitude, patience, resignation—of all the conflicts and all the sacrifices that ennoble us most. A sick chamber may often furnish the worth of volumes.'

'Yes,' said Mrs. Smith more doubtingly, 'sometimes it may,

though I fear its lessons are not often in the elevated style you describe. Here and there, human nature may be great in times of trial, but generally speaking it is its weakness and not its strength that appears in a sick chamber; it is selfishness and impatience rather than generosity and fortitude, that one hears of. There is so little real friendship in the world!—and unfortunately' (speaking low and tremulously) 'there are so many who forget to think seriously till it is almost too late.'

Anne saw the misery of such feelings. The husband had not been what he ought, and the wife had been led among that part of mankind which made her think worse of the world, than she hoped it deserved. It was but a passing emotion however with Mrs. Smith, she shook it off, and soon added in a different tone,

'I do not suppose the situation my friend Mrs. Rooke is in at present, will furnish much either to interest or edify me.—She is only nursing Mrs. Wallis of Marlborough-buildings— a mere pretty, silly, expensive, fashionable woman, I believe—and of course will have nothing to report but of lace and finery.—I mean to make my profit of Mrs. Wallis, however. She has plenty of money, and I intend she shall buy all the high-priced things I have in hand now.'

Anne had called several times on her friend, before the existence of such a person was known in Camden-place. At last, it became necessary to speak of her.—Sir Walter, Elizabeth and Mrs. Clay returned one morning from Laura-place, with a sudden invitation from Lady Dalrymple for the same evening, and Anne was already engaged, to spend that evening in Westgate-buildings. She was not sorry for the excuse. They were only asked, she was sure, because Lady Dalrymple being kept at home by a bad cold, was glad to make use of the relationship which had been so pressed on her,—and she declined on her own account with great alacrity—'She was engaged to spend the evening with an old school-fellow.' They were not much interested in any thing relative to Anne, but still there were questions enough asked, to make it understood what this old school-fellow was; and Elizabeth was disdainful, and Sir Walter severe.

'Westgate-buildings!' said he; 'and who is Miss Anne Elliot to be visiting in Westgate-buildings?—A Mrs. Smith. A widow Mrs. Smith,—and who was her husband? One of the five thousand Mr. Smiths whose names are to be met with every where. And what is her attraction? That she is old and sickly.—Upon my word, Miss

Anne Elliot, you have the most extraordinary taste! Every thing that revolts other people, low company, paltry rooms, foul air, disgusting associations are inviting to you. But surely, you may put off this old lady till to-morrow. She is not so near her end, I presume, but that she may hope to see another day. What is her age? Forty?'

'No, Sir, she is not one and thirty; but I do not think I can put off my engagement, because it is the only evening for some time which will at once suit her and myself.—She goes into the warm bath to-morrow, and for the rest of the week you know we are engaged.'

'But what does Lady Russell think of this acquaintance?' asked Elizabeth.

'She sees nothing to blame in it,' replied Anne; 'on the contrary, she approves it; and has generally taken me, when I have called on Mrs. Smith.'

'Westgate-buildings must have been rather surprised by the appearance of a carriage drawn up near its pavement!' observed Sir Walter.—'Sir Henry Russell's widow, indeed, has no honours to dis-tinguish her arms,* but still, it is a handsome equipage, and no doubt is well known to convey a Miss Elliot.—A widow Mrs. Smith, lodg-ing in Westgate-buildings!—A poor widow, barely able to live, between thirty and forty—a mere Mrs. Smith, an every day Mrs. Smith, of all people and all names in the world, to be the chosen friend of Miss Anne Elliot, and to be preferred by her, to her own family connections among the nobility of England and Ireland! Mrs. Smith, such a name!'

Mrs. Clay, who had been present while all this passed, now thought it advisable to leave the room, and Anne could have said much and did long to say a little, in defence of *her* friend's not very dissimilar claims to theirs, but her sense of personal respect to her father prevented her. She made no reply. She left it to himself to recollect, that Mrs. Smith was not the only widow in Bath between thirty and forty, with little to live on, and no sirname of dignity.

Anne kept her appointment; the others kept theirs, and of course she heard the next morning that they had had a delightful evening.— She had been the only one of the set absent; for Sir Walter and Elizabeth had not only been quite at her ladyship's service them-selves, but had actually been happy to be employed by her in collect-ing others, and had been at the trouble of inviting both Lady Russell and Mr. Elliot; and Mr. Elliot had made a point of leaving Colonel

Wallis early, and Lady Russell had fresh arranged all her evening engagements in order to wait on her. Anne had the whole history of all that such an evening could supply, from Lady Russell. To her, its greatest interest must be, in having been very much talked of between her friend and Mr. Elliot, in having been wished for, regretted, and at the same time honoured for staying away in such a cause.—Her kind, compassionate visits to this old school-fellow, sick and reduced, seemed to have quite delighted Mr. Elliot. He thought her a most extraordinary young woman; in her temper, manners, mind, a model of female excellence. He could meet even Lady Russell in a discussion of her merits; and Anne could not be given to understand so much by her friend, could not know herself to be so highly rated by a sensible man, without many of those agreeable sensations which her friend meant to create.

Lady Russell was now perfectly decided in her opinion of Mr. Elliot. She was as much convinced of his meaning to gain Anne in time, as of his deserving her; and was beginning to calculate the number of weeks which would free him from all the remaining restraints of widowhood* and leave him at liberty to exert his most open powers of pleasing. She would not speak to Anne with half the certainty she felt on the subject, she would venture on little more than hints of what might be hereafter, of a possible attachment on his side, of the desirableness of the alliance, supposing such attachment to be real, and returned. Anne heard her, and made no violent exclamations. She only smiled, blushed, and gently shook her head.

'I am no match-maker, as you well know,' said Lady Russell, 'being much too well aware of the uncertainty of all human events and calculations. I only mean that if Mr. Elliot should some time hence pay his addresses to you, and if you should be disposed to accept him, I think there would be every possibility of your being happy together. A most suitable connection every body must consider it—but I think it might be a very happy one.'

'Mr. Elliot is an exceedingly agreeable man, and in many respects I think highly of him,' said Anne; 'but we should not suit.'

Lady Russell let this pass, and only said in rejoinder, 'I own that to be able to regard you as the future mistress of Kellynch, the future Lady Elliot—to look forward and see you occupying your dear mother's place, succeeding to all her rights, and all her popularity, as well as to all her virtues, would be the highest possible gratification to me.—You are your mother's self in countenance and disposition; and if I might be allowed to fancy you such as she was, in situation, and name, and home, presiding and blessing in the same spot, and only superior to her in being more highly valued! My dearest Anne, it would give me more delight than is often felt at my time of life!'

Anne was obliged to turn away, to rise, to walk to a distant table, and, leaning there in pretended employment, try to subdue the feelings this picture excited. For a few moments her imagination and her heart were bewitched. The idea of becoming what her mother had been; of having the precious name of 'Lady Elliot' first revived in herself; of being restored to Kellynch, calling it her home again, her home for ever, was a charm which she could not immediately resist. Lady Russell said not another word, willing to leave the matter to its own operation; and believing that, could Mr. Elliot at that moment with propriety have spoken for himself!—She believed, in short, what Anne did not believe. The same image of Mr. Elliot speaking for himself, brought Anne to composure again. The charm of Kellynch and of 'Lady Elliot' all faded away. She never could accept him. And it was not only that her feelings were still adverse to any man save one; her judgment, on a serious consideration of the possibilities of such a case, was against Mr. Elliot.

Though they had now been acquainted a month, she could not be satisfied that she really knew his character. That he was a sensible man, an agreeable man,—that he talked well, professed good opinions, seemed to judge properly and as a man of principle,—this was all clear enough. He certainly knew what was right, nor could she fix on any one article of moral duty evidently transgressed; but yet she would have been afraid to answer for his conduct. She distrusted the past, if not the present. The names which occasionally dropt of former associates, the allusions to former practices and pursuits, suggested suspicions not favourable of what he had been. She saw that there had been bad habits; that Sunday-travelling had been a common thing;* that there had been a period of his life (and probably not a short one) when he had been, at least, careless on all serious matters; and, though he might now think very differently, who could answer for the true sentiments of a clever, cautious man, grown old enough to appreciate a fair character? How could it ever be ascertained that his mind was truly cleansed?

Mr. Elliot was rational, discreet, polished,—but he was not open.

There was never any burst of feeling, any warmth of indignation or delight, at the evil or good of others. This, to Anne, was a decided imperfection. Her early impressions were incurable. She prized the frank, the open-hearted, the eager character beyond all others. Warmth and enthusiasm did captivate her still. She felt that she could so much more depend upon the sincerity of those who sometimes looked or said a careless or a hasty thing, than of those whose presence of mind never varied, whose tongue never slipped.

Mr. Elliot was too generally agreeable. Various as were the tempers in her father's house, he pleased them all. He endured too well,—stood too well with everybody. He had spoken to her with some degree of openness of Mrs. Clay; had appeared completely to see what Mrs. Clay was about, and to hold her in contempt; and yet Mrs. Clay found him as agreeable as anybody.

Lady Russell saw either less or more than her young friend, for she saw nothing to excite distrust. She could not imagine a man more exactly what he ought to be than Mr. Elliot; nor did she ever enjoy a sweeter feeling than the hope of seeing him receive the hand of her beloved Anne in Kellynch church, in the course of the following autumn.

CHAPTER VI

It was the beginning of February; and Anne, having been a month in Bath, was growing very eager for news from Uppercross and Lyme. She wanted to hear much more than Mary communicated. It was three weeks since she had heard at all. She only knew that Henrietta was at home again; and that Louisa, though considered to be recovering fast, was still at Lyme; and she was thinking of them all very intently one evening, when a thicker letter than usual from Mary was delivered to her, and, to quicken the pleasure and surprise, with Admiral and Mrs. Croft's compliments.

The Crofts must be in Bath! A circumstance to interest her. They were people whom her heart turned to very naturally.

'What is this?' cried Sir Walter. 'The Crofts arrived in Bath? The Crofts who rent Kellynch? What have they brought you?'

'A letter from Uppercross Cottage, Sir.'

'Oh! those letters are convenient passports. They secure an

introduction. I should have visited Admiral Croft, however, at any rate. I know what is due to my tenant.'

Anne could listen no longer; she could not even have told how the poor Admiral's complexion escaped; her letter engrossed her. It had been begun several days back.

'February 1st,——.

'MY DEAR ANNE,

'I make no apology for my silence, because I know how little people think of letters in such a place as Bath. You must be a great deal too happy to care for Uppercross, which, as you well know, affords little to write about. We have had a very dull Christmas; Mr. and Mrs. Musgrove have not had one dinner-party all the holidays. I do not reckon the Hayters as any body. The holidays, however, are over at last: I believe no children ever had such long ones. I am sure I had not. The house was cleared yesterday, except of the little Harvilles; but you will be surprised to hear that they have never gone home. Mrs. Harville must be an odd mother to part with them so long. I do not understand it. They are not at all nice children, in my opinion; but Mrs. Musgrove seems to like them quite as well, if not better, than her grand-children. What dreadful weather we have had! It may not be felt in Bath, with your nice pavements; but in the country it is of some consequence. I have not had a creature call on me since the second week in January, except Charles Hayter, who has been calling much oftener than was welcome. Between ourselves, I think it a great pity Henrietta did not remain at Lyme as long as Louisa; it would have kept her a little out of his way. The carriage is gone to-day, to bring Louisa and the Harvilles to-morrow. We are not asked to dine with them, however, till the day after, Mrs. Musgrove is so afraid of her being fatigued by the journey, which is not very likely, considering the care that will be taken of her; and it would be much more convenient to me to dine there to-morrow. I am glad you find Mr. Elliot so agreeable, and wish I could be acquainted with him too; but I have my usual luck, I am always out of the way when any thing desirable is going on; always the last of my family to be noticed. What an immense time Mrs. Clay has been staying with Elizabeth! Does she never mean to go away? But perhaps if she were to leave the room vacant we might not be invited. Let me know what you think of this. I do not expect my children to be asked, you know.

I can leave them at the Great House very well, for a month or six weeks. I have this moment heard that the Crofts are going to Bath almost immediately; they think the admiral gouty.* Charles heard it quite by chance: they have not had the civility to give me any notice, or offer to take any thing. I do not think they improve at all as neighbours. We see nothing of them, and this is really an instance of gross inattention. Charles joins me in love, and every thing proper. Yours, affectionately,

'MARY M————.

'I am sorry to say that I am very far from well; and Jemima has just told me that the butcher says there is a bad sore-throat very much about. I dare say I shall catch it; and my sore-throats, you know, are always worse than anybody's.'

So ended the first part, which had been afterwards put into an envelop, containing nearly as much more.

'I kept my letter open, that I might send you word how Louisa bore her journey, and now I am extremely glad I did, having a great deal to add. In the first place, I had a note from Mrs. Croft yesterday, offering to convey any thing to you; a very kind, friendly note indeed, addressed to me, just as it ought; I shall therefore be able to make my letter as long as I like.* The admiral does not seem very ill, and I sincerely hope Bath will do him all the good he wants. I shall be truly glad to have them back again. Our neighbourhood cannot spare such a pleasant family. But now for Louisa. I have something to communicate that will astonish you not a little. She and the Harvilles came on Tuesday very safely, and in the evening we went to ask her how she did, when we were rather surprised not to find Captain Benwick of the party, for he had been invited as well as the Harvilles; and what do you think was the reason? Neither more nor less than his being in love with Louisa, and not choosing to venture to Uppercross till he had an answer from Mr. Musgrove; for it was all settled between him and her before she came away, and he had written to her father by Captain Harville. True, upon my honour. Are not you astonished? I shall be surprised at least if you ever received a hint of it, for I never did. Mrs. Musgrove protests solemnly that she knew nothing of the matter. We are all very well pleased, however; for though it is not equal to her marrying Captain Wentworth, it is infinitely better than Charles Hayter; and Mr. Musgrove has written his consent, and Captain Benwick is expected to-day. Mrs. Harville says her husband feels a good deal on his poor sister's account; but, however, Louisa is a great favourite with both. Indeed Mrs. Harville and I quite agree that we love her the better for having nursed her. Charles wonders what Captain Wentworth will say; but if you remember, I never thought him attached to Louisa; I never could see any thing of it. And this is the end, you see, of Captain Benwick's being supposed to be an admirer of yours. How Charles could take such a thing into his head was always incomprehensible to me. I hope he will be more agreeable now. Certainly not a great match for Louisa Musgrove; but a million times better than marrying among the Hayters.'

Mary need not have feared her sister's being in any degree prepared for the news. She had never in her life been more astonished. Captain Benwick and Louisa Musgrove! It was almost too wonderful for belief; and it was with the greatest effort that she could remain in the room, preserve an air of calmness, and answer the common questions of the moment. Happily for her, they were not many. Sir Walter wanted to know whether the Crofts travelled with four horses, and whether they were likely to be situated in such a part of Bath as it might suit Miss Elliot and himself to visit in; but had little curiosity beyond.

'How is Mary?' said Elizabeth; and without waiting for an answer. 'And pray what brings the Crofts to Bath?'

'They come on the Admiral's account. He is thought to be gouty.'

'Gout and decrepitude!' said Sir Walter. 'Poor old gentleman.'

'Have they any acquaintance here?' asked Elizabeth.

'I do not know; but I can hardly suppose that, at Admiral Croft's time of life, and in his profession, he should not have many acquaintance in such a place as this.'

'I suspect,' said Sir Walter coolly, 'that Admiral Croft will be best known in Bath as the renter of Kellynch-hall. Elizabeth, may we venture to present him and his wife in Laura-place?'

'Oh! no, I think not. Situated as we are with Lady Dalrymple, cousins, we ought to be very careful not to embarrass her with acquaintance she might not approve. If we were not related, it would not signify; but as cousins, she would feel scrupulous as to any proposal of ours. We had better leave the Crofts to find their own level. There are several odd-looking men walking about here, who, I am told, are sailors. The Crofts will associate with them!'

This was Sir Walter and Elizabeth's share of interest in the letter; when Mrs. Clay had paid her tribute of more decent attention, in an enquiry after Mrs. Charles Musgrove, and her fine little boys, Anne was at liberty.

In her own room she tried to comprehend it. Well might Charles wonder how Captain Wentworth would feel! Perhaps he had quitted the field, had given Louisa up, had ceased to love, had found he did not love her. She could not endure the idea of treachery or levity, or any thing akin to ill-usage between him and his friend. She could not endure that such a friendship as theirs should be severed unfairly.

Captain Benwick and Louisa Musgrove! The high-spirited, joyous, talking Louisa Musgrove, and the dejected, thinking, feeling, reading Captain Benwick, seemed each of them every thing that would not suit the other. Their minds most dissimilar! Where could have been the attraction? The answer soon presented itself. It had been in situation. They had been thrown together several weeks; they had been living in the same small family party; since Henrietta's coming away, they must have been depending almost entirely on each other, and Louisa, just recovering from illness, had been in an interesting state, and Captain Benwick was not inconsolable. That was a point which Anne had not been able to avoid suspecting before; and instead of drawing the same conclusion as Mary, from the present course of events, they served only to confirm the idea of his having felt some dawning of tenderness toward herself. She did not mean, however, to derive much more from it to gratify her vanity, than Mary might have allowed. She was persuaded that any tolerably pleasing young woman who had listened and seemed to feel for him, would have received the same compliment. He had an affectionate heart. He must love somebody.

She saw no reason against their being happy. Louisa had fine naval fervour to begin with, and they would soon grow more alike. He would gain cheerfulness, and she would learn to be an enthusiast for Scott and Lord Byron; nay, that was probably learnt already; of course they had fallen in love over poetry. The idea of Louisa Musgrove turned into a person of literary taste, and sentimental reflection, was amusing, but she had no doubt of its being so. The day at

Lyme, the fall from the Cobb, might influence her health, her nerves, her courage, her character to the end of her life, as thoroughly as it appeared to have influenced her fate.

The conclusion of the whole was, that if the woman who had been sensible of Captain Wentworth's merits could be allowed to prefer another man, there was nothing in the engagement to excite lasting wonder; and if Captain Wentworth lost no friend by it, certainly nothing to be regretted. No, it was not regret which made Anne's heart beat in spite of herself, and brought the colour into her cheeks when she thought of Captain Wentworth unshackled and free. She had some feelings which she was ashamed to investigate. They were too much like joy, senseless joy!

She longed to see the Crofts, but when the meeting took place, it was evident that no rumour of the news had yet reached them. The visit of ceremony was paid and returned, and Louisa Musgrove was mentioned, and Captain Benwick too, without even half a smile.

The Crofts had placed themselves in lodgings in Gay-street,* perfectly to Sir Walter's satisfaction. He was not at all ashamed of the acquaintance, and did, in fact, think and talk a great deal more about the Admiral, than the Admiral ever thought or talked about him.

The Crofts knew quite as many people in Bath as they wished for, and considered their intercourse with the Elliots as a mere matter of form, and not in the least likely to afford them any pleasure. They brought with them their country habit of being almost always together. He was ordered to walk, to keep off the gout, and Mrs. Croft seemed to go shares with him in every thing, and to walk for her life, to do him good. Anne saw them wherever she went. Lady Russell took her out in her carriage almost every morning, and she never failed to think of them, and never failed to see them. Knowing their feelings as she did, it was a most attractive picture of happiness to her. She always watched them as long as she could; delighted to fancy she understood what they might be talking of, as they walked along in happy independence, or equally delighted to see the Admiral's hearty shake of the hand when he encountered an old friend, and observe their eagerness of conversation when occasionally forming into a little knot of the navy, Mrs. Croft looking as intelligent and keen as any of the officers around her.

Anne was too much engaged with Lady Russell to be often walking herself, but it so happened that one morning, about a week or ten

days after the Crofts' arrival, it suited her best to leave her friend, or
her friend's carriage, in the lower part of the town, and return alone
to Camden-place; and in walking up Milsom-street,* she had the
good fortune to meet with the Admiral. He was standing by himself,
at a printshop window, with his hands behind him, in earnest contemplation of some print, and she not only might have passed him
unseen, but was obliged to touch as well as address him before she
could catch his notice. When he did perceive and acknowledge her,
however, it was done with all his usual frankness and good humour.
'Ha! is it you? Thank you, thank you. This is treating me like a
friend. Here I am, you see, staring at a picture. I can never get by this
shop without stopping. But what a thing here is, by way of a boat. Do
look at it. Did you ever see the like? What queer fellows your fine
painters must be, to think that any body would venture their lives in
such a shapeless old cockleshell as that. And yet, here are two
gentlemen stuck up in it mightily at their ease, and looking about
them at the rocks and mountains, as if they were not to be upset the
next moment, which they certainly must be. I wonder where that
boat was built!' (laughing heartily) 'I would not venture over a
horsepond in it. Well,' (turning away) 'now, where are you bound?
Can I go any where for you, or with you? Can I be of any use?'

'None, I thank you, unless you will give me the pleasure of your
company the little way our road lies together. I am going home.'

'That I will, with all my heart, and farther too. Yes, yes, we will
have a snug walk together; and I have something to tell you as we go
along. There, take my arm; that's right; I do not feel comfortable if I
have not a woman there. Lord! what a boat it is!' taking a last look at
the picture, as they began to be in motion.

'Did you say that you had something to tell me, sir?'

'Yes, I have. Presently. But here comes a friend, Captain Brigden; I
shall only say, "How d'ye do," as we pass, however. I shall not stop.
"How d'ye do." Brigden stares to see anybody with me but my wife.
She, poor soul, is tied by the leg. She has a blister on one of her heels,
as large as a three shilling piece.* If you look across the street, you will
see Admiral Brand coming down and his brother. Shabby fellows,
both of them! I am glad they are not on this side of the way. Sophy
cannot bear them. They played me a pitiful trick once—got away
some of my best men.* I will tell you the whole story another time.
There comes old Sir Archibald Drew and his grandson. Look, he

sees us; he kisses his hand to you; he takes you for my wife. Ah! the peace has come too soon for that younker.* Poor old Sir Archibald! How do you like Bath, Miss Elliot? It suits us very well. We are always meeting with some old friend or other; the streets full of them every morning; sure to have plenty of chat; and then we get away from them all, and shut ourselves into our lodgings, and draw in our chairs, and are as snug as if we were at Kellynch, ay, or as we used to be even at North Yarmouth* and Deal. We do not like our lodgings here the worse, I can tell you, for putting us in mind of those we first had at North Yarmouth. The wind blows through one of the cupboards just in the same way.'

When they were got a little farther, Anne ventured to press again for what he had to communicate. She had hoped, when clear of Milsom-street, to have her curiosity gratified; but she was still obliged to wait, for the Admiral had made up his mind not to begin, till they had gained the greater space and quiet of Belmont, and as she was not really Mrs. Croft, she must let him have his own way. As soon as they were fairly ascending Belmont, he began,

'Well, now you shall hear something that will surprise you. But first of all, you must tell me the name of the young lady I am going to talk about. That young lady, you know, that we have all been so concerned for. The Miss Musgrove, that all this has been happening to. Her christian name—I always forget her christian name.'

Anne had been ashamed to appear to comprehend so soon as she really did; but now she could safely suggest the name of 'Louisa.'

'Ay, ay, Miss Louisa Musgrove, that is the name. I wish young ladies had not such a number of fine christian names. I should never be out, if they were all Sophys, or something of that sort. Well, this Miss Louisa, we all thought, you know, was to marry Frederick. He was courting her week after week. The only wonder was, what they could be waiting for, till the business at Lyme came; then, indeed, it was clear enough that they must wait till her brain was set to right. But even then, there was something odd in their way of going on. Instead of staying at Lyme, he went off to Plymouth, and then he went off to see Edward. When we came back from Minehead,* he was gone down to Edward's, and there he has been ever since. We have seen nothing of him since November. Even Sophy could not understand it. But now, the matter has taken the strangest turn of all; for this young lady, this same Miss Musgrove, instead of being to marry Frederick, is to marry James Benwick. You know James Benwick.'

'A little. I am a little acquainted with Captain Benwick.'

'Well, she is to marry him. Nay, most likely they are married already, for I do not know what they should wait for.'

'I thought Captain Benwick a very pleasing young man,' said Anne, 'and I understand that he bears an excellent character.'

'Oh! yes, yes, there is not a word to be said against James Benwick. He is only a commander, it is true, made last summer, and these are bad times for getting on, but he has not another fault that I know of. An excellent, good-hearted fellow, I assure you, a very active, zealous officer too, which is more than you would think for, perhaps, for that soft sort of manner does not do him justice.'

'Indeed you are mistaken there, sir. I should never augur want of spirit from Captain Benwick's manners. I thought them particularly pleasing, and I will answer for it they would generally please.'

'Well, well, ladies are the best judges; but James Benwick is rather too piano* for me, and though very likely it is all our partiality, Sophy and I cannot help thinking Frederick's manners better than his. There is something about Frederick more to our taste.'

Anne was caught. She had only meant to oppose the too-common idea of spirit and gentleness being incompatible with each other, not at all to represent Captain Benwick's manners as the very best that could possibly be, and, after a little hesitation, she was beginning to say, 'I was not entering into any comparison of the two friends,' but the Admiral interrupted her with,

'And the thing is certainly true. It is not a mere bit of gossip. We have it from Frederick himself. His sister had a letter from him yesterday, in which he tells us of it, and he had just had it in a letter from Harville, written upon the spot, from Uppercross. I fancy they are all at Uppercross.'

This was an opportunity which Anne could not resist; she said, therefore, 'I hope, Admiral, I hope there is nothing in the style of Captain Wentworth's letter to make you and Mrs. Croft particularly uneasy. It did certainly seem, last autumn, as if there were an attachment between him and Louisa Musgrove; but I hope it may be understood to have worn out on each side equally, and without violence. I hope his letter does not breathe the spirit of an ill-used man.'

'Not at all, not at all; there is not an oath or a murmur from beginning to end.'

Anne looked down to hide her smile.

'No, no; Frederick is not a man to whine and complain; he has too much spirit for that. If the girl likes another man better, it is very fit she should have him.'

'Certainly. But what I mean is, that I hope there is nothing in Captain Wentworth's manner of writing to make you suppose he thinks himself ill-used by his friend, which might appear, you know, without its being absolutely said. I should be very sorry that such a friendship as has subsisted between him and Captain Benwick should be destroyed, or even wounded, by a circumstance of this sort.'

'Yes, yes, I understand you. But there is nothing at all of that nature in the letter. He does not give the least fling at Benwick; does not so much as say, "I wonder at it, I have a reason of my own for wondering at it." No, you would not guess, from his way of writing, that he had ever thought of this Miss (what's her name?) for himself. He very handsomely hopes they will be happy together, and there is nothing very unforgiving in that, I think.'

Anne did not receive the perfect conviction which the Admiral meant to convey, but it would have been useless to press the enquiry farther. She, therefore, satisfied herself with common-place remarks, or quiet attention, and the Admiral had it all his own way.

'Poor Frederick!' said he at last. 'Now he must begin all over again with somebody else. I think we must get him to Bath. Sophy must write, and beg him to come to Bath. Here are pretty girls enough, I am sure. It would be of no use to go to Uppercross again, for that other Miss Musgrove, I find, is bespoke by her cousin, the young parson. Do not you think, Miss Elliot, we had better try to get him to Bath?'

CHAPTER VII

WHILE Admiral Croft was taking this walk with Anne, and expressing his wish of getting Captain Wentworth to Bath, Captain Wentworth was already on his way thither. Before Mrs. Croft had written, he was arrived; and the very next time Anne walked out, she saw him.

Mr. Elliot was attending his two cousins and Mrs. Clay. They were in Milsom-street. It began to rain, not much, but enough to make shelter desirable for women, and quite enough to make it very desirable for Miss Elliot to have the advantage of being conveyed home in Lady Dalrymple's carriage, which was seen waiting at a little distance; she, Anne, and Mrs. Clay, therefore, turned into Molland's,* while Mr. Elliot stepped to Lady Dalrymple, to request her assistance. He soon joined them again, successful, of course; Lady Dalrymple would be most happy to take them home, and would call for them in a few minutes.

Her ladyship's carriage was a barouche,* and did not hold more than four with any comfort. Miss Carteret was with her mother; consequently it was not reasonable to expect accommodation for all the three Camden-place ladies. There could be no doubt as to Miss Elliot. Whoever suffered inconvenience, she must suffer none, but it occupied a little time to settle the point of civility between the other two. The rain was a mere trifle, and Anne was most sincere in preferring a walk with Mr. Elliot. But the rain was also a mere trifle to Mrs. Clay; she would hardly allow it even to drop at all, and her boots were so thick! much thicker than Miss Anne's; and, in short, her civility rendered her quite as anxious to be left to walk with Mr. Elliot, as Anne could be, and it was discussed between them with a generosity so polite and so determined, that the others were obliged to settle it for them; Miss Elliot maintaining that Mrs. Clay had a little cold already, and Mr. Elliot deciding on appeal, that his cousin Anne's boots were rather the thickest.

It was fixed accordingly that Mrs. Clay should be of the party in the carriage; and they had just reached this point when Anne, as she sat near the window, descried, most decidedly and distinctly, Captain Wentworth walking down the street.

Her start was perceptible only to herself; but she instantly felt that she was the greatest simpleton in the world, the most unaccountable and absurd! For a few minutes she saw nothing before her. It was all confusion. She was lost; and when she had scolded back her senses, she found the others still waiting for the carriage, and Mr. Elliot (always obliging) just setting off for Union-street on a commission of Mrs. Clay's.

She now felt a great inclination to go to the outer door; she wanted to see if it rained. Why was she to suspect herself of another motive?

Captain Wentworth must be out of sight. She left her seat, she would go, one half of her should not be always so much wiser than the other half, or always suspecting the other of being worse than it was. She would see if it rained. She was sent back, however, in a moment by the entrance of Captain Wentworth himself, among a party of gentlemen and ladies, evidently his acquaintance, and whom he must have joined a little below Milsom-street. He was more obviously struck and confused by the sight of her, than she had ever observed before; he looked quite red. For the first time, since their renewed acquaintance, she felt that she was betraying the least sensibility of the two. She had the advantage of him, in the preparation of the last few moments. All the overpowering, blinding, bewildering, first effects of strong surprise were over with her. Still, however, she had enough to feel! It was agitation, pain, pleasure, a something between delight and misery.

He spoke to her, and then turned away. The character of his manner was embarrassment. She could not have called it either cold or friendly, or any thing so certainly as embarrassed.

After a short interval, however, he came towards her and spoke again. Mutual enquiries on common subjects passed; neither of them, probably, much the wiser for what they heard, and Anne continuing fully sensible of his being less at ease than formerly. They had, by dint of being so very much together, got to speak to each other with a considerable portion of apparent indifference and calmness; but he could not do it now. Time had changed him, or Louisa had changed him. There was consciousness of some sort or other. He looked very well, not as if he had been suffering in health or spirits, and he talked of Uppercross, of the Musgroves, nay, even of Louisa, and had even a momentary look of his own arch significance as he named her; but yet it was Captain Wentworth not comfortable, not easy, not able to feign that he was.

It did not surprise, but it grieved Anne to observe that Elizabeth would not know him. She saw that he saw Elizabeth, that Elizabeth saw him, that there was complete internal recognition on each side; she was convinced that he was ready to be acknowledged as an acquaintance, expecting it, and she had the pain of seeing her sister turn away with unalterable coldness.

Lady Dalrymple's carriage, for which Miss Elliot was growing very impatient, now drew up; the servant came in to announce it. It was beginning to rain again, and altogether there was a delay, and a bustle, and a talking, which must make all the little crowd in the shop understand that Lady Dalrymple was calling to convey Miss Elliot. At last Miss Elliot and her friend, unattended but by the servant, (for there was no cousin returned) were walking off; and Captain Wentworth, watching them, turned again to Anne, and by manner, rather than words, was offering his services to her.

'I am much obliged to you,' was her answer, 'but I am not going with them. The carriage would not accommodate so many. I walk. I prefer walking.'

'But it rains.'

'Oh! very little. Nothing that I regard.'

After a moment's pause he said, 'Though I came only yesterday, I have equipped myself properly for Bath already,* you see,' (pointing to a new umbrella) 'I wish you would make use of it, if you are determined to walk; though, I think, it would be more prudent to let me get you a chair.'*

She was very much obliged to him, but declined it all, repeating her conviction, that the rain would come to nothing at present, and adding, 'I am only waiting for Mr. Elliot. He will be here in a moment, I am sure.'

She had hardly spoken the words, when Mr. Elliot walked in. Captain Wentworth recollected him perfectly. There was no difference between him and the man who had stood on the steps at Lyme, admiring Anne as she passed, except in the air and look and manner of the privileged relation and friend. He came in with eagerness, appeared to see and think only of her, apologised for his stay, was grieved to have kept her waiting, and anxious to get her away without further loss of time, and before the rain increased; and in another moment they walked off together, her arm under his, a gentle and embarrassed glance, and a 'good morning to you,' being all that she had time for, as she passed away.

As soon as they were out of sight, the ladies of Captain Wentworth's party began talking of them.

'Mr. Elliot does not dislike his cousin, I fancy?'

'Oh! no, that is clear enough. One can guess what will happen there. He is always with them; half lives in the family, I believe. What a very good-looking man!'

'Yes, and Miss Atkinson, who dined with him once at the

Wallises, says he is the most agreeable man she ever was in company with.'

'She is pretty, I think; Anne Elliot; very pretty, when one comes to look at her. It is not the fashion to say so, but I confess I admire her more than her sister.'

'Oh! so do I.'

'And so do I. No comparison. But the men are all wild after Miss Elliot. Anne is too delicate for them.'

Anne would have been particularly obliged to her cousin, if he would have walked by her side all the way to Camden-place, without saying a word. She had never found it so difficult to listen to him, though nothing could exceed his solicitude and care, and though his subjects were principally such as were wont to be always interesting—praise, warm, just, and discriminating, of Lady Russell, and insinuations highly rational against Mrs. Clay. But just now she could think only of Captain Wentworth. She could not understand his present feelings, whether he were really suffering much from disappointment or not; and till that point were settled, she could not be quite herself.

She hoped to be wise and reasonable in time; but alas! alas! she must confess to herself that she was not wise yet.

Another circumstance very essential for her to know, was how long he meant to be in Bath; he had not mentioned it, or she could not recollect it. He might be only passing through. But it was more probable that he should be come to stay. In that case, so liable as every body was to meet every body in Bath, Lady Russell would in all likelihood see him somewhere.—Would she recollect him? How would it all be?

She had already been obliged to tell Lady Russell that Louisa Musgrove was to marry Captain Benwick. It had cost her something to encounter Lady Russell's surprise; and now, if she were by any chance to be thrown into company with Captain Wentworth, her imperfect knowledge of the matter might add another shade of prejudice against him.

The following morning Anne was out with her friend, and for the first hour, in an incessant and fearful sort of watch for him in vain; but at last, in returning down Pulteney-street, she distinguished him on the right hand pavement at such a distance as to have him in view the greater part of the street. There were many other men about him, many groups walking the same way, but there was no mistaking him. She looked instinctively at Lady Russell; but not from any mad idea of her recognising him so soon as she did herself. No, it was not to be supposed that Lady Russell would perceive him till they were nearly opposite. She looked at her however, from time to time, anxiously; and when the moment approached which must point him out, though not daring to look again (for her own countenance she knew was unfit to be seen), she was yet perfectly conscious of Lady Russell's eyes being turned exactly in the direction for him, of her being in short intently observing him. She could thoroughly comprehend the sort of fascination he must possess over Lady Russell's mind, the difficulty it must be for her to withdraw her eyes, the astonishment she must be feeling that eight or nine years should have passed over him, and in foreign climes and in active service too, without robbing him of one personal grace!

At last, Lady Russell drew back her head.—'Now, how would she speak of him?'

'You will wonder,' said she, 'what has been fixing my eye so long; but I was looking after some window-curtains, which Lady Alicia and Mrs. Frankland were telling me of last night. They described the drawing-room window-curtains of one of the houses on this side of the way, and this part of the street, as being the handsomest and best hung of any in Bath, but could not recollect the exact number, and I have been trying to find out which it could be; but I confess I can see no curtains hereabouts that answer their description.'

Anne sighed and blushed and smiled, in pity and disdain, either at her friend or herself.—The part which provoked her most, was that in all this waste of foresight and caution, she should have lost the right moment for seeing whether he saw them.

A day or two passed without producing any thing.—The theatre or the rooms,* where he was most likely to be, were not fashionable enough for the Elliots, whose evening amusements were solely in the elegant stupidity of private parties, in which they were getting more and more engaged; and Anne, wearied of such a state of stagnation, sick of knowing nothing, and fancying herself stronger because her strength was not tried, was quite impatient for the concert evening. It was a concert for the benefit of a person patronised by Lady Dalrymple. Of course they must attend. It was really expected to be a good one, and Captain Wentworth was very fond of music. If she could only have a few minutes conversation with him again, she fancied she should be satisfied; and as to the power of addressing him she felt all over courage if the opportunity occurred. Elizabeth had turned from him, Lady Russell overlooked him; her nerves were strengthened by these circumstances; she felt that she owed him attention.

She had once partly promised Mrs. Smith to spend the evening with her; but in a short hurried call she excused herself and put it off, with the more decided promise of a longer visit on the morrow. Mrs. Smith gave a most good-humoured acquiescence.

'By all means,' said she; 'only tell me all about it, when you do come. Who is your party?'

Anne named them all. Mrs. Smith made no reply; but when she was leaving her, said, and with an expression half serious, half arch, 'Well, I heartily wish your concert may answer; and do not fail me to-morrow if you can come; for I begin to have a foreboding that I may not have many more visits from you.'

Anne was startled and confused, but after standing in a moment's suspense, was obliged, and not sorry to be obliged, to hurry away.

CHAPTER VIII

SIR WALTER, his two daughters, and Mrs. Clay, were the earliest of all their party, at the rooms in the evening; and as Lady Dalrymple must be waited for, they took their station by one of the fires in the octagon room.* But hardly were they so settled, when the door opened again, and Captain Wentworth walked in alone. Anne was the nearest to him, and making yet a little advance, she instantly spoke. He was preparing only to bow and pass on, but her gentle 'How do you do?' brought him out of the straight line to stand near her, and make enquiries in return, in spite of the formidable father and sister in the back ground. Their being in the back ground was a support to Anne; she knew nothing of their looks, and felt equal to every thing which she believed right to be done.

While they were speaking, a whispering between her father and Elizabeth caught her ear. She could not distinguish, but she must guess the subject; and on Captain Wentworth's making a distant bow, she comprehended that her father had judged so well as to give him that simple acknowledgment of acquaintance, and she was just in time by a side glance to see a slight curtsey from Elizabeth herself. This, though late and reluctant and ungracious, was yet better than nothing, and her spirits improved.

After talking however of the weather and Bath and the concert, their conversation began to flag, and so little was said at last, that she was expecting him to go every moment; but he did not; he seemed in no hurry to leave her; and presently with renewed spirit, with a little smile, a little glow, he said,

'I have hardly seen you since our day at Lyme. I am afraid you must have suffered from the shock, and the more from its not overpowering you at the time.'

She assured him that she had not.

'It was a frightful hour,' said he, 'a frightful day!' and he passed his hand across his eyes, as if the remembrance were still too painful; but in a moment half smiling again, added, 'The day has produced some effects however—has had some consequences which must be considered as the very reverse of frightful.—When you had the presence of mind to suggest that Benwick would be the properest person to fetch a surgeon, you could have little idea of his being eventually one of those most concerned in her recovery.'

'Certainly I could have none. But it appears—I should hope it would be a very happy match. There are on both sides good principles and good temper.'

'Yes,' said he, looking not exactly forward—'but there I think ends the resemblance. With all my soul I wish them happy, and rejoice over every circumstance in favour of it. They have no difficulties to contend with at home, no opposition, no caprice, no delays.—The Musgroves are behaving like themselves, most honourably and kindly, only anxious with true parental hearts to promote their daughter's comfort. All this is much, very much in favour of their happiness; more than perhaps—'

He stopped. A sudden recollection seemed to occur, and to give him some taste of that emotion which was reddening Anne's cheeks and fixing her eyes on the ground.—After clearing his throat, however, he proceeded thus,

'I confess that I do think there is a disparity, too great a disparity, and in a point no less essential than mind.—I regard Louisa Musgrove as a very amiable, sweet-tempered girl, and not deficient in understanding; but Benwick is something more. He is a clever man, a reading man—and I confess that I do consider his attaching himself to her, with some surprise. Had it been the effect of gratitude, had he learnt to love her, because he believed her to be preferring him, it would have been another thing. But I have no reason to suppose it so. It seems, on the contrary, to have been a perfectly spontaneous, untaught feeling on his side, and this surprises me. A man like him, in his situation! With a heart pierced, wounded, almost broken! Fanny Harville was a very superior creature; and his attachment to her was indeed attachment. A man does not recover from such a devotion of the heart to such a woman!—He ought not—he does not.'

Either from the consciousness, however, that his friend had recovered, or from some other consciousness, he went no farther; and Anne, who, in spite of the agitated voice in which the latter part had been uttered, and in spite of all the various noises of the room, the almost ceaseless slam of the door, and ceaseless buzz of persons walking through, had distinguished every word, was struck, gratified, confused, and beginning to breathe very quick, and feel an hundred things in a moment. It was impossible for her to enter on such a subject; and yet, after a pause, feeling the necessity of speaking, and having not the smallest wish for a total change, she only deviated so far as to say,

'You were a good while at Lyme, I think?'

'About a fortnight. I could not leave it till Louisa's doing well was quite ascertained. I had been too deeply concerned in the mischief to be soon at peace. It had been my doing—solely mine. She would not have been obstinate if I had not been weak. The country round Lyme is very fine. I walked and rode a great deal; and the more I saw, the more I found to admire.'

'I should very much like to see Lyme again,' said Anne.

'Indeed! I should not have supposed that you could have found any thing in Lyme to inspire such a feeling. The horror and distress you were involved in—the stretch of mind, the wear of spirits!—I should have thought your last impressions of Lyme must have been strong disgust.'

'The last few hours were certainly very painful,' replied Anne: 'but when pain is over, the remembrance of it often becomes a pleasure. One does not love a place the less for having suffered in it, unless it has been all suffering, nothing but suffering—which was by no means the case at Lyme. We were only in anxiety and distress during the last two hours; and, previously, there had been a great deal of enjoyment. So much novelty and beauty! I have travelled so little, that every fresh place would be interesting to me—but there is real beauty at Lyme: and in short' (with a faint blush at some recollections) 'altogether my impressions of the place are very agreeable.'

As she ceased, the entrance door opened again, and the very party appeared for whom they were waiting. 'Lady Dalrymple, Lady Dalrymple,' was the rejoicing sound; and with all the eagerness compatible with anxious elegance, Sir Walter and his two ladies stepped forward to meet her. Lady Dalrymple and Miss Carteret, escorted by Mr. Elliot and Colonel Wallis, who had happened to arrive nearly at the same instant, advanced into the room. The others joined them, and it was a group in which Anne found herself also necessarily included. She was divided from Captain Wentworth. Their interesting, almost too interesting conversation must be broken up for a time; but slight was the penance compared with the happiness which brought it on! She had learnt, in the last ten minutes, more of his feelings towards Louisa, more of all his feelings, than she dared to think of! and she gave herself up to the demands of the party, to the needful civilities of the moment, with exquisite, though agitated sensations. She was in good humour with all. She had received ideas which disposed her to be courteous and kind to all, and to pity every one, as being less happy than herself.

The delightful emotions were a little subdued, when, on stepping back from the group, to be joined again by Captain Wentworth, she saw that he was gone. She was just in time to see him turn into the concert room. He was gone—he had disappeared: she felt a moment's regret. But 'they should meet again. He would look for her—he would find her out long before the evening were over—and at present, perhaps, it was as well to be asunder. She was in need of a little interval for recollection.'

Upon Lady Russell's appearance soon afterwards, the whole party was collected, and all that remained, was to marshal themselves, and proceed into the concert room; and be of all the consequence in their power, draw as many eyes, excite as many whispers, and disturb as many people as they could.

Very, very happy were both Elizabeth and Anne Elliot as they

walked in. Elizabeth, arm in arm with Miss Carteret, and looking on
the broad back of the dowager Viscountess Dalrymple before her,
had nothing to wish for which did not seem within her reach; and
Anne——but it would be an insult to the nature of Anne's felicity, to
draw any comparison between it and her sister's; the origin of one all
selfish vanity, of the other all generous attachment.

Anne saw nothing, thought nothing of the brilliancy of the room.
Her happiness was from within. Her eyes were bright, and her
cheeks glowed,—but she knew nothing about it. She was thinking
only of the last half hour, and as they passed to their seats, her mind
took a hasty range over it. His choice of subjects, his expressions, and
still more his manner and look, had been such as she could see in
only one light. His opinion of Louisa Musgrove's inferiority, an
opinion which he had seemed solicitous to give, his wonder at Captain Benwick, his feelings as to a first, strong attachment,—
sentences begun which he could not finish—his half averted eyes,
and more than half expressive glance,—all, all declared that he had a
heart returning to her at least; that anger, resentment, avoidance,
were no more; and that they were succeeded, not merely by friendship and regard, but by the tenderness of the past; yes, some share of
the tenderness of the past. She could not contemplate the change as
implying less.—He must love her.

These were thoughts, with their attendant visions, which occupied and flurried her too much to leave her any power of observation;
and she passed along the room without having a glimpse of him,
without even trying to discern him. When their places were determined on, and they were all properly arranged, she looked round to
see if he should happen to be in the same part of the room, but he
was not, her eye could not reach him; and the concert being just
opening, she must consent for a time to be happy in an humbler way.

The party was divided, and disposed of on two contiguous
benches: Anne was among those on the foremost, and Mr. Elliot had
manœuvred so well, with the assistance of his friend Colonel Wallis,
as to have a seat by her. Miss Elliot, surrounded by her cousins, and
the principal object of Colonel Wallis's gallantry, was quite
contented.

Anne's mind was in a most favourable state for the entertainment
of the evening: it was just occupation enough: she had feelings for
the tender, spirits for the gay, attention for the scientific, and

patience for the wearisome; and had never liked a concert better, at least during the first act. Towards the close of it, in the interval succeeding an Italian song, she explained the words of the song to Mr. Elliot.—They had a concert bill between them.

'This,' said she, 'is nearly the sense, or rather the meaning of the words, for certainly the sense of an Italian love-song must not be talked of,—but it is as nearly the meaning as I can give; for I do not pretend to understand the language. I am a very poor Italian scholar.'

'Yes, yes, I see you are. I see you know nothing of the matter. You have only knowledge enough of the language, to translate at sight these inverted, transposed, curtailed Italian lines, into clear, comprehensible, elegant English. You need not say anything more of your ignorance.—Here is complete proof.'

'I will not oppose such kind politeness; but I should be sorry to be examined by a real proficient.'

'I have not had the pleasure of visiting in Camden-place so long,' replied he, 'without knowing something of Miss Anne Elliot; and I do regard her as one who is too modest, for the world in general to be aware of half her accomplishments, and too highly accomplished for modesty to be natural in any other woman.'

'For shame! for shame!—this is too much of flattery. I forget what we are to have next,' turning to the bill.

'Perhaps,' said Mr. Elliot, speaking low, 'I have had a longer acquaintance with your character than you are aware of.'

'Indeed!—How so? You can have been acquainted with it only since I came to Bath, excepting as you might hear me previously spoken of in my own family.'

'I knew you by report long before you came to Bath. I had heard you described by those who knew you intimately. I have been acquainted with you by character many years. Your person, your disposition, accomplishments, manner—they were all described, they were all present to me.'

Mr. Elliot was not disappointed in the interest he hoped to raise. No one can withstand the charm of such a mystery. To have been described long ago to a recent acquaintance, by nameless people, is irresistible; and Anne was all curiosity. She wondered, and questioned him eagerly—but in vain. He delighted in being asked, but he would not tell.

'No, no—some time or other perhaps, but not now. He would

mention no names now; but such, he could assure her, had been the fact. He had many years ago received such a description of Miss Anne Elliot, as had inspired him with the highest idea of her merit, and excited the warmest curiosity to know her.'

Anne could think of no one so likely to have spoken with partiality of her many years ago, as the Mr. Wentworth, of Monkford, Captain Wentworth's brother. He might have been in Mr. Elliot's company, but she had not courage to ask the question.

'The name of Anne Elliot,' said he, 'has long had an interesting sound to me. Very long has it possessed a charm over my fancy; and, if I dared, I would breathe my wishes that the name might never change.'*

Such she believed were his words; but scarcely had she received their sound, than her attention was caught by other sounds immediately behind her, which rendered every thing else trivial. Her father and Lady Dalrymple were speaking.

'A well-looking man,' said Sir Walter, 'a very well-looking man.'

'A very fine young man indeed!' said Lady Dalrymple. 'More air than one often sees in Bath.—Irish, I dare say.'

'No, I just know his name. A bowing acquaintance. Wentworth— Captain Wentworth of the navy. His sister married my tenant in Somersetshire,—the Croft, who rents Kellynch.'

Before Sir Walter had reached this point, Anne's eyes had caught the right direction, and distinguished Captain Wentworth, standing among a cluster of men at a little distance. As her eyes fell on him, his seemed to be withdrawn from her. It had that appearance. It seemed as if she had been one moment too late; and as long as she dared observe, he did not look again: but the performance was re-commencing, and she was forced to seem to restore her attention to the orchestra, and look straight forward.

When she could give another glance, he had moved away. He could not have come nearer to her if he would; she was so surrounded and shut in: but she would rather have caught his eye.

Mr. Elliot's speech too distressed her. She had no longer any inclination to talk to him. She wished him not so near her.

The first act was over. Now she hoped for some beneficial change; and, after a period of nothing-saying amongst the party, some of them did decide on going in quest of tea. Anne was one of the few who did not choose to move. She remained in her seat, and so did

Lady Russell; but she had the pleasure of getting rid of Mr. Elliot; and she did not mean, whatever she might feel on Lady Russell's account, to shrink from conversation with Captain Wentworth, if he gave her the opportunity. She was persuaded by Lady Russell's countenance that she had seen him.

He did not come however. Anne sometimes fancied she discerned him at a distance, but he never came. The anxious interval wore away unproductively. The others returned, the room filled again, benches were reclaimed and re-possessed, and another hour of pleasure or of penance was to be set out, another hour of music was to give delight or the gapes,* as real or affected taste for it prevailed. To Anne, it chiefly wore the prospect of an hour of agitation. She could not quit that room in peace without seeing Captain Wentworth once more, without the interchange of one friendly look.

In re-settling themselves, there were now many changes, the result of which was favourable for her. Colonel Wallis declined sitting down again, and Mr. Elliot was invited by Elizabeth and Miss Carteret, in a manner not to be refused, to sit between them; and by some other removals, and a little scheming of her own, Anne was enabled to place herself much nearer the end of the bench than she had been before, much more within reach of a passer-by. She could not do so, without comparing herself with Miss Larolles, the inimitable Miss Larolles,*—but still she did it, and not with much happier effect; though by what seemed prosperity in the shape of an early abdication in her next neighbours, she found herself at the very end of the bench before the concert closed.

Such was her situation, with a vacant space at hand, when Captain Wentworth was again in sight. She saw him not far off. He saw her too; yet he looked grave, and seemed irresolute, and only by very slow degrees came at last near enough to speak to her. She felt that something must be the matter. The change was indubitable. The difference between his present air and what it had been in the octagon room was strikingly great.—Why was it? She thought of her father—of Lady Russell. Could there have been any unpleasant glances? He began by speaking of the concert, gravely; more like the Captain Wentworth of Uppercross; owned himself disappointed, had expected better singing; and, in short, must confess that he should not be sorry when it was over. Anne replied, and spoke in defence of the performance so well, and yet in allowance for his feelings, so pleasantly, that his countenance improved, and he replied again with almost a smile. They talked for a few minutes more; the improvement held; he even looked down towards the bench, as if he saw a place on it well worth occupying; when, at that moment, a touch on her shoulder obliged Anne to turn round.—It came from Mr. Elliot. He begged her pardon, but she must be applied to, to explain Italian again. Miss Carteret was very anxious to have a general idea of what was next to be sung. Anne could not refuse; but never had she sacrificed to politeness with a more suffering spirit.

A few minutes, though as few as possible, were inevitably consumed; and when her own mistress again, when able to turn and look as she had done before, she found herself accosted by Captain Wentworth, in a reserved yet hurried sort of farewell. 'He must wish her good night. He was going—he should get home as fast as he could.'

'Is not this song worth staying for?' said Anne, suddenly struck by an idea which made her yet more anxious to be encouraging.

'No!' he replied impressively, 'there is nothing worth my staying for;' and he was gone directly.

Jealousy of Mr. Elliot! It was the only intelligible motive. Captain Wentworth jealous of her affection! Could she have believed it a week ago—three hours ago! For a moment the gratification was exquisite. But alas! there were very different thoughts to succeed. How was such jealousy to be quieted? How was the truth to reach him? How, in all the peculiar disadvantages of their respective situations, would he ever learn her real sentiments? It was misery to think of Mr. Elliot's attentions.—Their evil was incalculable.

CHAPTER IX

ANNE recollected with pleasure the next morning her promise of going to Mrs. Smith; meaning that it should engage her from home at the time when Mr. Elliot would be most likely to call; for to avoid Mr. Elliot was almost a first object.

She felt a great deal of good will towards him. In spite of the mischief of his attentions, she owed him gratitude and regard, perhaps compassion. She could not help thinking much of the extraordinary circumstances attending their acquaintance; of the right which he seemed to have to interest her, by every thing in situation, by his own sentiments, by his early prepossession. It was altogether very extraordinary.—Flattering, but painful. There was much to regret. How she might have felt, had there been no Captain Wentworth in the case, was not worth enquiry; for there was a Captain Wentworth: and be the conclusion of the present suspense good or bad, her affection would be his for ever. Their union, she believed, could not divide her more from other men, than their final separation.

Prettier musings of high-wrought love and eternal constancy, could never have passed along the streets of Bath, than Anne was sporting with from Camden-place to Westgate-buildings. It was almost enough to spread purification and perfume all the way.

She was sure of a pleasant reception; and her friend seemed this morning particularly obliged to her for coming, seemed hardly to have expected her, though it had been an appointment.

An account of the concert was immediately claimed; and Anne's recollections of the concert were quite happy enough to animate her features, and make her rejoice to talk of it. All that she could tell, she told most gladly; but the all was little for one who had been there, and unsatisfactory for such an enquirer as Mrs. Smith, who had already heard, through the short cut of a laundress and a waiter, rather more of the general success and produce of the evening than Anne could relate; and who now asked in vain for several particulars of the company. Every body of any consequence or notoriety in Bath was well known by name to Mrs. Smith.

'The little Durands were there, I conclude,' said she, 'with their mouths open to catch the music; like unfledged sparrows ready to be fed. They never miss a concert.'

'Yes. I did not see them myself, but I heard Mr. Elliot say they were in the room.'

'The Ibbotsons—were they there? and the two new beauties, with the tall Irish officer, who is talked of for one of them.'

'I do not know. I do not think they were.'

'Old Lady Mary Maclean? I need not ask after her. She never misses, I know; and you must have seen her. She must have been in your own circle, for as you went with Lady Dalrymple, you were in the seats of grandeur; round the orchestra, of course.'

'No, that was what I dreaded. It would have been very unpleasant to me in every respect. But happily Lady Dalrymple always chooses to be farther off; and we were exceedingly well placed—that is for hearing; I must not say for seeing, because I appear to have seen very little.'

'Oh! you saw enough for your own amusement.—I can understand. There is a sort of domestic enjoyment to be known even in a crowd, and this you had. You were a large party in yourselves, and you wanted nothing beyond.'

'But I ought to have looked about me more,' said Anne, conscious while she spoke, that there had in fact been no want of looking about; that the object only had been deficient.

'No, no—you were better employed. You need not tell me that you had a pleasant evening. I see it in your eye. I perfectly see how the hours passed—that you had always something agreeable to listen to. In the intervals of the concert, it was conversation.'

Anne half smiled and said, 'Do you see that in my eye?'

'Yes, I do. Your countenance perfectly informs me that you were in company last night with the person, whom you think the most agreeable in the world, the person who interests you at this present time, more than all the rest of the world put together.'

A blush overspread Anne's cheeks. She could say nothing.

'And such being the case,' continued Mrs. Smith, after a short pause, 'I hope you believe that I do know how to value your kindness in coming to me this morning. It is really very good of you to come and sit with me, when you must have so many pleasanter demands upon your time.'

Anne heard nothing of this. She was still in the astonishment and confusion excited by her friend's penetration, unable to imagine how any report of Captain Wentworth could have reached her. After another short silence—

'Pray,' said Mrs. Smith, 'is Mr. Elliot aware of your acquaintance with me? Does he know that I am in Bath?'

'Mr. Elliot!' repeated Anne, looking up surprised. A moment's reflection shewed her the mistake she had been under. She caught it instantaneously; and, recovering courage with the feeling of safety, soon added, more composedly, 'are you acquainted with Mr. Elliot?'

'I have been a good deal acquainted with him,' replied Mrs. Smith, gravely, 'but it seems worn out now. It is a great while since we met.'

'I was not at all aware of this. You never mentioned it before. Had I known it, I would have had the pleasure of talking to him about you.'

'To confess the truth,' said Mrs. Smith, assuming her usual air of cheerfulness, 'that is exactly the pleasure I want you to have. I want you to talk about me to Mr. Elliot. I want your interest with him. He can be of essential service to me; and if you would have the goodness, my dear Miss Elliot, to make it an object to yourself, of course it is done.'

'I should be extremely happy—I hope you cannot doubt my willingness to be of even the slightest use to you,' replied Anne; 'but I suspect that you are considering me as having a higher claim on Mr. Elliot—a greater right to influence him, than is really the case. I am sure you have, somehow or other, imbibed such a notion. You must consider me only as Mr. Elliot's relation. If in that light, if there is any thing which you suppose his cousin might fairly ask of him, I beg you would not hesitate to employ me.'

Mrs. Smith gave her a penetrating glance, and then, smiling, said,

'I have been a little premature, I perceive. I beg your pardon. I ought to have waited for official information. But now, my dear Miss Elliot, as an old friend, do give me a hint as to when I may speak. Next week? To be sure by next week I may be allowed to think it all settled, and build my own selfish schemes on Mr. Elliot's good fortune.'

'No,' replied Anne, 'nor next week, nor next, nor next. I assure you that nothing of the sort you are thinking of will be settled any week. I am not going to marry Mr. Elliot. I should like to know why you imagine I am.'

Mrs. Smith looked at her again, looked earnestly, smiled, shook her head, and exclaimed.

'Now, how I do wish I understood you! How I do wish I knew what you were at! I have a great idea that you do not design to be cruel, when the right moment comes. Till it does come, you know, we women never mean to have any body. It is a thing of course among us, that every man is refused—till he offers. But why should you be cruel? Let me plead for my—present friend I cannot call him—but for my former friend. Where can you look for a more suitable match? Where could you expect a more gentlemanlike, agreeable man? Let me recommend Mr. Elliot. I am sure you hear nothing but good of him from Colonel Wallis; and who can know him better than Colonel Wallis?'

'My dear Mrs. Smith, Mr. Elliot's wife has not been dead much above half a year. He ought not to be supposed to be paying his addresses to any one.'

'Oh! if these are your only objections,' cried Mrs. Smith, archly, 'Mr. Elliot is safe, and I shall give myself no more trouble about him. Do not forget me when you are married, that's all. Let him know me to be a friend of yours, and then he will think little of the trouble required, which it is very natural for him now, with so many affairs and engagements of his own, to avoid and get rid of as he can—very natural, perhaps. Ninety-nine out of a hundred would do the same. Of course, he cannot be aware of the importance to me. Well, my dear Miss Elliot, I hope and trust you will be very happy. Mr. Elliot has sense to understand the value of such a woman. Your peace will not be shipwrecked as mine has been. You are safe in all worldly matters, and safe in his character. He will not be led astray, he will not be misled by others to his ruin.'

'No,' said Anne, 'I can readily believe all that of my cousin. He seems to have a calm, decided temper, not at all open to dangerous impressions. I consider him with great respect. I have no reason, from any thing that has fallen within my observation, to do otherwise. But I have not known him long; and he is not a man, I think, to be known intimately soon. Will not this manner of speaking of him, Mrs. Smith, convince you that he is nothing to me? Surely, this must be calm enough. And, upon my word, he is nothing to me. Should he ever propose to me (which I have very little reason to imagine he has any thought of doing), I shall not accept him. I assure you I shall not. I assure you Mr. Elliot had not the share which you have been supposing, in whatever pleasure the concert of last night might afford:—not Mr. Elliot; it is not Mr. Elliot that—'

She stopped, regretting with a deep blush that she had implied so much; but less would hardly have been sufficient. Mrs. Smith would hardly have believed so soon in Mr. Elliot's failure, but from the perception of there being a somebody else. As it was, she instantly submitted, and with all the semblance of seeing nothing beyond; and Anne, eager to escape farther notice, was impatient to know why Mrs. Smith should have fancied she was to marry Mr. Elliot, where she could have received the idea, or from whom she could have heard it.

'Do tell me how it first came into your head.'

'It first came into my head,' replied Mrs. Smith, 'upon finding how much you were together, and feeling it to be the most probable thing in the world to be wished for by every body belonging to either of you; and you may depend upon it that all your acquaintance have disposed of you in the same way. But I never heard it spoken of till two days ago.'

'And has it indeed been spoken of?'

'Did you observe the woman who opened the door to you, when you called yesterday?'

'No. Was not it Mrs. Speed, as usual, or the maid? I observed no one in particular.'

'It was my friend, Mrs. Rooke—Nurse Rooke, who, by the by, had a great curiosity to see you, and was delighted to be in the way to let you in. She came away from Marlborough-buildings only on Sunday; and she it was who told me you were to marry Mr. Elliot. She had had it from Mrs. Wallis herself, which did not seem bad authority. She sat an hour with me on Monday evening, and gave me the whole history.'

'The whole history!' repeated Anne, laughing. 'She could not make a very long history, I think, of one such little article of unfounded news.'

Mrs. Smith said nothing.

'But,' continued Anne, presently, 'though there is no truth in my having this claim on Mr. Elliot, I should be extremely happy to be of use to you, in any way that I could. Shall I mention to him your being in Bath? Shall I take any message?'

'No, I thank you: no, certainly not. In the warmth of the moment, and under a mistaken impression, I might, perhaps, have endeavoured to interest you in some circumstances. But not now: no, I thank you, I have nothing to trouble you with.'

'I think you spoke of having known Mr. Elliot many years?'

'I did.'

'Not before he married, I suppose?'

'Yes; he was not married when I knew him first.'

'And—were you much acquainted?'

'Intimately.'

'Indeed! Then do tell me what he was at that time of life. I have a great curiosity to know what Mr. Elliot was as a very young man. Was he at all such as he appears now?'

'I have not seen Mr. Elliot these three years,' was Mrs. Smith's answer, given so gravely that it was impossible to pursue the subject farther; and Anne felt that she had gained nothing but an increase of curiosity. They were both silent—Mrs. Smith very thoughtful. At last,

'I beg your pardon, my dear Miss Elliot,' she cried, in her natural tone of cordiality, 'I beg your pardon for the short answers I have been giving you, but I have been uncertain what I ought to do. I have been doubting and considering as to what I ought to tell you. There were many things to be taken into the account. One hates to be officious, to be giving bad impressions, making mischief. Even the smooth surface of family-union seems worth preserving, though there may be nothing durable beneath. However, I have determined; I think I am right; I think you ought to be made acquainted with Mr. Elliot's real character. Though I fully believe that, at present, you have not the smallest intention of accepting him, there is no saying what may happen. You might, some time or other, be differently affected towards him. Hear the truth, therefore, now, while you are unprejudiced. Mr. Elliot is a man without heart or conscience; a designing, wary, cold-blooded being, who thinks only of himself; who, for his own interest or ease, would be guilty of any cruelty, or any treachery, that could be perpetrated without risk of his general character. He has no feeling for others. Those whom he has been the chief cause of leading into ruin, he can neglect and desert without the smallest compunction. He is totally beyond the reach of any sentiment of justice or compassion. Oh! he is black at heart, hollow and black!'

Anne's astonished air, and exclamation of wonder, made her pause, and in a calmer manner she added,

'My expressions startle you. You must allow for an injured, angry woman. But I will try to command myself. I will not abuse him. I will only tell you what I have found him. Facts shall speak. He was the intimate friend of my dear husband, who trusted and loved him, and thought him as good as himself. The intimacy had been formed before our marriage. I found them most intimate friends; and I, too, became excessively pleased with Mr. Elliot, and entertained the highest opinion of him. At nineteen, you know, one does not think very seriously, but Mr. Elliot appeared to me quite as good as others, and much more agreeable than most others, and we were almost always together. We were principally in town, living in very good style. He was then the inferior in circumstances, he was then the poor one; he had chambers in the Temple,* and it was as much as he could do to support the appearance of a gentleman. He had always a home with us whenever he chose it; he was always welcome; he was like a brother. My poor Charles, who had the finest, most generous spirit in the world, would have divided his last farthing with him; and I know that his purse was open to him; I know that he often assisted him.'

'This must have been about that very period of Mr. Elliot's life,' said Anne, 'which has always excited my particular curiosity. It must have been about the same time that he became known to my father and sister. I never knew him myself, I only heard of him, but there was a something in his conduct then with regard to my father and sister, and afterwards in the circumstances of his marriage, which I never could quite reconcile with present times. It seemed to announce a different sort of man.'

'I know it all, I know it all,' cried Mrs. Smith. 'He had been introduced to Sir Walter and your sister before I was acquainted with him, but I heard him speak of them for ever. I know he was invited and encouraged, and I know he did not choose to go. I can satisfy you, perhaps, on points which you would little expect; and as to his marriage, I knew all about it at the time. I was privy to all the fors and againsts, I was the friend to whom he confided his hopes and plans, and though I did not know his wife previously, (her inferior situation in society, indeed, rendered that impossible) yet I knew her all her life afterwards, or, at least, till within the last two years of her life, and can answer any question you wish to put.'

'Nay,' said Anne, 'I have no particular enquiry to make about her. I have always understood they were not a happy couple. But I should like to know why, at that time of his life, he should slight my father's acquaintance as he did. My father was certainly disposed to take very kind and proper notice of him. Why did Mr. Elliot draw back?'

'Mr. Elliot,' replied Mrs. Smith, 'at that period of his life, had one object in view—to make his fortune, and by a rather quicker process than the law. He was determined to make it by marriage. He was determined, at least, not to mar it by an imprudent marriage; and I know it was his belief, (whether justly or not, of course I cannot decide) that your father and sister, in their civilities and invitations, were designing a match between the heir and the young lady; and it was impossible that such a match should have answered his ideas of wealth and independance. That was his motive for drawing back, I can assure you. He told me the whole story. He had no concealments with me. It was curious, that having just left you behind me in Bath, my first and principal acquaintance on marrying, should be your cousin; and that, through him, I should be continually hearing of your father and sister. He described one Miss Elliot, and I thought very affectionately of the other.'

'Perhaps,' cried Anne, struck by a sudden idea, 'you sometimes spoke of me to Mr. Elliot?'

'To be sure I did, very often. I used to boast of my own Anne Elliot and vouch for your being a very different creature from—'

She checked herself just in time.

'This accounts for something which Mr. Elliot said last night,' cried Anne. 'This explains it. I found he had been used to hear of me. I could not comprehend how. What wild imaginations one forms, where dear self is concerned! How sure to be mistaken! But I beg your pardon; I have interrupted you. Mr. Elliot married, then, completely for money? The circumstance, probably, which first opened your eyes to his character.'

Mrs. Smith hesitated a little here. 'Oh! those things are too common. When one lives in the world, a man or woman's marrying for money is too common to strike one as it ought. I was very young, and associated only with the young, and we were a thoughtless, gay set, without any strict rules of conduct. We lived for enjoyment. I think differently now; time and sickness, and sorrow, have given me other notions; but, at that period, I must own I saw nothing reprehensible in what Mr. Elliot was doing. "To do the best for himself," passed as a duty.'

'But was not she a very low woman?'

'Yes; which I objected to, but he would not regard. Money, money, was all that he wanted. Her father was a grazier, her grandfather had been a butcher, but that was all nothing. She was a fine woman, had had a decent education, was brought forward by some cousins, thrown by chance into Mr. Elliot's company, and fell in love with him; and not a difficulty or a scruple was there on his side, with respect to her birth. All his caution was spent in being secured of the real amount of her fortune, before he committed himself. Depend upon it, whatever esteem Mr. Elliot may have for his own situation in life now, as a young man he had not the smallest value for it. His chance of the Kellynch estate was something, but all the honour of the family he held as cheap as dirt. I have often heard him declare, that if baronetcies were saleable, any body should have his for fifty pounds, arms and motto, name and livery included; but I will not pretend to repeat half that I used to hear him say on that subject. It would not be fair. And yet you ought to have proof; for what is all this but assertion? and you shall have proof.'

'Indeed, my dear Mrs. Smith, I want none,' cried Anne. 'You have asserted nothing contradictory to what Mr. Elliot appeared to be some years ago. This is all in confirmation, rather, of what we used to hear and believe. I am more curious to know why he should be so different now?'

'But for my satisfaction; if you will have the goodness to ring for Mary—stay, I am sure you will have the still greater goodness of going yourself into my bed-room, and bringing me the small inlaid box which you will find on the upper shelf of the closet.'

Anne, seeing her friend to be earnestly bent on it, did as she was desired. The box was brought and placed before her, and Mrs. Smith, sighing over it as she unlocked it, said,

'This is full of papers belonging to him, to my husband, a small portion only of what I had to look over when I lost him. The letter I am looking for, was one written by Mr. Elliot to him before our marriage, and happened to be saved; why, one can hardly imagine. But he was careless and immethodical, like other men, about those things; and when I came to examine his papers, I found it with others still more trivial from different people scattered here and there, while many letters and memorandums of real importance had been destroyed. Here it is. I would not burn it, because being even then very little satisfied with Mr. Elliot, I was determined to preserve every document of former intimacy. I have now another motive for being glad that I can produce it.'

This was the letter, directed to 'Charles Smith, Esq. Tunbridge Wells,' and dated from London, as far back as July, 1803.

'Dear Smith,

'I have received yours. Your kindness almost overpowers me. I wish nature had made such hearts as yours more common, but I have lived three and twenty years in the world, and have seen none like it. At present, believe me, I have no need of your services, being in cash again. Give me joy:* I have got rid of Sir Walter and Miss. They are gone back to Kellynch, and almost made me swear to visit them this summer, but my first visit to Kellynch will be with a surveyor, to tell me how to bring it with best advantage to the hammer.* The baronet, nevertheless, is not unlikely to marry again; he is quite fool enough. If he does, however, they will leave me in peace, which may be a decent equivalent for the reversion.* He is worse than last year.

'I wish I had any name but Elliot. I am sick of it. The name of Walter I can drop, thank God! and I desire you will never insult me with my second W. again, meaning, for the rest of my life, to be only yours truly,

WM. ELLIOT.'

Such a letter could not be read without putting Anne in a glow; and Mrs. Smith, observing the high colour in her face, said,

'The language, I know, is highly disrespectful. Though I have forgot the exact terms, I have a perfect impression of the general meaning. But it shews you the man. Mark his professions to my poor husband. Can any thing be stronger?'

Anne could not immediately get over the shock and mortification of finding such words applied to her father. She was obliged to recollect that her seeing the letter was a violation of the laws of honour, that no one ought to be judged or to be known by such testimonies, that no private correspondence could bear the eye of others, before she could recover calmness enough to return the letter which she had been meditating over, and say,

'Thank you. This is full proof undoubtedly, proof of every thing you were saying. But why be acquainted with us now?'

'I can explain this too,' cried Mrs. Smith, smiling.

'Can you really?'

'Yes. I have shewn you Mr. Elliot, as he was a dozen years ago, and I will shew him as he is now. I cannot produce written proof again, but I can give as authentic oral testimony as you can desire, of what he is now wanting, and what he is now doing. He is no hypocrite now.

He truly wants to marry you. His present attentions to your family are very sincere, quite from the heart. I will give you my authority; his friend Colonel Wallis.'

'Colonel Wallis! are you acquainted with him?'

'No. It does not come to me in quite so direct a line as that; it takes a bend or two, but nothing of consequence. The stream is as good as at first; the little rubbish it collects in the turnings, is easily moved away. Mr. Elliot talks unreservedly to Colonel Wallis of his views on you—which said Colonel Wallis I imagine to be in himself a sensible, careful, discerning sort of character; but Colonel Wallis has a very pretty silly wife, to whom he tells things which he had better not, and he repeats it all to her. She, in the overflowing spirits of her recovery, repeats it all to her nurse; and the nurse, knowing my acquaintance with you, very naturally brings it all to me. On Monday evening my good friend Mrs. Rooke let me thus much into the secrets of Marlborough-buildings. When I talked of a whole history therefore, you see, I was not romancing so much as you supposed.'

'My dear Mrs. Smith, your authority is deficient. This will not do. Mr. Elliot's having any views on me will not in the least account for the efforts he made towards a reconciliation with my father. That was all prior to my coming to Bath. I found them on the most friendly terms when I arrived.'

'I know you did; I know it all perfectly, but'

'Indeed, Mrs. Smith, we must not expect to get real information in such a line. Facts or opinions which are to pass through the hands of so many, to be misconceived by folly in one, and ignorance in another, can hardly have much truth left.'

'Only give me a hearing. You will soon be able to judge of the general credit due, by listening to some particulars which you can yourself immediately contradict or confirm. Nobody supposes that you were his first inducement. He had seen you indeed, before he came to Bath and admired you, but without knowing it to be you. So says my historian at least. Is this true? Did he see you last summer or autumn, "somewhere down in the west," to use her own words, without knowing it to be you?'

'He certainly did. So far it is very true. At Lyme; I happened to be at Lyme.'

'Well,' continued Mrs. Smith triumphantly, 'grant my friend the credit due to the establishment of the first point asserted. He saw you then at Lyme, and liked you so well as to be exceedingly pleased to meet with you again in Camden-place, as Miss Anne Elliot, and from that moment, I have no doubt, had a double motive in his visits there. But there was another, and an earlier; which I will now explain. If there is any thing in my story which you know to be either false or improbable, stop me. My account states, that your sister's friend, the lady now staying with you, whom I have heard you mention, came to Bath with Miss Elliot and Sir Walter as long ago as September, (in short when they first came themselves) and has been staying there ever since; that she is a clever, insinuating, handsome woman, poor and plausible, and altogether such in situation and manner, as to give a general idea among Sir Walter's acquaintance, of her meaning to be Lady Elliot, and as general a surprise that Miss Elliot should be apparently blind to the danger.'

Here Mrs. Smith paused a moment; but Anne had not a word to say, and she continued,

'This was the light in which it appeared to those who knew the family, long before your return to it; and Colonel Wallis had his eye upon your father enough to be sensible of it, though he did not then visit in Camden-place; but his regard for Mr. Elliot gave him an interest in watching all that was going on there, and when Mr. Elliot came to Bath for a day or two, as he happened to do a little before Christmas, Colonel Wallis made him acquainted with the appearance of things, and the reports beginning to prevail.—Now you are to understand that time had worked a very material change in Mr. Elliot's opinions as to the value of a baronetcy. Upon all points of blood and connexion, he is a completely altered man. Having long had as much money as he could spend, nothing to wish for on the side of avarice or indulgence, he has been gradually learning to pin his happiness upon the consequence he is heir to. I thought it coming on, before our acquaintance ceased, but it is now a confirmed feeling. He cannot bear the idea of not being Sir William. You may guess therefore that the news he heard from his friend, could not be very agreeable, and you may guess what it produced; the resolution of coming back to Bath as soon as possible, and of fixing himself here for a time, with the view of renewing his former acquaintance and recovering such a footing in the family, as might give him the means of ascertaining the degree of his danger, and of circumventing the lady if he found it material. This was agreed upon between the two friends, as the only thing to be done; and Colonel Wallis was to assist in every way that he could. He was to be introduced, and Mrs. Wallis was to be introduced, and every body was to be introduced. Mr. Elliot came back accordingly; and on application was forgiven, as you know, and re-admitted into the family; and there it was his constant object, and his only object (till your arrival added another motive) to watch Sir Walter and Mrs. Clay. He omitted no opportunity of being with them, threw himself in their way, called at all hours—but I need not be particular on this subject. You can imagine what an artful man would do; and with this guide, perhaps, may recollect what you have seen him do.'

'Yes,' said Anne, 'you tell me nothing which does not accord with what I have known, or could imagine. There is always something offensive in the details of cunning. The manœuvres of selfishness and duplicity must ever be revolting, but I have heard nothing which really surprises me. I know those who would be shocked by such a representation of Mr. Elliot, who would have difficulty in believing it; but I have never been satisfied. I have always wanted some other motive for his conduct than appeared.—I should like to know his present opinion, as to the probability of the event he has been in dread of; whether he considers the danger to be lessening or not.'

'Lessening, I understand,' replied Mrs. Smith. 'He thinks Mrs. Clay afraid of him, aware that he sees through her, and not daring to proceed as she might do in his absence. But since he must be absent some time or other, I do not perceive how he can ever be secure, while she holds her present influence. Mrs. Wallis has an amusing idea, as nurse tells me, that it is to be put into the marriage articles* when you and Mr. Elliot marry, that your father is not to marry Mrs. Clay. A scheme, worthy of Mrs. Wallis's understanding, by all accounts; but my sensible nurse Rooke sees the absurdity of it.— "Why, to be sure, ma'am," said she, "it would not prevent his marrying any body else." And indeed, to own the truth, I do not think nurse in her heart is a very strenuous opposer of Sir Walter's making a second match. She must be allowed to be a favourer of matrimony you know, and (since self will intrude) who can say that she may not have some flying visions of attending the next Lady Elliot, through Mrs. Wallis's recommendation?'

'I am very glad to know all this,' said Anne, after a little thoughtfulness. 'It will be more painful to me in some respects to be in company with him, but I shall know better what to do. My line of conduct will be more direct. Mr. Elliot is evidently a disingenuous, artificial, worldly man, who has never had any better principle to guide him than selfishness.'

But Mr. Elliot was not yet done with. Mrs. Smith had been carried away from her first direction, and Anne had forgotten, in the interest of her own family concerns, how much had been originally implied against him; but her attention was now called to the explanation of those first hints, and she listened to a recital which, if it did not perfectly justify the unqualified bitterness of Mrs. Smith, proved him to have been very unfeeling in his conduct towards her, very deficient both in justice and compassion.

She learned that (the intimacy between them continuing unimpaired by Mr. Elliot's marriage) they had been as before always together, and Mr. Elliot had led his friend into expenses much beyond his fortune. Mrs. Smith did not want to take blame to herself, and was most tender of throwing any on her husband; but Anne could collect that their income had never been equal to their style of living, and that from the first, there had been a great deal of several and joint extravagance. From his wife's account of him, she could discern Mr. Smith to have been a man of warm feelings, easy temper, careless habits, and not strong understanding, much more amiable than his friend, and very unlike him—led by him, and probably despised by him. Mr. Elliot, raised by his marriage to great affluence, and disposed to every gratification of pleasure and vanity which could be commanded without involving himself, (for with all his self-indulgence he had become a prudent man) and beginning to be rich, just as his friend ought to have found himself to be poor, seemed to have had no concern at all for that friend's probable finances, but, on the contrary, had been prompting and encouraging expenses, which could end only in ruin. And the Smiths accordingly had been ruined.

The husband had died just in time to be spared the full knowledge of it. They had previously known embarrassments enough to try the friendship of their friends, and to prove that Mr. Elliot's had better not be tried; but it was not till his death that the wretched state of his affairs was fully known. With a confidence in Mr. Elliot's regard, more creditable to his feelings than his judgment, Mr. Smith had appointed him the executor of his will; but Mr. Elliot would not act, and the difficulties and distresses which this refusal had heaped on her, in addition to the inevitable sufferings of her situation, had been such as could not be related without anguish of spirit, or listened to without corresponding indignation.

Anne was shewn some letters of his on the occasion, answers to urgent applications from Mrs. Smith, which all breathed the same stern resolution of not engaging in a fruitless trouble, and, under a cold civility, the same hard-hearted indifference to any of the evils it might bring on her. It was a dreadful picture of ingratitude and inhumanity; and Anne felt at some moments, that no flagrant open crime could have been worse. She had a great deal to listen to; all the particulars of past sad scenes, all the minutiæ of distress upon distress, which in former conversations had been merely hinted at, were dwelt on now with a natural indulgence. Anne could perfectly comprehend the exquisite relief, and was only the more inclined to wonder at the composure of her friend's usual state of mind.

There was one circumstance in the history of her grievances of particular irritation. She had good reason to believe that some property of her husband in the West Indies, which had been for many years under a sort of sequestration for the payment of its own incumbrances,* might be recoverable by proper measures; and this property, though not large, would be enough to make her comparatively rich. But there was nobody to stir in it. Mr. Elliot would do nothing, and she could do nothing herself, equally disabled from personal exertion by her state of bodily weakness, and from employing others by her want of money. She had no natural connexions to assist her even with their counsel, and she could not afford to purchase the assistance of the law. This was a cruel aggravation of actually streightened means. To feel that she ought to be in better circumstances, that a little trouble in the right place might do it, and to fear that delay might be even weakening her claims, was hard to bear!

It was on this point that she had hoped to engage Anne's good offices with Mr. Elliot. She had previously, in the anticipation of their marriage, been very apprehensive of losing her friend by it; but on being assured that he could have made no attempt of that nature, since he did not even know her to be in Bath, it immediately occurred, that something might be done in her favour by the influence of the woman he loved, and she had been hastily preparing to interest Anne's feelings, as far as the observances due to Mr. Elliot's character would allow, when Anne's refutation of the supposed engagement changed the face of every thing, and while it took from her the new-formed hope of succeeding in the object of her first anxiety, left her at least the comfort of telling the whole story her own way.

After listening to this full description of Mr. Elliot, Anne could not but express some surprise at Mrs. Smith's having spoken of him so favourably in the beginning of their conversation. 'She had seemed to recommend and praise him!'

'My dear,' was Mrs. Smith's reply, 'there was nothing else to be done. I considered your marrying him as certain, though he might not yet have made the offer, and I could no more speak the truth of him, than if he had been your husband. My heart bled for you, as I talked of happiness. And yet, he is sensible, he is agreeable, and with such a woman as you, it was not absolutely hopeless. He was very unkind to his first wife. They were wretched together. But she was too ignorant and giddy for respect, and he had never loved her. I was willing to hope that you must fare better.'

Anne could just acknowledge within herself such a possibility of having been induced to marry him, as made her shudder at the idea of the misery which must have followed. It was just possible that she might have been persuaded by Lady Russell! And under such a supposition, which would have been most miserable, when time had disclosed all, too late?

It was very desirable that Lady Russell should be no longer deceived; and one of the concluding arrangements of this important conference, which carried them through the greater part of the morning, was, that Anne had full liberty to communicate to her friend every thing relative to Mrs. Smith, in which his conduct was involved.

CHAPTER X

ANNE went home to think over all that she had heard. In one point, her feelings were relieved by this knowledge of Mr. Elliot. There was no longer any thing of tenderness due to him. He stood, as opposed to Captain Wentworth, in all his own unwelcome obtrusiveness; and the evil of his attentions last night, the irremediable mischief he might have done, was considered with sensations unqualified, unperplexed.—Pity for him was all over. But this was the only point of relief. In every other respect, in looking around her, or penetrating forward, she saw more to distrust and to apprehend. She was concerned for the disappointment and pain Lady Russell would be feeling, for the mortifications which must be hanging over her father and sister, and had all the distress of foreseeing many evils, without knowing how to avert any one of them.—She was most thankful for her own knowledge of him. She had never considered herself as entitled to reward for not slighting an old friend like Mrs. Smith, but here was a reward indeed springing from it!—Mrs. Smith had been able to tell her what no one else could have done. Could the knowledge have been extended through her family!—But this was a vain idea. She must talk to Lady Russell, tell her, consult with her, and having done her best, wait the event with as much composure as possible; and after all, her greatest want of composure would be in that quarter of the mind which could not be opened to Lady Russell, in that flow of anxieties and fears which must be all to herself.

She found, on reaching home, that she had, as she intended, escaped seeing Mr. Elliot; that he had called and paid them a long morning visit; but hardly had she congratulated herself, and felt safe till to-morrow, when she heard that he was coming again in the evening.

'I had not the smallest intention of asking him,' said Elizabeth, with affected carelessness, 'but he gave so many hints; so Mrs. Clay says, at least.'

'Indeed I do say it. I never saw any body in my life spell harder for an invitation. Poor man! I was really in pain for him; for your hard-hearted sister, Miss Anne, seems bent on cruelty.'

'Oh!' cried Elizabeth, 'I have been rather too much used to the game to be soon overcome by a gentleman's hints. However, when I found how excessively he was regretting that he should miss my father this morning, I gave way immediately, for I would never really omit an opportunity of bringing him and Sir Walter together. They appear to so much advantage in company with each other! Each behaving so pleasantly! Mr. Elliot looking up with so much respect!'

'Quite delightful!' cried Mrs. Clay, not daring, however, to turn her eyes towards Anne. 'Exactly like father and son! Dear Miss Elliot, may I not say father and son?'

'Oh! I lay no embargo on any body's words. If you will have such ideas! But, upon my word, I am scarcely sensible of his attentions being beyond those of other men.'

'My dear Miss Elliot!' exclaimed Mrs. Clay, lifting up her hands and eyes, and sinking all the rest of her astonishment in a convenient silence.

'Well, my dear Penelope, you need not be so alarmed about him. I did invite him, you know. I sent him away with smiles. When I found he was really going to his friends at Thornberry-park for the whole day to-morrow, I had compassion on him.'

Anne admired the good acting of the friend, in being able to shew such pleasure as she did, in the expectation, and in the actual arrival of the very person whose presence must really be interfering with her prime object. It was impossible but that Mrs. Clay must hate the sight of Mr. Elliot; and yet she could assume a most obliging, placid look, and appear quite satisfied with the curtailed license of devoting herself only half as much to Sir Walter as she would have done otherwise.

To Anne herself it was most distressing to see Mr. Elliot enter the room; and quite painful to have him approach and speak to her. She had been used before to feel that he could not be always quite sincere, but now she saw insincerity in every thing. His attentive deference to her father, contrasted with his former language, was odious; and when she thought of his cruel conduct towards Mrs. Smith, she could hardly bear the sight of his present smiles and mildness, or the sound of his artificial good sentiments. She meant to avoid any such alteration of manners as might provoke a remonstrance on his side. It was a great object with her to escape all enquiry or eclat;* but it was her intention to be as decidedly cool to him as might be compatible with their relationship, and to retrace, as quietly as she could, the few steps of unnecessary intimacy she had been gradually led along. She was accordingly more guarded, and more cool, than she had been the night before.

He wanted to animate her curiosity again as to how and where he could have heard her formerly praised; wanted very much to be gratified by more solicitation; but the charm was broken: he found that the heat and animation of a public room were necessary to kindle his modest cousin's vanity; he found, at least, that it was not to be done now, by any of those attempts which he could hazard among the too-commanding claims of the others. He little surmised that it was a subject acting now exactly against his interest, bringing immediately into her thoughts all those parts of his conduct which were least excusable.

She had some satisfaction in finding that he was really going out of Bath the next morning, going early, and that he would be gone the greater part of two days. He was invited again to Camden-place the very evening of his return; but from Thursday to Saturday evening his absence was certain. It was bad enough that a Mrs. Clay should be always before her; but that a deeper hypocrite should be added to their party, seemed the destruction of every thing like peace and comfort. It was so humiliating to reflect on the constant deception practised on her father and Elizabeth; to consider the various sources of mortification preparing for them! Mrs. Clay's selfishness was not so complicate nor so revolting as his; and Anne would have compounded for the marriage at once, with all its evils, to be clear of Mr. Elliot's subtleties, in endeavouring to prevent it.

On Friday morning she meant to go very early to Lady Russell, and accomplish the necessary communication; and she would have gone directly after breakfast but that Mrs. Clay was also going out on some obliging purpose of saving her sister trouble, which determined her to wait till she might be safe from such a companion. She saw Mrs. Clay fairly off, therefore, before she began to talk of spending the morning in Rivers-street.

'Very well,' said Elizabeth, 'I have nothing to send but my love. Oh! you may as well take back that tiresome book she would lend me, and pretend I have read it through. I really cannot be plaguing myself for ever with all the new poems and states of the nation that come out. Lady Russell quite bores one with her new publications. You need not tell her so, but I thought her dress hideous the other night. I used to think she had some taste in dress, but I was ashamed of her at the concert. Something so formal and *arrangé* in her air! and she sits so upright! My best love, of course.'

'And mine,' added Sir Walter. 'Kindest regards. And you may say, that I mean to call upon her soon. Make a civil message. But I shall only leave my card. Morning visits are never fair by women at her time of life, who make themselves up so little. If she would only wear rouge, she would not be afraid of being seen; but last time I called, I observed the blinds were let down immediately.'

While her father spoke, there was a knock at the door. Who could it be? Anne, remembering the preconcerted visits, at all hours, of Mr. Elliot, would have expected him, but for his known engagement seven miles off. After the usual period of suspense, the usual sounds of approach were heard, and 'Mr. and Mrs. Charles Musgrove' were ushered into the room.

Surprise was the strongest emotion raised by their appearance; but Anne was really glad to see them; and the others were not so sorry but that they could put on a decent air of welcome; and as soon as it became clear that these, their nearest relations, were not arrived with any views of accommodation in that house, Sir Walter and Elizabeth were able to rise in cordiality, and do the honours of it very well. They were come to Bath for a few days with Mrs. Musgrove, and were at the White Hart.* So much was pretty soon understood; but till Sir Walter and Elizabeth were walking Mary into the other drawing-room, and regaling themselves with her admiration, Anne could not draw upon Charles's brain for a regular history of their coming, or an explanation of some smiling hints of particular business, which had been ostentatiously dropped by Mary, as well as of some apparent confusion as to whom their party consisted of.

She then found that it consisted of Mrs. Musgrove, Henrietta, and Captain Harville, beside their two selves. He gave her a very plain, intelligible account of the whole; a narration in which she saw a great deal of most characteristic proceeding. The scheme had received its first impulse by Captain Harville's wanting to come to Bath on business. He had begun to talk of it a week ago; and by way of doing something, as shooting was over, Charles had proposed coming with him, and Mrs. Harville had seemed to like the idea of it very much, as an advantage to her husband; but Mary could not bear to be left, and had made herself so unhappy about it that, for a day or two, every thing seemed to be in suspense, or at an end. But then, it had been taken up by his father and mother. His mother had some old friends in Bath, whom she wanted to see; it was thought a good opportunity for Henrietta to come and buy wedding-clothes for herself and her sister; and, in short, it ended in being his mother's party, that every thing might be comfortable and easy to Captain Harville; and he and Mary were included in it, by way of general convenience. They had arrived late the night before. Mrs. Harville, her children, and Captain Benwick, remained with Mr. Musgrove and Louisa at Uppercross.

Anne's only surprise was, that affairs should be in forwardness enough for Henrietta's wedding-clothes to be talked of: she had imagined such difficulties of fortune to exist there as must prevent the marriage from being near at hand; but she learned from Charles that, very recently, (since Mary's last letter to herself) Charles Hayter had been applied to by a friend to hold a living for a youth* who could not possibly claim it under many years; and that, on the strength of this present income, with almost a certainty of something more permanent long before the term in question, the two families had consented to the young people's wishes, and that their marriage was likely to take place in a few months, quite as soon as Louisa's. 'And a very good living it was,' Charles added, 'only five-and-twenty miles from Uppercross, and in a very fine country—fine part of Dorsetshire. In the centre of some of the best preserves in the kingdom, surrounded by three great proprietors, each more careful and jealous than the other;* and to two of the three, at least, Charles Hayter might get a special recommendation. Not that he will value it as he ought,' he observed, 'Charles is too cool about sporting. That's the worst of him.'

'I am extremely glad, indeed,' cried Anne, 'particularly glad that this should happen: and that of two sisters, who both deserve equally well, and who have always been such good friends, the pleasant prospects of one should not be dimming those of the other—that they should be so equal in their prosperity and comfort. I hope your father and mother are quite happy with regard to both.'

'Oh! yes. My father would be as well pleased if the gentlemen were richer, but he has no other fault to find. Money, you know, coming down with money—two daughters at once—it cannot be a very agreeable operation, and it streightens him as to many things. However, I do not mean to say they have not a right to it. It is very fit they should have daughters' shares; and I am sure he has always been a very kind, liberal father to me. Mary does not above half like Henrietta's match. She never did, you know. But she does not do him justice, nor think enough about Winthrop. I cannot make her attend to the value of the property. It is a very fair match, as times go; and I have liked Charles Hayter all my life, and I shall not leave off now.'

'Such excellent parents as Mr. and Mrs. Musgrove,' exclaimed Anne, 'should be happy in their children's marriages. They do every thing to confer happiness, I am sure. What a blessing to young people to be in such hands! Your father and mother seem so totally free from all those ambitious feelings which have led to so much misconduct and misery, both in young and old! I hope you think Louisa perfectly recovered now?'

He answered rather hesitatingly, 'Yes, I believe I do—very much recovered; but she is altered: there is no running or jumping about, no laughing or dancing; it is quite different. If one happens only to shut the door a little hard, she starts and wriggles like a young dab chick in the water; and Benwick sits at her elbow, reading verses, or whispering to her, all day long.'

Anne could not help laughing. 'That cannot be much to your taste, I know,' said she; 'but I do believe him to be an excellent young man.'

'To be sure he is. Nobody doubts it; and I hope you do not think I am so illiberal as to want every man to have the same objects and pleasures as myself. I have a great value for Benwick; and when one can but get him to talk, he has plenty to say. His reading has done him no harm, for he has fought as well as read. He is a brave fellow. I got more acquainted with him last Monday than ever I did before. We had a famous set-to at rat-hunting all the morning, in my father's great barns; and he played his part so well, that I have liked him the better ever since.'

Here they were interrupted by the absolute necessity of Charles's following the others to admire mirrors and china; but Anne had heard enough to understand the present state of Uppercross, and rejoice in its happiness; and though she sighed as she rejoiced, her sigh had none of the ill-will of envy in it. She would certainly have risen to their blessings if she could, but she did not want to lessen theirs.

The visit passed off altogether in high good humour. Mary was in excellent spirits, enjoying the gaiety and the change; and so well satisfied with the journey in her mother-in-law's carriage with four horses, and with her own complete independence of Camden-place, that she was exactly in a temper to admire every thing as she ought, and enter most readily into all the superiorities of the house, as they were detailed to her. She had no demands on her father or sister, and her consequence was just enough increased by their handsome drawing-rooms.

Elizabeth was, for a short time, suffering a good deal. She felt that Mrs. Musgrove and all her party ought to be asked to dine with them, but she could not bear to have the difference of style, the reduction of servants, which a dinner must betray, witnessed by those who had been always so inferior to the Elliots of Kellynch. It was a struggle between propriety and vanity; but vanity got the better, and then Elizabeth was happy again. These were her internal persuasions.—'Old fashioned notions—country hospitality—we do not profess to give dinners—few people in Bath do—Lady Alicia never does; did not even ask her own sister's family, though they were here a month: and I dare say it would be very inconvenient to Mrs. Musgrove—put her quite out of her way. I am sure she would rather not come—she cannot feel easy with us. I will ask them all for an evening; that will be much better—that will be a novelty and a treat. They have not seen two such drawing-rooms before. They will be delighted to come to-morrow evening. It shall be a regular party—small, but most elegant.' And this satisfied Elizabeth: and when the invitation was given to the two present, and promised for the absent, Mary was as completely satisfied. She was particularly asked to meet Mr. Elliot, and be introduced to Lady Dalrymple and Miss Carteret, who were fortunately already engaged to come; and she could not have received a more gratifying attention. Miss Elliot was to have the honour of calling on Mrs. Musgrove in the course of the morning, and Anne walked off with Charles and Mary, to go and see her and Henrietta directly.

Her plan of sitting with Lady Russell must give way for the present. They all three called in Rivers-street for a couple of minutes; but Anne convinced herself that a day's delay of the intended communication could be of no consequence, and hastened forward to the White Hart, to see again the friends and companions of the last autumn, with an eagerness of good-will which many associations contributed to form.

They found Mrs. Musgrove and her daughter within, and by themselves, and Anne had the kindest welcome from each. Henrietta was exactly in that state of recently-improved views, of fresh-formed happiness, which made her full of regard and interest for every body she had ever liked before at all; and Mrs. Musgrove's real affection had been won by her usefulness when they were in distress. It was a heartiness, and a warmth, and a sincerity which Anne delighted in the more, from the sad want of such blessings at home. She was intreated to give them as much of her time as possible, invited for every day and all day long, or rather claimed as a part of the family; and in return, she naturally fell into all her wonted ways of attention and assistance, and on Charles's leaving them together, was listening to Mrs. Musgrove's history of Louisa, and to Henrietta's of herself, giving opinions on business, and recommendations to shops; with intervals of every help which Mary required, from altering her ribbon to settling her accounts, from finding her keys, and assorting her trinkets, to trying to convince her that she was not ill used by any body; which Mary, well amused as she generally was in her station at a window overlooking the entrance to the pump-room,* could not but have her moments of imagining.

A morning of thorough confusion was to be expected. A large party in an hotel ensured a quick-changing, unsettled scene. One five minutes brought a note, the next a parcel, and Anne had not been there half an hour, when their dining-room, spacious as it was, seemed more than half filled: a party of steady old friends were seated round Mrs. Musgrove, and Charles came back with Captains Harville and Wentworth. The appearance of the latter could not be more than the surprise of the moment. It was impossible for her to have forgotten to feel, that this arrival of their common friends must be soon bringing them together again. Their last meeting had been most important in opening his feelings; she had derived from it a delightful conviction; but she feared from his looks, that the same unfortunate persuasion, which had hastened him away from the concert room, still governed. He did not seem to want to be near enough for conversation.

She tried to be calm, and leave things to take their course; and tried to dwell much on this argument of rational dependance—'Surely, if there be constant attachment on each side, our hearts must understand each other ere long. We are not boy and girl, to be captiously irritable, misled by every moment's inadvertence, and wantonly playing with our own happiness.' And yet, a few minutes afterwards, she felt as if their being in company with each other, under their present circumstances, could only be exposing them to inadvertencies and misconstructions of the most mischievous kind.

'Anne,' cried Mary, still at her window, 'there is Mrs. Clay, I am sure, standing under the colonnade, and a gentleman with her. I saw them turn the corner from Bath-street just now. They seem deep in talk. Who is it?—Come, and tell me. Good heavens! I recollect.—It is Mr. Elliot himself.'

'No,' cried Anne quickly, 'it cannot be Mr. Elliot, I assure you. He was to leave Bath at nine this morning, and does not come back till to-morrow.'

As she spoke, she felt that Captain Wentworth was looking at her; the consciousness of which vexed and embarrassed her, and made her regret that she had said so much, simple as it was.

Mary, resenting that she should be supposed not to know her own cousin, began talking very warmly about the family features, and protesting still more positively that it was Mr. Elliot, calling again upon Anne to come and look herself; but Anne did not mean to stir, and tried to be cool and unconcerned. Her distress returned, however, on perceiving smiles and intelligent glances pass between two or three of the lady visitors, as if they believed themselves quite in the secret. It was evident that the report concerning her had spread; and a short pause succeeded, which seemed to ensure that it would now spread farther.

'Do come, Anne,' cried Mary, 'come and look yourself. You will be too late, if you do not make haste. They are parting, they are shaking hands. He is turning away. Not know Mr. Elliot, indeed!—You seem to have forgot all about Lyme.'

To pacify Mary, and perhaps screen her own embarrassment, Anne did move quietly to the window. She was just in time to ascertain that it really was Mr. Elliot (which she had never believed), before he disappeared on one side, as Mrs. Clay walked quickly off on the other; and checking the surprise which she could not but feel at such an appearance of friendly conference between two persons of totally opposite interests, she calmly said, 'Yes, it is Mr. Elliot certainly. He has changed his hour of going, I suppose, that is all—or I may be mistaken; I might not attend;' and walked back to her chair, recomposed, and with the comfortable hope of having acquitted herself well.

The visitors took their leave; and Charles, having civilly seen them off, and then made a face at them, and abused them for coming, began with—

'Well, mother, I have done something for you that you will like. I have been to the theatre, and secured a box for to-morrow night. A'n't I a good boy? I know you love a play; and there is room for us all. It holds nine. I have engaged Captain Wentworth. Anne will not be sorry to join us, I am sure. We all like a play. Have not I done well, mother?'

Mrs. Musgrove was good humouredly beginning to express her perfect readiness for the play, if Henrietta and all the others liked it, when Mary eagerly interrupted her by exclaiming,

'Good heavens, Charles! how can you think of such a thing? Take a box for to-morrow night! Have you forgot that we are engaged to Camden-place to-morrow night? and that we were most particularly asked on purpose to meet Lady Dalrymple and her daughter, and Mr. Elliot—all the principal family connexions—on purpose to be introduced to them? How can you be so forgetful?'

'Phoo! phoo!' replied Charles, 'what's an evening party? Never worth remembering. Your father might have asked us to dinner, I think, if he had wanted to see us. You may do as you like, but I shall go to the play.'

'Oh! Charles, I declare it will be too abominable if you do! when you promised to go.'

'No, I did not promise. I only smirked and bowed, and said the word "happy." There was no promise.'

'But you must go, Charles. It would be unpardonable to fail. We were asked on purpose to be introduced. There was always such a great connexion between the Dalrymples and ourselves. Nothing ever happened on either side that was not announced immediately. We are quite near relations, you know: and Mr. Elliot too, whom you ought so particularly to be acquainted with! Every attention is due to Mr. Elliot. Consider, my father's heir—the future representative of the family.'

'Don't talk to me about heirs and representatives,' cried Charles. 'I am not one of those who neglect the reigning power to bow to the rising sun. If I would not go for the sake of your father, I should think it scandalous to go for the sake of his heir. What is Mr. Elliot to me?'

The careless expression was life to Anne, who saw that Captain Wentworth was all attention, looking and listening with his whole soul; and that the last words brought his enquiring eyes from Charles to herself.

Charles and Mary still talked on in the same style; he, half serious and half jesting, maintaining the scheme for the play; and she, invariably serious, most warmly opposing it, and not omitting to make it known, that however determined to go to Camden-place herself, she should not think herself very well used, if they went to the play without her. Mrs. Musgrove interposed.

'We had better put it off. Charles, you had much better go back, and change the box for Tuesday. It would be a pity to be divided, and we should be losing Miss Anne too, if there is a party at her father's; and I am sure neither Henrietta nor I should care at all for the play, if Miss Anne could not be with us.'

Anne felt truly obliged to her for such kindness; and quite as much so, moreover, for the opportunity it gave her of decidedly saying—

'If it depended only on my inclination, ma'am, the party at home (excepting on Mary's account) would not be the smallest impediment. I have no pleasure in the sort of meeting, and should be too happy to change it for a play, and with you. But, it had better not be attempted, perhaps.'

She had spoken it; but she trembled when it was done, conscious that her words were listened to, and daring not even to try to observe their effect.

It was soon generally agreed that Tuesday should be the day, Charles only reserving the advantage of still teasing his wife, by persisting that he would go to the play to-morrow, if nobody else would.

Captain Wentworth left his seat, and walked to the fireplace; probably for the sake of walking away from it soon afterwards, and taking a station, with less barefaced design, by Anne.

'You have not been long enough in Bath,' said he, 'to enjoy the evening parties of the place.'

'Oh! no. The usual character of them has nothing for me. I am no card-player.'

'You were not formerly, I know. You did not use to like cards; but time makes many changes.'

'I am not yet so much changed,' cried Anne, and stopped, fearing she hardly knew what misconstruction. After waiting a few moments he said—and as if it were the result of immediate feeling—'It is a period, indeed! Eight years and a half is a period!'

Whether he would have proceeded farther was left to Anne's imagination to ponder over in a calmer hour; for while still hearing the sounds he had uttered, she was startled to other subjects by Henrietta, eager to make use of the present leisure for getting out, and calling on her companions to lose no time, lest somebody else should come in.

They were obliged to move. Anne talked of being perfectly ready, and tried to look it; but she felt that could Henrietta have known the regret and reluctance of her heart in quitting that chair, in preparing to quit the room, she would have found, in all her own sensations for her cousin, in the very security of his affection, wherewith to pity her.

Their preparations, however, were stopped short. Alarming sounds were heard; other visitors approached, and the door was thrown open for Sir Walter and Miss Elliot, whose entrance seemed to give a general chill. Anne felt an instant oppression, and, wherever she looked, saw symptoms of the same. The comfort, the freedom, the gaiety of the room was over, hushed into cold composure, determined silence, or insipid talk, to meet the heartless elegance of her father and sister. How mortifying to feel that it was so!

Her jealous eye was satisfied in one particular. Captain Wentworth was acknowledged again by each, by Elizabeth more graciously than before. She even addressed him once, and looked at him more than once. Elizabeth was, in fact, revolving a great measure. The sequel explained it. After the waste of a few minutes in saying the proper nothings, she began to give the invitation which was to comprise all the remaining dues of the Musgroves. 'To-morrow evening, to meet a few friends, no formal party.' It was all said very gracefully, and the cards with which she had provided herself, the 'Miss Elliot at home,' were laid on the table, with a courteous, comprehensive smile to all; and one smile and one card more decidedly for Captain Wentworth. The truth was, that Elizabeth had been long enough in Bath, to understand the importance of a man of such an air and appearance as his. The past was nothing. The present was that Captain Wentworth would move about well in her drawing-room. The card was pointedly given, and Sir Walter and Elizabeth arose and disappeared.

The interruption had been short, though severe; and ease and animation returned to most of those they left, as the door shut them out, but not to Anne. She could think only of the invitation she had with such astonishment witnessed; and of the manner in which it had been received, a manner of doubtful meaning, of surprise rather than gratification, of polite acknowledgment rather than acceptance. She knew him; she saw disdain in his eye, and could not venture to believe that he had determined to accept such an offering, as atonement for all the insolence of the past. Her spirits sank. He held the card in his hand after they were gone, as if deeply considering it.

'Only think of Elizabeth's including every body!' whispered Mary very audibly. 'I do not wonder Captain Wentworth is delighted! You see he cannot put the card out of his hand.'

Anne caught his eye, saw his cheeks glow, and his mouth form itself into a momentary expression of contempt, and turned away, that she might neither see nor hear more to vex her.

The party separated. The gentlemen had their own pursuits, the ladies proceeded on their own business, and they met no more while Anne belonged to them. She was earnestly begged to return and dine, and give them all the rest of the day; but her spirits had been so long exerted, that at present she felt unequal to more, and fit only for home, where she might be sure of being as silent as she chose.

Promising to be with them the whole of the following morning, therefore, she closed the fatigues of the present, by a toilsome walk to Camden-place, there to spend the evening chiefly in listening to the busy arrangements of Elizabeth and Mrs. Clay for the morrow's party, the frequent enumeration of the persons invited, and the continually improving detail of all the embellishments which were to make it the most completely elegant of its kind in Bath, while harassing herself in secret with the never-ending question, of whether Captain Wentworth would come or not? They were reckoning him as certain, but, with her, it was a gnawing solicitude never appeased for five minutes together. She generally thought he would come, because she generally thought he ought; but it was a case which she could not so shape into any positive act of duty or discretion, as inevitably to defy the suggestions of very opposite feelings.

She only roused herself from the broodings of this restless agitation, to let Mrs. Clay know that she had been seen with Mr. Elliot three hours after his being supposed to be out of Bath; for having watched in vain for some intimation of the interview from the lady herself, she determined to mention it; and it seemed to her that there was guilt in Mrs. Clay's face as she listened. It was transient, cleared

away in an instant, but Anne could imagine she read there the consciousness of having, by some complication of mutual trick, or some
overbearing authority of his, been obliged to attend (perhaps for half
an hour) to his lectures and restrictions on her designs on Sir Walter.
She exclaimed, however, with a very tolerable imitation of nature,

'Oh dear! very true. Only think, Miss Elliot, to my great surprise I
met with Mr. Elliot in Bath-street! I was never more astonished. He
turned back and walked with me to the Pump-yard. He had been
prevented setting off for Thornberry, but I really forget by what—
for I was in a hurry, and could not much attend, and I can only
answer for his being determined not to be delayed in his return. He
wanted to know how early he might be admitted to-morrow. He was
full of "to-morrow;" and it is very evident that I have been full of it
too ever since I entered the house, and learnt the extension of your
plan, and all that had happened, or my seeing him could never have
gone so entirely out of my head.'

CHAPTER XI

ONE day only had passed since Anne's conversation with Mrs.
Smith; but a keener interest had succeeded, and she was now so little
touched by Mr. Elliot's conduct, except by its effects in one quarter,
that it became a matter of course the next morning, still to defer her
explanatory visit in Rivers-street. She had promised to be with the
Musgroves from breakfast to dinner. Her faith was plighted, and Mr.
Elliot's character, like the Sultaness Scheherazade's head,* must live
another day.

She could not keep her appointment punctually, however; the
weather was unfavourable, and she had grieved over the rain on her
friends' account, and felt it very much on her own, before she was
able to attempt the walk. When she reached the White Hart, and
made her way to the proper apartment, she found herself neither
arriving quite in time, nor the first to arrive. The party before her
were Mrs. Musgrove, talking to Mrs. Croft, and Captain Harville to
Captain Wentworth, and she immediately heard that Mary and Henrietta, too impatient to wait, had gone out the moment it had cleared,
but would be back again soon, and that the strictest injunctions had
been left with Mrs. Musgrove, to keep her there till they returned.

She had only to submit, sit down, be outwardly composed, and feel herself plunged at once in all the agitations which she had merely laid her account of tasting a little before the morning closed. There was no delay, no waste of time. She was deep in the happiness of such misery, or the misery of such happiness, instantly. Two minutes after her entering the room, Captain Wentworth said,

'We will write the letter we were talking of, Harville, now, if you will give me materials.'

Materials were all at hand, on a separate table; he went to it, and nearly turning his back on them all, was engrossed by writing.

Mrs. Musgrove was giving Mrs. Croft the history of her eldest daughter's engagement, and just in that inconvenient tone of voice which was perfectly audible while it pretended to be a whisper. Anne felt that she did not belong to the conversation, and yet, as Captain Harville seemed thoughtful and not disposed to talk, she could not avoid hearing many undesirable particulars, such as 'how Mr. Musgrove and my brother Hayter had met again and again to talk it over; what my brother Hayter had said one day, and what Mr. Musgrove had proposed the next, and what had occurred to my sister Hayter, and what the young people had wished, and what I said at first I never could consent to, but was afterwards persuaded to think might do very well,' and a great deal in the same style of open-hearted communication—Minutiæ which, even with every advantage of taste and delicacy which good Mrs. Musgrove could not give, could be properly interesting only to the principals. Mrs. Croft was attending with great good humour, and whenever she spoke at all, it was very sensibly. Anne hoped the gentlemen might each be too much self-occupied to hear.

'And so, ma'am, all these things considered,' said Mrs. Musgrove in her powerful whisper, 'though we could have wished it different, yet altogether we did not think it fair to stand out any longer; for Charles Hayter was quite wild about it, and Henrietta was pretty near as bad; and so we thought they had better marry at once, and make the best of it, as many others have done before them. At any rate, said I, it will be better than a long engagement.'

'That is precisely what I was going to observe,' cried Mrs. Croft. 'I would rather have young people settle on a small income at once, and have to struggle with a few difficulties together, than be involved in a long engagement. I always think that no mutual—'

'Oh! dear Mrs. Croft,' cried Mrs. Musgrove, unable to let her finish her speech, 'there is nothing I so abominate for young people as a long engagement. It is what I always protested against for my children. It is all very well, I used to say, for young people to be engaged, if there is a certainty of their being able to marry in six months, or even in twelve, but a long engagement!'

'Yes, dear ma'am,' said Mrs. Croft, 'or an uncertain engagement; an engagement which may be long. To begin without knowing that at such a time there will be the means of marrying, I hold to be very unsafe and unwise, and what, I think, all parents should prevent as far as they can.'

Anne found an unexpected interest here. She felt its application to herself, felt it in a nervous thrill all over her, and at the same moment that her eyes instinctively glanced towards the distant table, Captain Wentworth's pen ceased to move, his head was raised, pausing, listening, and he turned round the next instant to give a look—one quick, conscious look at her.

The two ladies continued to talk, to re-urge the same admitted truths, and enforce them with such examples of the ill effect of a contrary practice, as had fallen within their observation, but Anne heard nothing distinctly; it was only a buzz of words in her ear, her mind was in confusion.

Captain Harville, who had in truth been hearing none of it, now left his seat, and moved to a window; and Anne seeming to watch him, though it was from thorough absence of mind, became gradually sensible that he was inviting her to join him where he stood. He looked at her with a smile, and a little motion of the head, which expressed, 'Come to me, I have something to say;' and the unaffected, easy kindness of manner which denoted the feelings of an older acquaintance than he really was, strongly enforced the invitation. She roused herself and went to him. The window at which he stood, was at the other end of the room from where the two ladies were sitting, and though nearer to Captain Wentworth's table, not very near. As she joined him, Captain Harville's countenance reassumed the serious, thoughtful expression which seemed its natural character.

'Look here,' said he, unfolding a parcel in his hand, and displaying a small miniature painting, 'do you know who that is?'

'Certainly, Captain Benwick.'

'Yes, and you may guess who it is for. But (in a deep tone) it was not done for her. Miss Elliot, do you remember our walking together at Lyme, and grieving for him? I little thought then—but no matter. This was drawn at the Cape. He met with a clever young German artist at the Cape, and in compliance with a promise to my poor sister, sat to him, and was bringing it home for her. And I have now the charge of getting it properly set for another! It was a commission to me! But who else was there to employ? I hope I can allow for him. I am not sorry, indeed, to make it over to another. He undertakes it— (looking towards Captain Wentworth) he is writing about it now.' And with a quivering lip he wound up the whole by adding, 'Poor Fanny! she would not have forgotten him so soon!'

'No,' replied Anne, in a low feeling voice. 'That, I can easily believe.'

'It was not in her nature. She doated on him.'

'It would not be the nature of any woman who truly loved.'

Captain Harville smiled, as much as to say, 'Do you claim that for your sex?' and she answered the question, smiling also, 'Yes. We certainly do not forget you, so soon as you forget us. It is, perhaps, our fate rather than our merit. We cannot help ourselves. We live at home, quiet, confined, and our feelings prey upon us. You are forced on exertion. You have always a profession, pursuits, business of some sort or other, to take you back into the world immediately, and continual occupation and change soon weaken impressions.'

'Granting your assertion that the world does all this so soon for men, (which, however, I do not think I shall grant) it does not apply to Benwick. He has not been forced upon any exertion. The peace turned him on shore at the very moment, and he has been living with us, in our little family-circle, ever since.'

'True,' said Anne, 'very true; I did not recollect; but what shall we say now, Captain Harville? If the change be not from outward circumstances, it must be from within; it must be nature, man's nature, which has done the business for Captain Benwick.'

'No, no, it is not man's nature. I will not allow it to be more man's nature than woman's to be inconstant and forget those they do love, or have loved. I believe the reverse. I believe in a true analogy between our bodily frames and our mental; and that as our bodies are the strongest, so are our feelings; capable of bearing most rough usage, and riding out the heaviest weather.'

'Your feelings may be the strongest,' replied Anne, 'but the same spirit of analogy will authorise me to assert that ours are the most tender. Man is more robust than woman, but he is not longer-lived; which exactly explains my view of the nature of their attachments. Nay, it would be too hard upon you, if it were otherwise. You have difficulties, and privations, and dangers enough to struggle with. You are always labouring and toiling, exposed to every risk and hardship. Your home, country, friends, all quitted. Neither time, nor health, nor life, to be called your own. It would be too hard indeed' (with a faltering voice) 'if woman's feelings were to be added to all this.'

'We shall never agree upon this question'—Captain Harville was beginning to say, when a slight noise called their attention to Captain Wentworth's hitherto perfectly quiet division of the room. It was nothing more than that his pen had fallen down, but Anne was startled at finding him nearer than she had supposed, and half inclined to suspect that the pen had only fallen, because he had been occupied by them, striving to catch sounds, which yet she did not think he could have caught.

'Have you finished your letter?' said Captain Harville.

'Not quite, a few lines more. I shall have done in five minutes.'

'There is no hurry on my side. I am only ready whenever you are.—I am in very good anchorage here,' (smiling at Anne) 'well supplied, and want for nothing.—No hurry for a signal at all.—Well, Miss Elliot,' (lowering his voice) 'as I was saying, we shall never agree I suppose upon this point. No man and woman would, prob-ably. But let me observe that all histories are against you, all stories, prose and verse. If I had such a memory as Benwick, I could bring you fifty quotations in a moment on my side the argument, and I do not think I ever opened a book in my life which had not something to say upon woman's inconstancy. Songs and proverbs, all talk of woman's fickleness. But perhaps you will say, these were all written by men.'

'Perhaps I shall.—Yes, yes, if you please, no reference to examples in books. Men have had every advantage of us in telling their own story. Education has been theirs in so much higher a degree; the pen has been in their hands.* I will not allow books to prove any thing.'

'But how shall we prove any thing?'

'We never shall. We never can expect to prove any thing upon such a point. It is a difference of opinion which does not admit of proof. We each begin probably with a little bias towards our own sex, and upon that bias build every circumstance in favour of it which has occurred within our own circle; many of which circumstances (perhaps those very cases which strike us the most) may be precisely such as cannot be brought forward without betraying a confidence, or in some respect saying what should not be said.'

'Ah!' cried Captain Harville, in a tone of strong feeling, 'if I could but make you comprehend what a man suffers when he takes a last look at his wife and children, and watches the boat that he has sent them off in, as long as it is in sight, and then turns away and says, "God knows whether we ever meet again!" And then, if I could convey to you the glow of his soul when he does see them again; when, coming back after a twelvemonth's absence perhaps, and obliged to put into another port, he calculates how soon it be possible to get them there, pretending to deceive himself, and saying, "They cannot be here till such a day," but all the while hoping for them twelve hours sooner, and seeing them arrive at last, as if Heaven had given them wings, by many hours sooner still! If I could explain to you all this, and all that a man can bear and do, and glories to do for the sake of these treasures of his existence! I speak, you know, only of such men as have hearts!' pressing his own with emotion.

'Oh!' cried Anne eagerly, 'I hope I do justice to all that is felt by you, and by those who resemble you. God forbid that I should undervalue the warm and faithful feelings of any of my fellow-creatures. I should deserve utter contempt if I dared to suppose that true attachment and constancy were known only by woman. No, I believe you capable of every thing great and good in your married lives. I believe you equal to every important exertion, and to every domestic forbearance, so long as—if I may be allowed the expression, so long as you have an object. I mean, while the woman you love lives, and lives for you. All the privilege I claim for my own sex (it is not a very enviable one, you need not covet it) is that of loving longest, when existence or when hope is gone.'

She could not immediately have uttered another sentence; her heart was too full, her breath too much oppressed.

'You are a good soul,' cried Captain Harville, putting his hand on her arm quite affectionately. 'There is no quarrelling with you.— And when I think of Benwick, my tongue is tied.'

Their attention was called towards the others.—Mrs. Croft was taking leave.

'Here, Frederick, you and I part company, I believe,' said she. 'I am going home, and you have an engagement with your friend.— To-night we may have the pleasure of all meeting again, at your party,' (turning to Anne.) 'We had your sister's card yesterday, and I understood Frederick had a card too, though I did not see it— and you are disengaged, Frederick, are you not, as well as ourselves?'

Captain Wentworth was folding up a letter in great haste, and either could not or would not answer fully.

'Yes,' said he, 'very true; here we separate, but Harville and I shall soon be after you, that is, Harville, if you are ready, I am in half a minute. I know you will not be sorry to be off. I shall be at your service in half a minute.'

Mrs. Croft left them, and Captain Wentworth, having sealed his letter with great rapidity, was indeed ready, and had even a hurried, agitated air, which shewed impatience to be gone. Anne knew not how to understand it. She had the kindest 'Good morning, God bless you,' from Captain Harville, but from him not a word, nor a look. He had passed out of the room without a look!

She had only time, however, to move closer to the table where he had been writing, when footsteps were heard returning; the door opened; it was himself. He begged their pardon, but he had forgotten his gloves, and instantly crossing the room to the writing table, and standing with his back towards Mrs. Musgrove, he drew out a letter from under the scattered paper, placed it before Anne with eyes of glowing entreaty fixed on her for a moment, and hastily collecting his gloves, was again out of the room, almost before Mrs. Musgrove was aware of his being in it—the work of an instant!

The revolution which one instant had made in Anne, was almost beyond expression. The letter, with a direction hardly legible, to 'Miss A. E.—.' was evidently the one which he had been folding so hastily. While supposed to be writing only to Captain Benwick, he had been also addressing her! On the contents of that letter depended all which this world could do for her! Any thing was possible, any thing might be defied rather than suspense. Mrs. Mus- grove had little arrangements of her own at her own table; to their protection she must trust, and sinking into the chair which he had occupied, succeeding to the very spot where he had leaned and written, her eyes devoured the following words:

'I can listen no longer in silence. I must speak to you by such means as are within my reach. You pierce my soul. I am half agony, half hope. Tell me not that I am too late, that such precious feelings are gone for ever. I offer myself to you again with a heart even more your own, than when you almost broke it eight years and a half ago. Dare not say that man forgets sooner than woman, that his love has an earlier death. I have loved none but you. Unjust I may have been, weak and resentful I have been, but never inconstant. You alone have brought me to Bath. For you alone I think and plan.—Have you not seen this? Can you fail to have understood my wishes?—I had not waited even these ten days, could I have read your feelings, as I think you must have penetrated mine. I can hardly write. I am every instant hearing something which overpowers me. You sink your voice, but I can distinguish the tones of that voice, when they would be lost on others.—Too good, too excellent creature! You do us justice indeed. You do believe that there is true attachment and constancy among men. Believe it to be most fervent, most undeviating in

F. W.

'I must go, uncertain of my fate; but I shall return hither, or follow your party, as soon as possible. A word, a look will be enough to decide whether I enter your father's house this evening, or never.'

Such a letter was not to be soon recovered from. Half an hour's solitude and reflection might have tranquillized her; but the ten minutes only, which now passed before she was interrupted, with all the restraints of her situation, could do nothing towards tranquillity. Every moment rather brought fresh agitation. It was an overpowering happiness. And before she was beyond the first stage of full sensation, Charles, Mary, and Henrietta all came in.

The absolute necessity of seeming like herself produced then an immediate struggle; but after a while she could do no more. She began not to understand a word they said, and was obliged to plead indisposition and excuse herself. They could then see that she looked very ill—were shocked and concerned—and would not stir without her for the world. This was dreadful! Would they only have gone away, and left her in the quiet possession of that room, it would have been her cure; but to have them all standing or waiting around her was distracting, and, in desperation, she said she would go home.

'By all means, my dear,' cried Mrs. Musgrove, 'go home directly and take care of yourself, that you may be fit for the evening. I wish Sarah was here to doctor you, but I am no doctor myself. Charles, ring and order a chair. She must not walk.'

But the chair would never do. Worse than all! To lose the possibility of speaking two words to Captain Wentworth in the course of her quiet, solitary progress up the town (and she felt almost certain of meeting him) could not be borne. The chair was earnestly protested against; and Mrs. Musgrove, who thought only of one sort of illness, having assured herself, with some anxiety, that there had been no fall in the case; that Anne had not, at any time lately, slipped down, and got a blow on her head; that she was perfectly convinced of having had no fall, could part with her cheerfully, and depend on finding her better at night.

Anxious to omit no possible precaution, Anne struggled, and said,

'I am afraid, ma'am, that it is not perfectly understood. Pray be so good as to mention to the other gentlemen that we hope to see your whole party this evening. I am afraid there has been some mistake; and I wish you particularly to assure Captain Harville, and Captain Wentworth, that we hope to see them both.'

'Oh! my dear, it is quite understood, I give you my word. Captain Harville has no thought but of going.'

'Do you think so? But I am afraid; and I should be so very sorry! Will you promise me to mention it, when you see them again? You will see them both again this morning, I dare say. Do promise me.'

'To be sure I will, if you wish it. Charles, if you see Captain Harville any where, remember to give Miss Anne's message. But indeed, my dear, you need not be uneasy. Captain Harville holds himself quite engaged, I'll answer for it; and Captain Wentworth the same, I dare say.'

Anne could do no more; but her heart prophesied some mischance, to damp the perfection of her felicity. It could not be very lasting, however. Even if he did not come to Camden-place himself, it would be in her power to send an intelligible sentence by Captain Harville.

Another momentary vexation occurred. Charles, in his real concern and good-nature, would go home with her; there was no preventing him. This was almost cruel! But she could not be long ungrateful; he was sacrificing an engagement at a gunsmith's to be of use to her; and she set off with him, with no feeling but gratitude apparent.

They were in Union-street, when a quicker step behind, a something of familiar sound, gave her two moments preparation for the sight of Captain Wentworth. He joined them; but, as if irresolute whether to join or to pass on, said nothing—only looked. Anne could command herself enough to receive that look, and not repulsively. The cheeks which had been pale now glowed, and the movements which had hesitated were decided. He walked by her side. Presently, struck by a sudden thought, Charles said,

'Captain Wentworth, which way are you going? only to Gay-street, or farther up the town?'

'I hardly know,' replied Captain Wentworth, surprised.

'Are you going as high as Belmont? Are you going near Camden-place? Because if you are, I shall have no scruple in asking you to take my place, and give Anne your arm to her father's door. She is rather done for this morning, and must not go so far without help. And I ought to be at that fellow's in the market-place. He promised me the sight of a capital gun he is just going to send off, said he would keep it unpacked to the last possible moment, that I might see it; and if I do not turn back now, I have no chance. By his description, a good deal like the second-sized double-barrel of mine, which you shot with one day, round Winthrop.'

There could not be an objection. There could be only a most proper alacrity, a most obliging compliance for public view; and smiles reined in and spirits dancing in private rapture. In half a minute, Charles was at the bottom of Union-street again, and the other two proceeding together; and soon words enough had passed between them to decide their direction towards the comparatively quiet and retired gravel-walk,* where the power of conversation would make the present hour a blessing indeed; and prepare for it all the immortality which the happiest recollections of their own future lives could bestow. There they exchanged again those feelings and those promises which had once before seemed to secure every thing, but which had been followed by so many, many years of division and estrangement. There they returned again into the past, more exquisitely happy, perhaps, in their re-union, than when it had been first projected; more tender, more tried, more fixed in a knowledge of each other's character, truth, and attachment; more equal to act, more justified in acting. And there, as they slowly paced the gradual ascent, heedless of every group around them, seeing neither sauntering politicians, bustling house-keepers, flirting girls, nor nurserymaids and children, they could indulge in those retrospections and acknowledgments, and especially in those explanations of what had directly preceded the present moment, which were so poignant and so ceaseless in interest. All the little variations of the last week were gone through; and of yesterday and to-day there could scarcely be an end.

She had not mistaken him. Jealousy of Mr. Elliot had been the retarding weight, the doubt, the torment. That had begun to operate in the very hour of first meeting her in Bath; that had returned, after a short suspension, to ruin the concert; and that had influenced him in every thing he had said and done, or omitted to say and do, in the last four-and-twenty hours. It had been gradually yielding to the better hopes which her looks, or words, or actions occasionally encouraged; it had been vanquished at last by those sentiments and those tones which had reached him while she talked with Captain Harville; and under the irresistible governance of which he had seized a sheet of paper, and poured out his feelings.

Of what he had then written, nothing was to be retracted or qualified. He persisted in having loved none but her. She had never been supplanted. He never even believed himself to see her equal. Thus much indeed he was obliged to acknowledge—that he had been constant unconsciously, nay unintentionally; that he had meant to forget her, and believed it to be done. He had imagined himself indifferent, when he had only been angry; and he had been unjust to her merits, because he had been a sufferer from them. Her character was now fixed on his mind as perfection itself, maintaining the loveliest medium of fortitude and gentleness; but he was obliged to acknowledge that only at Uppercross had he learnt to do her justice, and only at Lyme had he begun to understand himself.

At Lyme, he had received lessons of more than one sort. The passing admiration of Mr. Elliot had at least roused him, and the scenes on the Cobb, and at Captain Harville's, had fixed her superiority.

In his preceding attempts to attach himself to Louisa Musgrove (the attempts of angry pride), he protested that he had for ever felt it to be impossible; that he had not cared, could not care for Louisa; though, till that day, till the leisure for reflection which followed it, he had not understood the perfect excellence of the mind with which Louisa's could so ill bear a comparison; or the perfect, unrivalled hold it possessed over his own. There, he had learnt to distinguish between the steadiness of principle and the obstinacy of self-will, between the darings of heedlessness and the resolution of a collected mind. There, he had seen every thing to exalt in his estimation the woman he had lost, and there begun to deplore the pride, the folly, the madness of resentment, which had kept him from trying to regain her when thrown in his way.

From that period his penance had become severe. He had no sooner been free from the horror and remorse attending the first few days of Louisa's accident, no sooner begun to feel himself alive again, than he had begun to feel himself, though alive, not at liberty.

'I found,' said he, 'that I was considered by Harville an engaged man! That neither Harville nor his wife entertained a doubt of our mutual attachment. I was startled and shocked. To a degree, I could contradict this instantly; but, when I began to reflect that others might have felt the same—her own family, nay, perhaps herself, I was no longer at my own disposal. I was hers in honour if she wished it. I had been unguarded. I had not thought seriously on this subject before. I had not considered that my excessive intimacy must have its danger of ill consequence in many ways; and that I had no right to be trying whether I could attach myself to either of the girls, at the risk of raising even an unpleasant report, were there no other ill effects. I had been grossly wrong, and must abide the consequences.'

He found too late, in short, that he had entangled himself; and that precisely as he became fully satisfied of his not caring for Louisa at all, he must regard himself as bound to her, if her sentiments for him were what the Harvilles supposed. It determined him to leave Lyme, and await her complete recovery elsewhere. He would gladly weaken, by any fair means, whatever feelings or speculations concerning him might exist; and he went, therefore, to his brother's, meaning after a while to return to Kellynch, and act as circumstances might require.

'I was six weeks with Edward,' said he, 'and saw him happy. I could have no other pleasure. I deserved none. He enquired after you very particularly; asked even if you were personally altered, little suspecting that to my eye you could never alter.'

Anne smiled, and let it pass. It was too pleasing a blunder for a reproach. It is something for a woman to be assured, in her eight-and-twentieth year, that she has not lost one charm of earlier youth: but the value of such homage was inexpressibly increased to Anne, by comparing it with former words, and feeling it to be the result, not the cause of a revival of his warm attachment.

He had remained in Shropshire, lamenting the blindness of his own pride, and the blunders of his own calculations, till at once released from Louisa by the astonishing and felicitous intelligence of her engagement with Benwick.

'Here,' said he, 'ended the worst of my state; for now I could at least put myself in the way of happiness, I could exert myself, I could do something. But to be waiting so long in inaction, and waiting only for evil, had been dreadful. Within the first five minutes I said, "I will be at Bath on Wednesday," and I was. Was it unpardonable to think it worth my while to come? and to arrive with some degree of hope? You were single. It was possible that you might retain the feelings of the past, as I did; and one encouragement happened to be mine. I could never doubt that you would be loved and sought by others, but I knew to a certainty that you had refused one man at least, of better pretensions than myself: and I could not help often saying, Was this for me?'

Their first meeting in Milsom-street afforded much to be said, but the concert still more. That evening seemed to be made up of exquisite moments. The moment of her stepping forward in the octagon-room to speak to him, the moment of Mr. Elliot's appearing and tearing her away, and one or two subsequent moments, marked by returning hope or increasing despondence, were dwelt on with energy.

'To see you,' cried he, 'in the midst of those who could not be my well-wishers, to see your cousin close by you, conversing and smil-ing, and feel all the horrible eligibilities and proprieties of the match! To consider it as the certain wish of every being who could hope to influence you! Even, if your own feelings were reluctant or indiffer-ent, to consider what powerful supports would be his! Was it not enough to make the fool of me which I appeared? How could I look on without agony? Was not the very sight of the friend who sat

behind you, was not the recollection of what had been, the knowledge of her influence, the indelible, immoveable impression of what
persuasion had once done—was it not all against me?'

'You should have distinguished,' replied Anne. 'You should not
have suspected me now; the case so different, and my age so different. If I was wrong in yielding to persuasion once, remember that it
was to persuasion exerted on the side of safety, not of risk. When I
yielded, I thought it was to duty; but no duty could be called in aid
here. In marrying a man indifferent to me, all risk would have been
incurred, and all duty violated.'

'Perhaps I ought to have reasoned thus,' he replied, 'but I could
not. I could not derive benefit from the late knowledge I had
acquired of your character. I could not bring it into play: it was
overwhelmed, buried, lost in those earlier feelings which I had been
smarting under year after year. I could think of you only as one who
had yielded, who had given me up, who had been influenced by any
one rather than by me. I saw you with the very person who had
guided you in that year of misery. I had no reason to believe her of
less authority now.—The force of habit was to be added.'

'I should have thought,' said Anne, 'that my manner to yourself
might have spared you much or all of this.'

'No, no! your manner might be only the ease which your engagement to another man would give. I left you in this belief; and yet—
I was determined to see you again. My spirits rallied with the
morning, and I felt that I had still a motive for remaining here.'

At last Anne was at home again, and happier than any one in that
house could have conceived. All the surprise and suspense, and every
other painful part of the morning dissipated by this conversation,
she re-entered the house so happy as to be obliged to find an alloy in
some momentary apprehensions of its being impossible to last. An
interval of meditation, serious and grateful, was the best corrective of
every thing dangerous in such high-wrought felicity; and she went to
her room, and grew steadfast and fearless in the thankfulness of her
enjoyment.

The evening came, the drawing-rooms were lighted up, the company assembled. It was but a card-party, it was but a mixture of those
who had never met before, and those who met too often—a
common-place business, too numerous for intimacy, too small for
variety; but Anne had never found an evening shorter. Glowing and

lovely in sensibility and happiness, and more generally admired than she thought about or cared for, she had cheerful or forbearing feelings for every creature around her. Mr. Elliot was there; she avoided, but she could pity him. The Wallises; she had amusement in understanding them. Lady Dalrymple and Miss Carteret; they would soon be innoxious cousins to her. She cared not for Mrs. Clay, and had nothing to blush for in the public manners of her father and sister. With the Musgroves, there was the happy chat of perfect ease; with Captain Harville, the kind-hearted intercourse of brother and sister; with Lady Russell, attempts at conversation, which a delicious consciousness cut short; with Admiral and Mrs. Croft, every thing of peculiar cordiality and fervent interest, which the same consciousness sought to conceal;—and with Captain Wentworth, some moments of communication continually occurring, and always the hope of more, and always the knowledge of his being there!

It was in one of these short meetings, each apparently occupied in admiring a fine display of green-house plants, that she said—

'I have been thinking over the past, and trying impartially to judge of the right and wrong, I mean with regard to myself; and I must believe that I was right, much as I suffered from it, that I was perfectly right in being guided by the friend whom you will love better than you do now. To me, she was in the place of a parent. Do not mistake me, however. I am not saying that she did not err in her advice. It was, perhaps, one of those cases in which advice is good or bad only as the event decides; and for myself, I certainly never should, in any circumstance of tolerable similarity, give such advice. But I mean, that I was right in submitting to her, and that if I had done otherwise, I should have suffered more in continuing the engagement than I did even in giving it up, because I should have suffered in my conscience. I have now, as far as such a sentiment is allowable in human nature, nothing to reproach myself with; and if I mistake not, a strong sense of duty is no bad part of a woman's portion.'*

He looked at her, looked at Lady Russell, and looking again at her, replied, as if in cool deliberation.

'Not yet. But there are hopes of her being forgiven in time. I trust to being in charity with her soon. But I too have been thinking over the past, and a question has suggested itself, whether there may not have been one person more my enemy even than that lady? My own self. Tell me if, when I returned to England in the year eight, with a few thousand pounds, and was posted into the Laconia, if I had then written to you, would you have answered my letter? would you, in short, have renewed the engagement then?'

'Would I!' was all her answer; but the accent was decisive enough.

'Good God!' he cried, 'you would! It is not that I did not think of it, or desire it, as what could alone crown all my other success. But I was proud, too proud to ask again. I did not understand you. I shut my eyes, and would not understand you, or do you justice. This is a recollection which ought to make me forgive every one sooner than myself. Six years of separation and suffering might have been spared. It is a sort of pain, too, which is new to me. I have been used to the gratification of believing myself to earn every blessing that I enjoyed. I have valued myself on honourable toils and just rewards. Like other great men under reverses,' he added with a smile, 'I must endeavour to subdue my mind to my fortune. I must learn to brook being happier than I deserve.'

CHAPTER XII

Who can be in doubt of what followed? When any two young people take it into their heads to marry, they are pretty sure by perseverance to carry their point, be they ever so poor, or ever so imprudent, or ever so little likely to be necessary to each other's ultimate comfort. This may be bad morality to conclude with, but I believe it to be truth; and if such parties succeed, how should a Captain Wentworth and an Anne Elliot, with the advantage of maturity of mind, consciousness of right, and one independent fortune between them, fail of bearing down every opposition? They might in fact have borne down a great deal more than they met with, for there was little to distress them beyond the want of graciousness and warmth.—Sir Walter made no objection, and Elizabeth did nothing worse than look cold and unconcerned. Captain Wentworth, with five-and-twenty thousand pounds, and as high in his profession as merit and activity could place him,* was no longer nobody. He was now esteemed quite worthy to address the daughter of a foolish, spend-thrift baronet, who had not had principle or sense enough to maintain himself in the situation in which Providence had placed him, and who could give his daughter at present but a small part of the share of ten thousand pounds which must be hers hereafter.

Sir Walter indeed, though he had no affection for Anne, and no vanity flattered, to make him really happy on the occasion, was very far from thinking it a bad match for her. On the contrary, when he saw more of Captain Wentworth, saw him repeatedly by daylight and eyed him well, he was very much struck by his personal claims, and felt that his superiority of appearance might be not unfairly balanced against her superiority of rank; and all this, assisted by his well-sounding name, enabled Sir Walter at last to prepare his pen with a very good grace for the insertion of the marriage in the volume of honour.

The only one among them, whose opposition of feeling could excite any serious anxiety, was Lady Russell. Anne knew that Lady Russell must be suffering some pain in understanding and relinquishing Mr. Elliot, and be making some struggles to become truly acquainted with, and do justice to Captain Wentworth. This however was what Lady Russell had now to do. She must learn to feel that she had been mistaken with regard to both; that she had been unfairly influenced by appearances in each; that because Captain Wentworth's manners had not suited her own ideas, she had been too quick in suspecting them to indicate a character of dangerous impetuosity; and that because Mr. Elliot's manners had precisely pleased her in their propriety and correctness, their general politeness and suavity, she had been too quick in receiving them as the certain result of the most correct opinions and well regulated mind. There was nothing less for Lady Russell to do, than to admit that she had been pretty completely wrong, and to take up a new set of opinions and of hopes.

There is a quickness of perception in some, a nicety in the discernment of character, a natural penetration, in short, which no experience in others can equal, and Lady Russell had been less gifted in this part of understanding than her young friend. But she was a very good woman, and if her second object was to be sensible and well-judging, her first was to see Anne happy. She loved Anne better than she loved her own abilities; and when the awkwardness of the beginning was over, found little hardship in attaching herself as a mother to the man who was securing the happiness of her other child.

Of all the family, Mary was probably the one most immediately gratified by the circumstance. It was creditable to have a sister married, and she might flatter herself with having been greatly instrumental to the connexion, by keeping Anne with her in the autumn; and as her own sister must be better than her husband's sisters, it was very agreeable that Captain Wentworth should be a richer man than either Captain Benwick or Charles Hayter.—She had something to suffer perhaps when they came into contact again, in seeing Anne restored to the rights of seniority,* and the mistress of a very pretty landaulette;* but she had a future to look forward to, of powerful consolation. Anne had no Uppercross-hall before her, no landed estate, no headship of a family; and if they could but keep Captain Wentworth from being made a baronet, she would not change situations with Anne.

It would be well for the eldest sister if she were equally satisfied with her situation, for a change is not very probable there. She had soon the mortification of seeing Mr. Elliot withdraw; and no one of proper condition has since presented himself to raise even the unfounded hopes which sunk with him.

The news of his cousin Anne's engagement burst on Mr. Elliot most unexpectedly. It deranged his best plan of domestic happiness, his best hope of keeping Sir Walter single by the watchfulness which a son-in-law's rights would have given. But, though discomfited and disappointed, he could still do something for his own interest and his own enjoyment. He soon quitted Bath; and on Mrs. Clay's quitting it likewise soon afterwards, and being next heard of as established under his protection in London, it was evident how double a game he had been playing, and how determined he was to save himself from being cut out by one artful woman, at least.

Mrs. Clay's affections had overpowered her interest, and she had sacrificed, for the young man's sake, the possibility of scheming longer for Sir Walter. She has abilities, however, as well as affections; and it is now a doubtful point whether his cunning, or hers, may finally carry the day; whether, after preventing her from being the wife of Sir Walter, he may not be wheedled and caressed at last into making her the wife of Sir William.

It cannot be doubted that Sir Walter and Elizabeth were shocked and mortified by the loss of their companion, and the discovery of their deception in her. They had their great cousins, to be sure, to resort to for comfort; but they must long feel that to flatter and follow others, without being flattered and followed in turn, is but a state of half enjoyment.

Anne, satisfied at a very early period of Lady Russell's meaning to love Captain Wentworth as she ought, had no other alloy to the happiness of her prospects than what arose from the consciousness of having no relations to bestow on him which a man of sense could value. There she felt her own inferiority keenly. The disproportion in their fortune was nothing; it did not give her a moment's regret; but to have no family to receive and estimate him properly; nothing of respectability, of harmony, of good-will to offer in return for all the worth and all the prompt welcome which met her in his brothers and sisters, was a source of as lively pain as her mind could well be sensible of, under circumstances of otherwise strong felicity. She had but two friends in the world to add to his list, Lady Russell and Mrs. Smith. To those, however, he was very well disposed to attach himself. Lady Russell, in spite of all her former transgressions, he could now value from his heart. While he was not obliged to say that he believed her to have been right in originally dividing them, he was ready to say almost every thing else in her favour; and as for Mrs. Smith, she had claims of various kinds to recommend her quickly and permanently.

Her recent good offices by Anne had been enough in themselves; and their marriage, instead of depriving her of one friend, secured her two. She was their earliest visitor in their settled life; and Captain Wentworth, by putting her in the way of recovering her husband's property in the West Indies; by writing for her, acting for her, and seeing her through all the petty difficulties of the case, with the activity and exertion of a fearless man and a determined friend, fully requited the services which she had rendered, or ever meant to render, to his wife.

Mrs. Smith's enjoyments were not spoiled by this improvement of income, with some improvement of health, and the acquisition of such friends to be often with, for her cheerfulness and mental alacrity did not fail her; and while these prime supplies of good remained, she might have bid defiance even to greater accessions of worldly prosperity. She might have been absolutely rich and perfectly healthy, and yet be happy. Her spring of felicity was in the glow of her spirits, as her friend Anne's was in the warmth of her heart. Anne was tenderness itself, and she had the full worth of it in

Captain Wentworth's affection. His profession was all that could ever make her friends wish that tenderness less; the dread of a future war all that could dim her sunshine. She gloried in being a sailor's wife, but she must pay the tax of quick alarm for belonging to that profession which is, if possible, more distinguished in its domestic virtues than in its national importance.

APPENDIX A

THE ORIGINAL ENDING OF *PERSUASION*

CHAP. 10

July 8.

With all this knowledge of M^r E— & this authority to impart it, Anne left Westgate Build^{gs}—her mind deeply busy in revolving what she had heard, feeling, thinking, recalling & forseeing everything; shocked at Mr Elliot—sighing over future Kellynch, and pained for Lady Russell, whose confidence in him had been entire.—The Embarrassment which must be felt from this hour in his presence!—How to behave to him?—how to get rid of him?—what to do by any of the Party at home?—where to be blind? where to be active?—It was altogether a confusion of Images & Doubts—a perplexity, an agitation which she could not see the end of—and she was in Gay S^t & still so much engrossed, that she started on being addressed by Adm^l Croft, as if he were a person unlikely to be met there. It was within a few steps of his own door.—'You are going to call upon my wife, said he, she will be very glad to see you.'—Anne denied it 'No—she really had not time, she was in her way home'—but while she spoke, the Adm^l had stepped back & knocked at the door, calling out, 'Yes, yes, do go in; she is all alone, go in & rest yourself.'—Anne felt so little disposed at this time to be in company of any sort, that it vexed her to be thus constrained—but she was obliged to stop. 'Since you are so very kind, said she, I will just ask Mrs Croft how she does, but I really cannot stay 5 minutes.—You are sure she is quite alone.'—The possibility of Capt. W. had occurred—and most fearfully anxious was she to be assured—either that he was within or that he was not; *which*, might have been a question.—'Oh! yes, quite alone—Nobody but her Mantuamaker* with her, & they have been shut up together this half hour, so it must be over soon.'—'Her Mantua maker!—then I am sure my calling now, w^d be most inconvenient.—Indeed you must allow me to leave my Card & be so good as to explain it afterwards to Mrs C.' 'No, no, not at all, not at all. She will be very happy to see you. Mind—I will not swear that she has not something particular to say to you—but *that* will all come out in the right place. I give no hints.—Why, Miss Elliot, we begin to hear strange things of you—(smiling in her face)—But you have not much the Look of it—as Grave as a little Judge.'—Anne blushed.—'Aye, aye, that will do. Now, it is right. I *thought* we were not mistaken.' She was left to guess at the direction of his Suspicions;—the first wild idea had been of some disclosure from his B^r in law—but she was ashamed the next moment—& felt how far more probable that he should be meaning Mr E.—The door was opened—& the Man evidently beginning to *deny* his Mistress, when the sight of his Master stopped him. The Adm^l enjoyed the joke exceedingly. Anne thought his triumph over Stephen rather too long. At last however, he was able to invite her upstairs, & stepping before her said—'I will just go up with you myself & shew you in—.I cannot stay, because I must go to the P. Office, but if you will only sit down for 5 minutes I am sure Sophy will come—and you will find nobody to disturb you—there is nobody but Frederick here—' opening the door as he spoke.—Such a person to be passed over as a Nobody to *her*!—After being allowed to feel quite secure—indifferent—at her ease, to have it burst on her that she was to be the next moment in the same room with him!—No time for recollection!—for planning behaviour, or regulating manners!—There was time only to turn pale, before she had passed through the door, & met the astonished eyes of Capt. W—. who was sitting by the fire pretending to read & prepared for no greater surprise than the Admiral's hasty return.—Equally unexpected was the meeting, on each side. There was nothing to be done however, but to stifle feelings & be quietly polite;—and the Admiral was too much on the alert, to leave any troublesome pause.— He repeated again what he had said before about his wife & everybody— insisted on Anne's sitting down & being perfectly comfortable, was sorry he must leave her himself, but was sure Mrs Croft w^d be down very soon, & w^d go upstairs & give her notice directly.—Anne *was* sitting down, but now she arose again—to entreat him not to interrupt M^rs C— & re-urge the wish of going away & calling another time.—But the Adm^l would not hear of it;—and if she did not return to the charge with unconquerable Perseverance, or did not with a more passive Determination walk quietly out of the room—(as certainly she might have done) may she not be pardoned?—If she *had* no horror of a few minutes Tète a Tète with Capt. W—, may she not be pardoned for not wishing to give him the idea that she *had*?—She reseated herself, & the Adm^l took leave; but on reaching the door, said, 'Frederick, a word with *you*, if you please.'—Capt. W— went to him; and instantly, before they were well out of the room, the Adm^l continued—'As I am going to leave you together, it is but fair I should give you something to talk of—& so, if you please—' Here the door was very firmly closed; she could guess by which of the two; and she lost entirely what immediately followed; but it was impossible for her not to distinguish parts of the rest, for the Adm^l on the strength of the Door's being shut was speaking without any management of voice, tho' she c^d hear his companion trying to check him.—She could not doubt their being speaking of her. She heard her own name & *Kellynch* repeatedly—she was very much distressed. She knew not what to do, or what to expect—and among other agonies felt the possibility of Capt. W—'s not returning into the room at all, which after *her* consenting to stay would have been—too bad for Language.—They seemed to be talking of the Adm^ls Lease of Kellynch. She heard him say something of 'the Lease being signed or not signed'—*that* was not likely to be a very agitating subject—but then followed 'I hate to be at an uncertainty—I must know at once—Sophy thinks the same.' Then, in a lower tone, Capt. W— seemed remonstrating—wanting to be excused—wanting to put something off. 'Phoo, Phoo—answered the Admiral now is the Time. If *you* will not speak, I will stop & speak myself.'—'Very well Sir, very well Sir, followed with some impatience from his companion, opening the door as he spoke.—'You will then—you promise you will?' replied the Admiral, in all the power of his natural voice, unbroken even by one thin door.—'Yes—Sir—Yes.' And the Adm^l was hastily left, the door was closed, and the moment arrived in which Anne was alone with Capt. W—. She could not attempt to see how he looked; but he walked immediately to a window, as if irresolute & embarrassed;—and for about the space of 5 seconds, she repented what she had done—censured it as unwise, blushed over it as indelicate.—She longed to be able to speak of the weather or the Concert—but could only compass the releif of taking a Newspaper in her hand.—The distressing pause was soon over however; he turned round in half a minute, and coming towards the Table where she sat, said, in a voice of effort & constraint—'You must have heard too much already Madam to be in any doubt of my having promised Adm^l Croft to speak to you on some particular subject—& this conviction determines me to do it—however repugnant to my—to all my sense of propriety, to be taking so great a liberty.—You will acquit me of Impertinence I trust, by considering me as speaking only for another, and speaking by Necessity;—and the Adm^l is a Man who can never be thought Impertinent by one who knows him as you do—. His Intentions are always the kindest & the Best;—and you will perceive that he is actuated by none other, in the application which I am now with—with very peculiar feelings—obliged to make.'—He stopped—but merely to recover breath;—not seeming to expect any answer.—Anne listened, as if her Life depended on the issue of his Speech.—He proceeded, with a forced alacrity.—'The Adm^l, Madam, was this morning confidently informed that you were—upon my word I am quite at a loss, ashamed—(breathing & speaking quick)—the awkwardness of *giving* Information of this sort to one of the Parties—You can be at no loss to understand me—It was very confidently said that Mr Elliot—that everything was settled in the family for an Union between Mr Elliot—& yourself. It was added that you were to live at Kellynch—that Kellynch was to be given up. This, the Admiral knew could not be correct—But it occurred to him that it might be the *wish* of the Parties—And my commission from him Madam, is to say, that if the Family wish is such, his Lease of Kellynch shall be cancel'd, & he & my sister will provide themselves with another home, without imagining themselves to be doing anything which under similar circumstances w^d not be done for *them*.—This is all Madam.—A very few words in reply from you will be sufficient.—That *I* should be the person commissioned on this subject is extraordinary!—and believe me Madam, it is no less painful.—A very few words however will put an end to the awakwardness & distress we may *both* be feeling.' Anne spoke a word or two, but they were un-intelligible—And before she could command herself, he added,—'If you only tell me that the Adm^l may address a Line to Sir Walter, it will be enough. Pronounce only the words, *he may*.—I shall immediately follow him with your message.—' This was spoken, as with a fortitude which seemed to meet the message.—'No Sir—said Anne—There is no message.—You are misin—the Adm^l is mis-informed.—I do justice to the kindness of his Intentions, but he is quite mistaken. There is no Truth in any such report.'—He was a moment silent.—She turned her eyes towards him for the first time since his re-entering the room. His colour was varying—& he was looking at her with all the Power & Keenness, which she beleived no other eyes than his, possessed. '*No* Truth in any such report!—he repeated.—No Truth in any *part* of it?'—'None.'—He had been standing by a chair—enjoying the relief of leaning on it—or of playing with it;—he now sat down—drew it a little nearer to her—& looked, with an expression which had something more than penetration in it, something softer;—Her Countenance did not discourage.—It was a silent, but a very powerful Dialogue;—on his side, Supplication, on her's acceptance.—Still, a little nearer—and a hand taken and pressed—and 'Anne, my own dear Anne!'—bursting forth in the fullness of exquisite feeling—and all Suspense & Indecision were over.—They were re-united. They were restored to all that had been lost. They were carried back to the past, with only an increase of attachment & confidence, & only such a flutter of present Delight as made them little fit for the interruption of Mrs Croft, when she joined them not long after-wards.—*She* probably, in the observations of the next ten minutes, saw something to suspect—& tho' it was hardly possible for a woman of her description to wish the Mantuamaker had imprisoned her longer, she might be very likely wishing for some excuse to run about the house, some storm to break the windows above, or a summons to the Admiral's Shoe-maker below.—Fortune favoured them all however in another way—in a gentle, steady rain—just happily set in as the Admiral returned & Anne rose to go.—She was earnestly invited to stay dinner;—a note was dispatched to Camden Place—and she staid;—staid till 10 at night. And during that time, the Husband & wife, either by the wife's contrivance, or by simply going on in their usual way, were frequently out of the room together—gone up stairs to hear a noise, or down stairs to settle their accounts, or upon the Landing place to trim the Lamp.—And these precious moments were turned to so good an account that all the most anxious feelings of the past were gone through.—Before they parted at night, Anne had the felicity of being assured in the first place that—(so far from being altered for the worse!)—she had *gained* inexpressibly in personal Loveliness; & that as to Character—her's was now fixed on his Mind as Perfection itself—maintaining the just Medium of Fortitude & Gentleness;—that he had never ceased to love & prefer her, though it had been only at Uppercross that he had learn't to do her Justice—& only at Lyme that he had begun to understand his own sensations;—that at Lyme he had received Lessons of more than one kind;—the passing admiration of Mr Elliot had at least *roused* him, and the scenes on the Cobb & at Capt. Harville's had fixed her superiority.—In his preceding *attempts* to attach himself to Louisa Musgrove, (the attempts of Anger & Pique)—he protested that he had continually felt the impossibility of really caring for Louisa, though till *that day*, till the leisure for reflection which followed it, he had not understood the perfect excellence of the Mind, with which Louisa's could so ill bear a comparison, or the perfect, the unrivalled hold it possessed over his own.—There he had learnt to distinguish between the steadiness of Principle & the Obstinacy of Self-will, between the Darings of Heedlessness, & the Resolution of a collected Mind—there he had seen everything to exalt in his estimation the Woman he had lost, & there begun to deplore the pride, the folly, the madness of resentment which had kept him from trying to regain her, when thrown in his way. From that period to the present had his penance been the most severe.— He had no sooner been free from the horror & remorse attending the first few days of Louisa's accident, no sooner begun to feel himself alive again, than he had begun to feel himself though alive, not at liberty.—He found that he was considered by his friend Harville, as an engaged Man. The Harvilles entertained not a doubt of a mutual attachment between him & Louisa—and though this to *a degree*, was contradicted instantly—it yet made him feel that perhaps by *her* family, by everybody, by *herself* even, the same idea might be held—and that he was not *free* in honour— though, if such were to be the conclusion, too free alas! in Heart.—He had never thought justly on this subject before—he had not sufficiently considered that his excessive Intimacy at Uppercross must have it's danger of ill consequence in many ways, and that while trying whether he c^d attach himself to either of the Girls, he might be exciting unpleasant reports, if not, raising unrequited regard!—He found, too late, that he had entangled himself—and that precisely as he became thoroughly satisfied of his not *caring* for Louisa at all, he must regard himself as bound to her, if her feelings for him, were what the Harvilles supposed.—It determined him to leave Lyme—& await her perfect recovery elsewhere. He would gladly weaken, by any *fair* means, whatever sentiments or speculations concerning him might exist; and he went therefore into Shropshire meaning after a while, to return to the Crofts at Kellynch, & act as he found requisite.— He had remained in Shropshire, lamenting the Blindness of his own Pride, & the Blunders of his own Calculations, till at once released from Louisa by the astonishing felicity of her engagement with Benwicke. Bath, Bath—had instantly followed, in *Thought*; & not long after, in *fact*. To Bath, to arrive with Hope, to be torn by Jealousy at the first sight of M^r E—, to experience all the changes of each at the Concert, to be miserable by this morning's circumstantial report, to be now, more happy than Language could express, or any heart but his own be capable of.

He was very eager & very delightful in the description of what he had felt at the Concert.—The Even^g seemed to have been made up of exquisite moments;—the moment of her stepping forward in the Octagon Room to speak to him—the moment of M^r E's appearing & tearing her away, & one or two subsequent moments, marked by returning hope, or increasing Despondence, were all dwelt on with energy. 'To see you, cried he, in the midst of those who could not be *my* well-wishers, to see your Cousin close by you—conversing & smiling—& feel all the horrible Eligibilities & Proprieties of the Match!—to consider it as the certain wish of every being who could hope to influence you—even, if your own feelings were reluctant, or indifferent—to consider what powerful supports would be his!—Was not it enough to make the fool of me, which my behaviour expressed?—How could I look on without agony?—Was not the very sight of the *Friend* who sat behind you?—was not the recollection of what *had* been—the knowledge of her Influence—the indelible, immoveable Impression of what *Persuasion* had *once* done, was not it all against me?'—

'You should have distinguished—replied Anne—You should not have suspected me *now*;—The case so different, & my age so different!—If I *was* wrong, in yeilding to Persuasion once, remember that it was to Persuasion exerted on the side of Safety, not of Risk. When I yeilded, I thought it was to *Duty*.—But no *Duty* could be called in aid here.—In marrying a Man indifferent to me, all Risk would have been incurred, & all Duty violated.'—'Perhaps I ought to have reasoned thus, he replied, but I could not.—I could not derive benefit from the later knowledge of your Character which I had acquired, I could not bring it into play, it was overwhelmed, buried, lost in those earlier feelings, which I had been smarting under Year after Year.—I could think of you only as one who *had* yeilded, who *had* given me up, who *had* been influenced by any one rather than by *me*—I saw you with the very Person who had guided you in that year of Misery—I had no reason to think her of less authority now;—the force of Habit was to be added.'—'I should have thought, said Anne, that my Manner to yourself, might have spared you much, or all of this.'—'No—No—Your manner might be only the ease, which your engagement to another Man would give.—I left you with this belief.—And yet—I was determined to see you again.—My spirits rallied with the morning, & I felt that I had still a motive for remaining here.—The Admirals news indeed, was a revulsion. Since that moment, I have been decided what to do—and had it been confirmed, this would have been my *last day* in Bath.'

There was time for all this to pass—with such Interruptions only as enhanced the charm of the communication—and Bath c^d scarcely contain any other two Beings at once so rationally & so rapturously happy as during that even^g occupied the Sopha of Mrs Croft's Drawing room in Gay S^t.

Capt. W.—had taken care to meet the Adm^l as he returned into the house, to satisfy him as to M^r E— & Kellynch;—and the delicacy of the Admiral's good nature kept him from saying another word on the subject to Anne.—He was quite concerned lest he might have been giving her pain by touching a tender part. Who could say?—She might be liking her Cousin, better than he liked her.—And indeed, upon recollection, if they had been to marry at all why should they have waited so long?—

When the Even^g closed, it is probable that the Adm^l received some new Ideas from his Wife;—whose particularly friendly manner in parting with her, gave Anne the gratifying persuasion of her seeing & approving.

It had been such a day to Anne!—the hours which had passed since her leaving Camden Place, had done so much!—She was almost bewildered, almost too happy in looking back.—It was necessary to sit up half the Night & lie awake the remainder to comprehend with composure her present state, & pay for the overplus of Bliss, by Headake & Fatigue.—

CHAPTER 11

Who can be in doubt of what followed?—When any two Young People take it into their heads to marry, they are pretty sure by perseverance to carry their point—be they ever so poor, or ever so imprudent, or ever so

little likely to be necessary to each other's ultimate comfort. This may be
bad Morality to conclude with, but I beleive it to be Truth—and if such
parties succeed, how should a Capt. W— & an Anne E—, with the advantage of maturity of Mind, consciousness of Right, & one Independant
Fortune between them, fail of bearing down every opposition? They
might in fact, have born down a great deal more than they met with, for
there was little to distress them beyond the want of Graciousness &
Warmth. Sir W. made no objection, & Elizth did nothing worse than look
cold & unconcerned. Capt. W— with £25,000—& as high in his Profession as Merit & Activity c^d place him, was no longer nobody. He was now
esteemed quite worthy to address the Daughter of a foolish spendthrift
Baronet, who had not had Principle or sense enough to maintain himself
in the Situation in which Providence had placed him, & who c^d give his
Daughter but a small part of the share of ten Thousand pounds which
must be her's hereafter.—Sir Walter indeed tho' he had no affection for
his Daughter & no vanity flattered to make him really happy on the
occasion, was very far from thinking it a bad match for her.—On the
contrary when he saw more of Capt. W.— & eyed him well, he was very
much struck by his personal claims & felt that *his* superiority of appearance might be not unfairly balanced against *her* superiority of Rank;—and
all this, together with his well-sounding name, enabled Sir W. at last to
prepare his pen with a very good grace for the insertion of the Marriage in
the volume of Honour.—The only person among them whose opposition
of feelings c^d excite any serious anxiety, was Lady Russel.—Anne knew
that Lady R— must be suffering some pain in understanding & relinquishing M^r E—& be making some struggles to become truly acquainted with
& do justice to Capt. W.—This however, was what Lady R— had now to
do. She must learn to feel that she had been mistaken with regard to
both—that she had been unfairly influenced by appearances in each—
that, because Capt. W.'s manners had not suited her own ideas, she had
been too quick in suspecting them to indicate a Character of dangerous
Impetuosity, & that because Mr Elliot's manners had precisely pleased her
in their propriety & correctness, their general politeness & suavity, she had
been too quick in receiving them as the certain result of the most correct
opinions & well regulated Mind. There was nothing less for Lady R. to do
than to admit that she had been pretty completely wrong, & to take up a
new set of opinions & hopes.—There *is* a quickness of perception in some,
a nicety in the discernment of character—a natural Penetration in short
which no Experience in others can equal—and Lady R. had been less
gifted in this part of Understanding than her young friend;—but she was
a very good Woman; & if her second object was to be sensible & well
judging, her first was to see Anne happy. She loved Anne better than she
loved her own abilities—and when the awkwardness of the Beginning was

over, found little hardship in attaching herself as a Mother to the Man who was securing the happiness of her Child. Of all the family, Mary was probably the one most immediately gratified by the circumstance. It was creditable to have a Sister married, and she might flatter herself that she had been greatly instrumental to the connection, by having Anne staying with her in the Autumn; & as her own Sister must be better than her Husbands Sisters, it was very agreable that Capt[n] W— should be a richer Man than either Capt. B. or Charles Hayter.—She had something to suffer perhaps when they came into contact again, in seeing Anne restored to the rights of Seniority & the Mistress of a very pretty Landaulet—but *she* had a *future* to look forward to, of powerful consolation—Anne had no Uppercross Hall before her, no Landed Estate, no Headship of a family, and if they could but keep Capt. W— from being made a Baronet, she would not change situations with Anne.—It would be well for the *Eldest* Sister if she were equally satisfied with *her* situation, for a change is not very probable there.—She had soon the mortification of seeing M[r] E. withdraw, & no one of proper condition has since presented himself to raise even the unfounded hopes which sunk with *him*. The news of his Cousin Anne's engagement burst on M[r] Elliot most unexpectedly. It deranged his best plan of domestic Happiness, his best hopes of keeping Sir Walter single by the watchfulness which a son in law's rights w[d] have given—But tho' discomfited & disappointed, he c[d] still do something for his own interest & his own enjoyment. He soon quitted Bath and on M[rs] Clay's quitting it likewise soon afterwards & being next heard of, as established under his Protection in London, it was evident how double a Game he had been playing, & how determined he was to save himself from being cut out by *one* artful woman at least.—M[rs] Clay's affections had overpowered her Interest, & she had sacrificed for the Young Man's sake, the possibility of scheming longer for Sir Walter;—she has Abilities however as well as Affections, and it is now a doubtful point whether his cunning or hers may finally carry the day, whether, after preventing her from being the wife of Sir Walter, he may not be wheedled & caressed at last into making her the wife of Sir William.—

It cannot be doubted that Sir Walter & Eliz: were shocked & mortified by the loss of their companion & the discovery of their deception in her. They had their great cousins to be sure, to resort to for comfort—but they must long feel that to flatter & follow others, without being flattered & followed themselves is but a state of half enjoyment.

Anne, satisfied at a very early period, of Lady Russel's *meaning* to love Capt. W— as she ought, had no other alloy to the happiness of her prospects, than what arose from the consciousness of having no relations to bestow on him which a Man of Sense could value.—There, she felt her own Inferiority keenly.—The disproportion in their fortunes was nothing;—it did not give her a moment's regret;—but to have no Family to receive & estimate him properly, nothing of respectability, of Harmony, of Goodwill to offer in return for all the Worth & all the prompt welcome which met her in his Brothers & Sisters, was a source of as lively pain, as her Mind could well be sensible of, under circumstances of otherwise strong felicity.—She had but two friends in the World, to add to his List, Lady R. & Mrs Smith.—To those however, he was very well-disposed to attach himself. Lady R— inspite of all her former transgressions, he could now value from his heart;—while he was not obliged to say that he beleived her to have been right in originally dividing them, he was ready to say almost anything else in her favour;—& as for Mrs Smith, she had claims of various kinds to recommend her quickly & permanently.—Her recent good offices by Anne had been enough in themselves—and their marriage, instead of depriving her of one friend secured her two. She was one of their first visitors in their settled Life—and Capt. Wentworth, by putting her in the way of recovering her Husband's property in the W. Indies, by writing for her, & acting for her, & seeing her through all the petty Difficulties of the case, with the activity & exertion of a fearless Man, & a determined friend, fully requited the services she had rendered, or had ever meant to render, to his Wife. Mrs Smith's enjoyments were not *spoiled* by this improvement of Income, with some improvement of health, & the acquisition of such friends to be often with, for her chearfulness & mental Activity did not fail her, & while those prime supplies of Good remained, she might have bid defiance even to greater accessions of worldly Prosperity. She might have been absolutely rich & perfectly healthy, & yet be happy.—*Her* spring of Felicity was in the glow of her Spirits—as her friend Anne's was in the warmth of her Heart.—Anne was Tenderness itself;—and she had the full worth of it in Captn Wentworth's affection. His Profession was all that could ever make her friends wish *that* Tenderness less; the dread of a future War, all that could dim her Sunshine.—She gloried in being a Sailor's wife, but she must pay the tax of quick alarm, for belonging to that Profession which is—if possible—more distinguished in it's Domestic Virtues, than in it's National Importance.—

FINIS

July 18.–1816.

APPENDIX B

RANK AND SOCIAL STATUS

The drama and the comedy of Austen's novels are dependent on a sharp awareness of fine social distinctions. As she famously told her niece Anna, '3 or 4 Families in a Country Village is the very thing to work on', and an understanding of the subtle social differences between those families is crucial to an understanding of the meanings of her novels.[1] Which is not to say that Austen herself necessarily approves of the obsession with differences of rank manifested by some of her characters (the obsequious Mr Collins, fawning on Lady Catherine de Bourgh in *Pride and Prejudice*, for example, or Sir Walter Elliot, never tired of reading his name in the *Baronetage*, in *Persuasion*); rather that, as the daughter of a far from wealthy rural clergyman who nevertheless had much wealthier family connections (her brother Edward was adopted by a rich landowning cousin, and inherited estates in Kent and Hampshire), she was astutely realistic about the effects that differences of status and income could have on people's lives—and particularly on the lives of women.

Austen writes about a very specific social group: the rural élite during the period of the Napoleonic Wars. But 'rural élite' needs careful definition. Austen deals hardly at all, and never sympathetically, with the aristocracy, the great titled families; and though she is sometimes loosely described as writing about 'the gentry', the traditional rural gentry, those whose income and status were dependent on long-standing ownership of land, are not really her main focus. Members of the traditional gentry often appear in her fiction—Darcy in *Pride and Prejudice*, for example, or Mr Knightley in *Emma* (whose name, rather than any actual title, indicates his status), or, less promisingly, Sir John Middleton in *Sense and Sensibility*, or Mr Rushworth in *Mansfield Park*—but Austen is much more interested in the types of people who lived more precariously on the margins of the gentry proper, but whose connections, education, or role in the community gave them the right, like her father the rector, to 'mix in the best society of the neighbourhood'.[2] Critics have coined a variety of terms to describe this shifting, heterogeneous group, some of whom

[1] *Jane Austen's Letters*, 3rd edn., ed. Deirdre Le Faye (Oxford and New York: Oxford University Press, 1995), 275.
[2] James Edward Austen-Leigh, *A Memoir of Jane Austen* (1871), in *A Memoir of Jane Austen and Other Family Recollections*, ed. Kathryn Sutherland (Oxford: Oxford University Press, 2002), 26.

aspired to imitate a traditional gentry lifestyle, some of whom, though they might mix socially and marry into the gentry, identified much more closely with professional, meritocratic values. Terry Lovell refers to them simply as the 'lesser gentry'; for Nancy Armstrong, playing suggestively with two nevertheless inappropriate terms, they are a 'middle-class aristocracy'; and, perhaps most usefully, David Spring adopts the historian Alan Everitt's category 'pseudo-gentry'—though, as Jan Fergus points out, there are also drawbacks to a term which 'carries too many connotations of fraudulence'.[3] However problematic, such labels indicate the inadequacy simply of 'gentry', and they also importantly avoid the suggestion that Austen's characters are 'bourgeois', a term more appropriate to the dominantly urban class system of later nineteenth-century industrial society, rather than to the hierarchy of rank, rather than class, which governed the rural social order familiar to Austen.

In Austen's world, money certainly matters. Austen always makes sure we know precisely what her main characters are worth in financial terms. And her professionally based perspective is evident from the way in which, as Edward Copeland points out, she gives that information in terms of annual income rather than, for example, numbers of acres owned—even in the case of someone like Darcy, whose wealth is land based.[4] But, in Austen's world, there is no straightforward equivalence between income and social status, and certainly none between income or social status and moral approval. Some members of the 'pseudo-gentry' are upwardly mobile, having bought their way into a leisured gentry lifestyle, usually with the proceeds of trade: Bingley, for example, in *Pride and Prejudice*, is renting Netherfield, having inherited a fortune from his father, who 'had intended to purchase an estate, but did not live to do it'.[5] Such characters have to shore up their merely financial status by cultivating social connections with the traditional gentry—sometimes with mixed success. More often, however, Austen's pseudo-gentry, and particularly the professional classes, are more complexly involved with the landowning

---

[3] Terry Lovell, 'Jane Austen and the Gentry: A Study in Literature and Ideology', in Diana Laurenson (ed.), *The Sociology of Literature: Applied Studies* (Keele: Sociological Review Monographs, 1978), 21; Nancy Armstrong, *Desire and Domestic Fiction: A Political History of the Novel* (Oxford and New York: Oxford University Press, 1987), 160; David Spring, 'Interpreters of Jane Austen's Social World: Literary Critics and Historians', in Janet Todd (ed.), *Jane Austen: New Perspectives, Women and Literature*, 3 (New York and London: Holmes and Meier, 1983), 60; Jan Fergus, *Jane Austen: A Literary Life* (Basingstoke and London: Macmillan, 1991), 47.

[4] Edward Copeland, 'Jane Austen and the Consumer Revolution', in J. David Grey *et al.* (eds.), *The Jane Austen Handbook* (London: Athlone Press, 1986), 77; Edward Copeland, 'Money', in Edward Copeland and Juliet McMaster (eds.), *The Cambridge Companion to Jane Austen* (Cambridge: Cambridge University Press, 1997), 134.

[5] *Pride and Prejudice*, vol. I, ch. iv.

gentry, whose system of property inheritance worked to the financial disadvantage of daughters and younger sons. Primogeniture, which sought to preserve estates by passing them down through the male line rather than dividing them equally between several children, is responsible for the precarious circumstances of many of Austen's characters. Though the social respectability of younger sons like Henry Tilney in *Northanger Abbey*, Edmund Bertram in *Mansfield Park*, or John Knightley in *Emma* is assured by their family connections, financially they are much less secure since they have to make their own living. Typically, they do so by entering one of the traditional professions, where, theoretically at least, they would be in competition with young men from lowlier backgrounds seeking to improve their social standing by way of a successful career. In practice, personal merit could be considerably less important in securing a comfortable position than the systems of patronage open to younger sons through family connections. Most often, Austen's male professionals are clergymen, like two of her brothers and her father, whose rectorships at Steventon and Deane, in Hampshire, were in the gift of a wealthy relation. Occasionally, they are lawyers, like John Knightley—and like the uncle who paid for Austen's father's education out of the proceeds of his legal practice and a highly advantageous marriage to a rich widow. The other favoured profession is that of naval officer where, again—as Austen well knew from the experiences of her two sailor brothers, and as William Price learns in *Mansfield Park*—successful promotion often depended on securing the favour of an influential patron.

Daughters almost never inherit, of course, and, like the Bennets in *Pride and Prejudice* or the Dashwood sisters in *Sense and Sensibility*, might even lose their home at their father's death to a sometimes quite remote male relative, through the system of 'entail'. Nor are they expected to earn their own living, since for women of this class to work—as a governess, for example, like Jane Fairfax in *Emma*—was to risk losing all respectability. Their father's will might have provided them with a settlement of capital which yields a more or less adequate annual income, but their (and their family's) best hope of financial and social security is to marry well, which is much more likely on Emma's fortune of thirty thousand pounds (or £1,500 per year) than on Elizabeth Bennet's one thousand (£40). For the unmarried daughters of professional men without property or capital— like Miss Bates in *Emma*, and like Austen herself—the death of their father could bring both significant financial hardship and the consequent prospect of slipping down the social hierarchy.

Austen expects her readers to be alert to the subtle signals of status within this narrow, but still various, world. At the most obvious level, income is displayed through consumer items such as carriages or furnishings (an annual income of £800 was needed to run a carriage), or in domestic arrangements like the number of servants employed or the ability to go up to London or to Bath for the season. The full notes to this edition help modern readers to read the telling, but now unfamiliar, details whose meanings Austen could take for granted in her contemporary audience, just as today we are adept at interpreting the social meanings of a particular car or designer label. But Austen also expects us to recognize a different hierarchy, of moral rather than monetary value, evident through less tangible signs—a character's language, for example, or their readiness (or not) to treat those lower down the social scale with respect. The status of 'gentleman' is an important one for Austen, but it is much more than simply a label of rank. This is evident when Austen introduces the Gardiners, the Bennet sisters' uncle and aunt, in *Pride and Prejudice*, for example. Mr Gardiner is one of the most 'sensible, gentlemanlike' men, and his wife is one of the most 'amiable, intelligent, elegant' women in her fiction. Yet the Gardiners '[live] by trade, and within view of his own warehouses', a social and physical location which would horrify the superficial, snobbish Bingley sisters. And in the same novel the heroine Elizabeth Bennet proudly claims the status of 'gentleman's daughter', and has to educate Austen's richest hero into behaving in 'a more gentleman-like manner'.[6] Though her heroines obediently marry up, they carry with them Austen's meritocratic moral instincts. Unlike the inherited estates of the traditional gentry, the title of gentleman, and the respect and love of the heroine, must be earned.

V. J.

Further Reading

Butler, Marilyn, 'History, Politics, and Religion', in J. David Grey *et al.* (eds.), *The Jane Austen Handbook* (London: Athlone Press, 1986), 190–208.

Copeland, Edward, 'Jane Austen and the Consumer Revolution', in Grey *et al.* (eds.), *Jane Austen Handbook*, 77–92.

——'Money', in Edward Copeland and Juliet McMaster (eds.), *The Cambridge Companion to Jane Austen* (Cambridge: Cambridge University Press, 1997), 131–48.

——'What is a Competence? Jane Austen, her Sister Novelists, and the 5%'s', *Modern Language Studies*, 9 (1979), 161–8.

McMaster, Juliet, 'Class', in Copeland and McMaster (eds.), *Cambridge Companion*, 115–30.

---

[6] *Pride and Prejudice*, vol. II, ch. ii; vol. III, ch. xiv; vol. II, ch xi.

Spring, David, 'Interpreters of Jane Austen's Social World: Literary Critics and Historians', in Janet Todd (ed.), *Jane Austen: New Perspectives, Women and Literature*, 3 (New York and London: Holmes and Meier, 1983), 53–72.

Williamson, Tom, and Bellamy, Liz, *Property and Landscape: A Social History of Land Ownership and the English Countryside* (London: George Philip, 1987).

APPENDIX C

DANCING

Whether it took place in private houses, or at public assemblies held at inns or purpose-built assembly rooms, social dancing in polite society was governed in Austen's time by strict rules of etiquette, the broad outlines of which dated back to Beau Nash's 'Rules to be observ'd at Bath' of 1706. Designed to facilitate social mixing, to involve strangers, and to prevent anyone from being monopolized by a single partner (whether or not they wished to be), such rules were posted outside public assembly rooms, or taken as read at private balls. The 'Rules' for the Assembly Rooms at Maidstone in Kent are typical:

> Places in Country Dances to be drawn for, and Partners to be changed after every second Dance.

> Every Lady who does not go down the set, except prevented by indisposition, precludes herself from dancing during the evening . . .

> Gentlemen, Officers on duty excepted, are not admissible in boots.

> Strangers will be introduced to Partners by applying to the Gentlemen of the Committee; each of whom is, in rotation, to act as Master of Ceremonies for the night . . .[1]

Other rules are listed in a contemporary *Companion to the Ball Room*. For example, same-sex couples were not allowed, 'without the permission of the Master of Ceremonies; nor can permission be given while there are an equal number of Ladies and Gentlemen'.[2] Men did the asking, of course, with the help of the Master of Ceremonies if an introduction was required, and there was often manœuvring in advance to book particular dances with a favoured partner. To neglect to ask someone in need of a partner to dance (as Darcy does to Elizabeth in *Pride and Prejudice*, and Mr Elton does to Harriet in *Emma*), to dance with someone else after refusing an invitation from another partner (a mistake made by Frances Burney's Evelina), or to give up on a dance before the end, was considered grossly impolite.[3] Young women at public assemblies were accompanied

[1] 'Rules' [1797?], Assembly Room, Maidstone, Kent, courtesy of Maidstone Museum and Art Gallery.

[2] Thomas Wilson, *A Companion to the Ball Room* (London, Edinburgh, Dublin, 1816), 222.

[3] *Pride and Prejudice*, vol. I, ch. iii; *Emma*, vol. III, ch. ii; Frances Burney, *Evelina* (1778), vol. I, letter xi, ed. Vivien Jones (Oxford: Oxford University Press, 2002), 34–5.

by a chaperone—usually their mother or some other older woman who was expected to pass the time playing cards or chatting, rather than dancing herself. Austen registers the transition from dancer to onlooker in one of her letters to her sister Cassandra, written when she was thirty-seven: 'By the bye, as I must leave off being young, I find many Douceurs in being a sort of Chaperon for I am put on the Sofa near the Fire & can drink as much wine as I like.'[4]

By the early nineteenth century, dances like the waltz, danced by individual couples and in close physical contact with your partner—and considered dangerously improper as a result—were being imported from Europe and beginning to gain popularity in the most fashionable London circles. But the assembly room rules refer to the traditional 'country dances', which still held sway at the balls Austen herself attended, and at those described in her fiction. Balls usually began with minuets, which were more stately and elegant than the country dances which followed but which, like country dances, involved holding your partner by the hand only, and at arm's length. Unlike country dances, minuets danced the same steps to different tunes. Country dances (which included French dances like the 'Boulanger' and traditional English dances such as 'Gathering Peascods') were performed to particular tunes, sometimes in a circle, but most often in a 'set', in which an indefinite number of couples faced each other. They typically involved very complicated figures in which each couple worked their way from the top to the bottom of the set by completing the dance figure with every other couple in turn. The 'Lady who does not go down the set' is thus spoiling the dance for everyone else. A long dance or a large set could mean quite a lot of standing and waiting, and thus the opportunity (or pressure) to converse with one's partner, an obligation Elizabeth Bennet draws to Darcy's attention in *Pride and Prejudice*.[5] The higher you stood in the set, the more attention you drew. At Maidstone, evidently, places were decided by drawing lots, but at Bath, for example, it was done strictly according to social rank. At special balls— like the one held for Fanny in *Mansfield Park*—the person honoured would be expected to lead the set, just as the bridal couple today traditionally start the dancing at weddings.

Dancing was much encouraged in manuals on polite behaviour, and taught at fashionable schools:

This is one of the most genteel and polite Accomplishments which a young Lady can possess. It will give a natural, easy and graceful Air to all the Motions of your Body, and enable you to behave in Company with a

---

[4] *Letters*, ed. Le Faye, 251.
[5] *Pride and Prejudice*, vol. I, ch. xviii.

modest Assurance and Address. Besides, it is an Art in which you will frequently be obliged to shew your Skill, in the fashionable Balls and Assemblies . . .; to appear ignorant or aukward on these Occasions, would not fail to put you to the Blush.[6]

But the necessary personal display involved was also a source of anxiety to the writers of books on moral conduct. The Evangelical Thomas Gisborne, for example, whose *Enquiry into the Duties of the Female Sex* (1797) Austen read and approved, acknowledged that dancing was 'an amusement in itself both innocent and salubrious, and therefore by no means improper, under suitable regulations', but that it also provided young women with 'the stage for displaying the attractions, by the possession of which a young woman is apt to be most elated' and 'if a young woman cannot partake of the amusements of a ball-room, except at the expence of benevolence, of friendship, of diffidence, of sincerity, of good-humour, at the expence of some Christian disposition . . . she has no business there'.[7]

Austen loved dancing and, according to family memoirs, she was good at it. Her letters to her sister Cassandra are full of descriptions of the participants, the flirting and the displays of fashion (including her own) at the neighbourhood balls she attended: 'There were twenty Dances & I danced them all, & without any fatigue . . . in cold weather & with few couples I fancy I could just as well dance for a week together as for half an hour.—My black Cap was openly admired by M[rs] Lefroy, & secretly I imagine by every body else in the room.'[8] But they also ironically register the anxieties and the jealousies warned against in more moralistic terms by Gisborne: 'I do not think I was very much in request—. People were rather apt not to ask me till they could not help it.' And on another occasion: 'The room was tolerably full, & there were perhaps thirty couple of Dancers;—the melancholy part was to see so many dozen young Women standing by without partners, & each of them with two ugly naked shoulders!'[9] Scenes set at balls and assemblies are an important structural feature of all Austen's novels. In such scenes, she subtly explores the pleasures and pains of dancing, and of the matchmaking and social mixing ritualized in its elaborate rules of polite behaviour.

V. J.

[6] *The Polite Academy; or, School of Behaviour for Young Gentlemen and Ladies. Intended as a Foundation for Good Manner and Polite Address* . . ., 4th edn. (London: R. Baldwin and Salisbury: B. Collins, 1768), p. xxxv.

[7] Thomas Gisborne, *An Enquiry into the Duties of the Female Sex*, 3rd edn., corrected (London: Cadell and Davies, 1798), 190–1; and see *Letters*, ed. Le Faye, 112: 'I am glad you recommended "Gisborne", for having begun, I am pleased with it, and I had quite determined not to read it.'

[8] *Letters*, ed. Le Faye, 29–30.

[9] Ibid. 35, 156–7.

Further Reading

Franks, Arthur Henry, *Social Dance: A Short History* (London: Routledge and Kegan Paul, 1963).

Lee-Riffe, Nancy M., 'The Role of Country Dance in the Fiction of Jane Austen', *Women's Writing*, 5: 1 (1998), 103–12.

Monaghan, David, *Jane Austen: Structure and Social Vision* (London: Macmillan, 1980).

Richardson, Philip J. S., *The Social Dances of the Nineteenth Century in England* (London: Herbert Jenkins, 1960).

APPENDIX D
AUSTEN AND THE NAVY

Austen had personal as well as patriotic reasons for her interest in the Navy, which plays a significant role in *Mansfield Park* and is central to *Persuasion*. For most of Austen's adult life, Britain was at war with post-Revolutionary and Napoleonic France and this had a direct influence on the careers of three of her six brothers. For a fairly brief period during the 1790s, Henry Austen was a lieutenant in the Oxford Militia, one of the non-regular regiments (like the one stationed near Meryton in *Pride and Prejudice*) which were dedicated to home defence in the event of an invasion; after resigning from the militia in 1801, he used his military contacts to set up business as an army agent and banker in London, a business which failed in 1816, the year after the war ended. Austen's youngest brothers, Francis and Charles, had lifelong careers in the Navy, rising eventually—after Austen's death—to become Admirals, and between them they were involved in all the major naval theatres of war: carrying troops and supplying the British Army; blockading the French fleet in the English Channel, the Mediterranean, and off the Atlantic coast of Spain; and protecting British trading vessels on the North American seaboard and in the East Indies. Austen clearly favours the Navy: partly in tribute both to her brothers and to the service publicly celebrated as largely responsible for the eventual victory over Napoleon; but also because the Navy's cultural cachet, as well as its particular conditions of service, allowed her to explore issues of professionalism and social status, patronage and individual merit, and patriotic manliness.

The careers of Austen's brothers typified the way in which the modernization of the Navy during the Napoleonic period was still dogged by entrenched systems of favouritism and patronage. Mary Wollstonecraft, writing in 1790 against Edmund Burke's defence of English systems of inherited authority in the face of French Revolutionary ideas, used the Navy as an iniquitous example, where men, 'press[ed] for the sea service', were 'compelled to pull a strange rope at the surly command of a tyrannic boy, who probably obtained his rank on account of his family connections'.[1] Austen's family had no naval contacts who might have been used

---

[1] Mary Wollstonecraft, *A Vindication of the Rights of Men* (1790), in *A Vindication of the Rights of Men and A Vindication of the Rights of Woman*, ed. Janet Todd (Oxford: Oxford University Press, 1994), 13–14.

to find sea-going apprenticeships for Frank and Charles, so they were entered for the Royal Naval Academy at Portsmouth, where they received an officer's education. Though the Academy dated back to the early eighteenth century, there was still considerable prejudice among traditionally minded officers against those who joined the Navy by this professional route, and promotion thereafter was often still dependent on securing patronage. Both Frank and Charles achieved gradual promotion through a mixture of merit and influence. Through the marriages of their brother James and their cousin, Jane Cooper, into families with naval connections, the Austens were able to mobilize influence to get their sons promoted to more prestigious ships. 'Frank is made.—He was yesterday raised to the Rank of Commander . . . & likewise . . . Lieut. Charles John Austen is removed to the *Tamer* Frigate', Austen wrote to her sister Cassandra in 1798.[2] The experience is directly reflected in *Mansfield Park*, where William Price, whose immediate family have none of the right connections, is dependent for his promotion from midshipman to lieutenant on Henry Crawford's intervention with his dissolute uncle the Admiral.

But, at other points in their careers, both Frank and Charles also achieved promotion and honours through their involvement in significant battles or the capture of enemy ships: the kind of professional reward for merit romantically represented in the heroic career of Captain Wentworth in *Persuasion*. Like Captain Wentworth, whose fortune is the result of 'prize-money', naval officers could make considerable fortunes out of the war. 'Prize-money' was awarded by the government to a ship's crew when they had sunk or, even better, captured an enemy military or trading vessel, the amount due being based on an evaluation of the ship's assets. But substantial financial gifts or other trophies were also offered to naval commanders by commercial enterprises like Lloyd's insurance or the East India Company in payment for protecting the merchant fleet, or carrying valuable freight for merchant companies. Austen presents Captain Wentworth's financial success in a wholly positive light, and celebrates in her letters the (comparatively small) prize-money awarded to her brothers, but these rewards were much more controversial, both inside and outside the Navy, than her representation of them acknowledges. Though they are used by Austen to suggest a properly meritocratic system which rewards heroism and ability, for many commentators they were not equitable enough. They were vociferously attacked by the radical William Cobbett, for example, whose principles—more egalitarian than Austen's—were offended by an unequal system of distribution according to which the captain's share of prize-money was three-eighths or, after a review of 1808,

---

[2] *Letters*, ed. Le Faye, 32.

one-quarter of the total, with the remainder divided among the rest of the crew. Brian Southam quotes a distribution of prizes from 1799, for example, in which 'each Captain's share represented his pay for over 300 years and a seaman's pay (of £12) for fifteen years'.[3]

Austen's romantic representation of the Navy also ignores the notorious brutality meted out to sailors to enforce discipline, and it plays down the sheer hazardousness of a naval career—though danger is acknowledged in the 'tax of quick alarm' which Anne, as a naval wife, must pay for her happiness with Wentworth.[4] During the Napoleonic period 80 per cent of deaths at sea were due to disease or accidents; 13 per cent to natural disasters; and only 7 per cent to death in battle.[5] Instead, through the female perspective of the domestic novel, Austen contributes to the idealization of the Navy and of naval heroes which was dominant in British culture both during and immediately after the Napoleonic Wars: a popularity reflected and sustained in publications such as Robert Southey's *Life of Nelson* of 1813, which Austen was willing to read 'if Frank is mentioned in it'.[6] In Austen's selective representation, the Navy's meritocratic professionalism stands for vigorous, manly Englishness—William Price, 'working his way to fortune and consequence with so much self-respect and happy ardour'; or the 'intelligence, spirit and brilliancy' of Captain Wentworth[7]—in contrast to the inadequacies of the landed gentry: Sir Thomas Bertram's irresponsibility, or the effete self-preening of Sir Walter Elliot, totally unable to appreciate the merits of Admiral Croft. But, in *Persuasion*, the Navy stands, too, for new ideals of domestic behaviour: in the 'picture of repose and domestic happiness' which Anne finds at the Harvilles' lodgings in Lyme; and, more daringly, in the successful partnership of the Crofts' marriage. Mrs Croft's insistence on accompanying her husband to sea ('as long as we could be together, nothing ever ailed me'), and her assertion that women are 'rational creatures' rather than 'fine ladies', suggest that women, too, might aspire to share in the new professionalism which has saved the nation.[8]

V. J.

[3] Brian Southam, *Jane Austen and the Navy* (London and New York: Hambledon and London, 2000), 121, and on Cobbett, see ibid. 119.

[4] *Persuasion*, vol. II, ch. xii.

[5] Southam, *Jane Austen and the Navy*, 67–8.

[6] *Letters*, ed. Le Faye, 235.

[7] *Mansfield Park*, vol. II, ch. vi; *Persuasion*, vol. I, ch. iv.

[8] *Persuasion*, vol. I, ch. xi; vol. I, ch. viii; and see Roger Sales, *Jane Austen and Representations of Regency England* (London and New York: Routledge, 1994), 180–1.

Further Reading

Cohen, Monica, 'Persuading the Navy Home: Austen and Married Women's Professional Property', *Novel: A Forum on Fiction*, 29: 3 (1996), 346–66.

Fulford, Tim, 'Romanticizing the Empire: The Naval Heroes of Southey, Coleridge, Austen, and Marryat', *Modern Language Quarterly*, 60: 2 (1999), 161–96.

Morriss, Roger, *The Royal Dockyards during the Revolutionary and Napoleonic Wars* (Leicester: Leicester University Press, 1983).

Parkinson, C. Northcote, *Britannia Rules: The Classic Age of Naval History 1793–1815* (Gloucester: Sutton, 1987).

Southam, Brian, *Jane Austen and the Navy* (London and New York: Hambledon and London, 2000).

TEXTUAL NOTES

In the list that follows, references are to page and line in the present volume; the adopted text is given first, followed by the alternative reading. Commentary is given in italics.

A = the first edition, 1818

VOLUME I

9.7   contempt, as] contempt. As *A*

9.15   1801] 1800 *A. Cf. pp. 10, 13 infra: she had been dead 13 years by summer 1814*

11.8   daughters'] daughter's *A*

48.15 was,] was *A*

48.24 in reply] to reply *A*

72.37 and 'No] 'And no *A*

78.12 us] them *A*

85.16 endurance] endurances *A*

VOLUME II

100.33 room now] now room *A*

102.39 owners'] owners *A*

135.14 joyous,] joyous *A*

164.3   yours] your *A*

168.19 several] general *A*

183.18 more] move *A*

184.16 out of my] out my *A*

184.27 friends'] friend's *A*

193.35 for it] it for *A*

195.17 begun] began *A*

EXPLANATORY NOTES

Abbreviations

Johnson	Samuel Johnson, *A Dictionary of the English Language*, 4th edn. (London, 1773).
Letters	*Jane Austen's Letters*, 3rd edn., ed. Deirdre Le Faye (Oxford and New York: Oxford University Press, 1995).
Lewis	Samuel Lewis, *A Topographical Dictionary of England*, 4 vols. (London, 1831).
New Bath Guide	*The New Bath Guide; Or, Useful Pocket Companion. For all Persons residing at or resorting to this Antient City*, new edn. (Bath: W. Taylor, 1784).
OED	*Oxford English Dictionary*, 2nd edn.
Treatise on Carriages	William Felton, *A Treatise on Carriages: Comprehending Coaches, Chariots, Phaetons, Curricles, Whiskies, &c. Together With Their Proper Harness. In Which The Fair Prices of Every Article Are Accurately Stated* (London, 1794; rpt. Mendham, NJ: The Astragal Press, 1995).

Biographical Notice

4 *a D'Arblay and an Edgeworth*: two of the most esteemed novelists publishing during Austen's lifetime, Frances Burney (1752–1840), known as Madame D'Arblay following her 1793 marriage, and Maria Edgeworth (1767–1849). *Northanger Abbey* pays tribute to both when the narrator, defending the novel form from the condescension of its critics, points to Burney's *Cecilia* (1782) and *Camilla* (1796) and to Edgeworth's *Belinda* (1801) as proof that some novels display 'the greatest powers of the mind . . . [,] the most thorough knowledge of human nature, the happiest delineation of its varieties, the liveliest effusions of wit and humour' (vol. I, ch. v).

symptoms of a decay, deep and incurable: examining Austen's letters and other family records, some historians of medicine have conjectured that Austen died of a failure of the adrenal glands, the disorder that since her time has come to be known as Addison's disease. Others have identified the disorder as Hodgkin's disease.

some stanzas: the verses entitled 'When Winchester races' (included in Austen, *Catharine and Other Writings*, ed. Margaret Anne Doody and Douglas Murray (Oxford: Oxford University Press, 1993), 245). They use the occasion of Winchester's July horse races to retell the legend which holds that rain on St Swithun's Day, 15 July, heralds another forty days of precipitation. This reference to the verses, which Austen probably dictated to her sister, Cassandra, was omitted from the version of the

'Biographical Notice' that Henry Austen published in 1833, as well as from the first full-scale biography of Austen, James Edward Austen-Leigh's *A Memoir of Jane Austen* (1870). As proper Victorians, Austen's surviving relations found their aunt's light-hearted way of occupying her deathbed an embarrassment.

5 *her eloquent blood spoke through her modest cheeks*: while testifying to his sister's properly feminine modesty, Henry Austen echoes John Donne's lines mourning Elizabeth Drury in 'The Second Anniversary' (published 1612): '. . . her pure, and eloquent blood | Spoke in her cheeks, and so distinctly wrought, | That one might almost say, her body thought' (ll. 244–6).

6 *Neither the hope of fame nor profit mixed with her early motives*: in minimizing his sister's professionalism, Henry Austen means, here as elsewhere, to protect her reputation for femininity and gentility. Her letters, however, suggest an author who is attentive to sales and canny in her dealings with publishers (dealings in which Henry, often but not always, acted as a mediator). See, for instance, the letter to her brother Francis she writes shortly after the publication of *Pride and Prejudice*: 'I have now therefore written myself into £250.—which only makes me long for more' (*Letters*, 217).

Gilpin on the Picturesque: Revd William Gilpin's accounts of British scenery, in books such as *Observations on the River Wye . . . Relative Chiefly to Picturesque Beauty* (1782), taught readers new modes of appreciating the landscape and a new language with which to flaunt their aesthetic sensibilities. Gilpin was popular in part because he offered an alternative to the Grand Tours of the Continent favoured by eighteenth-century aristocratic gentlemen: his picturesque tours of Britain suited lower gentry and middle-class budgets.

Johnson in prose, and Cowper in verse: Samuel Johnson (1709–84), who owed his fame to his essay series *The Rambler* (see note to p. 85), and William Cowper (1731–1800), the poet of rural domesticity whose quality of feeling and love of nature are much admired by the heroines Marianne Dashwood of *Sense and Sensibility* and Fanny Price of *Mansfield Park*.

'Sir Charles Grandison': the last of the three long novels-in-letters written by Samuel Richardson (1689–1761), *The History of Sir Charles Grandison* (1753–4) inspired Austen, sometime between 1800 and 1805, to write (in an amazing feat of abridgement) the play 'Sir Charles Grandison, or the Happy Man. A Comedy in Five Acts'. See *Jane Austen's 'Sir Charles Grandison'*, ed. B. C. Southam (Oxford: Oxford University Press, 1980).

7 *She did not rank any work of Fielding quite so high*: comparisons of Samuel Richardson and Henry Fielding (1707–54)—identified in early nineteenth-century histories of the novel as the duo who had simultaneously begun the fashion of novel-writing in England—frequently assumed that the former was more appropriate reading for ladies than the latter. Recalling the sexual appetites of the hero of Fielding's *Tom Jones* (1749), or

Tom's bastardy, Henry Austen may, with this claim, be taking pains once again to project a prim and proper image of his sister.

7 *a young relation*: James Edward Austen-Leigh, son of Austen's eldest brother and, decades later, his aunt's biographer. Henry Austen has reworded the letter, which Austen began writing to 'Edward' on her own birthday, 16 December 1816 (see *Letters*, 322–4).

your manly, vigorous sketches . . . a little bit of ivory: Austen arguably intended this self-deprecating characterization of her own art jokingly, and as a pat on the back for her teenaged nephew. But because critics during the last decade of her life had begun to insist on the distinctions ostensibly separating 'masculine' from 'feminine' novels, this excerpt from her correspondence has, since its publication, often been read unironically, as proof that this woman novelist knew her feminine limitations.

8 *with rather longer petticoats than last year*: the original of this letter has never been discovered, and it is known only through Henry Austen's extracts in the 'Biographical Notice'. The reference to the short petticoats of Captain——'s wife and sister was omitted from later versions of the 'Notice', for the same reasons that the reference to the 'stanzas replete with fancy and vigour' was (on these omissions see Jo Modert, *Jane Austen's Manuscript Letters in Facsimile* (Carbondale, Ill.: Southern Illinois University Press, 1990), pp. xxii–xxiii).

Persuasion

9 *the Baronetage*: numerous listings of the baronets of England and accounts of their genealogies were issued and reissued from the late seventeenth century on. The book Sir Walter consults to read his own history may be Debrett's *Baronetage of England*, which was issued in two volumes in 1808.

limited remnant of the earliest patents: a title was also referred to as a *patent*: 'a writ conferring some exclusive right or privilege' (Johnson). Sir Walter regrets the passing away of the families whose titles date back to the seventeenth century. James I had created the title of baronet in 1611 and had used the financial support he obtained from the baronets he created to fund his army in Northern Ireland.

endless creations of the last century: Sir Walter's contempt for the low-born recipients of the new titles that the government had distributed would extend to those who, like the commander of the Fleet, Lord Nelson (the son of a mere country clergyman), had recently been rewarded with newly created peerages for their war service.

Dugdale: William Dugdale's *The Ancient Usage in Bearing of Such Ensigns of Honour as are Commonly Call'd Arms. With a Catalogue of the present Nobility of England* (1682), which supplied the nineteenth-century compilers of peerages with a means of identifying families whose honours were of long standing.

High Sheriff: the chief representative of the Crown in county government, the High Sheriff presided over parliamentary elections and the administration of justice. Holders of the office (which is now a mainly ceremonial one) were chosen annually from among the principal landowners of the county.

exertions of loyalty, and dignity of baronet, in the first year of Charles II.: this indicates that the Elliots' title originated with the restoration of the Stuart monarchy in 1660 and that it was, like many baronetcies, an ancestor's reward for loyalty to that royal family. Charles II's 1660 return from exile put a close to a historical chapter which included the Civil War, the execution of Charles I, and England's short-lived experiment with republicanism. This detail would be noticed by Austen's first readers: radical political reformers in her lifetime had often taken inspiration from seventeenth-century political crises or were accused by their opponents of doing so. (The year after Austen's death the poet Percy Bysshe Shelley began a drama entitled *Charles the First*.) With the failure of the French Revolution and the subsequent restoration in 1815 of the Bourbon monarchy, history had recently appeared to be repeating itself. On the rank of baronet, see note to p. 15.

duodecimo: a duodecimo page, so called because it is produced by folding a large printer's sheet into twelve parts, measures about four by seven inches.

10 *Heir presumptive*: Sir Walter's annotation reminds us that he has no son and also suggests that the property of Kellynch Hall is, in the legal terminology of the period, entailed and subject to strict settlement. Sir Walter's daughters are not and cannot be heirs to his estate. Instead, the legal device that some Elliot ancestor must have employed to ensure that Kellynch Hall would never pass from the male line of the family makes Mr William Walter Elliot, though a distant relation, the heir to the estate, barring the future birth of a son to Sir Walter.

an awful legacy: here as elsewhere Austen uses 'awful' to denote '[t]hat which strikes with awe' (Johnson): 'awesome'.

11 *his dear daughters' sake*: this is how most modern editions render this passage. In the first edition, however, perhaps because of an error the printer made in positioning the apostrophe, Sir Walter remained single for 'his dear daughter's sake'. However, it is quite possible that the reference to 'daughter' in the singular rather than 'daughters' in the plural might not be an error but an instance of Austen's irony. Sir Walter is capable of forgetting two of his three daughters at the very moment when he is thinking about what a good father he has been.

12 *the chaise and four*: although an expensive purchase, given that it carried ordinarily no more than three passengers, the chaise was one of the lighter enclosed carriages used in the period. The use of four horses to power it, where fewer would do, marks the Elliots' extravagance.

opening every ball: the rules of etiquette that governed balls assigned the place of honour in the sets formed for the country dances to the couple of the highest rank. As testimony to her status as the eldest daughter of the neighbourhood's only baronet, Elizabeth, with a partner, has the honour of beginning the dancing at these balls, and the other couples in the set follow them. See Appendix C on 'Dancing' in this volume, and compare the episode in *Mansfield Park* in which Fanny Price discovers to her surprise that she herself is expected 'to lead the way and open the ball': Mr Crawford conducts her to their assigned place at the top of the room, where the other couples join them, and Fanny muses to herself, 'To be placed above so many elegant young women! The distinction was too great' (vol. II, ch. x).

13 *Tattersal's*: visits to Richard Tattersall's auction house for the sale of bloodstock (thoroughbred and pedigree horses), founded in 1766, might be to Sir Walter's taste simply because Sir Walter shares with breeders of bloodstock their solicitude about pedigree. Tattersall's premises near Hyde Park, which included club rooms for members of the Jockey Club as well as stables and a riding ring, were also a place where gentlemen could place bets on races. The prestige of being seen in this particular locale would be considerable: Tattersall's friends included the Prince Regent (later King George IV). Austen also uses the names of her characters to allude to Tattersall's world of thoroughbred horse racing: stallions owned and bred by the Wentworth family of Yorkshire were frequent race winners during Austen's youth. I am grateful to my colleague Richard Nash for sharing his knowledge of the history of the turf.

wearing black ribbons for his wife: the black ribbons trimming her gowns and caps are Elizabeth's inexpensive way of acknowledging Mr Elliot's loss of his wife. Full mourning would be deemed an unnecessarily costly sign of respect for the death of so distant a relation, but some acknowledgement was obligatory.

14 *Mr. Shepherd, his agent*: manager of Sir Walter's estate, who probably oversees the farming of the Kellynch property by its tenants.

15 *had every acre been alienable*: another suggestion that the Elliot estate is subject to strict settlement. Aside from the small part of his estate (likely a recent acquisition) that Sir Walter may sell on the open market, i.e. that he may 'alienate', Kellynch Hall must, under the terms of the settlement, be transmitted intact to Sir Walter's heir.

the widow of only a knight: a knighthood, less prestigious than a baronetcy, was awarded for particular services. In *Pride and Prejudice*, for example, Austen introduces Sir William Lucas with the explanation that he was 'formerly in trade in Meryton, where he had made a tolerable fortune and risen to the honour of knighthood by an address to the King, during his mayoralty' (vol. I, ch. v). A knight could not pass his title to an heir. As a baronet, and someone who could, Sir Walter Elliot outranks Lady Russell, although he is technically not a member of the aristocracy but belongs instead to the uppermost rank of the gentry. The rank of baronet hovers between the gentry and the aristocracy, and this in-between position may account for Sir Walter's preoccupation with differences of rank.

17 *Bath*: a city in Somerset, which owes its fame to its hot springs of mineral waters, reputed to be medicinal for those who drink or bathe in them. *The New Bath Guide* reports that 'This place was originally a resort of cripples and diseased persons, but is now as much frequented by the gay and healthy for their pleasure, as the sick for their health' (p. 4). Throughout the eighteenth century, sites such as Bath's theatre and assembly rooms were as frequented as the baths themselves. By Austen's day, however, Bath's glamour as a 'vortex of amusement' was on the wane (*New Bath Guide*, 26). Fashion had begun to follow the Prince Regent to Brighton, where the Prince built himself a Marine Pavilion; and other south coast resorts, such as Weymouth and Lyme Regis (see note to p. 79), had also gained in popularity as holiday sites, in part because, from the middle of the eighteenth century on, sea air and salt water bathing had acquired more and more advocates amongst medical practitioners.

19 *returned, after an unprosperous marriage, to her father's house*: along with Lady Russell and Mrs Smith, Mrs Clay should be considered one of the novel's widows. Divorce rarely ended marriages in this era, except among the very rich.

complaisance: here, as elsewhere in the novel, used as a synonym for 'civility: desire of pleasing' (Johnson).

20 *This peace*: the Peace of Paris, signed 30 June 1814 in the wake of Napoleon Bonaparte's abdication as emperor, ended hostilities between Britain and France for the first time since the year-long interval that had succeeded the Peace of Amiens in 1802. The original readers of *Persuasion* would, however, have known, as the characters do not, that in March 1815 Bonaparte, having escaped from his exile on the island of Elba, would resume power in Paris. Bonaparte's escape brought a renewal of hostilities, which were terminated, following the interval known as the Hundred Days, by France's decisive defeat at the Battle of Waterloo on 18 June 1815.

A prize indeed: Sir Walter alludes through his pun to the source of the wealth that some naval officers brought ashore with them: the money that they and (to a lesser degree) the other members of the crew were awarded for the enemy ships (for the *prizes*) that they had sunk or captured. See Appendix D on 'Austen and the Navy' in this volume. Prizes were a sailor's sole route to wealth, since the salaries the Navy paid even to commissioned officers were modest. (The net pay in 1814 for the commander of a sloop was £272 a year. In *Sense and Sensibility*, Colonel Brandon cautions that, although Edward Ferrars might live comfortably as a bachelor on £200 a year, that income, even when it comes with a rectory in which to live rent-free, 'cannot enable him to marry' (vol. III, ch. iv).)

20 *liberal notions*: when Mr Shepherd commends Navy officers for their liberal notions, his verbal agility and ability to defer to Sir Walter's prejudices in favour of family and rank while simultaneously keeping an eye on financial matters are evident. The word 'liberal' can mean either 'becoming a gentleman' or 'generous; bountiful, not parcimonious' (Johnson).

23 *the quarter sessions at Taunton*: civil and criminal trials were conducted under the auspices of the county courts, whose quarterly sessions in towns such as Taunton (the county seat of Somerset) would bring together the county's professional men and country gentlemen in their guise as justices of the peace and as jury men.

24 *rear admiral of the white*: rear admirals were junior to vice-admirals, who were in turn outranked by admirals. Within each rank, there were three grades, which were, in order of seniority, the Red, White, and Blue (the names derive from the colours of the flags that each division of the Fleet had carried in the seventeenth century).

the Trafalgar action: the decisive naval victory over the Napoleonic Fleet that occurred off the southern coast of Spain on 21 October 1805. Lord Nelson, the Commander-in-Chief of the Mediterranean Fleet, did not survive the battle, but his victory ensured Britain's supremacy in the Mediterranean and its security from the prospect of a future invasion.

would be glad of the deputation: a law of 1671 restricted the right to shoot game (pheasants, partridge, grouse, rabbits) to gentlemen who met certain property qualifications. Sir Walter has the power, however, to 'deputize' his tenant to shoot, by virtue of his own right to do so.

25 *nothing to do with the Strafford family*: the Wentworths of Yorkshire were ennobled when King Charles I made their ancestor Thomas Wentworth the first Earl of Strafford for his services in Ireland. In the early days of the Civil War, Strafford was impeached and executed at the urging of Parliament. The title 'Earl of Strafford' was subsequently revived with the Restoration, and Wentworth's son became the Second Earl, but by Sir Walter Elliot's day it had died out altogether.

26 *the action off St. Domingo*: Santo Domingo, the Caribbean island that is the present-day location of Haiti and the Dominican Republic, was, because of the riches of its sugar plantations, a prize for which the British and French imperial powers vied repeatedly between 1793 and 1815. Their rivalry was complicated by the struggles for freedom engaging the enslaved population of the island, led by Toussaint L'Ouverture, which culminated in the establishment in 1804 of Haiti as an independent black republic. At the beginning of 1806 a French squadron broke the Continental blockade and sailed to Santo Domingo to begin a concerted disruption of Britain's trade in the West Indies. On 6 February its ships were routed by the British squadron in which Austen's brother Francis was serving as captain.

28 *the nice tone of her mind*: Austen here, as elsewhere, uses 'nice' in a now obsolete sense as a synonym for 'fastidious' or 'refined' (Johnson).

29 *the other step in rank*: the promotion from commander to captain proper, which would have qualified Wentworth for the captaincy of larger, better-armed ships than the sloops or gun brigs assigned to commanders. This promotion would have enhanced his chances of capturing enemy vessels.

navy lists: listings of the commissioned officers or of the ships in the fleet, which would often supply records of the battles in which men and ships had been engaged. These were available in numerous formats: Anne might have consulted an official Admiralty publication like *An alphabetical list of the post captains, commanders, and lieutenants of His Majesty's Fleet* or the cheap pamphlets that were issued monthly by the bookseller David Steel, *Steel's original and correct list of the Royal Navy and Honourable East-India Company's shipping*.

31 *'This indenture sheweth'*: the customary preamble to a legal contract.

will never set the Thames on fire: a proverbial expression. According to the Admiral, Sir Walter will never do anything remarkable.

Michaelmas: 29 September, one of the four days, fixed by custom, on which quarterly rents were paid and on which tenancy of houses would begin and end.

33 *more dangerous attractions than any merely personal*: attractions that are merely 'personal' are limited to those that are 'Exterior; corporal' (Johnson). Mrs Clay is not physically attractive, but in her company Sir Walter might nonetheless begin to contemplate a second marriage.

38 *the usual stock of accomplishments*: in providing for their daughters' schooling, parents were concerned less for their education than for their fate in a competitive marriage market. The curriculum designed for the woman of fashion focused, accordingly, on 'accomplishments': the instruction in piano or harp, in drawing, and in modern languages such as French that would certify her gentility, make her a good conversation partner for her husband, and give her (as Hester Chapone in her popular *Letters on the Improvement of the Mind* proposed) 'the power of filling up agreeably those intervals of time, which too often hang heavily on the hands of a woman' (*Letters on the Improvement of the Mind* (London, 1773; rpt. Hagers-Town, Md., 1819), letter viii, vol. ii, p. 193). However, girls were also warned, and with increasing frequency during Austen's lifetime, not to be too zealous in their pursuit of accomplishments. To leave school a 'prodigy', i.e. to get too proficient at music or art, was an outcome to be avoided, because of the damage it might do to a girl's reputation for modesty.

39 *none of your Queen-squares for us*: the lively Musgrove sisters may consider Queen Square—which was one of the earliest products of Bath's eighteenth-century building boom—an outmoded backwater where the company would be too staid for their taste. The sisters' preference is the more piquant when one knows that in 1799 Austen's wealthy brother Edward leased a rather grand house in Queen Square, which Austen visited.

39 *repulsive*: 'repellent—intended or tending to repel by denial, coldness of manner' (*OED*).

41 *give her the precedence that was her due*: according to proper etiquette, Mary is, as the daughter of a baronet, entitled to take precedence over her mother-in-law (precedence that Mary could not claim merely as the wife of the Musgroves' eldest son). If she stands on ceremony, Mary can, for instance, elect to precede the elder Mrs Musgrove when they are entering or leaving a room or to lead the way when they are taking their places in a carriage. See also the note to p. 12 on how Elizabeth Elliot is entitled to open every ball.

43 *country dances*: for details on how these were danced, see Appendix C on 'Dancing' in this volume. In an 1808 letter Austen writes of practising country dances on the pianoforte at Chawton, so that 'we may have some amusement for our nephews and nieces when we have the pleasure of their company' (*Letters*, 161).

there being no means of her going: Charles drives a curricle (see p. 80 and note) and would not have room to carry a third passenger in comfort.

46 *frigate*: one of the smaller vessels used in the Navy, reserved mainly for convoy duty, although captains of frigates would also cruise for French privateers (armed vessels that were commanded not by naval officers but by civilians and which concentrated their efforts on capturing merchant shipping).

Clifton: a fashionable spa town 14 miles north-west of Bath.

47 *the school-master*: Captain Wentworth's concern for Dick Musgrove's schooling seemed excessive to Dick himself, but it was also mandatory. The Navy employed schoolmasters (often the ships' chaplains) to provide education to all its midshipmen. The schoolmasters would instruct 'the youngsters', as they were known, in the mathematical and astronomical knowledge that was required for navigation and gunnery. After at least six years on a ship's muster (an apprenticeship period which a boy could begin as early as age 11), a midshipman would be examined in these topics and on his record. If he passed, he could be appointed lieutenant and begin his career as an officer. In many ways, the Fleet provided offshore boarding schools to the parents of this period, especially to those who were rich or well connected politically and whose recommendations would therefore have some weight with the Navy captains, who could choose which boys they put on their ships' musters.

48 *Her brother's return*: it is Charles Musgrove who returns. 'Brother', as Austen and her contemporaries use the term, can include a brother-in-law. See also p. 96, where Mary refers to herself as Louisa Musgrove's sister, rather than sister-in-law, and see the reference on p. 202 to Captain Wentworth's 'brothers and sisters', a group including both Admiral Croft and the woman who by marrying his brother Edward became Captain Wentworth's 'sister'.

56 *old built sloop*: a sloop was the smallest Navy vessel and carried no more than eighteen guns. But Wentworth's first command may have made up for its smallness with its seaworthiness. Commenting on Admiral Croft's assertion, Brian Southam observes that because there was a shortage of wood as the war dragged on, old built ships were constructed from a better grade of timber than newer ones (*Jane Austen and the Navy* (London and New York: Hambledon and London, 2000), 270).

with no more interest than his: promotion to the rank of commander, which Wentworth received in 1806, did not automatically lead to an appointment as the captain of a specific ship. There were more commissioned officers than there were appointments, and Wentworth is lucky that he was not obliged to wait longer (on shore and on half-pay) for the opportunities that his active service provided him for supplementing his captain's salary with prize-money. Wentworth is the novel's figure of self-reliance, but in the Navy of this era the claims of individual merit were only beginning to count for as much as the individual's connections and the influence or 'interest' those connections exercised. For further detail, see Appendix D on 'Austen and the Navy' in this volume.

57 *pelisse*: an ankle-length overcoat worn by women.

Plymouth . . . the Sound: Plymouth is a south coast sea-port, one of the chief 'naval and military stations in the kingdom, and during war, the most important, as commanding the entrance of the English Channel, and being the grand rendezvous of the channel fleet' (Lewis, iii. 541). The Sound is the inlet that leads from the English Channel into Plymouth Harbour.

the Great Nation: France.

Gibraltar: the Rock of Gibraltar off the southern tip of Spain, a British territory since 1713. The base the Royal Navy maintained there gave Britain control of the strategically important straits connecting the Atlantic to the Mediterranean.

58 *her name and rate, and present non-commissioned class*: there were six classes of Navy ships, which were rated according to the number of guns they carried. The highest were the first-rates: these three-deckers carried 120 cannon. At the bottom of the scale, as the fifth- or sixth-rates, were the frigates (such as the *Laconia*, the ship Wentworth is commanding when Dick Musgrove ends up as one of his midshipmen), which would carry between thirty-two and forty-four cannon. Below them came the unrated ships. The latter category included the sloops (such as Wentworth's first command, the *Asp*), as well as brigs, schooners, and cutters. A ship that was non-commissioned, like the *Laconia*, had been taken out of service and was manned by a skeleton crew only.

the Western Islands: the West Indies.

59 *never willingly admit any ladies*: strictly speaking, regulations prohibited a captain from carrying 'any Woman to Sea' (*Regulations and Instructions*

Relating to His Majesty's Service at Sea (1790), cited in Southam, *Jane Austen and the Navy*, 276). But to his brother-in-law and sister, Wentworth's embargo on female passengers appears overscrupulous and even irrational. It was not that unusual for the wives or mistresses of the officers and of the men of other ranks to find accommodation—and in the case of working-class women, employment—on board.

60 *a man of war*: the term used for any ship equipped for battle, no matter what its size.

61 *Cork, and Lisbon*: bases for the Navy's Irish Squadron and Mediterranean Fleet respectively.

never went beyond the Streights: the Straits of Gibraltar (see note to p. 57); Mrs Croft is explaining that her voyages have never taken her east into the Mediterranean.

Deal: a seaport on the coast of Kent, important because of its proximity to the Downs Anchorage. This was an area between the coast and the outlying sands, where ships awaiting favourable winds or their orders could lie in safety, protected from the weather.

the assizes: 'The sessions held periodically in each county of England, for the purpose of administering civil and criminal justice' (*OED*). Unlike the quarter sessions (see note to p. 23), which were presided over by local justices of the peace, the assizes were presided over by professional judges travelling on circuit.

63 *a gig*: the plainest, least expensive style of carriage, drawn by one horse. The passengers in a gig, unlike those in a closed carriage such as a coach, would be exposed to the elements and, on rough country roads, liable to be tossed out (see p. 72).

66 *freehold property*: property that is held for life, as opposed to property held through a lease.

72 *conscious*: the word is formed from the Latin for 'knowing' (*scio*) and 'with' (*con*), and although Austen in *Persuasion* sometimes uses 'conscious', 'consciousness', and 'consciously' to communicate the familiar sense of being 'aware of what one is doing', she also, with her contemporaries, uses these terms in an older sense that approaches that etymological emphasis on 'knowing something with others'. In that older sense, to be 'conscious' was to share a knowledge, like a secret, with a witness, including the witness of one's own sense of better judgement. According to this older usage, which might appropriately evoke Henrietta's sense of wrongdoing where cousin Charles is concerned, someone who is 'conscious' has a secret on her mind. See also, e.g., p. 198, 'attempts at conversation, which a delicious consciousness cut short'.

73 *stile*: 'A set of steps to pass from one inclosure to another' (Johnson). People would be able to climb a stile to get into or out of an enclosed field or pasture, but it would be impassable to sheep and cattle.

74 *Captain Wentworth and Louisa in the hedge-row . . . down the centre*: describing the lie of the land around Winthrop, Austen probably draws on her memories of the countryside surrounding her childhood home of Steventon, where, as James Edward Austen-Leigh reports in the *Memoir*, the hedgerows enclosing the fields were planted in double rows. Between these rows of 'copse-wood and timber' there would be a channel 'wide enough to contain within it a winding footpath, or a rough cart track' (ch. 2). In an 1813 letter Austen asks her sister to investigate 'whether Northamptonshire is a country of Hedgerows' (*Letters*, 202); the request suggests that this episode in *Persuasion* might have been intended originally for *Mansfield Park*, which Austen was beginning at that time.

75 *The listener's proverbial fate*: 'Listeners never hear good of themselves.'

78 *spread a little more canvas*: nautical jargon. Canvas is the material from which sails are made. Admiral Croft, who, if he wished one of his ships to go more swiftly, would order his crew to raise more sails, is saying that he wishes that Captain Wentworth would stop delaying and start hurrying up.

79 *Lyme*: or Lyme Regis, port on the south coast of England. By the end of the eighteenth century, trade there had declined, because the enlarged scale on which merchant ships had come to be built meant that they could no longer enter Lyme's harbour. However, the town in the meantime was metamorphosing into a popular seaside resort. Austen's contemporary, the courtesan memoirist Harriette Wilson, described Lyme 'as a sort of Brighton, in miniature, all bustle and confusion, assembly-rooms, donkey-riding, raffling, &c. &c.' (*Memoirs of Harriette Wilson* (London, 1825), iii. 263). Austen and members of her family visited Lyme in 1803 and 1804, when Austen attended a ball at the Assembly Rooms, took walks, and bathed in the sea, most likely using a bathing machine (see note to p. 80).

80 *Mr. Musgrove's coach . . . and Charles's curricle*: a coach would ordinarily hold as many as six persons and was recommended to prospective buyers of this period as the most convenient form of transportation for large families (*Treatise on Carriages*, i. 36). A curricle is a two-wheeled open carriage, said to be favoured by 'those who are partial to drive their own horses' (*Treatise on Carriages*, ii. 95). It held only two persons and could be purchased for approximately one-third the price of a coach.

bathing machines: invented in the mid-eighteenth century, the bathing machine was a mobile hut which would be wheeled into the sea, where its inmate, holding onto a harness of sorts, would be dipped into the waves. This device enabled users to receive the health benefits of salt water without compromising their modesty.

the Cobb itself, its old wonders and new improvements: the Cobb was a semicircular stone breakwater that had been built in the Middle Ages to create a harbour for Lyme and to protect the town from storms. Its rebuilt masonry was deemed one of the modern architectural wonders of

England. The Cobb incorporated two causeways, which were linked by a steep staircase.

80 *Charmouth . . . Up Lyme*: Charmouth is a small village and resort for sea-bathing, located two miles north-east of Lyme. Up Lyme is located one mile and a quarter to the north-west and, as its name suggests, up the hill from the town.

81 *Pinny, with its green chasms between romantic rocks*: many readers encountering this description of the scenery of Pinny, just west of Lyme, have detected an echo of the poet Samuel Taylor Coleridge's 'Kubla Khan' (composed 1798; published 1816). See lines 12–13: 'But oh! that deep romantic chasm which slanted | Down the green hill athwart a cedarn cover. . . .' The romance of the landscape is the product of a series of landslides, which have carried into Pinny Bay some of the cliff paths on which Austen must have walked during her stay in Lyme.

the far-famed Isle of Wight: a large island just off the south coast of England, immediately south of Southampton. Austen's brother Francis (another naval officer) lived with his young family for a time in Yarmouth, then the Island's principal town.

83 *constant employment within*: in making himself useful around the house, Harville is likely continuing habits acquired on board ship. It was common for sailors to while away time during a long voyage by taking up handicrafts, and Austen in letters often mentions how good her brother Francis is with his hands and how well he keeps himself occupied while home on shore. In February 1807, for instance, Francis busies himself crafting a 'very nice fringe for the Drawingroom-Curtains' (*Letters*, 123).

new netting-needles and pins with improvements: at this moment in her account of Captain Harville's handiwork, Austen is having fun mixing up male and female spheres. Since Harville may be preparing to make the nets that would be used on board ship to stow the sails and hammocks, and since the pins he improves may be belaying pins, used on board ship to secure ropes, he is in some ways keeping up his connection with the naval profession. Netting was, in fact, a drawing-room occupation men might engage in with impunity. Yet netting also invokes the world of female handicraft (net purses were popular accessories), and the reference to needles and pins inevitably reminds readers of the paraphernalia that was supposed to define the domestic woman.

84 *'no-thorough-fare of Lyme'*: Lyme was not well served by Britain's inland road system. Because of their distance from any major coaching road, the town's innkeepers would presumably have difficulty in obtaining any great variety of provisions for their guests and at the close of the season may have abandoned the effort altogether.

whether Marmion or The Lady of the Lake were to be preferred, and how ranked the Giaour and The Bride of Abydos: the first two titles refer to long narrative poems, romances of medieval times, published by Sir Walter Scott in 1808 and 1810; the third and fourth refer to 'Turkish tales' published by rival poet Lord Byron in 1813. The poets' representations of warrior heroes committing doughty deeds in picturesque settings probably contributed to their wartime popularity. Still, the notes that Byron appended to his poems adopt a more cynical view of their heroes' sabre-rattling than do the poems themselves, in ways that distinguish their account of heroism from *Persuasion*'s idealistic view of its chivalric war hero. Anne and Benwick prove themselves faithful observers of the literary scene when they attempt to adjudicate between Scott and Byron (an attempt they resume on p. 90). Similar efforts at a comparative evaluation of the decade's two most commercially successful poets are pursued in William Hazlitt's *The Spirit of the Age* (1825) and the anonymous *A Discourse on the Comparative Merits of Scott and Byron* (1824).

85 *our best moralists*: the texts Anne prescribes to Benwick would very probably include works by Samuel Johnson. Throughout the second half of the eighteenth century readers made an almost medicinal use of the essay series *The Rambler* (first published 1750–2), in which Johnson treats such topics as the dangers of solitude and the necessity of resignation in the face of loss. Johnson's biographer James Boswell claimed of *The Rambler* that 'In no writings whatever can be found . . . more that can brace and invigorate every manly and noble sentiment' (*Life of Johnson*, ed. R. W. Chapman (Oxford: Oxford University Press, 1983), 154).

86 *procuring a dispensation*: Dr Shirley would have to procure permission to reside away from his parish and to hire the curate who would perform his pastoral duties in his absence. (Henrietta understandably considers Charles Hayter to be perfect for that job.) The Church of England did not make such dispensations difficult to procure. At various points in his career Austen's father, Revd George Austen, exercised his rectorship *in absentia*, while continuing to collect the parish tithes.

88 *from Sidmouth . . . for Crewkherne*: Sidmouth is another of the south coast's seaside resorts, located 17 miles from Lyme in Devonshire. Crewkerne (as it is now spelled) is an inland market town in the county of Somerset.

89 *I wonder the arms did not strike me!*: the Elliot coat of arms would have been painted on the side of the carriage.

90 *just made into the Grappler*: i.e. having just been promoted in rank and assigned the command of the *Grappler*. Compare Austen's 1798 letter, in which she passes on the latest news of her brother Francis: 'Frank is made.—He was yesterday raised to the Rank of Commander' (*Letters*, 32).

I would as soon have been run up to the yard-arm: one punishment meted out on board Navy ships involved hanging or ducking the offender from the yard or yard-arm ('a wooden . . . spar, . . . slung at its centre from, and forward of a mast and serving to support and extend a square sail' (*OED*)).

91 *Lord Byron's 'dark blue seas'*: Benwick and Anne perhaps recall the second
    canto of *Childe Harold's Pilgrimage* (1812). Its description of the hero's
    voyage from Greece and of the 'little warlike world within' (ii. 154) he
    enters when he boards the ship certainly glamorizes nautical life: 'He
    that has sail'd upon the dark blue sea, | Has view'd at times, I ween, a full
    fair sight' (ii. 145–6). They may also be remembering the lines that open
    The Corsair (1814), a description of the freedom that the poem's pirates
    enjoy as outlaws: 'O'er the glad waters of the dark blue sea, | Our
    thoughts as boundless and our souls as free'. In a letter of 1814 Austen
    sounds jaded about the Byronic heroes, such as Harold and Conrad the
    Corsair, who enthuse Captain Benwick: 'I have read the Corsair, mended
    my petticoat, & have nothing else to do' (*Letters*, 257).

96 *Anne, who was nothing to Louisa, while she was her sister*: we would say 'sis-
    ter-in-law' rather than 'sister': see note to p. 48.

97 *an Emma towards her Henry*: in Matthew Prior's much anthologized
    'Henry and Emma, A Poem' (1709; based on the sixteenth-century ballad
    'The Nut-Brown Maid'), the hero, who suspects that all women are
    fickle, determines to put his lover's constancy on trial. Emma passes the
    test that Henry sets her: she responds to his announcement that he has
    transferred his affections to a younger, more beautiful woman by offer-
    ing, in extravagantly self-abnegating fashion, to cater to her (non-
    existent) rival's every demand.

98 *when the horses were baited*: when the horses were rested and fed.

99 *the mansion-house*: that is, the Great House, and not Uppercross Cottage,
    where Anne had previously stayed with her sister and brother-in-law.

    blains: probably an abbreviation of *chilblains*, inflammations 'produced by
    exposure to cold, affecting the hands and feet' (*OED*).

101 *the house in Camden-place*: the Elliots have landed in an expensive block of
    houses in a newer neighbourhood of Bath. Camden Place overlooks the
    city centre to the south from the slope of Beacon Hill.

103 *breaking a head and giving a plaister*: proverbial expression. *Plaister* is the
    obsolete spelling of *plaster*, the 'curative application used for the local
    application of a medicament, or for closing a wound' (*OED*). Admiral
    Croft is using the proverb to comment jokingly on Wentworth's way of
    courting Louisa—on how Wentworth's 'love-making' (a term that in
    1818 did not imply sexual intercourse) ministers to wounds that Went-
    worth himself has caused.

110 *pattens*: a patten is a 'shoe of wood with an iron ring, worn under the
    common shoe by women to keep them from the dirt' (Johnson).

112 *having cards left by people of whom they knew nothing*: calling or visiting
    cards could be left in lieu of personal visits. This was a new device,
    coming into use at around 1800 in the large towns, for policing the
    boundaries of 'good' society—and it would have assisted the Elliots in
    their determination to know nothing of a great number of people.

'Ideally a lady seated in her carriage handed her card to her servant who took it to the door and handed it to the servant of the house who took it to his mistress who could then decide whether or not she was "At Home" to the caller' (Leonore Davidoff, *The Best Circles: Society, Etiquette and the Season* (London: Cresset, 1986), 42). Cards acquired in this manner would be displayed in the hall to let visitors see who had preceded them (see also p. 121).

114 *under-hung*: having a projecting lower jaw (*OED*).

117 *'eleven with its silver sounds'*: the literary allusion has not been traced. In 1921 Herbert Grierson conjectured that Austen was here misremembering the description of the coquette's morning rituals that Alexander Pope gives in *The Rape of the Lock* (1712): 'Thrice rung the Bell, the Slipper knock'd the Ground, | And the press'd Watch return'd a silver Sound' (i. 17–18).

118 *Gowland*: a lotion whose use would eliminate all varieties of skin disorders, or so its manufacturers promised in the many advertisements that they issued in prose and verse. Gowland's manufacturers advertised in the *Bath Chronicle*, the journal a Bath resident like Sir Walter would read in order to keep track of the whereabouts of members of high society, whose arrivals in Bath the *Chronicle* would announce. Perhaps these advertisements suggested to him that Gowland would assist Mrs Clay with her freckles.

119 *who drinks the water*: since the medicinal effects of Bath water were thought to be of most benefit if the water were drunk hot each morning, the visitor to Bath would have to allot time in her daily schedule for attendance at the Pump Room, where the water was pumped directly from the springs (*New Bath Guide*, 13–14). In *Northanger Abbey* Austen includes an hour-long visit to the Pump Room—considered here, however, as a site for people-watching—among the 'regular duties' that Catherine Morland, Austen's heroine, and Catherine's chaperone, Mrs Allen, punctually fulfil each morning on first arriving in Bath (vol. I, ch. iii).

candid: the older meanings of the word include 'Free from malice; not desirous to find faults' (Johnson). In *Pride and Prejudice*, Elizabeth Bennet both teases and applauds her sister Jane for being 'candid'; Jane, Elizabeth says, takes 'the good of every body's character . . . and say[s] nothing of the bad' (vol. I, ch. iv).

120 *the crape round his hat*: a sign of mourning. Crape for mourning was a type of black silk gauze.

the Dowager Viscountess Dalrymple, and her daughter, the Honourable Miss Carteret: as Margaret Kirkham notes in *Jane Austen: Feminism and Fiction* ((Brighton: Harvester Press, 1983), 140), the names Dalrymple and Carteret both appear in the new arrivals lists appearing in Bath news papers during the winter of 1801–2, when Austen herself was an inhabitant of the city. As the widow (as the word 'Dowager' indicates) of a viscount, Lady Dalrymple is positioned nearer the top of the social ladder than any other figure in the novel. She and her daughter are the only characters who belong to the nobility.

121 *letters of ceremony*: the letters of congratulation and condolence required by etiquette.

122 *a little learning*: Mr Elliot's witticism inverts the poet Alexander Pope's dictum in his *Essay on Criticism* (1711): 'A little learning is a dang'rous thing' (l. 215).

123 *a welcome which depends so entirely upon place*: in this sentence Anne uses 'place' in a complex way, both as a synonym for social position or 'rank' (one definition that Johnson gives for 'place'), and as a way of referring to the scale of 'precedence' sustained by the etiquette of the period ('precedence' is another synonym mentioned in Johnson's definition). Anne's complaint is that her aristocratic relations value the Elliots not for who they are, but what they are (how they rank) and, worse, for where they are: their acquaintance is valued more highly now than in the past only because Lady Dalrymple and her daughter find themselves at loose ends in Bath.

126 *she disposes of my merchandize*: the appealing portrait of women's economic solidarity the modern reader glimpses here is complicated by considerations of class. It is worth noting that Mrs Smith uses the profits from Nurse Rooke's sale of her handicrafts to dispense charity to the 'poor families in [the] neighbourhood'. Their arrangement thus permits Mrs Smith the luxury, despite her poverty, of preserving a genteel class identity that was in new ways pegged to fantasies of female benevolence and to the notion that it was incumbent on a lady to aid and to superintend the poor. These emerging definitions of the gentlewoman's duty—and the ways in which they made benevolence an alibi for the gentlewoman's class-consciousness and perhaps as well her entrepreneurial energies—could occasion controversy. The Bath episodes of Susan Ferrier's novel *Marriage* (1818) include a caustic portrait of a wealthy woman whose hobby is instructing her poor protégées in such 'little female works' as the making of pincushions and card-racks (racks for holding visiting cards). By aggressively pressing their wares on all who call on her, she has turned her house into 'a beggar's repository' (*Marriage*, ed. Herbert Foltinek (Oxford: Oxford University Press, 1986), vol. III, ch. xi, pp. 375–6).

au fait: a French phrase meaning 'thoroughly conversant in'.

128 *no honours to distinguish her arms*: Sir Walter refers to the fact that emblems of special achievement (such as those denoting his status as a baronet) are absent from the coat of arms that appears on Lady Russell's carriage.

129 *remaining restraints of widowhood*: the period of mourning that followed the death of a spouse was supposed to last a full year.

130 *Sunday-travelling had been a common thing*: Anne's misgivings about Mr Elliot's past failure to observe the Sabbath indicate her strict moral and religious principles. They perhaps express, as well, the increasing sympathy with the Evangelical strands of Anglican religious practice that some biographers, looking at the last decade of her life in particular, have ascribed to Austen herself.

133 *they think the admiral gouty*: in modern medicine, gout names a form of arthritis that occurs when crystals of uric acid are deposited in the joints of the body, the feet especially. The diagnosis is less common today than in the eighteenth and early nineteenth centuries: then, painful 'fits' of the gout were thought to menace, in spring and autumn especially, men 'upwards of thirty' and, in particular, 'persons of acute parts, who follow their studies too closely' and 'those who live high and indulge their appetites, drinking plenty of rich, generous wines' ('Medicine', *Encyclopaedia Britannica, Or, a Dictionary of Arts and Sciences* (Edinburgh, 1771), iii. 126). As these quotations suggest, gout was a malady that medical science correlated with gentlemanly leisure, and, fittingly, George IV came to be numbered among the gouty. The *Encyclopaedia Britannica* recommends taking the waters at Bath to alleviate gouty symptoms.

make my letter as long as I like: a letter that extended onto a second sheet of notepaper would require double the postage. Such double letters would not necessarily be welcomed by their recipients, as they, rather than the senders, paid for letters at the time of delivery. Mrs Croft has spared the Elliots that expense by carrying the letter with her to Bath.

136 *lodgings in Gay-street*: the high price the Crofts would pay for lodging at that address might be what satisfies the status-conscious Sir Walter. When the Austen family began house-hunting in Bath in 1801, the houses available in Gay Street were initially ruled out because of their cost (*Letters*, 67). So were the houses in Laura Place, the address (the grandest in the novel) where Austen places the Elliots' aristocratic cousins, Lady Dalrymple and Miss Carteret (see p. 121). After the death of Jane Austen's father, Austen, her mother, and sister did rent lodgings at no. 25 Gay Street for a few months in 1805, just before leaving the city for Southampton.

137 *walking up Milsom-street*: 'the very magnet of Bath, the centre of attraction and, till the hour of dinner-time, the peculiar resort of the *beau monde*—where the familiar nod and the "How do you do" are repeated fifty times in the course of the morning': Pierce Egan, *Walks through Bath, describing every thing worthy of interest* (Bath: Meynell and Sons, 1819), walk 1, pp. 74–5. The street was a fashionable site for upmarket shopping and (as Egan suggests) promenading and people-watching. Bath is a city of steep hills, and Anne's readiness to return home to Camden-place by the uphill walk from the lower part of town is another sign that her health has improved since Volume I.

137 *a blister on one of her heels, as large as a three shilling piece*: Admiral Croft's analogy is remarkable not for what it tells us about Mrs Croft's heel (he must be exaggerating the blister's size), but rather for what it says about the care Austen has taken to locate her novel's action at a very precise historical moment. Three-shilling pieces, also known as 'three-shilling bank tokens', were struck only between 1811 and 1816 and ceased to be legal tender in 1817. They were not in fact coins issued by the Royal Mint. The latter were in short supply, in part because anxieties about the war led people to hoard their silver coinage rather than keeping it in circulation. In response to this problem, the machinery of the Royal Mint was gradually refurbished in preparation for a new coinage. In the meantime, to ensure that there was enough money available during the interval in which Britain awaited the Mint's new issues, Parliament empowered the industrialist Matthew Boulton to manufacture an unofficial silver coinage. Boulton's 'Bank of England tokens', as they were known, included the three-shilling piece.

got away some of my best men: desertions, disease, accidents, and fatalities in battle meant that Navy ships were chronically undermanned. To make up the numbers on their ship, Admiral Brand and his brother have contrived to press-gang members of Croft's crew while the latter are on shore.

138 *that younker*: 'A boy or junior seaman on board ship' (*OED*).

North Yarmouth: a minor naval base on the Norfolk coast, used by the North Sea and Baltic fleets.

Minehead: town on the shore of the Bristol Channel, 'occasionally visited by invalids from Bristol, Bath &c., for the purpose of sea-bathing, but its reputation is as yet not sufficient to give it the title of a bathing-place' (Lewis, iii. 307).

139 *rather too piano*: slang for 'gentle, mild, weak' (*OED*).

141 *Molland's*: this was the name of a shop selling sweets and pastries on Milsom Street.

a barouche: a four-wheeled carriage, whose top could be raised or let down according to the wish of its passengers. It had a seat in front for the driver and seats inside that would enable two couples to sit facing each other. The high cost of a barouche can be gauged from an observation in *Sense and Sensibility*: Edward Ferrars's snobbish family would like to see him in Parliament or connected with great men, we learn, but 'till one of these superior blessings could be attained,' it would quiet the ambition of his sister 'to see him driving a barouche' (vol. I, ch. iii).

143 *I have equipped myself properly for Bath already*: in calling attention to his umbrella, Captain Wentworth refers obliquely to Bath's notoriously wet weather. In Tobias Smollett's novel *The Expedition of Humphry Clinker* (1771) the grumpy protagonist Matt Bramble, visiting Bath to treat his gout, writes a letter to his physician in which he complains bitterly of the

city's 'almost perpetual' rain (*The Expedition of Humphry Clinker*, ed. Lewis M. Knapp, rev. Paul-Gabriel Boucé (Oxford: Oxford University Press, 1984), 34).

let me get you a chair: hired sedan chairs, mounted on poles and carried by two men, were common means of conveyance used by the wealthy.

145 *the rooms*: Bath's two sets of assembly rooms, where, after taking out a subscription, people gathered to drink tea, play cards, listen to music, and, on certain evenings each week, to dance. '[T]he entertainments are so widely regulated,' *The New Bath Guide* promises, 'that although there is never a cessation of them, there is never a lassitude from bad hours or from an excess of dissipation.' It also adds that 'Every one mixes in the Rooms upon an equality' (p. 26): hence Sir Walter's and Elizabeth's inclination to stay away.

146 *the octagon room*: the centre of the New Assembly Rooms (opened 1771). The card-room, the ballroom, the tea-room (which did double duty as a concert-room), and a vestibule opened out from it.

152 *my wishes that the name might never change*: if she married Mr Elliot, Anne would remain an Elliot. Though worded very cautiously, this is a proposal of marriage. Compare the narrator's account on p. 28 of how, three years after the break-up with Wentworth, Anne had been 'solicited [by Charles Musgrove] to change her name'.

153 *the gapes*: a fit of yawning.

the inimitable Miss Larolles: a character in Frances Burney's *Cecilia* (1782), who, uninvited, acts as Cecilia's guide to the amusements of London, and who gives her unsolicited advice as to where one should sit when visiting tea rooms, theatres, and the like. In book IV, chapter 6, Miss Larolles has just tried to draw a certain supercilious gentleman into conversation, but her usual stratagem has failed: 'Though I am sure he saw me, for I sat at the outside on purpose to speak to a person or two, that I knew would be strolling about; for if one sits on the inside, there's no speaking to a creature, you know, so I never do it at the Opera, nor . . . any where' (*Cecilia*, ed. Margaret Anne Doody and Peter Sabor (Oxford: Oxford University Press, 1988), 286).

161 *chambers in the Temple*: Mr Elliot lived in the quarter of London known as the Temple, where there were lodging houses reserved for attorneys and students of law.

164 *Give me joy*: congratulate me.

how to bring it with best advantage to the hammer: how to auction off the house and its contents. The reference is to the hammer wielded by an auctioneer, who raps with it to indicate the sale of an article.

reversion: 'right of succession' (Johnson). Mr Elliot claims to welcome the prospect of Sir Walter's remarriage, despite the possibility that a son born of this second marriage would replace him as the legitimate heir to Kellynch Hall and to the title of baronet.

167 *the marriage articles*: the private legal contract, made prior to a marriage, which established property rights within the union (setting up, for instance, the regular allowance or 'pin-money' that the husband was to pay out to his wife) and which also established future rights of succession (including those of any daughters or younger sons born of the marriage).

169 *sequestration for the payment of its own incumbrances*: in conformity to the terms of a legal judgement, the income that is produced by this property (possibly a sugar cane plantation) has been appropriated by the late Mr Smith's creditors so as to pay off his remaining debts.

172 *eclat*: from the French 'faire éclat'—to create a stir or a scandal. To 'escape all . . . eclat' is to avoid a scene.

174 *the White Hart*: an inn, one of the biggest in Bath and, because almost all the post coaches entering and leaving the city collected passengers and parcels there, one of the busiest. It was located across from the Pump Room, where genteel invalids assembled to take the waters.

175 *hold a living for a youth*: Charles Hayter will, as curate, and for a salary, exercise the pastoral duties for this parish, on the understanding that he will give up the position to this youth when the latter attains the age of 24 (the minimum age for ordination according to the Clergy Ordination Act of 1801).

the best preserves in the kingdom . . . each more careful and jealous than the other: *preserves* are the grounds that have been set apart from the rest of an estate for the rearing of game. In emphasizing that their owners are *jealous*, Charles Musgrove uses the term in a now obsolete sense as a synonym for *vigilant*. He commends the sportsmanlike care they show in ensuring that each season they have (as the narrator earlier observes in reference to both Charles and his father) plenty of 'game to guard, and to destroy' (p. 39).

178 *the pump-room*: see notes to pp. 119 and 174.

184 *the Sultaness Scheherazade's head*: the character in the *Arabian Nights' Entertainment* (first translated into English in 1706–8 from the French of Antoine Galland) whose name has become a byword for women's imaginative powers, because her skill in narration enables her to escape from the beheading her husband has reserved for her. To avenge himself for the inconstancy of his first wife, the Sultan has vowed to marry a wife every night and have each one executed when the sun rises the next morning. Managing to keep him hooked on her stories night after night until he at last revokes his vow, Scheherezade saves her life and the lives of many other women.

188 *the pen has been in their hands*: even as she has Anne object to examples from books, Austen echoes the precedents set by figures in the literary tradition who have previously commented on men's monopoly of the written word. Anne sounds like the Wife of Bath in Geoffrey Chaucer's *Canterbury Tales*, who is exasperated by male clerics' representations of

women, and, closer to Austen's time, like Richard Steele's character Arietta, who recounts the story of Inkle, the mercenary Englishman, and Yarico, the native woman of Jamaica whom Inkle betrays, so as to counter her male visitor's trite examples of female inconstancy. Arietta observes, 'You Men are Writers, and can represent us Women as Unbecoming as you please in your Works, while we are unable to return the Injury' (*Spectator*, 11 (13 Mar. 1711)).

193 *the comparatively quiet and retired gravel-walk*: a path that the late eighteenth-century architect John Wood the Younger designed to link the old and new quarters of Bath. Skirting the gardens behind Gay Street, the gravel walk climbs from Queen Square (the architectural project built for Wood's father, John Wood, between 1728 and 1735) to the Royal Crescent (built to the design of Wood the Younger between 1767 and 1774). As they pace 'the gradual ascent' (p. 194), Anne and Captain Wentworth are in some sense leaving the past behind them.

198 *a woman's portion*: a portion is what a woman inherits—the share of her parent's estate to which a daughter would be entitled under the terms of the previous generation's marriage settlement.

199 *as high in his profession as merit and activity could place him*: promotion beyond the rank of captain was based exclusively on seniority. From that point, one moved up the ladder of rank as posts opened up, and the individual with the longest period of service behind him would move first.

201 *Anne restored to rights of seniority*: by marrying, Anne ascends a notch in the scale of precedence sustained by the etiquette of the period. Although Mary is younger than Anne, she has hitherto, by virtue of her marriage, been entitled to take precedence over her elder, unmarried sister. Mary values these petty honours to the point of apparently regretting that Anne's marriage will take them away again.

a very pretty landaulette: also known as a demi- or half-landau, a light carriage for two passengers. Its top could be opened, 'which gives the advantage of air and view to the passengers' (*Treatise on Carriages*, i. 39).

Appendix A

204 *Mantuamaker*: dressmaker.

ANTHONY TROLLOPE

The American Senator
An Autobiography
Barchester Towers
Can You Forgive Her?
The Claverings
Cousin Henry
The Duke's Children
The Eustace Diamonds
Framley Parsonage
He Knew He Was Right
Lady Anna
Orley Farm
Phineas Finn
Phineas Redux
The Prime Minister
Rachel Ray
The Small House at Allington
The Warden
The Way We Live Now

ANTON CHEKHOV	About Love and Other Stories
	Early Stories
	Five Plays
	The Princess and Other Stories
	The Russian Master and Other Stories
	The Steppe and Other Stories
	Twelve Plays
	Ward Number Six and Other Stories
FYODOR DOSTOEVSKY	Crime and Punishment
	Devils
	A Gentle Creature and Other Stories
	The Idiot
	The Karamazov Brothers
	Memoirs from the House of the Dead
	Notes from the Underground and The Gambler
NIKOLAI GOGOL	Dead Souls
	Plays and Petersburg Tales
ALEXANDER PUSHKIN	Eugene Onegin
	The Queen of Spades and Other Stories
LEO TOLSTOY	Anna Karenina
	The Kreutzer Sonata and Other Stories
	The Raid and Other Stories
	Resurrection
	War and Peace
IVAN TURGENEV	Fathers and Sons
	First Love and Other Stories
	A Month in the Country